THE PROTECTORATE WARS:
Rise

S.A. Shaffer, Esq.

The Protectorate Wars : Rise

Copyright © 2019 by S. A. Shaffer, Esq.

Cover Art by Austin Reddington
(AustinReddington.com)

2nd edition

ISBN: 9781673397796

Map Of The Fertile Plains

CONTENTS

PROLOGUE

"Yoni, you give Mercy back this instant, or I'm telling father!" Mercedes said, stamping her foot so hard her auburn tresses danced across her forehead. She put on her most fierce pout, bunching up her eyebrows and crossing her arms over her chest. Why did she have to be so little? It wasn't fair that the boys were bigger than her.

"I'll give her back, I promise. I just want to borrow her for a minute. I'm using her as a test dummy for my new rocket!" Yoni, her brother and a few cycles older, wore his thick black goggles and oversized lab coat. He held the doll just out of reach as Mercedes stood on her tiptoes, hopping around him. While her hair was a deep red, his had mellowed with time, softening into a copper brown. They argued in a field on the outskirts of Armstad, just beyond notice of any casual observer.

"You will not," She shrieked in horror as she danced around him. "Last time you used Eleanor and burnt off all her hair."

"A simple miscalculation in my fuel mixtures. It won't

happen again." Yoni held his sister back as he strapped her doll into a wooden seat at the top of a fathom long cylinder, a cylinder that looked rather like a missile.

"That's what you said when you put Alexandra in your air cannon. It blew all of her clothes off, and I still can't find them." Mercedes rested her fists on her hips and stamped her foot again for emphasis.

"But she came back all in one piece, just like I said she would." Yoni finished tying the doll into the rocket and then, taking Mercedes by the hand, he walked back a few dozen paces.

"...one piece completely covered in mud. Yoni, you give her back or... or... or I will never speak to you again." Mercedes looked at him in earnest, lip quivering. She wondered if she had gone too far.

"Well, if this is our last conversation, I should ask you if I can borrow Lorraine tomorrow when I test my concept focus lens. I think I've really got it this time."

Mercedes gasped, mouth falling open in absolute shock. Then she closed her eyes and sniffed, pointedly turning away from Yoni.

Yoni bent down and fiddled on an intricate device with several buttons and triggers. He extended an antenna and then nudged Mercedes with an extra pair of goggles.

She ignored him. She said she would never speak to him again, and she meant it. Yoni continued to nudge her with the goggles.

"I'm not speaking to you," she whispered without looking at him, for everybody knows that whispers don't count as speaking. She heard him sigh and pocket the extra goggles. Then he began the count down.

"Launching in three, two, one!"

Mercedes turned at the last moment and looked at her poor doll. Her brother pressed a button and sucked in his breath with excited anticipation. Nothing happened.

"Ha! It didn't work, now give her here!" Then Mercedes remembered her vow. "I mean, I'm not talking to you," she whispered as she shut her eyes and looked away. However, she kept one eye squinted, so she could see if Yoni would give her back her doll.

"I can't understand it. It should have—"

Suddenly the rocket shot off the ground, propelled by a jet of flame. It reached a dozen fathoms, broke apart and exploded into a spectacular ball of fire. Mercedes' eyes shot open as she looked on in shock, wondering which one of the falling pieces of debris was her doll. Yoni whooped as he jumped up and down. Evidently, that was what his latest contraption was supposed to do.

"Look!" He said, pointing at one of the larger pieces that fell into some of the longer grass. He grabbed Mercedes' hand and dragged her after him.

"I told you," Yoni said as he bent down and picked up a splintered piece of wood and pulled something off of it. He held up her doll in a triumphant fist. It looked all right, but for the smoke wafting from its head.

"You see, good as new!"

Then the head rolled off. Mercedes screamed. She screamed louder than she ever had before. She screamed, and she screamed, and she screamed.

In retrospect, she probably overdid it. As it turned out,

the combination of Yoni's rocket exploding and her screams convinced a nearby patrol station that the second Protectorate War had finally begun. Within minutes Armstad sprang to action. A citywide claxon rang out, and not just any claxon, the *high alert* claxon. Such were the circumstances that the city guard forewent the two proceeding levels of alert and implemented a full evacuation. People began the well-rehearsed procedures, filing into lines that led to their famed fortresses. They lived in constant fear of invasion, and that fear granted considerable motivation.

However, the general populous was not alone in their fervor. Airships filled the sky and spread out to forestall the supposed invasion. Airships filled with young men prepared to trade their lives for the safety of their country—trade them to give the people a few more precious moments to find shelter. The local militia loaded bunkers and manned flack cannons. The Prime Minister's office even sent a message off to the Houselands of Alönia, requesting aide.

It didn't take the Armstad Armada very long to find the would-be-invaders: a wide-eyed boy and a hysterical little girl. But by that time, it was too late to call off the national emergency.

The cost of the false alarm was impossible to calculate in money and resources: the loss of business, the expenditure of fuel, and all the other incidentals that result from shutting down and relocating an entire populous. Whatever the cost may have been, it could not compare to the resultant shock and pandemonium in the hearts and minds of the locals.

But Mercedes didn't know any of this. She didn't know why some soldiers herded her and her brother into a gunship and flew them to the Megiddo Fortress. Or why the Armada General personally escorted them home that day and stayed to speak with her father. As she watched her father take Yoni by the arm and lead him back into his bedroom, she only felt sorry. She cried when she heard the four, sharp smacks and saw Yoni walking out of the bedroom holding his backside. She didn't care about the doll that much; she still had three others. And as they sat down to dinner, she couldn't meet Yoni's eyes, choosing instead to look at her lap. Binyamin sat across from her, silent, as always, but keeping a constant vigil with his quick dark eyes. He was the next eldest above Yonatan. His hands fidgeted, as always, spinning his fork between his fingers.

Mercedes cheered up a bit when Corvin arrived home in a rush, slamming the door behind himself.

"Father! Father, did you hear, it was all a false alarm." He ran into the dining room, his long legs carrying him across the house in a matter of seconds.

"It was a false alarm! Some idiot kid lit off a bomb on the outskirts of the city and scared the devil out of a little… What?" Corvin faltered as everyone looked at him.

"It's already been addressed, Corvin," Father said. "No need to rehash the past."

Corvin looked around the room, head on a swivel until he spotted Yoni, who at that moment trying to disappear into his chair, eyes still teary.

"Yoni! Not again! That's the third time."

"Let it be, Corvin," Father said as he poured juice and passed it around the table. "Now sit down. Your mother is bringing in the dinner."

Corvin looked like he wanted to say more on the topic, but he held his tongue and sat with a huff.

"How was class?" Father asked as he straightened the cutlery next to his plate.

"Other than the evacuation?" Corvin asked.

Father rolled his eyes before giving him a stern look.

"Right," Corvin said with a wince. "Well, my linguistics instructor passed me on Viörn and transferred me into Bergish."

"You're fluent?" Mother asked as she entered the room carrying a tray of roasted Mountain Lamb.

Corvin nodded. "Got my certificate this morning. Professor Rubin said it was the fastest certification he'd ever seen."

"Well, it doesn't surprise me one bit," Mother said as she walked back into the kitchen. "You always did have a knack for languages."

"True," Father said with a nod, "… and, now that you have Viörn out of the way, you can spend more time on your Alönian."

"What's wrong with my Alönian?" Corvin asked with an indignant look.

Yoni snorted as he took a drink of juice and some of it shot out his nose. He coughed a few times before saying, "Even Mercedes' Alönian is better than yours."

"That's because she's an intelligent young lady," Corvin said with a nod at his sister, to which Mercedes blushed. "Even so," Corvin continued, "what good will Alönian do me. They aren't our enemy."

"Communication is the fuel of friendship," Father said. "How do you expect them to remain our ally if we do not speak to them?"

"Father," Corvin said in exasperation. "Everyone in Armstad is fluent in Alönian. If one citizen speaks with an accent, I'm not sure how that will lead to the breakdown of a 50-cycle-old alliance."

"Corvin," Father began in a matter-of-fact tone, "it does no good to learn something half-heartedly. If you are going to learn Alönian, learn it with all your might."

Corvin looked down and nodded.

Father continued. "Your aspirations to join the Sneaks is noble, and I have no doubt Armstad will be better for it, but it does not excuse you from pursuing a well-rounded education."

"Yes, Father."

"How about you Binyamin?" Father said as he turned to his second oldest. "How was your day? When's that hand-to-hand tournament?"

Binyamin looked up from the platter of Mountain Lamb that his eyes were already devouring. "Tomorrow," he said, and then looked back at the lamb. He always seemed hungry these days, looking perpetually half-starved, and no matter how much he ate, he never seemed satisfied.

Father nodded, apparently satisfied with the exchange.

He looked at Yoni next and pursed his lips. Yoni tried to look up and down at the same time in a self-deprecating manner.

Father cleared his throat before speaking. "Yoni, was your experiment successful?"

Yoni lit up with the question. "I achieved what I wanted to. It didn't explode until it was at least fifty feet in the air."

"Well, you know I want you to continue your experiments, but I trust you will *never again forget* to wait for me before testing them." Father didn't shout, he didn't even look stern, but his words had a way of resonating in your ears.

Yoni looked down again. "Yes, Father," he said.

"And how about you, Mercedes? Did you practice numbers today?"

Mercedes looked at her father as her mother brought in the rest of the food.

"Yes, father. Three times, just like you asked."

"Good girl. What else did you do today?"

"I watched Yoni blow up my doll and knock her head off, but it's ok, I forgive him." And she meant it, for she did not want Yoni to receive any further punishment. She wondered if she had said something she shouldn't have when Yoni slouched even further in his chair. Corvin choked on some of his water, and father glared at Yoni, who offered a half-smile, half-shrug.

Mother pursed her lips as she started dishing everyone up.

"We will get you another doll," Father said.

Mercedes felt herself smile, but as mother dished up her plate with Mountain Lamb, Sea-Grass salad, freshly baked tuber, and Skyfish skewers, her smile transformed into a frown. She hated Skyfish.

"Mercedes?" Mother asked with a stern look. "What did I tell you about making faces at your food?"

"Yes, Mother," Mercedes said as she forced a smile back onto her face.

"That's better," Her mother said, nodding as she sat down.

With a nod from father, the family held hands and bowed their heads while father prayed. He prayed as he always did, thanking Jeshua for his many blessings and his wondrous creation and asking for continued protection for their small country. He asked for wisdom for their leaders and confusion to their enemies. In all, he prayed for peace.

While Mercedes may have been young—missing or misunderstanding much of what happened around her— she knew the fear in which her family lived and the dangers they faced every day. So as she went to sleep that night, she said her own prayers. She prayed for her family, the people she loved the most in all the Fertile Plains, and she vowed with the tenacity of a girl in her sixth season that she would do anything to keep them safe.

Chapter One
REPRESENTING DEPRAVITY

It could have been the high whine of the Vielle or the garish laughter from intoxicated patrons. Then again, it might have been the fawning words of sycophants and the general clamor of flattery. Whatever it was, it made David feel uncomfortable as he sat in the middle of the Speaker's Gala of the New Cycle. His head ached from the sparkle of gold and crystal and gems, and he jumped every time someone barked out a boisterous laugh at an unamusing joke. Hundreds of women flitted around in thousand sterling gowns wearing ten thousand sterling jewelry—gold rings in pigs' snouts. The older women buried their sorrows in wine glasses, drowning out the ghosts of their wild youths. The younger women pretended to be intoxicated, as they prowled and prattled about the high-profile husbands of the older women. The men, whether young or old, stalked the banquet with loose lips, loose hands, and looser morals. Debauchery reigned supreme.

This cycle the Chateau de Bolitona, a luxurious residence on the Braxton coastland, hosted the Gala. Grand dining rooms and luscious gardens overlooked staggering views of ocean waves and far away storms. Rumor had it that this was the most expensive Speaker's Gala in Alönian history, an ironic achievement for the Equalist party. Even more ironic, Alönia's generous taxpayers funded the entire event. The longer David worked amongst Equalists, the more hypocrisy he seemed to uncover. Perhaps the condition ran deeper than Blythe. Their ideology seemed sound, but at some point along its implementation, the message distorted.

David longed to leave the saturnalia, but things were not as they used to be. He could no longer slip into the background as he once did. People knew him now, at least, they knew of him. They knew he was Blythe's aide, and more than one bootlicker had tried flattering him in hopes of meeting the speaker, as if he were some sort of gatekeeper. How little they understood. David would give anything to have never known the speaker, anything to undo the past cycles' events that catapulted a lowly aide into the highest tier of society and placed a murderer in the speakership. Yes, people knew him now, but they did not respect him, not for who he really was. A casual glance around the room convinced David that very little respect suffered this banquet. Most didn't even know the meaning of the word. It was a collection of individuals seeking to use other individuals for personal gain. Greedy. Selfish. Licentious. Was that all they were? Did they even know the constituents their offices represented? What of all those people?

David supported the Equalist party because they helped people. Yet, all this extravagance gave him pause. He'd always blamed the greedy Pragmatics for the underfunded social assistance programs, but was the problem elsewhere? Perhaps the issue was not the lack of water in the bucket, but rather too many holes in its base.

He thought this and many other things as he sat at the speaker's table, rubbing the top of his wine goblet with a finger yet never lifting it to his lips. This table really bore no difference to any other table, despite its title, as the speaker had not graced it since the evening began. Speaker Blythe intermingled with his guests, shaking their hands and speaking their names—*all* of their names. Somehow he remembered every single one. Not for the first time, David marveled at the man's ability to play the crowd. Then again, Blythe really didn't have to play this crowd. They were putty in his hands the moment he took the speaker's oath a season and a half ago. The man was an entertainer, and no one could take that away from him.

A beautiful young woman clung to his arm, the latest in a long line of young ladies accompanying the speaker, though anyone privy to the situation knew that she was little more than an escort. Regardless, this one made David ache as she flitted around sending her deep auburn tresses through the air in wisps. Her pleasing face and matching figure complimented her magenta gown. David shut his eyes, reminiscing on a time long past.

"What's the matter, David?" ask Eric Himpton. "Too

much high class for you? I'll wager this is more opulence than you've ever seen."

David stiffened in his meditations as the dark, handsome aide leaned over from the seat beside him. Eric was the latest addition to the Blythe campaign. While it took some time for David to allow Blythe to fill Mercy's position, his horror was complete when Blythe selected Eric Himpton as his second aide. Eric had never forgiven David for beating his score on the PLAEE and had treated David abominably ever since they met that first day in the assembly room. However, Eric thrived in his position. He was an intelligent young man, and what else would an intelligent young man do in a campaign of envy, self-gratification, and sex, other than thrive. The lad fit right in as he partook in the wiles.

Of course, the Blythe campaign looked professional from the perspective of an onlooker. *The Blythe Campaign: Truthful and Diligent. Working to better your society by fulfilling your needs.* That's the way the tabloids portrayed it anyway. But on the inside, Eric and everyone else in the campaign, save David and one or two others, used Houseland funds to further their own lusts.

"I don't think *anyone* has ever seen this much opulence before, Eric," David said as he squeezed the neck of his wine goblet, not meeting the tan boy's lazy gaze.

Eric snickered. "If I didn't know any better, I'd say you weren't excited to be at the most coveted party of the cycle. That's a very interesting prospect for Speaker Blythe's first and strongest supporter."

David rolled his head around and looked at Eric with a

forced smile. "Well, you don't know any better, so shut up."

Eric frowned but didn't say anything as he drained his glass and raised it for the waiters to refill.

David looked up as the audiences' cheer rose to a crescendo, cheering for Blythe as he deposited the redheaded beauty in a chair and stepped up to a podium beside the speaker's table. He raised his hands to quiet the rabble, but they were too excited, or too drunk, to realize. They roared on, praising his name through sputtering speech. One man elbowed David in his exuberance, spilling half a goblet of wine on the woman next to him in the process. She laughed, hardly even noticing.

Blythe continued with his attempts to placate the people with dancing hands, but they would not have it. He laughed at their enthusiasm and stepped back to await their attention. Eventually, they grew thirsty and went looking for their wine.

"Friends! I cannot thank you enough for your support, and I am glad to be amongst such caring people as we welcome in a new cycle, the dawning of a new age."

A lone patron interrupted him as he shouted out from the crowd, "Thanks for the wine, William."

Blythe laughed with the rest of the crowd, and it was some time until he could resume his speech.

"You're welcome, Edward. Remind me next cycle to limit your intake. Now, we are here tonight to honor Alönia's remarkable achievements, struggles, and triumphs in the past cycle, notably, the final triumph and the crowning victory of the Equalist party!"

Everybody in the room jumped to their feet and shouted their approval. Fists rose, women squealed, and more wine spilled. David joined them for fear of standing out.

"Yes, a remarkable achievement, to be sure, but we celebrate the future more so than the past. We are here to imagine an even more remarkable 3242nd cycle. We must not stop to marvel at the changes of last cycle or the last hundred before it. We must dream of the changes still to come. Memories are fruitless. We must look to our dreams. For when our memories outgrow our dreams, we will fade into memory ourselves. I pledge to you that we will never fade, nor will we ever relinquish the trust and power that the people of Alönia have bestowed upon us!"

As the crowd applauded yet again, David snickered at the hidden meaning in the words. Blythe had just announced himself a tyrant. Did anyone else in the room hear? Or perhaps, they didn't care?

"We must look forward to new and evolving ideas in an effort to create a more perfect Houseland," Blythe continued. "We must not fear change. Instead, let us welcome it, embrace it, and nourish it. The great story of Alönia's recent past was the triumph in the Protectorate Wars. But I challenge you this evening as the last moments of 3241 pass us by, who are we if our proudest moment is the destruction of our neighbors? Our greatest hero a warrior? What of the unsung heroes? What of the struggling poor? The struggle for equal rights? The triumph over entrepreneurial government?"

The people grew silent at this as their lips puckered to

a frown and they nodded their heads. David felt his face flush at the slight toward his grandfather. Had they forgotten the destruction of Armstad? Had they forgotten the violent natures of those *so-called* neighbors? But of course they had; they had abandoned fruitless memory in favor of baseless dreams.

"We must never forget the meaning of the Fertile Plains," Blythe said. "It is a place where all peoples, regardless of their realm, can come together and find shelter from the harshness of the Southern Ocean, the heat of the desert, and the cold of the frozen wastes. I have been in contact with our Neighbors, the Viörn and the Berg. They desire peace more than any of us, and as proof of their sentiments, they are unifying their two great realms through marriage, a Viörn princess for a Bergish prince. This marks the end of ancient hostilities and the healing of old wounds. But I ask you: will Alönia resist such sentiments? If the story of the past was the triumph over our neighbors, what will the story of the future be? Let it be of healing and unification. To bring peace to a land where we shed our differences and honor our commonality."

The people applauded, more subdued this time as a few wiped eyes and blew noses. Several even called out blessings on the new couple.

So it was true, then. David thought back to the conversation he had overheard between Walker and the mysterious Armstadi. Peace was never a bad thing, but the very prospect that Blythe desired gave David pause. What was the angle? He always had an angle. He'd surprised David already when he got caught looking the wrong way. Never again. Besides, did they not already have peace in the Fertile Plains? How else would one describe sixty cycles without war?

But Blythe wasn't finished. "But such a triumph will require great effort from us all and great sacrifice. We must stand against hatred and bigotry, nationalism and domination. We must continue to alleviate poverty, not only here, but all across the Fertile Plains. We must bridle our prosperity with service in our communities. We must encourage the greaters among us to serve the lessers through carefully crafted legislation. And we must find new ways to better care for these Fertile Plains we all call home."

"Here! Here!" Representative Arnold shouted from his seat across from David. Albert Arnold headed up the newly minted Fertile Plains restoration committee, and Blythe nodded to him before he continued.

"There will be resistance, particularly from our *Pragmatic* friends." A collective boo rang out among the patrons. "We may not be able to eliminate all oppression, greed, and intolerance, but we can create new hatred for such characteristics and an intolerance among the masses as has never been seen before. For the rich are few, but many are equal."

As the people applauded and shouted once again, David let his eyebrows shoot up. This man wanted a cultural war, one sown with the seeds of envy, and this didn't trouble anyone? Sure, use some tax funds to help out those in need, but when did hate become a part of it?

"There will be consequences for our actions, ones that we cannot fully eliminate," Blythe said. "There will be resistance from the final death throes of our political opponents. But the equality of our Fertile Plains is well worth the risk. In short, if we want the story of 3242, the cycle the Equalists came to power, to be of triumph and unification, we must redirect the resources of Alönia toward new horizons. For this reason, I am implementing two new directives. First, we must absorb the resources of our wealthier districts in favor of those in need. I have crafted legislation that I will propose and implement in the next season for just such a purpose. Second, I will encourage peace amongst our neighbors with a gesture of good faith. I intend to issue a speaker's order for the immediate deconstruction of our forward fleet groups. Peace and unification are impossible when we hold a gun in our hands." The crowd started cheering again, but Blythe shouted over the top of them. "We are only moments from our new cycle. And when the sun rises tomorrow, it will rise to a new era of Alönian history."

The people went wild as the clock struck midnight, and the cycle of the Fertile Plains restarted. David did not partake in the revelry; he couldn't. As the people cheered around him, he slipped out of the dining room, walking down golden halls and plush carpets until he found the washroom. He turned on the sink and leaned over it as he felt bile rise in his stomach, but a few splashes of water soon set him right.

David wondered as he leaned over the sink. What on earth were they thinking? It was one thing to slow the expansion of the armada, but to deconstruct more than 75% of it, and that 75% representing the newer, more-sophisticated airships. That was a level of vulnerability Alönia had never known before. A gesture of good faith? The sentiment seemed honorable, but perhaps misguided and untimely. A strong armada had guided them through 60 cycles of peace. Should they change a successful strategy? Again, David recalled what he had heard several seasons earlier when he stalked Speaker Walker's residence. Viörn and Berg were both massing their armadas along the Armstad borders. Perhaps it was a defensive move, but what if it wasn't? What would be the outcome of a war with a defenseless Alönia?

The common decency of man versus the natural depravity. That was the central difference between Equalists and Pragmatics. At the core, every conflict between the two political parties grew out of a differing perspective on mankind's basic nature. Either the Viörn and Berg were simply building fleets out of fear, or they were preparing for the conquest of the Fertile Plains. Decency or depravity? David still clung to the common decency perspective, but it had been quite some time since he'd seen common decency.

He looked in the mirror, the only surface of the room that was not gold or silver, and he gazed at the man he'd become. His breath caught in his throat as he slid a finger down the lapel of his midnight blue suit; the very suit a beautiful young lady had bought him earlier that cycle. He could afford new suits after Blythe's elevation to the speakership, but this one would always be his favorite.

Mercy, oh how he missed her. That wound would not heal, not as long as her killer still lived and ruled Alönia. But it had been a cycle and a half since he'd reached out to the Man in the Shadows or at least attempted to do so. He sighed. His attempt to communicate had always been a fool's hope, a fool's hope in a man that might not even exist. No, he stood alone. A man without a country or a friend or a cause. A man betrayed. A man who hoped in false hope. He would remain alone as he watched the sun set on Alönian history, powerless to do anything about it. He rinsed his face in the sink one more time, using his real fingers to massage his temples.

Merciful Jeshua, if you're out there, we could use your help right about now.

As he walked back toward the dining room and the general sound of frivolity, he found himself walking past the entrance. He wasn't ready to rejoin the others; he wasn't ready to resume his false face, not yet. He could spare a few more minutes.

He followed the hallway along the outside of the mansion, not caring where it led, as long as it was away from Blythe and his flatterers. The hall deposited him into the gardens overlooking Fisherman's Gulf. He took a deep, soothing breath of the fresh, salty air. No stars shone this evening, and the moon gave only a dull glow from beneath the clouds. Crisp air wafted by as he meandered through the hand-carved shrubberies, many of them dormant, waiting for the golden days to coax them back into life and vigor. And, as surely as the new cycle began, so too did the mists of Úoi Season start to churn and coalesce, drifting in on the ocean breeze.

David knew he should be heading back to the party, but he convinced himself that a few additional minutes couldn't hurt, and the garden attracted him. He passed fruit trees and spice gardens, cutting beds, and water features. A pair of double-winged owls swooped and dove in a romantic air dance as they crossed the evening sky. At some point along the way, David passed one row of hedges into another exiting the glow of the mansion's lights into dense shadow. The change eluded him. He walked on, lost in his thoughts, and did not rouse until he heard the sharp snap of a twig. He whirled around, looking into the shadows and seeing nothing. His neck prickled with anxiety, and he searched the shadows with careful eyes. But there was nothing. Just as he decided it might be best to return to the house, a shadow passed in front of him, and a spray of aerosol hissed in his face. David opened his mouth to yell, but no sound came out. His eyes felt hooded and his body, weightless. Lightheadedness passed over him as his knees buckled. Then the shadows closed in, and all went silent.

Chapter Two
ANSWERS AND QUESTIONS

David regained consciousness and struggled to free his arms as he pieced together what was going on. Darkness surrounded him, and he could hear his panicked breath echoing off some unseen walls. He squirmed and kicked on a wooden chair, but his hands and feet were tied. He called out, but no one answered. Calming himself with long slow breaths, he considered his options. He tried wiggling his wrists out of the knots, but it was useless. He only succeeded in rubbing his skin raw. Perhaps, if he tipped his chair over, he might be able to wriggle his hands in front of him so that he could loosen the knots with his teeth. He was about to try when something behind him clicked. A shaft of light speared out from behind him and illuminated the five-stride circular room. He could tell that several people had entered the room by the sound of the shuffling feet, and then the shaft of light narrowed and disappeared with another click. David sucked in a breath. He could still hear the people in the room, their breaths, and the shuffling of their feet. Then, a single light bulb illumined above him. He heard a few whispers and a muffled assent. He couldn't help but wonder if this is the way Paula, Samantha, and Mercy's interrogations began. Had his turn finally arrived? Had Blythe suspected his disloyalty and ordered his elimination... via torture?

"So, David, how was the party?" A voice said from behind him.

It wasn't Mr. Blythe's voice. David worked his shoulders back and forth, craning his neck, but he couldn't see who was addressing him.

"Um... fancy," David said.

"That's all? Just... fancy?"

"I don't think you kidnaped me to ask me if I enjoyed the gala. What do you want with me?"

"My, but you are blunt. To business then. We want to know what you think of Speaker Blythe?"

David wasn't sure how to answer or if it even mattered. Was his fate already decided? "He's my boss, gave me my first job. Why, what do you think of him?"

"Well," the man said, "I think he's a criminal. I know of two murders in this cycle alone. Not to mention his financial fraud." he sighed. "Not very good boss material, wouldn't you agree?"

David's mind raced. Was he goading him, trying to prod him into betraying his true feelings about Blythe? Was this a test? Or, was the man in earnest? He started to wonder if this interrogation had any connection with Blythe. Was this someone else? "Who... Who are you, and which murders are you speaking of?"

The man didn't answer for a moment. Then David heard footsteps echo on concrete, and a tall man in a knee-length leather jacket walked around and stood in front of him. The light hung low in the room, so shadows still obscured the man's face. "I've gone by many names, but the one you gave me is the best of all. I even scare myself sometimes. You see, I'm the *Man-in-the-shadows*."

David's mouth fell open, but he quickly shut it. Had he ever told Mr. Blythe about the Man-in-the-shadows? Had he ever told anyone?

"Who told you that name?"

"Mercy did."

"Mercy!" David said, his stiffening limbs almost knocking him over.

"Yes, I thought that might get a reaction out of you. Mercy was one of ours. We inserted her into Blythe's office after his bid for power."

"Inserted her? How? I was there at her interview, and she came directly from Representative Herald's office where she had a two-cycle record?"

"Come now, David, you're a smart lad, you should be able to work it out."

David tried to calm himself so he could think, but his racing heart made that problematic. "If— If she was with you from the beginning, that means you placed her in Representative Herald's campaign two cycles ago. That would follow, as two cycles ago, Herald was the biggest threat to the Pragmatics."

The Man-in-the-shadows started to clap, the sound

echoing around the room. "You see, now it all makes sense. Mercy was a gorgeous girl, and Blythe's weakness for beautiful women was well known to us long before Ms. Samantha. We knew he wouldn't be able to resist her or her résumé. We did have concerns about you, though. You're a very bright young man. I've manipulated politics for cycles, and no one has ever foiled me, save you."

"She told you about the wall of questions at my apartment." David let his head hang. He felt a twinge of betrayal poking at his heart.

"She did. She told us many things about you. She told us you were a sincere, honorable young man deceived and entrapped by Mr. Blythe. She told us you were the son of a skilled airship captain, who was also the son of a skilled airship captain. It didn't take us long to work out who you were after that. Isn't that right, Mr. Ike." The man leaned forward a little bit, just enough for David to see the sparkle of his eyes in the shadows. It made him feel uncomfortable like someone was peeling back the layers of his past.

"At long last, the only living heir of the Ike legend, the grandson of the great Admiral Ike, reemerges, and in the most peculiar of places. What a strange life we live."

David Gulped. These people knew who he was… who he actually was. After so many cycles of keeping it secret, they knew.

"I should have known when you flew that Sunbeam like the devil himself, evading my prowlers like they were paper gliders." The man chuckled when David looked up in astonishment, guessing the reason. "Yes, we have a few prowlers at our beck and call. We have a friendship of sorts with the outlanders."

"Seems like a fragile friendship," David said.

"Perhaps."

"Did Mercy know who I was? My... heritage?" David asked.

"Not at first. She was shocked when I told her. But as all the pieces of your past folded together, she saw the truth."

David nodded. He'd wanted to tell her while she lived. He'd wanted to impress her, but it frightened him. In the end, she'd already known.

"Which is why we were looking when you wrote this." The man produced a slip of paper from his breast pocket and showed it to David. It was the very same slip of paper he had left in his copy of *House Law* during Blythe's acceptance speech. He remembered the words like he had written them yesterday. *I know the truth now, and I'm ready to meet.* He'd written them in hopes that the Man-in-the-shadows would find them. He'd longed for him to find them, but now that the moment had arrived, he didn't know what to do. Then again, he didn't have much of a choice. He either took a chance or watched as Mr. Blythe tore the Houselands apart. He swallowed before speaking.

"You're wrong about Speaker Blythe, you know."

"I'm sorry?" The man said with some surprise.

"He committed three murders, not just two. Paula, Samantha, and Mercy."

The man looked down at the note in his hand and nodded. "I was forgetting Ms. Paula."

"I... I can't find Mercy's body," David said, and he felt his eyes fill with tears. "I've looked everywhere. It disappeared from evidence not long after she died. I think Mr. Blythe disposed of it."

The man folded his hands behind his back and started walking around David, pacing the circular room. "No. We have the body. We slipped in and got it. She's... at peace now."

David let out a breath and sniffed. "Good. I couldn't bear the thought of it lying in a gutter somewhere." He stretched his neck and wiped his face on his collar, noticing several other figures at the side of the room as he did so. "Did you order her to commit voter's fraud?"

"No, that was her own idea. Her last great scheme to unseat Blythe before the census. It probably would have worked... if she'd had more time."

David nodded and tried not to think about those few awful days that culminated in Mercy's death. "Well, you know who I am; you have me here, tied to a chair. What do you want?"

"On the contrary, you are the one who wanted to meet," the man said as he passed in front of David holding up the note as he did. "You tell me, Mr. Ike? What do you want with the Man-in-the-shadows?" The man snickered. "That name is just too dramatic. Why don't you call me Mit for short?"

"Mit?" David asked. "M-I-T, as in man-in-the-shadows?"

"That's right," Mit said with a nod. "The *s* is silent,"

David snorted. "Alright, Mit." He said, his tone

betraying a hint of mockery. "How do I know that's who you are, or if I can trust you? You haven't told me anything about yourself. If you are the man in the shadows, you ordered a Prowler attack on our ship. We might have been killed."

"If you recall, other than a harmless warning shot, you were not fired upon. The only danger you were in you caused yourself by taking command of a ship you knew nothing about and flying it like a cross-eyed Viörn. If nothing else, let that prove our conscientiousness and that we do not rashly extinguish life, no matter the reason." Mit paused, seemingly to let his words sink in. "As for proof of who we are, we have no proof except the treasonous acts we participate in. If you're tired of working for Blythe and want to do some good, then you're at the right place. Otherwise, we will dump you off where we found you, and you can continue to flounder. Now, answer the question: what do you want?"

David paused to think, planning his words. "He's a murderer and a thief. He killed Paula, Samantha, and Mercy, and he's probably done a lot more. I— I want to bring Blythe to justice. I want him to answer for the crimes he's committed, even if it means crushing the Equalist party."

Mit nodded as he passed in front of David again, folding the note in his hands and replacing it in his breast pocket. "Tell me, did your family ever talk to you about politics?"

David shook his head. "My father and grandfather were military, so they avoided politics. Part of the job. My dad always said our political beliefs didn't attach to a party, but rather the characters of individuals."

"Well, no matter what he might have said, he was a Pragmatic through and through, as was your grandfather."

"How do you know what they were?" David said with another snort. He looked at Mit with a smile. "Did you know them?"

"I did," Mit said as he paused in front of David.

David's smile vanished, and he looked at the man in earnest.

"I only met your grandfather on one occasion. It was in passing, and I could hardly claim him as an acquaintance. Your father, on the other hand, was one of my comrades in arms. We were on a mission together early in our careers."

"Maybe what you say is true," David said, "but how do you know they were Pragmatics?"

"They are gone, David, and I have no way to prove what I am telling you. What I do know is that your father and grandfather's Pragmatic views caused some conflict within the Armada, and eventually led to their retirement."

David looked at his lap as he thought back to the day of the Academy Skiff Race. His father told him about a conflict, but he never revealed the source. "They never told me. I didn't even know he'd resigned from the Armada until after he died."

Mit sighed, turning his back to David. "I only bring it up because causing the downfall of the Equalist party may not be such a bad thing. Perhaps knowing your parents were opposed to Equalist ideals will harden your resolve in bringing down Blythe, and in time, you might perceive politics as they did."

"I need no hardening of resolve to bringing the speaker to justice, on that you have my word." David said as he stared at Mit's back.

"And how would you go about achieving such a feat?" Mit asked as he turned to face David.

"We could start with convicting him of murder."

"How's that? We might know it was him that did it, but we have no proof, and even if we did, no one would charge him."

"There's a man, Inspector Kenneth Winston. He was the Inspector looking into the murders. He helped me figure out it was Mr. Blythe who murdered all three women. Find him, and you will have all the evidence you need and somebody to press charges."

"Well, where is he then? I'll have my men pick him up tonight."

"I don't know. The last time I saw him was the evening of the census. I've called the Capital City police a dozen times, and I can't get ahold of him. I finally stopped. If he's *missing*, it probably means he's dead, and my calling would only raise suspicion."

"Not exactly your best plan, finding a man who's probably dead."

David shrugged. "It's all I have to work with at the moment. You did sort'a catch me unprepared."

Mit snickered and nodded. "It's not much, but we'll

look into it."

"Well, I've answered your questions. Are you going to answer mine?" David asked and felt rude in the asking, but the ropes on his wrists and ankles weren't precisely common courtesy. "What do you have in mind for me? I assume it entails more than being tied to a chair? Trust goes both ways, does it not?"

"Well, since you put it that way, there is something you could do for us," Mit said as he clasped his hands. "We need you to steal something?"

"Steal something? But I'm not a thief?"

"... and after we've had a look at it, we need you to put it back. *Borrow* is probably a better description than steal."

"Oh, that does make me feel better about it. If anybody catches me, I'll be sure to tell them that." David sighed. "What is it you want me to steal?"

"Inside Mr. Blythe's office, there's a records vault. You know the one I mean?"

David nodded.

"Well, it just so happens that there are only three people with the combination to open it: Mr. Blythe and his two aides, which includes you."

"I've been through all those records. I don't think any of them are of use."

"Oh, we're not after a record. There's a small black cylinder about the size of a shoe. We know Blythe put it in the vault recently, so you may not have noticed it. We need you to steal it, pass it off to one of our agents, and then put it back in the vault after they've had a look at it.

If all goes according to plan, Speaker Blythe will never know it was missing."

"It's not exactly in my line of expertise." David gave an idle twist of his wrists and felt the rope bite into his skin again. "If I refuse?"

"As I said before, refuse or accept, you will be released. You know nothing of us, neither where we are nor who we are. We have not shared any sensitive information with you that you didn't already know. And, I am convinced that you truly believe, as we do, that Blythe must be brought to justice. Releasing you will not cause us harm. However, as we are an organization that can only prove who we are by the treasonous activities we perform, we only accept membership from individuals who participate in treasonous acts. If you accept and gain our trust, we will train you as a sneak and equip you with what you need to crush Blythe. That I can promise you. If you refuse, this will be our last conversation. Just remember, you made Speaker Blythe, and if we cannot bring him down, you will have to live with the consequences, knowing all the while that you did nothing to stop him."

That made David cringe. "I'm not afraid for myself," he said as he looked at Mit. "If mine were the only life I had to be concerned with, I would have shot Speaker Blythe last season. But it's not. I have a mother to worry about, and she cannot survive in my absence. What you are asking me to do… it affects more than just myself."

Mit nodded as if he already expected this answer. "We know about your mother and her condition. Like I said,

Mercy told us many things about you. We've been watching your apartment for some time. If anything were to happen to you, we would care for your mother. In that, you have my word. Her future need not worry you. Now, what is it going to be, David? Are you ready to commit treason?

David looked at Mit, knowing the gravity of the decision he was about to make, and understanding there would be no going back after today. Could he trust this Man-in-the-shadows, a man he had never met, who'd told him things he'd never known about his own parents? His better judgment urged caution, but something else— something deep down—wanted to trust the stranger. David made up his mind and clenched his jaw with determination.

* * * * *

Mercy watched as they questioned David. She listened to his answers. She fought back tears when he talked about looking for her body, silent tears rolling down her cheek. She almost gasped when he turned his head and looked right at her, but she never said a word as she watched. That was the agreement. She could observe from the shadows, but only if she remained absolutely silent. She wanted to cry out. She wanted to tell him she was still alive if only to heal the wound he felt so deeply. But she kept to the agreement. Even when they put a sack on David's head and marched him out of the room, she kept silent. If she'd reach out, she could have touched him. Then he was gone, airshipped back to his apartment.

"Will he do it?" someone asked.

Mercy looked up with a start. Everyone had left the room, save Mit.

"Yes," she said, nodding slowly. "Blythe's crimes have transformed David's admiration into loathing. As long as he feels his mother is safe, he'll help us bring Blythe down."

"Can he do it? Not the burglary—that will be a cinch, and Francisco will be there to smooth things over. Can he unseat Blythe before the war starts?"

Mercy didn't answer for a moment. "He has the capability, but he's lost a lot of his drive since last I saw him. He needs hope again."

"No, Mercy," Mit said. "I know where you are going with this, and the answer is no."

"But if you just let him know I'm alive." She countered. "Give him hope again."

"This is not a love story, Mercy. It's a war, a bloody deadly war. David hardly trusts us as it is. What would happen if he knew your death was a fake? If the limp body he held in his arms, and the blood that seeped into his clothes was nothing more than a ruse? Your death was the catalyst that pushed him onto our side. We can't take that away, not yet. Not when all our plans hinge on the lad."

Mercy sighed and nodded.

"The truth is, I knew his father very well. I also hated him with every fiber of my being. He betrayed my confidence. Thus, it's difficult for me to trust the son, but after this job, we'll take incremental steps, the last of which will be revealing you."

"Last!" Mercy said with a gasp.

Mit nodded. "I'll see about giving him hope again. Maybe when he has a cause, it will reinvigorate him. Giving a man a mission he believes in always invigorates his efforts."

"Perhaps, but only when that cause helps the people he cares about," Mercy said in one last desperate attempt to change Mit's mind.

Mit laughed. "Did anyone ever tell you that you argue too much?"

Mercy smiled, her first one in a while. "My brothers, all the time."

Mit took her arm and led her out of the small room. "I'll bet they did."

As they passed out of the room, Mercy found it ironic that this room was both where she discovered who David really was, and where David discovered who she really was. They moved down a hallway with wide bay windows overlooking several massive laboratories. "Well, more to the point. I want you to cement your role as Don Johnson's assistant. You shouldn't come into contact with anyone from your previous life, and if you do, your disguise should suffice."

"When do you want me to start diluting the Pharmaceuticals?"

"Blythe sent out his request to the Don last week. Let's allow him to see some results before we pull the plug, but only administer his modified drug in the Capital

City. That should be enough to convince him."

Mercy nodded. Mit was right in a way, having something to do certainly gave her motivation, if only because she didn't have to think about David. But as she climbed into her skiff and headed to her new apartment, she continued to ponder over David. What would he do when he finally discovered she still lived? Would he hate her for what she'd done? Would he be able to forgive her?

Chapter Three

CAUGHT IN THE ACT

As the private steam lift arrived at the speaker's offices and the door opened in front of him, David took a careful step into the foyer. It was just like any other day. Soft music played from a phonograph, and the sweet smell of fresh-cut orchids hung in the air. Light poured in from above and below as the early morning sun shone through both glass ceiling and glass floor. He heard soft giggling from one of the many female assistants as she both resisted and invited the attentions of an orbital guardsman. And that was the source of his hesitation. At least a dozen guards patrolled the office, ever vigilant.

I can do this. Just act normal. David thought as he blew out a breath. He walked through the foyer, smiled, and greeted the first guard he passed, something he'd never done before.

The speaker's offices covered ten times the surface area of the old 3rd district offices, bisecting all three floors of the orbital and conveniently situated one door away from the Assembly Room. A spectacular stairway spiraled up the center of the floors, from the first to the third. Amenities included washrooms on all three levels, a fully stocked kitchen, and enough couches to sleep the entire Assembly. Evidently, it had been done. The steam lift he had just exited came directly from a private dock on the bottom of the orbital. No more security checkpoints; no more lines, just a flash of the pass.

David walked into the center part of the office and started up the stairs. He spotted the giggling girl chatting in a dark corner with a guard – Chanel, that was her name. If she played this game with any more guards, she was likely to have a riot on her hands. He continued up the stairs, hand on the golden railing until he reached the second floor and his own private office. It was a comfortable space without any window-floors located between Bethany and Francisco's offices. However, before he stepped off onto the second floor, he climbed a few additional stairs and spotted a very stern looking Gerald and Hans, Blythe's personal guards, where they stood flanking the doorway of the speaker's office.

The third floor consisted of two doors: one to Speaker Blythe's palatial office, an apartment really, and one to the open-air promenade deck. David dropped his satchel and coat on a chair as he entered his office. He rested his hands on his hips and chewed his cheek. If Gerald and Hans were here, Blythe was too, something David didn't expect after the gala. A black cylinder the size of a shoe was not something he could slip under his shirt and walk away with. He had to do this the smart way. David squared his shoulders and walked up the last flight of stairs towards Blythe's office, but as he reached the top step and looked at Gerald and Hans, his confidence faltered. He stepped up to the office door, knocked, and waited for a moment. When there was no reply, he raised an eyebrow at Hans.

"He was here overnight after the gala," Hans said, "but got up early to take his lady friend home."

David smiled, wondering how the fiery redhead would handle the dismissal speech Blythe eventually gave all his young women. What Hans said also told him that the office was empty.

David nodded. "Could you go to the concierge's desk and see if he arrived back at the docks yet?"

Hans scowled, but before he could offer protest, David pushed the door open and slipped inside. He stood behind the door just long enough to hear Hans stomp off, grumbling to himself. Then, he ran across the office toward the document vault.

"Just another day at the office, just another day at the office," David mumbled to himself as he reached the large, ebony-iron door and started turning the combination dials. He hardly noticed the sheets and comforter laid out on one of the oversized couches, or the three empty bottles of spirits sitting on the coffee table. The desk appeared untouched with its rows of pens perfectly aligned, and stacks of paper precisely arranged. It didn't take a genius to know that the type of work that went on there was less political and more romantic. David turned the final dial and heard a sharp click as the vault unlocked. He heaved the door open and turned on the light. A room twenty paces in length stretched out in front of him with a double row of file shelves on either side. He poked around the vault, but all he saw were documents. He pulled open the few drawers, but nothing resembled a shoe-sized cylinder. Knowing that any minute his window of opportunity would shut, he grew more frantic as the seconds ticked by. He climbed on top of a box and looked along the top of the shelves. He rifled through reams of documents marked *top-secret*, and he saw nothing. He stepped back to the door, considering giving up, when he noticed a space between the shelves of files and the floor. He dropped to his hands and knees and peeked under the four-inch gap. Something caught his eye toward the middle of the vault. He slid across the floor and reached his arm under the shelf, grabbing hold of a curious object and scraping it along the floor. It caught on the lip of the shelf. He pulled a few times with panicked grunts before he thought to turn in sideways. It slid free, and he looked at what he had found: a black, oblong cylinder, about a foot in length and five inches in diameter.

David didn't pause to celebrate. He scooped it up and ran out of the vault. Switching off the light and swinging the massive door shut, he sprinted across the office. He paused before exiting long enough to position the black cylinder against his chest, cradling it with his mechanical arm. He shouldered the door open so that his back faced Gerald. To David's great relief, Hans hadn't returned to his post on the left side of the door, and no one was there to see what he had pressed against his chest as he walked down the corridor. He allowed a smirk to slither across his face until he reached the top of the stairs and realized he was trapped. Blythe and Hans rounded the bend in the spiraling stairway, deep in conversation as they climbed the last flight to the third floor. Without missing a step, David continued down the hall and out the exit that led to the promenade deck. He prayed they had not seen him.

Once outside, he shivered as the icy wind chilled him. The sun hung a hand's width above the horizon, giving the cloud carpet a brilliant golden sheen. The promenade deck of the orbital was initially designed for representatives to stroll in-between sessions of Assembly, though few people used it these days. Manicured shrubberies filled the polymer boxes that scattered the walkway around the tops of Orbital balloons. Here and there a fountain burbled in brass-colored basins. David stepped out onto the Promenade and wished he had remembered his coat, not only to protect from the cold but also to conceal his pilfered goods. He walked around a few planter boxes to the edge of the deck and leaned against the railing.

What was he to do now? He held something of more importance than top-secret documents, and he had no way to conceal it. He could walk all the way around the promenade and enter the orbital at one of the other entrances, but, there again, he had no way of concealing what he carried, and he'd forgot his pass in his coat pocket. There were any number of guards along the way, and a security checkpoint before he could enter the speaker's offices. He let out a steamy breath as the cold started to prickle his nose. That's when he heard the door shut, and Blythe's voice call out.

"David, are you up here?"

David whirled around and saw the speaker rounding a planter less than twenty paces away. David looked down at the cylinder in his arm and gulped. He searched around, and, on a whim, he tossed the object into the planter box beside him. When he looked up, Blythe was striding toward him from around the planter box, Gerald and Hans on his heals. David tried on a smile, but it ill-suited him. The guards only escorted the speaker when there was something amiss or trouble in the air. However, Blythe stepped up to him with the same warm smile he always wore.

"I've been worried about you. You disappeared so suddenly last night and missed most of the party. I hope everything is ok?"

"Um, yes. I had to leave because of my mother. I don't like staying away for too long at a time."

"Hmm, I see. She's feeling alright, though? No concerns?" As Blythe asked the question, David noticed his eyes flick ever so quickly to the bushes where he had tossed the cylinder. A simple motion, but it brought a flash of heat to David's face so suddenly that a trickle of sweat slid down his neck.

"No, no, none at all. She's fine."

"You're sure?"

David nodded with a content purse of his lips.

"I see," Blythe said, nodding as he spoke, but then he

put a hand on David's shoulder and looking him full in the face. "David, you've been acting very strange these past few days. You're not your usual self. So I'm only going to ask you this once, and I want the truth. Is there anything you wish to tell me?"

David fought to keep his face placid as he shook his head. "No sir, I'm fine, honestly."

Blythe nodded along with David as he straightened up and crossed his arms. Then the man sighed as he reached into the planter box and retrieved the black cylinder. David's heart sank. Blythe held the device in front of him with a questioning look, but David said nothing as he hung his head, unable to hide the guilt as he examined his shoes. Blythe turned the object over in his hands a few times before grasping one end and sliding off a cap with a hollow pop. He looked inside the cylinder, and then down at David.

It started as a smile, then rolled into a chuckle, and finally, an all-out laugh. Blythe laughed until he held his sides and moaned.

"David, I just spent an evening with a woman 20 cycles my junior in the most scandalous fashion. And yet, you're the one blushing about something as trivial as a smoking ban on the orbital. Aw, David," Blythe said as he massaged his forehead. "Sometimes, I forget how young you are."

David looked down at the cylinder as perplexed as ever. Blythe pulled out some loose straw, and a waft of musky scent filled David's nose. He tried to laugh, but his body had experienced such a range of emotions it came out as a whine. Blythe slid out a seven-inch stick and held it up to the sun.

"Hang on," he said as he brought the cigar closer to his face and squinted at the label. "David, do you have any idea what these are?" He looked at David with wide eyes. "Royal Empress Cigars! These are Viörn and just about the finest I've ever seen." He turned the cylinder's cap over and read the inscription. "Great maker, 2277! These are vintage, hand-rolled cigars, and the most coveted cycle. Speaker Spencer smoked cigars like these during the protectorate wars. The Assembly used to complain because they couldn't understand him, as he habitually spoke with one in his mouth. My goodness, David, where in the Fertile Plains did you find them? They probably cost 100 sterling apiece."

David's mouth fell open, but he quickly shut it and struggled to spin a tail. "My, well, my grandfather had a few boxes. He's gone now, and I've been going through his things. I had no idea they were worth so much money."

Blythe ran the fat cigar under his nose and closed his eyes as he breathed in. Then he looked around in a quick motion, and back at David. "I'd love a good smoke. How about we light up a pair." He didn't wait for David to answer. "Hans, Gerald, see to it nobody sees us." Blythe walked around the planter and sat on a bench on the other side, motioning for David to join him. "Got a light?" He asked as he nipped off one end of his cigar and spit the bits off the side of the orbital.

"Um, in my haste I left it in my office."

Blythe chuckled as he shook his head. He handed David the cigar case, and David did his best to imitate him, as he had never smoked a cigar in his life.

"Hans, you have any matches?" Blythe asked.

The burly man walked over and handed Blythe a little box of matches, before returning to his watch. Blythe struck up a match and sheltered it from the wind as he lit his cigar. After a few moments, a puff of rolling smoke wafted from his mouth and carried away in the breeze. He handed the matches to David as he leaned back on the bench and closed his eyes, breathing out a contented sigh.

David used several matches as the wind kept blowing them out. He was glad Blythe had his eyes closed. Finally, David lit up a match and jammed the cigar into the flame until it started to smoke. He sucked the head until his cheeks drew inward, but nothing happened. He'd forgot to bite off the cap. By the time he'd done so, his cigar had nearly smothered itself. He blew some life back into the cinders, took a long pull, and promptly swallowed. The thick smoke billowed out of his nose, and he fought convulsions.

Blythe opened his eyes and looked at him. "Are you alright?"

"Yeah, fine. I got some smoke in my eyes, that's all."

The speaker nodded and sighed again. "This is the life, is it not? Beautiful women, fine parties, fine wines, and excellent cigars. You know, I'm not sure I can say I've ever been as happy."

David nodded his assent as he swallowed away a

cough. "Agreed," he added in a raspy voice. He looked at the cigar in his hand and inwardly groaned as he put it to his lips for another drag.

"Everything is going according to plan," Blythe said as another waft of smoke poured from his lips. He made it look so easy. "My scientists have come up with a drug solution for both children and adults. It will reduce depression and increase cognitive function in all our citizens. I met with Don Johnson last week, and he is ecstatic. His facilities are working overtime to produce the compound by next week. Imagine it, David: Our people free of depression and anxiety, free to go about their day without hindrance. Children learning in schools without any intellectual stunting."

"Sounds like utopia," David said in between stomach contractions.

"That it does. We aren't perfect, though. I'm already beginning to feel resistance from the few Pragmatics left in the Assembly. Hopefully, my next economic plan will force them right out of office."

"You mentioned that in your speech last night. What do you have in mind?"

Blythe crossed his legs and took another puff on his cigar. He put his arm around David and squinted the way he always did right before he wanted to have an intellectual conversation.

"Do you know how to generate a political base?" He asked.

David shrugged. "Serve the peoples' needs?"

Blythe shook his head. "Before that. You have to

generate a need, or a crisis, something only you have the solution to fix." He poked a finger in David's chest a few times for emphasis. "It forces people to believe in your campaign because you were the first one to see the problem and provide the solution. Honestly, at its base, there really isn't much need for the Assembly beyond keeping the peace and promoting trade. Wars are few and far between, and the dons could promote trade just as easily as we could. You have to convince people you're needed; the greater the need, the greater the support. That's what my economic plan is all about. I'm going to convince people, not only in Equalist districts but in the remaining Pragmatic district as well, that they need our help." Blythe finished his explanation with a pull from his cigar.

"How's that?"

"By taking away pragmatic money and giving it to Equalists," Blythe said with a smile. "It's that simple. I'm going to pull funds from wealthy businesses, particularly in the 6th, and shunt it to our poorer district. The poorer district will love me for it."

"But how will that convince people from Pragmatic districts that they need your help? They won't exactly thank you for taking their money?"

"Only the business owners. The common workers, which outnumber the owners 100 to 1, will be the first to feel the hurt. The business owner will no longer be able to pay them as they once did, and the common workers will turn to me for a solution. It won't take much, only a little shove for them to blame their woes on their employers and their Pragmatic representatives. How long after that will it be before the Equalists have complete control?"

"Not long," David said with a nod of his head and a frown at his cigar. "Will it harm our economy?"

"At first, but we can fix that later in a controlled environment."

"What of the Fertile Plains unification and the deconstruction of the Armada? You mentioned that too. Have the Viörn and Berg reached out to you for a peace summit?"

Blythe nodded. "I'm to attend the Royal wedding, and, while there, we plan to have talks of a unified Fertile Plains."

"Wouldn't that be something," David said, feeling his guts turn inside out. Something was not right with his innards.

"That it would," Blythe said as he slapped David on the back. The movement caused David to choke as he swallowed back a gulp of bile. Blythe stood as he continued to puff on his cigar.

"Well, I best be off. Many things to do this season before our golden day retreat." He started to walk away toward Hans and Gerald, but he stopped halfway to them.

"Oh, and if you want to smoke in your office, I think I can let it slip." He put the cigar between smiling lips as he continued toward the door.

David sat there for a moment and watched the three men leave the Promenade deck. Then he leaned over the railing and spewed sick into the Alönian sky. He looked down at his cigar and tossed it over the side after his breakfast. David picked up the case and slid the lid on, loathing the sight of it. After exiting the Promenade deck, he passed by Bethany's office and saw her slumped over her desk in a mess of blond hair. No sooner had he entered his own office, he felt another bout of nausea. He leaned over his wastebasket and dry-heaved.

"Mate, you're an absolute moron," a voice said as a light switched on.

David looked up from his trashcan, spittle dripping from his chin, at a man sitting with his feet crossed on top of the desk. "Francisco? What on earth are you doing in…" but the rest was lost in a gag.

Francisco picked up the case of cigars, where it lay rolling around on the desk. "How did you manage to turn such a work of art into a puking nightmare?" He took one of the cigars out and rolled it between his fingers. "For future reference, never swallow cigar smoke."

David used a tissue to wipe his chin. "How are you supposed to smoke it if you can't swallow?"

"How am I supposed to get my job done when I have to work with an imbecile like yourself? First, answer me that? You were supposed to retrieve an experimental Viörn transponder, not custom Viörn cigars."

"Well, they didn't tell me it was a transponder… Wait, you? You're the agent?"

"It doesn't matter what they told you. What idiot would come back with a case of cigars? I suppose it's for the best, given that you botched it anyway."

"I didn't know it was a cigar case. It was the only black cylinder in the vault."

Francisco held up his own black cylinder, only this one had a black sheen to its surface and looked to be made of metal. "Did you try looking in the box in the middle of the floor?"

"Yeah... No," David said with a frown. Thinking back to the box he'd stood upon to look on top of the shelves. "I didn't think to look there. Hang on, how do you have it?"

"I went in after you scuttled off with your cigars... like a panicked Loper. Somebody conveniently forgot to relock the vault. Despite how hard you tried to thwart this job, you actually did manage to do one thing of use. It was rather simple work with the guards gone."

David flushed with embarrassment. Everything about this was unsettling, especially the fact that Francisco had said more words in the last five minutes than David had heard him use during their entire acquaintance. Not to mention, he spoke with a strange accent he had never heard before. "Well, I'm sorry, alright. It's not exactly my line of work. I'm just trying to help. How did you see all of that anyway? There was nobody else on the third floor but myself and the guards."

Francisco folded his arms. "We all have our areas of expertise."

Even if he didn't say it, David speculated the bionic eye played a part. "Well, don't you have to copy it or something."

"Already did that while you were turning green on the

top deck. But, since you're so eager to help, how about you find a way to put it back before he notices it's missing."

David jumped as Francisco tossed him the transponder. "But... what do I do after that?"

"We'll be in touch," Francisco said as he stood from the chair and walked toward the office door. "Oh, and this time, try not to confuse the cigar case with the cylinder."

David watched Francisco leave, spittle still dripping from his chin. He stood up from the wastebasket, trying to think of a way to get the case back into the vault while also holding down his nausea. All the excitement of the past hour had drained him, and returning to Blythe's office was the last thing he wanted to do. He decided to start small—cleaning his face and the wastebasket in the washroom sink—but as he returned to his office, he looked at the wastebasket in his arms, and he had a thought. Grabbing his satchel, David took one of the financial reports he'd been working on and stuffed it and the transponder inside. He took a deep breath, picked up the cigar case, and ascended the stairs once again. After knocking and receiving permission, he entered Blythe's office. Blythe sat at his desk on the far end of the office, pouring through some papers and sipping from a glass filled with his favorite pink liquid.

"Ahh, David. Something you need?"

"No, sir, I'm just returning a report I took from the vault this morning."

"Very good, well, go right ahead. You remember the

combination?"

David nodded as he spun the dials and pulled the door open. Regardless, Blythe stood from his desk and meandered across the room toward him. David opened the vault as quick as his fingers would allow and slipped in before while Blythe was still several strides away. As Blythe entered the vault, David was just sliding his insignificant financial report in between a massive stack of classified Armstad Defense specs.

"I still can't believe you have a 2277 case of Royal Empress cigars," Blythe said as he reached inside David's satchel and pulled out the black cylinder. He grabbed either end of the cylinder and pulled. Nothing happened. Blythe hunched over and pulled again with considerable force. This time the top of the cylinder came free with a pop. Blythe looked inside and smiled, smelling the cigars one more time.

"Marvel upon marvel, David, you never cease to surprise me."

He replaced the cap and handed the cigars back to David. But as David took the case, he let it fall to the floor and roll under the shelves."

"Damn," Blythe said. "No, no, let me." He added when David started to bend down.

When Blythe lay on the vault floor and reached under the shelf at the exact same spot David had found the cigars, David reached beside the stack of classified Armstad Defense specs and grabbed the communication cylinder. As quick as he could, he stepped over Blythe and slipped it back into the box that Francisco had described. As Blythe sat up from the floor with the cigars in hand, David stood there with his hands clasped and a grateful look on his face.

"Hang on to those, lad," Blythe said. "It would be a shame if they were to be lost."

David nodded as sheepishly as he knew how.

Blythe walked him through the office with a hand on his shoulder and even opened the door to let him out. This time, as David smirked at the top of the stairs, he felt as though he'd earned it.

Chapter Four
THE SILENT PRAYER

Marguerite awoke to the hum of voices around her, the sound of men whispering. Her eyes opened on their own account, at least, that's how it seemed. She didn't remember opening them herself. She lay in a bright room, so bright the light compelled her to squint, but now that her eyes were opened, she found she could not squint or close them.

Why was she in a bright room? How had she got there? It smelled sterile, like disinfectant. Rhythmic beeps, whistles, and hisses of a dozen different machines all added to the general din of the strange place. Yet, as her eyes prickled with the sting of a thousand needles, a reaction to the light she could not avoid, her memories returned. She'd been on an airship, yes, an airship in the mountains with her husband and her son.

The trickle of memories became a flood, and with them an excruciating pain in her heart. Her husband, her love, she had watched him die, his body incinerated with their airship. She felt the pain of his passing, but she could not feel the tears that she knew she must be crying. In fact, other than the pain rending her soul, she could not feel a thing. She could hear herself breathing, but she couldn't feel it. She could hear the throb of her heart, but she couldn't feel the blood pumping. But that was not what troubled her most of all.

Her son... her David! Where was her son? She remembered their perilous fall in the mountains. She remembered their combined weight was too much for their life balloon. She grew frantic, but to all the world, there was no outward sign of it. She screamed, but no sound escaped her mouth. She thrashed, but there was no movement. She persisted for some time, but eventually, her inner self grew fatigued, and she quieted her soul and listened.

The voices were still in the room, though she could not see them. But as she lay there beneath the bright lights, she began to understand them.

"... the lad should be out of surgery soon, the sooner, the better. They've been here too long already."

"Martin, how could you say such a thing?" A second man said. "These two have lost so much in recent days. Have a heart."

"I see turmoil every day." She heard Martin reply. "How are they any different than all the other sad cases that roll through our hospital? I've heard too many screams and seen too many broken bodies. I've exhausted my supply of sympathy. No, I find if I ignore my heart and focus on my job, I endure quite well."

"But how will they live? Does that not concern you? The boy has but half a body left and the mother, none at all. Where will they go?"

They said more, but Marguerite was no longer listening. Half a body? They weren't speaking of her son; they couldn't be. He was young and healthy and still growing. She had seen him yesterday... or the day before. How long had it been? What had happened while she slept? Where was David? Merciful Jeshua, please let him be alright. She had to see him! She had to! She had to see him...

But her weakened body couldn't withstand the stress, and she drifted away in a wakeful sleep. Voices visited her in her dreams, voices she did not know. Sounds of people walking roused her on several occasions, but she never roused for long.

Then she heard a voice she recognized, and the sound of it made her alert. It was David's voice, and he was close.

"... What's wrong with her? Why won't she look at me?"

"She's paralyzed, lucky to be alive. One of the worst breaks I've ever seen, several actually."

"Will she be ok?"

"She'll be fine. We are doing everything we can. Come along, it's time to attach your prosthetic."

"But I want to speak to her."

"Um, no. It's perhaps not a good time for that. She is very tired. Rest is what she needs right now. Come on, let's away. Don't you want your arm back?"

Then they were gone, and Marguerite was left with her thoughts. She felt weightless like the world was underwater. A nurse came in some time later and washed her. She panicked at first when the nurse forced a tube down her throat, but the gag never came. What had the doctor said? Paralyzed. She realized with horror then that this would be her method of feeding for the rest of her life. The weight of the word took effect as she struggled in vain to lift her arms. The nurse left, and Marguerite started crying as worry, turmoil, and loss threatened to drown her in their endless depths. But before she succumbed, she reached out to the only support she had left, an anchor in the storm her life had become.

Merciful Jeshua! Help Me! Please!

She prayed and prayed, and eventually her prayers brought her peace in the form of sleep.

* * * * *

"Why has nothing been done for her?"

Marguerite came awake as she heard David's voice again.

"Well, I'm afraid your hospital bills have wiped out whatever meager funds you possessed when you entered. On top of that, we already used the maximum amount of governmental support funds available per family. There simply wasn't enough money to perform surgery on both you and your mother. And besides, your mother's condition is tenuous, and the results of such an experimental operation are uncertain, at best. We selected you over her for surgery due to your age and your greater potential for society."

"But… but you don't understand, my father was a captain in the armada. We had indemnification for exactly this kind of incident."

There was a sigh. "My boy, our records indicate that your father resigned from the armada nearly a season ago. We checked the records. His early retirement forwent all health indemnification or stipends."

Marguerite felt herself burning up inside. He didn't resign! He was forced out! They hadn't told David because they didn't want to upset him, especially not when he had his own troubles to deal with at the academy."

"Oh… I didn't know." She heard David say. "But what about me? I'm in the academy. That has to be good for something?"

"Your benefits only apply to yourself, and only for incidents occurring during academy activities. You see… there simply isn't anything we can do."

"But where will we go?" David asked. "If you send us from here, how will my mother live?"

"There are many people sick in the Houselands." The stranger sounded tired of the conversation. "The public hospital cannot expend more resources on one citizen simply because of the heartbreaking condition. We must spend our resources where we expect to see the greatest return."

"Yes, of course. I'm sorry," David said. "We are grateful for everything you've done so far."

There was a pause.

"If... If you need a place to go, might I suggest the Third District of Braxton?" The Doctor said. "Representative Blythe has recently implemented some social assistance programs. Maybe you'll find help there."

The voices moved away, and for a moment Marguerite thought she was alone. Then she saw him; she saw David as he walked over beside her bed, but she couldn't turn her head to look him in the eyes. She could only see half of him, and the half she saw made her heart ache. His left arm was missing at the shoulder and replaced with a hideous mechanical monstrosity. It was oversized to his 14-cycle-old frame, and the weight of it made him slouch. Everything in her wanted to cry out, to hold her son, but she could not. All she could do was lie there as tears flowed down her cheeks. She heard more than felt him begin to brush her hair. She could tell he wanted to say something, even though she couldn't see him, if only because she knew her son better than he knew himself. Then he sniffed a few times.

"Grandfather died last night," He said as he choked off a sob. "The— The doctor said his heart gave out upon hearing the news of Father's..." He sniffed again.

"Don't worry, mother. I'll take care of us." His voice took on a false cheer. Her wonderful son was trying to hide his own pain to comfort her. Marguerite felt her heart breaking.

"Everything is going to be fine. I... I'll—" But whatever else David wanted to say choked off in a sob. She saw the room jostle as David fell into her chest and cried. He hugged her, but she could not hug him back. He spoke to her, and she said nothing. He came to her in pain, and she could not make him feel better with her kisses. She was powerless. Her boy needed her now, more than ever before, and all she could do was watch him suffer. Memories of running her fingers through his hair and holding him close plagued her immobile limbs. She could never do it again.

"I don't know what to do, Mother. I don't know where to go. We have no money, no benefactors. Any day now I expect I'll receive a letter from the academy medically discharging me. All our family is dead. I don't know what to do. I don't know what to do!"

He continued like that, clinging to her, shaking with the sobs that racked his body until at last, sleep took him. Sleep for him, but not for her. She could not sleep, not anymore. She doubted she ever would again.

Sometime later—she did not know how long—there came a knock at the door. David awoke and was careful not to rock the bed as he sat up. He stood and walked to the door. It was her doctor coming to check on her.

"Ah, David. How are we today? Your arm giving you any trouble? No, of course it's not. I'm here to give your mother one last checkup before she's good to go. You'll both be free to get out of this dingy old hospital." The man had a box under his arm that he sat aside as he checked some machines beside Marguerite's bed. "Yes, I think she is doing marvelously. She'd tell you herself if she could."

"When do we have to leave?" David asked.

"You can leave this afternoon if you wish. We are all good here. She's fit as a fiddle."

"No, when do we *have to* leave? When will the hospital kick us out?"

"I'm afraid I won't be able to let you stay any longer than absolutely necessary. Since both you and your mother are no longer in any immediate danger, and because there really isn't anything else we can do for you... Well, you understand, don't you?"

"Can we stay the night? Just one more?"

"There really isn't any need. You are both in quite good health."

"Just one more night, sir. I have no idea where we are going to go after this, and another night would give me enough time to make some arrangements."

There was a pause, and then the doctor signed. "I suppose I can delay signing off on your release for another night. But I'm afraid that's it. You will have to leave by tomorrow."

"Thank you, sir, I appreciate it."

Marguerite saw the doctor wave his hands in exasperation and walked back toward the door. He opened it, but before she heard it shut, the doctor spoke. "By the by, those packages arrived for you. A letter and the box beneath." Then a door thumped shut, and the sound of footsteps faded into the distance.

Marguerite heard David lift the box and bring it over to her bed. He sat it beside her and tore open the letter on top. She could see his face as he read it. His eyes teared, but he didn't let himself cry. He sniffed and let his hands fall to his sides as he looked at the ceiling. From her vantage point, she only saw the top of the letter, but the academy crest spoke volumes. David's dream of becoming an aeronaut, his chief pursuit of following in his father and grandfather's footsteps had been cut off with a simple letter.

"Well, we both knew that was coming," David said as he refolded the letter and laid it aside.

Next, he opened the box and looked inside. He gasped and pulled out the contents with eager fingers.

"It's the strongbox from the airship. It survived."

David had it out and open in an instant. Then he froze as he saw what was inside. Marguerite couldn't see what it was, but then she caught a glimpse of the family revolver when he laid it on the bed. She had been with her husband when he purchased it from an Armstad vendor. While she never understood its value while he lived, it was invaluable to her now simply because it was his in life. The gun brought back sweet memories, or perhaps bittersweet.

David wrapped the pistol in a cloth and moved on to the other items in the strongbox. There was pocketbook with a modest amount of sterling—thank Jeshua for small favors—and her husband's old satchel. David held the bag for a long time, looking at it but not opening it. Finally, he lifted the cover and pulled out the only thing inside. It was a book, and she saw David examine it with a puzzled expression.

Marguerite watched him eye it for a moment as he turned it end over end. They had never told David about his father's early retirement from the armada, nor had they told him their plans to pursue a future in politics. They were going to tell him everything at the end of their holiday in the mountains. It pained her to see David struggling to understand why his father had a PLAEE study book in his satchel. Father had taken the exam not three weeks previous, and the vacation was partly a celebration of his high marks. After a cycle as an aide, he hoped to steal a seat as a Braxton representative. It was all planned out. Now, it was merely a future that could never be.

She watched David flip through a few pages in the book, stopping when he found some marked pages. But it didn't seem to be the pages that gave him pause. Instead, it was the bookmarks. David held up the photos that father had used as bookmarks. Marguerite couldn't see them, but she knew her husband well enough to know he'd use pictures of his family to mark pages in his studies. David looked at the photos for a long moment before he reverently replaced them in the book. He had a look at the book cover with a contemplative expression. Then, he started pacing, and he continued to do so long into the night.

Marguerite caught glimpses of him as he walked back and forth. While she couldn't help physically, she could still pray, an escape into the arms of Jeshua. She prayed even after David stopped pacing and inventoried all their possessions on the bed. He counted and recounted the few sterlings he'd found in the pocketbook. He wrapped and rewrapped the pistol in its cloth and stowed it in the satchel. Then, as the first light of dawn filtered through the room's only window, David sat on the edge of the bed with the PLAEE book and started to read.

They left the hospital that day and moved to a city, though Marguerite could not tell which. She remembered the air smelling rank, and after a few nights of moving about, they settled in a tiny little apartment that overlooked a dirty city. From there, she lived her life, watching her son fight for his own in the midst of tragedy. At first, she did not want to live, knowing that her life was only a burden on an already suffering boy. But in time, she realized that her presence was something David needed. She was the only one who listened when the rest of the Fertile Plains drown him out. And, she once again found solace in prayer, the one activity her debilitated body could manage with no difficulty at all. It was her fortress, her only hope.

Chapter Five
EQUIPMENT UPGRADE

A week passed after David's *vault heist*, as he liked to call it. However, after more than a season of idleness, a week tried his patience to its limit. Ever since Blythe ascended to the speakership, He found himself idle during the working hours. He arrived early for work purely on principle, though he hardly ever did anything. Most of the office staff never arrived at all, and nobody seemed to notice or care. This week David either spent his time pacing his workspace or fidgeting with random objects. He reorganized his desk twice. All the while, he wondered when Mit would contact him again, and what results his vault heist had wrought.

What made it all the worse was the knowledge that Francisco sat three doors down the hall and possessed all the answers David desired, yet he refused to capitulate any. Daily David visited the spy's office, asking, in code of course, when he was to expect another assignment, or at the very least, news regarding the mysterious object he helped steal. But the exchanges always came to the same result.

"Have you heard any news from our mutual friend and the cigars I procured for him?" David asked on several occasions, and then he would proffer a very bold wink.

But Francisco never accommodated; rather, he feigned ignorance, and on occasion, spoke in riddles, saying:

"What the devil are you talking about?" or "I'm afraid you've got the wrong man. I only ever use prescription drugs."

And so, after a week's time, David grew tired of asking and vowed he would wait in silence until the little snot decided to speak. But all that was about to change.

David walked home after work from the transportation facility, hands in pockets, and whistling a very off-key tune. There he happened upon Ella, his mother's nurse, as she ran out of the Lousy Lodgings steam lift.

"Oh, David, thank the maker," She said in-between gasps. "Come quickly, it's your mother."

"What about her?" David asked. "Is she ok?"

"She's suffering from a fever, and despite my ministrations, it only seems to worsen."

David didn't wait to hear more. He ran the rest of the way back to his apartment and burst into his mother's room. Placing a hand on her forehead, he sensed what Ella had described. Her skin felt as though she'd been sitting to close to a fire. It also had a yellow tinge to it. David stooped and looked into his mother's eyes and noticed the same tinge there; though, even in sickness, his mother made no response. The faint breath that came from her nose felt hot and moist. David didn't waste any more time, as he lifted his mother's emaciated frame and charged out of the room.

"Where are you taking her?" Ella asked from the door.

"The hospital. I don't think this is an ordinary sickness."

"But David, they won't have room—"

David didn't listen. He rushed into the steam lift and ran through the twilight of the dirty streets he knew so well until he arrived at a Third District public hospital a few blocks away. He entered the center for emergencies, and his mouth fell open at what he saw. People packed the square room to capacity, all dressed in dingy old clothes that smelled of urine. Rusty girders arched across the ceiling giving the space an industrial feel.

David ignored the rabble and pushed his way to the reception desk at the back where a middle-aged man in a dirty lab coat sifted through some files. The tag on his jacket only designated him as a *doctor* without any surname.

"Hello, doctor. It's my mother she's—"

"Fill in your name and have a seat. We will be with you as soon as we can." The doctor never looked up from his files, and he spoke with a dejected voice.

"But… But she needs to be seen right away."

The doctor looked up then. His eyes were ringed with fatigue. "We are required to see patients in the order they arrive. You will have to wait your turn. I'm sorry, but there is nothing I can do to alter that."

David opened and closed his mouth several times before leaning his mother against a table, which was the only available space nearby, and stepping up to the sign-in sheet. He filled in her name as well as her date of birth. However, he put his name down as her guardian, and after a moment's thought, he added his occupation in hopes that it might open some doors.

David turned to pick up his mother, but when he saw the throng in that stuffy waiting room, he despaired. Turning back to the doctor, he pressed his case again.

"Sir, are all these people waiting to be seen?"

"They are."

"And how long would you estimate it to take for my mother to be seen?"

The doctor looked around David at all the people behind him and winced.

"Perhaps, sometime tomorrow."

"Tomorrow!" David said with shock.

"Or the next day, it's difficult to say," the doctor added, and then he put his hands up in a placating gesture in response to David's frustrated face. "We don't have a choice. Our beds are packed to capacity."

"What if I made an appointment and returned?"

"Appointments are booked two seasons out. The hospital doesn't have enough rooms or personnel to deal with this kind of volume."

"But, wasn't legislation passed last season that boosted the public hospital funding?"

"Yes, and with that funding came a drastic increase in

patients." The doctor sighed and rested his hands on the counter. "You see, when the populace realized they could enter the hospital for free and receive beds, meals, and treatment for their self-imposed illnesses, mostly caused by illegal usage of antipsychotics, they came by the droves. As you can see, most of the people here are homeless reprobates." He whispered the last part in a conspiratorial manner.

"What about a private doctor?" David said.

But the man shook his head. "There aren't any left. The city requisitioned every doctor to meet the public hospitals' growing demands, and they issued an ordinance to revoke any private practitioner's license to dissuade any from practicing outside the hospital."

"So there's nothing I can do? My mother might be dead by tomorrow!" David said as his frustration mounted.

The doctor looked at Mother for a moment where she lay against the table. Then he reached out a hand and placed it on her forehead. He leaned across the counter and used a thumb and forefinger to hold open one of her eyes.

"Why is she non-responsive? How long has she been like this?" The doctor asked with a quick look at David.

"She's been paralyzed for the past five cycles. Airship Accident."

The doctor pulled his hand back very slowly as he pursed his lips. "It must have been a terrible accident. Did... Did the doctors tell you about potential health problems after the accident?"

David nodded. "They said she only had a few cycles before her organs would begin to fail. Is that what's happening?"

"Your right about her needing immediate attention." The doctor said, ignoring the question. He lowered his voice as some of the others in the waiting room murmured, clearly suspicious that he giving David aid ahead of his turn.

"Listen to me, you won't find any help here. The hospital implemented immediate provisions to speed up patient care. When we see patients, our diagnoses are based on their age and probability of recovery. Your mother may have some time left, but on paper, her condition is mortal, and she is in the final stages. If you wait through this interminable line, and by some miracle your mother is still alive at the end of it, the only thing the hospital will do is give her a sedative and send you on your way."

David opened his mouth to berate the doctor, but the man pressed on before David could say anything.

"I desperately want to help you, but if I did, the hospital would throw us both out before I could do anything useful."

"So, am I just supposed to watch her die?" David said amidst a feeling of hopelessness.

The doctor was at a loss for words at that. He looked around for a moment before he held up a finger and disappeared around the corner. After a good while, David feared the doctor might not return, but then he reemerged walking with forced casualness. He placed his hand on the counter palm down and heaved a great sigh.

"I'm sorry. You're just going to have to wait your turn, sir. I can have some more chairs brought in if you would like?"

David wanted to shout at the man, but then the doctor removed his hand from the counter, leaving behind a small brown pouch. He looked David in the eye and gave a barely perceptible nod.

"Um... no, the chairs won't be necessary," David said as he grabbed the pouch and retrieved his mother.

"You're sure? It's no trouble."

"Yes, I think we will tough it out at home. Thank you for your help, doctor."

The doctor nodded. "Bear in mind, even with medication," he placed special emphasis on that word, "your mother only has a short time. She needs significant help if she is to survive the week."

David swallowed hard and nodded. Turning, he left the pungent reception room and stepped out into now dark streets. He held the small pouch in his fist, which he suspected was filled with pills. They didn't give him much hope. Although the doctor hadn't said it, he guessed the organ failure he'd feared for so long was finally ravaging his mother's body.

As soon as he entered the night air, the sounds of the city assaulted him, and chilled mist swept over him. He shivered and held his mother even closer, not knowing where he should go next. Home to spend his last few days with her? Or should he seek help elsewhere? Such was the depth of his desperation that he actually considered going to see Blythe.

But as he stood there contemplating, an air-taxi descended from the murky clouds, landing several strides away. It struck David as strange, as this was not an appropriate landing zone. Presently, the rear hatch opened, and to David's shock, out stepped Francisco.

David gawked at the man, but Francisco gave him his usual drab look.

"Are you going to gape like that all night?" Francisco asked. "Get in, it's bloody chilly out here."

David recovered from his surprise enough to nod and stumble toward the skiff. He laid his mother down on one of its plush benches. Then he took a seat across from her and held her hand as the airship ascended. David looked around the air-taxi's interior and at Francisco, who sat beside him.

"How did you know where to find me?"

Francisco jerked a thumb behind him. Only then did David see a figure sitting in the shadows on the far side of the ship.

"We were watching your apartment, remember?" a voice said from the darkness. "They notified me that you took your mother to the hospital, and I came directly. What's wrong with her?"

"I think she's going into organ failure," David said as he felt his mother's forehead yet again. "The hospital said they weren't able to do anything for her other than a few pills."

"That would figure after the last medical directive out of Blythe's office," Mit said from the shadows.

David nodded. "So the doctor told me."

"Well, don't you worry," Mit said. "I'll have my doctors take a look at her."

David continued to hold his mother's hand for the journey, which was far shorter than he imagined. In no time at all, he felt the taxi bump up to a dock at the base of an old factory and heard some clamps fasten. The rear hatch lowered, and David jumped as a medical team raced into the skiff and lifted his mother onto a gurney. As the team wheeled her away, he stepped out of the skiff into a long hallway with armed guards flanking either side. Without thinking about it, David followed the medical team as they wound through a few corridors. He passed several rooms, some filled with people, some filled with munitions. They took his mother to a surgical room, one of many in a long line. A man in a lab coat, presumably a doctor, did a quick vitals check and then gave some orders to his colleagues. The last thing David saw before they shut the door was his mother's pale, weary face.

She is in the very best of hands, David" a man said from behind David as he stood staring at the closed door.

David nodded as the man gave him a gentle squeeze on the shoulder. But as his mind shifted from thoughts of his mother to thoughts of where he was, he got a chill, especially as he realized who it was squeezing his shoulder. David turned around very slowly and faced the man in the shadows, except there were no shadows here. He looked up at a man in his late forties with a stern yet an honest disposition. Some might describe him as handsome, others, brooding. He had a shaved head, something that concealed his receding hairline, and his brown eyes shown with intelligence. David had to look up a long way to meet those eyes, but when he did, he saw no danger in them.

"Aren't you concerned at revealing yourself to me?" David asked.

"You've proved yourself trustworthy," Mit said. "Besides, after seeing me, do you have any idea who I am?"

David shook his head.

Mit smiled and nodded down the hall. "Walk with me."

He led David down one corridor and rounded a corner into an observatory that overlooked an airship hanger with a few dozen military-grade skiffs docked three high in elevated berths. There was a table there with a steaming pot of tea and a pair of mugs. They sat down, and Mit poured himself and David each a cup of tea. Other than Francisco, who stood a few paces back, no one else was in the room.

David massaged his forehead with his clenched fists and let out a long breath, the stress of the evening taking its toll. He stopped when he realized he had something in his hand. It was the brown pouch the doctor had given him.

"What do you have there?" Mit asked before sliding a mug of tea across the table.

"The public doctor gave me some medicine for my mother," David said. "I completely forgot to give it to your doctor."

Mit motioned for the pouch, and David handed it to him. Mit opened it, poured some of the pills into his hand, and held them up to the light.

"I wouldn't trouble the doctor with these," he said after squinting at a code on the pill. "These are an antiseptic, and not even a very strong one. Our supply is much better."

"Lousy doctor told me it was the best he could do." David said with a bitter scowl.

"I wouldn't be too hard on the good doctor," Mit said. "He couldn't help you even if he wanted to. You're lucky you got this much."

"He said as much," David said with a shake of his head. "I don't know what I would have done if you hadn't picked me up. Speaking of which, what is this place?"

"It doesn't really have an official name," Mit said. "Most of my men call it the underground. After Blythe came to power, we went dark. Most of us are ex-armada, commandos, or old sneaks who know Alönia is headed to ruin unless something changes."

"But all this costs money and a lot of it. Where do you get the funds?"

"All that is to come. But first, you'll be happy to know that the transmitter you helped steal..." Mit paused as chuckling issued from Francisco. "Be nice, Francisco, He did help us," Mit reiterated with a glare at Francisco before continuing. "The transmitter that you helped us steal has been extremely informative. Were you told exactly what it was you were stealing?"

David shook his head.

"Well, it's a long-range communication device, highly experimental. We've known for some time that Blythe's been talking with people some distance away, but we haven't been able to establish who. While you were having a smoke on top of the orbital, as it were, Francisco cloned the device, and we've been listening in on Blythe's communications. Most are in code, so we still have no idea who Blythe is speaking with, but we did piece together a discussion about a meeting to take place on the twelfth golden day at 11:00 pm."

"That's during the speaker's retreat in House Thornton," David said.

Mit nodded. "We want to eavesdrop on that meeting, in person if we can. If we can get an eyeball on whoever Blythe's mysterious friends are, we might be able to discern his future plans. The trouble is: security will be quite strict at this event. We probably won't be able to implant any of our own people into the retreat. That means you and Francisco will have to do the eavesdropping by yourselves."

David looked over at Francisco, who sat with his head in his hands. "I'm certainly willing, but won't I just get in Francisco's way? I don't see how I can add to the operation."

Francisco looked up and nodded vigorously in agreement.

"Francisco is a sneak, not a politician. You have a knowledge of politics and foreign policy that is nearly unmatched in the Fertile Plaines. It's possible you're one of the only people capable of identifying these mysterious friends on sight. We will send you with insta-cameras, but there might not be a good opportunity to snap a picture."

"Oh, I see," David said slowly. "Well, if Francisco is willing, I certainly am."

"Oh, Francisco is willing whether he is willing or not. Aren't you Francisco?"

Francisco grunted and looked away.

"Well now that that is settled, there is one other matter I wanted to discuss with you." Mit leaned forward in his chair and took a sip of tea. "Do you remember my promise? I told you that if you worked with us, we would give you some training and an equipment upgrade."

David nodded.

"Well, for starters, how would you like a new arm?"

David gaped at Mit. "I... You'd do that?"

"Well, I always send my men in with the best possible equipment, and no offense, but you'd probably be better off with one arm than with that rusty, old contraption."

David looked down, unsure of what to say. It was what he'd always dreamed of but never thought could be a reality.

"Of course, if you're attached to it, we can just see about cleaning it up..."

"No sir, you misunderstand my speechlessness. This arm may be attached to me, but I am not attached to it. I'd be very grateful for a replacement."

"Excellent!" Mit said as he drained his tea in one gulp and stood. "You can write Blythe a note telling him you're having surgery to replace your arm, and we will begin right away."

"Now?" David said in surprise as he stood with Mit.

"Why wait?" Mit said. "You'll need a season to get used to it before you and Francisco snoop about in Thornton."

David stammered for a moment, but before he knew it, he was jotting down a simple note to Blythe informing him that he would be out for a week due to his mechanical arm. It was hardly necessary, as Blythe would probably not even notice his absence. Little in the way of real work happened at the office, and Blythe had expected nothing from him after his rise to the speakership. David also checked on his mother. Her condition had stabilized after the doctor administered some very strong antibiotics. Seeing the way the underground cared for her convinced him he was doing the right thing. She was in the best of care. An hour later he found himself in a surgical room lying on a gurney beneath a bright light and beside a long table of intricate, sharp instruments. He shivered as his bear skin touched cold metal. A doctor gave him something to drink, and in a matter of moments, his eyes fluttered, and he drifted off to sleep.

* * * * *

David awoke in a most unnatural manner. He lay for a long while unable to rouse himself. He could hear beeping from somewhere nearby, and he squinted beneath the bright lights, but his body felt sluggish. In time, he awoke fully and sat on the side of his bed. To his surprise, he lay in naught but his shorts. He felt strange, and when he tried stretching, pain lanced across his shoulders. He looked down and gaped at a mechanical arm unlike any he had ever seen.

It looked remarkably similar to his natural hand, with the exception of the polished black surface. He opened and closed the fingers with fascination. This new mechanical arm shone with a sleek black finish, and it felt light, considerably lighter than his old one. He glanced around and saw a mirror on the far side of the room. Sliding off the bed, he stepped onto the cold floor with his bare feet and gasped when he felt the same excruciating pain shoot up his weak leg. It buckled beneath his weight, and he fell on top of a surgical table, sending dozens of intricate instruments skittering across the floor. His fall against the table jarred his shoulders, causing more pain. He breathed between clenched teeth and looked down at his leg. What he saw shocked him: two legs of the same length. He rotated his former gimpy leg and saw a row of incisions stitching down one side of his knee and calf. He looked back at the mirror, and despite the aches and pains that throbbed across his shoulder and leg, he straightened and walked across the small room with stiffness. He grunted with every step, but he would see himself in the mirror!

He reached the mirror and fell against a table, sending another lance of pain through his shoulders, but he shrugged it off and looked into the mirror. His mouth fell open, and all the pain seemed to vanish. He reached his mechanical arm up and touched the glass with a coal-black finger. He cocked his head and noted that his shoulders sat level without their usual slant. He worked them back and forth for a bit, admiring their mobility. But that wasn't all: he was taller! Either that or everything else in the room was a few inches shorter.

He looked at his legs again. Having two of the same length made him considerably taller. David smiled and looked back across the room, determined to take another few steps. He'd walked with a limp for so long that stepping with an even gate sounded wonderful. He stepped, and his even stride felt as though he was walking on somebody else's legs, and he loved it. The pain reassured him that they were indeed his own. He walked by the mirror again and couldn't help but admired his new physique, in spite of the grimacing pain. As he looked down at the table beneath the mirror, he noticed a large hand-shaped dent in the metal. He examined his ebony hand and furrowed his brow, wondering if it had caused the damage.

David curled his fingers into a fist and punched one of the beams in the middle of the room. His eyes widened, and he bellowed a cry so loud he was sure the entire city heard him. He leaned forward and panted as the pain subsided. When his wits returned, he noticed a scrape in the beam but not even a scratch on his fist. David stood very still, holding his arms outstretched. At that moment, the door opened, and Mit and a doctor rushed in.

"Are you alright?" Mit asked with concern, but then he surveyed the room and chuckled. "Oh, I see you're just getting used to your new limbs."

The doctor was not so amused. He scowled at David but held his tongue.

"Everything is… different," David said, between gasps as he scooted back to his bed, holding his mechanical arm above his head.

"Perhaps if you'd stayed in bed—" The doctor began before Mit cut him off.

"Nonsense Dr. Abraham. Sometimes you have to run before you can walk. You may prefer an idle patient, but I prefer active sneaks."

"Well, for the sake of my surgical center, please refrain from running," Abraham said, and then he stepped over to David and began examining him.

His fingers were cold to the touch, and David's skin prickled with every contact. All the while, Abraham mumbled to himself.

"That has healed nicely. I do the best work, I always say. Lift your shoulder, lad. That's right. Any resistance? No, of course not."

Mit stood for a moment, but then he busied himself cleaning up the wrecked surgical room. He snickered when he saw the handprint in the table. David, feeling uncomfortable enough as it was, remained silent as Abraham prodded him, prattling on about his expert work. At last, Abraham sat back in a chair and nodded.

"Before you stand again, and wreck another room, understand exactly what it is I did. Your accident in cycles past, not only severed your arm but broke your leg in such a way that it stunted its growth—hence your limp. The mechanical contraption those beastly butchers attached to your shoulder worsened the condition. It weighed nearly a kilogram more than your natural arm, and over the cycles it contorted your skeletal structure. I didn't simply replace your arm; I also did a bit of work with your shoulders, spine, and leg in order to straighten your posture. In particular, I lengthened your leg and augmented it to the point where it is just a slight bit stronger than your regular leg—this is why you might feel a poor sense of balance. Your back and shoulders are now in a position where you will not feel the need to slouch. Do you understand what I'm saying?"

David, who had been nodding along, stopped and shook his head, no.

Dr. Abraham sighed. "Suffice it to say, you are going to be in a lot of pain for about two weeks. I've given you some supplements and serums to accelerate the regular healing process, but science can only do so much. The rest is up to you. We will steadily increase your exercise over time. Yes?"

David nodded.

"Now, your arm," Abraham rubbed his hands together in greedy self-approval. "Your arm is a work of art designed in my home country of Armstad. The dent you put in that table is only a fraction of its capabilities. For starters, it's fashioned from ebony iron."

"What?" David said with astonishment. He looked at his arm in newfound wonder. "Ebony iron? But that must have cost a fortune. This arm is worth more than an airship!"

"A very nice airship," Mit said as he straightened the

surgical instruments he'd put back on the table.

"Quite so," said Abraham. "That means it's the same weight as your natural arm yet nearly indestructible. You could take the full firepower of a super fortress and still be able to bequeath that arm in your will. You'll also find the appendage to be extremely agile. Strength wise, your body will give out far before your arm, so you must understand your limits. That's probably all you need to know for now to help you familiarize yourself with the appendage. Once you feel as comfortable with this new arm as you are with your natural one, we'll talk about upgrades and attachments."

David gulped. "Upgrades? Attachments? I can't imagine anything upgrading this beyond what it already is." He looked at Abraham and then at Mit. "I'm not sure I will ever be able to thank you for such a treasure. Not only the arm," David said as he spun the wrist a few revolutions, "but also the ability to stand without a stoop."

"Trust me, lad," Mit said. "You will earn the right to wear that arm… if Francisco has anything to say about it. You'll train with him every night for the rest of the season until the golden days. By the time your Thornton mission arrives, you won't be able to recognize yourself."

David continued to smile, in spite of himself, flexing the arm and admiring its superior quality. It had been so long since he'd known anything… normal. But, at the same time, it wasn't normal. It was extraordinarily strong, sleek, and compact, a beautiful marriage of man and machinery. If he had known then exactly how much work training with Francisco meant and how sore he was going to be for the next season, he might have given the appendage back right then and there.

Chapter Six
OLD FRIENDS

Mit desperately wanted to scratch his back as he lay in the snow at the base of the Rorand Mountains, but four cycles of hard training taught him self-control. This mission, the first of his career, was not at all what he expected it to be. For cycles he'd dreamed of excitement, daring sprints, and glorious firefights. Thus far, he had sat in an airship flying through chilling winds only to take up a position on a half-frozen hill to wait in four feet of freezing snow. Berg, he decided, was the most unpleasant country in the Fertile Plains. No wonder the Bergish people had such an itch to conquer other lands. They desperately needed a beach where they could thaw their frostbitten limbs.

Mit clenched his muscles to ward off a shiver. Despite the weather, and the boredom, he still possessed a thrill in his throbbing heart, the thrill of knowing he was singled out of an entire class of sneaks to perform this mission. How he had swelled with pride the day his instructor called him in and outlined the mission. Berg, a long silent enemy, had a turncoat, or at least a self-proclaimed turncoat. His mission was to cross the Bergish border, flying close to the foothills of the Rorand Mountains until they got to Vojh Nović's Mound—a hill with a statue of the famed Bergish Admiral erected in honor of his brave sacrifice, or suicidal butchery as Mit described it. There, at midnight on the 37th day of Derecho Season, they would meet their turncoat friend. Mit liked the mission brief, up until the part about his escort. The armada wanted a hand in this mission. If Alönia was going to disturb the waters and cross a long-established line, the armada wanted to make the most of it. They insisted that one of their own recent graduates fly Mit in on a skiff and be ready for evacuation if the mission boded ill. While Mit's mission was to meet and assess the possible turncoat, the armada's representative was to update the Alönian annals on Berg's military might. Mit disliked the idea about as much as all Sneaks disliked Armada officers. But what was to be done about it?

His escort was a legend at his academy in the same way that Mit was a legend at his. He was a four-time champion of their oh-so-blessed academy skiff race, a feat only the legendary Admiral Ike had accomplished. This Ensign Ike even shared the same name as the legend, though anyone who knew him could tell there was no connection with the famed Admiral. He was too quiet to be the son of a famous admiral.

Mit felt a light nudge at his shoulder that brought him out of his musings. There was movement at the edge of the frozen tree line, and the Armada Ensign had spotted it first. Mit gave an almost imperceptible nod, something he hoped would communicate that he already knew about the movement. So far, this Ensign Ike had been a quiet fellow following Mit's lead as the mission parameters required. He only offered suggestions when Mit was unsure how to proceed, and only then when Mit looked to him. The lad was tall, not as tall as Mit, but taller than average and about Mit's age. His athletic bearing made Mit wonder if he could take him in a fight. He piloted them through the night along the Rorand Mountains with almost careless ease, as if flying and breathing flowed from the same instinctual source. Their stealth vessel never left the mists, yet, they arrived ahead of schedule at the precise location without any deviation in course, a navigational wonder. If Mit had to pair with an Armada Officer, Ike seemed probably the best choice.

The movement at the base of the mountain transformed into a man extricating himself from the shadows of the tree line. Only the light of the moon revealed the figure. He trudged through the knee-high snow until he reached the base of the embankment. He looked around for a moment before he started the slow assent to the top of the mound. Mit and Ike chose a knoll at the top of the mound a few strides to the right of the statue as their hiding place. They lay there for a moment as the turncoat walked thrice around the statue, ignorant of their presence. At last he stood and leaned against the statue, checking his wristwatch and breathing out clouds of steam. Only after an additional five minutes did Mit climb from the snow in his all white camouflage and approach the turncoat. The man jumped when he saw Mit, seemingly shocked that a person had materialized out of the frigid air. Mit approached him slowly and with his arms cradling his repeater, a gesture that was one part friendly and two parts forceful. He reached the turncoat in a dozen strides upon which the stranger raised his hands in a solute.

"Strength to Alönia," He said with his Bergish lilt.

"Peace friend," Mit replied in perfect Bergish. "What brings you to this dismal monument?"

The man paused for a moment, apparently surprised at hearing his own tongue in such fluency from a foreign mouth. But the traitor persisted in his own broken Alönian.

"You who I'm supposed to meet, yes?" He said, reaching out his hand.

Mit did not take it, but he did switch to Alönian as the man insisted on speaking it. "If you are a traitor, then yes. I am who you're supposed to meet. What information do you have for me?"

"No," said the traitor with a shake of his head. "Leave Berg first. How many come? Can we get out and safe?"

"I can get you safely out, but only when I know what you're willing to give us. Your message promised information. We will not leave until you tell me the quality of the information you possess."

"You only?" The traitor said in apparent frustration. "Where the rest? Where your airship?"

Mit balked. "Airship? How the devil did you expect

me to get a whole airship across Berg without being seen? I came alone through a pass in the mountains. I have enough gear to get us back to Armstad and then Alönia." The traitor looked aghast. "You? Alone? No airship? Impossible! Crossing Mountain is death."

"Perhaps, but it all depends on how determined you are," Mit said. "So tell me, Mr. Bergish traitor, how badly do you want to leave Berg?"

"No airship," the traitor said with a sigh and a nod. Then he snorted and gave Mit a sly smile. "No Berg would ever leave. We are strength, and Berg is power." In an instant the turncoat pulled a pistol from his sleeve and pointed it at Mit. At the snap of his fingers, a squad of soldiers rushed out of the tree line around the mound and ascended.

"Drop weapon," the traitor said. "Or I shoot."

"No information then?" Mit said as he dropped his repeater in the snow.

The Berg laughed. "You information. We wanted airship, but you will do."

By that time, the squad of soldiers had reached the top of the mound and surrounded Mit and the would-be-informer in a tight ring. Mit placed his hands on his head and closed his eyes. He could hear the hum of an airship approaching from the east, no doubt to collect him and his capturers. He could hear a soldier approaching from behind him with a pair of jingling arm restraints. As he heard the men around him prattling on in their guttural tongue, he squeezed his eyes shut as tight as he could and waited.

It happened quickly, a flash so bright Mit could see it through his shut eyes followed by the growl of a repeater. As soon as Mit heard the sound of the gunshots, he lunged forward onto the spot where he'd thrown his own weapon. It was well he did, for bullets pelted all around the place he'd stood mere moments after he landed in the snow. A red splotch stained a place right next to where he lay. It oozed from the man he'd come to meet, a rather ironic turn of events. The traitor of a turncoat had trapped himself within his own trap.

Mit grasped his repeater with firm hands, rolled over in the snow, and unloaded his magazine on the soldiers that still stood. The situation was unfair in the extreme. The Bergs ran wild in their blindness firing their weapons at the sound of gunfire. Half the squad fell to friendly fire; the remainder fell to Mit and Ike's precise and deadly repeaters. As the last body fell, the two Alönians were on their feet and racing up the foothills of the Rorand Mountains. They reached the cover of the trees as the approaching airship found their carnage with a wandering searchlight.

"It appears you were right about the trap," Mit said as the two of them darted around trees. They could hear the sound of multiple airships now, and the trees around them glinted as spotlights searched their shadows.

"I didn't know there was going to be a trap," Ike said as he lurched over a fallen tree. "I just didn't want to get caught in one."

The chemical flash was Ike's idea, and Mit was very thankful for it in his present condition. At the time, he'd doubted its necessity, but allowed Ike his cautions after the Ensign stressed the necessity to plan for the unexpected. They'd implanted the chemical flashes three days prior to the meeting and agreed that Mit would place his hands on his head and shut his eyes in the event of an emergency.

"Well, I'm bloody glad you thought of it," Mit said between breaths. "Now, how about we scuttle our airship and make for the border. Perhaps in a season or two we can thaw our frostbit toes in the Armstad hot springs."

"No," Ike said breathlessly, "I'll take my chances with the airship."

"What? We'll never make it out with all of Berg on our trail."

"Listen," Ike said as he grabbed onto Mit's sleeve and pulled him to a stop. He held a gloved finger to his lips.

Mit slowed his panting breaths and focused on the silence, and then he heard what Ike was talking about, the baying of Bergish red hounds.

"We won't make it one hour with those on our track. Our only chance is the airship."

Ike let go of Mit's Sleeve and charged on.

Mit followed. "But don't you see, all they wanted was the airship. If you fly out of here, they will shoot you down and recover it from the wreckage. We have to scuttle it."

"The only way they will get this airship is if it rains from the sky in fire and ash," Ike said with confidence. "Trust me, there will be less of it left if they shoot it down than if we try and scuttle it."

By that time, they'd reached the place where they'd landed. Ike bent at the base of a small hill and reached into the snow. He jerked on the corner of a tarp, and the whole hill slid away revealing the two-man skiff beneath.

"Ensign Ike, I cannot allow this. I'm in command of this—"

"Wrong," Ike said as he checked over the airship's twin tail and intakes. "You are in command of the meeting; I am in command of infiltration and extraction. This," Ike waved his hand around, "is called *extraction*. Now you can either join me or walk, but either way, I am flying this ship back to Armstad."

The moment hung in the air. Mit gritted his teeth. He didn't like it, but he knew his place. And he knew Ike was correct about the extraction command structure. It dawned on him that this disagreement stemmed from their vastly different areas of expertise. Ike knew airships and would rely on them in his moment of need. Mit was a sneak. Hounds didn't trouble him. Seasons in the frozen Bergish wastes didn't trouble him. Confinement in an airship a thousand fathoms above the ground with hundreds of enemies giving chase through the sky... that *definitely* trouble him.

"You're sure," Mit asked. "You're sure you can make the flight?"

Ike smiled in that way that only airship pilots could manage. "I'll bet my life on it," he said.

To his amazement, Mit found himself climbing into the gunner's seat behind the daring Ensign. The man's bearing inspired his confidence. Ike seemed like so much more than a lowly Ensign. He carried himself like an admiral, relying on the efforts of others, yet stepping in and taking command when needed. It was this bearing that drove Mit to trust him—that and the prospect of freezing to death in Berg.

Ike started up the burner. Within a few moments the lift gas flash heated, and the skiff rose into the air. It only took the Berg seconds to pinpoint their location after the whine of their airship reverberated through the forest. Mit could see half a dozen airships swirling like vultures above the scraggly, white trees. How Ike hoped to climb past them without getting shot to pieces, Mit did not know. He was already starting to regret his decision when Ike slammed the accelerator down. But the skiff rocketed forward... not up!

Mit realized Ike intended to fly *beneath* the tree canopy, and he really started regretting his decision. He gripped his seat with white-knuckled fingers as the airship lurched back and forth dodging trunks, limbs, and stumps. Ike was insane. No pilot could fly through such debris at this speed. Mit looked out the windscreen and then regretted it as the motion twisted his vision in knots. He took deep breaths and pushed away the nausea.

Chain-gun fire riddled the trees around them. Mit swiveled his chair to man the rear gun, but Ike stopped him from firing.

"Wait till we are out of the woods. Their shooting at shadows right now. They don't know where we are. Firing will give us away."

What he said was true. As Ike banked the ship up the

side of the Rorands, the enemy's fire continued along their original course. The Berg lost the Alönians to the cover of shadow, the whine of their engines, and the howl of their chain-guns. Ike kept the ship beneath the canopy yet climbing and climbing up the side of the slope. All at once, the trees fell away as the airship passed the invisible line where flora ceased to live. Mit looked down the steep slope they had just climbed and saw the squad of Berg airships continuing along the valley where they had begun the chase. He'd never even needed to fire his chain-gun. Ike pulled the airship away from the mountain and cut across the sky toward a cloudbank.

"Get ready," Ike called from up front.

"For what?" Mit said.

"They are in that cloud bank; I'm sure of it," Ike said. "I'm going to try and get above them, but I have no idea what they are hiding in there. I think this is the test they wanted all along."

"What do you mean?"

"Well, if you can't have an Alönian airship, what's the next best thing? A dogfight between their ship and yours. They're testing themselves."

"But Berg doesn't have skiff craft," Mit said as he tightened his restraints and checked his chain-gun.

"I very much doubt that to be the case anymore," Ike said as he let off the throttle and split power between lift and thrust.

Mit wished the aeronaut would get it wrong for once, but not a moment after they began their climb over the wisp of clouds, three airships shot out of the mist. They were unlike any Bergish ships Mit had ever seen, small and sharp against the moonlit sky.

"There it is. I give you a bergish skiff," Ike said. "I think we may learn more on this trip than originally planned. Hold tight."

Mit checked his mirrors and noticed that the Bergish gunships below had broken off their chase of the phantom in the forest and now climbed toward them at an alarming rate. Berg above and Berg below. He felt hopelessness closing in around him as the Bergish skiffs started firing. But Ike wasn't about to go down without a fight; in fact, he didn't seem interested in going down at all. Mit was first slammed against one side of his seat and then thrown to the opposite as Ike resumed his sporadic maneuvers. He felt weightless as they dove away from the skiffs. He swallowed down some bile as he tried to call out at Ike. High ground was everything, and this insane pilot was giving it away before even firing a shot.

"If you plan on using that chain-gun, now's the time," Ike said as he committed to the dive.

Mit kept his comments to himself and sighted in on the enemy, determined to kill at least one of the ships before he went to his grave. He squeezed the trigger and watched one of the skiffs erupt into flame and break apart.

"I got one!" Mit said with excitement, but then he checked himself as he aimed at another skiff and pulled the trigger. He realized the skiffs did not return fire. "Why aren't they firing back?" He asked.

"Because their foolish compatriots from below have

climbed into their crossfire," Ike said as the ships forward chain-guns barked. "Also, I don't think they knew this ship had a tail gun. You may find them a harder target from now on."

Ike was right, again. The two remaining enemy skiffs in pursuit bounced around as Mit squeezed off bursts of rounds. Then, he felt his seat press into him as Ike leveled off their dive. Three ships from their original pursuers sped by as Ike passed through their formation. These were larger ships with multiple gun emplacements and at least five crewmembers.

"Weren't there six of those?" Mit asked as he peppered one of the floundering gunships with bullets. It listed to the side as its balloon hissed with sealant.

"Actually, whatever you see behind us is all that's left of them."

Mit gaped as he realized Ike had downed three gunships in one dive.

"Don't worry about the last of the gunships," Ike called as he veered the ship back and forth and bullets whizzed by. "They're too slow to cause us concern. Fire on those last two skiffs."

Mit begged to differ as to what was, and what was not a concern, but he did as asked and fired a burst at the closer of the two skiffs, which were overtaking them as they completed their dive. The vessel spun away as his tracer rounds passed over it. He might have landed a hit if Ike wasn't hopping about the sky like a kite in a storm.

"Can't you fly this thing in a straight line?" Mit said as he missed his shot yet again.

"Priorities, my man. Do you want to kill the enemy, or survive?"

Mit groaned as the ship bobbed again, and he felt his stomach churning.

"Oh... I don't think mommy likes us beating up on her children," Ike said, and Mit spun his chair forward to see what he meant. He wished he hadn't.

The most enormous airship he had ever seen dropped through the clouds into their flight path.

"Well, I think we've seen enough," Ike said, and Mit fell back into his seat as their airship's velocity halved. At the same moment, the two pursuing skiffs shot past. A few bursts of the main chain-guns later, and both were falling from the sky in flame. Mit saw the corner of a dangerous grin on the side of Ike's face.

Then Ike pointed their skiff at the enormous airship and accelerated to full throttle.

"That's no ordinary Super Fortress. I think we need a closer look." Ike said.

By this time, Mit had exhausted his stores of surprise and shock. So he found himself nodding along with Ike's insane idea.

"Sure, that's... that's fine. Sounds good to me." he replied.

As they neared firing range of the ships long guns, Mit saw that it was indeed different from any Super Fortress he had ever seen. It bore the same shape as standard fortresses—a multi-decked armored spire—but this one had an unusual compartment in the middle. As he looked at it, large bay doors opened along the strange compartment, and several dozen skiffs zoomed out.

"A Super Carrier!" Ike said. "And no doubt the first of its kind. Too bad it's filled with garbage skiffs. Be sure to give them a proper solute with your gun as we fly by, will you?"

Mit rotated his chair around, but not before he saw Ike flip a safety cover from a small red button. He looked down his sights and prepared himself for one last fight. All of a sudden, their skiff bucked so hard Mit thought his head might fall off as he was flung into his restraints. Flame consumed the entire view of his tail gun port. His buckle pressed into his stomach, and the nausea he'd been fighting the entire flight forced itself upon him once again. In the midst of his panic, he heard the most peculiar sound: Laughter. Ike was laughing.

As quickly as it had begun, it stopped. The flames behind them extinguished, and the ship resumed its normal flight pattern, and the Super Carrier was far in their wake. Ike still chuckled as he banked the ship into the clouds and prepared for the journey home. Mit grabbed the small bag beside his chair and emptied his stomach in three long wretches. Ike said nothing, but he did pass back a handkerchief and some water.

"What the devil just happened!" Mit said as he slowly swiveled his chair around and faced the front of the skiff again.

"That, my friend," Ike said, "was a little something our scientists attached to this skiff in preparation for the mission. They call it the *afterburner.*"

"Why the devil did you turn it off?" Mit said as he

wiped his mouth. "Why not rocket all the way back to Armstad."

"I'm afraid it's still in the experimental phase. If I power it for more than a few seconds, we will either burn our engines out or set the ship alight. Still, I wish I could have seen their faces as we passed them by."

Mit swallowed and rubbed his face. "I forgot to salute them."

Ike leaned around his chair and looked at Mit. "Damn. Well, we could always go back...?"

"You're the Devil, Ike," Mit said as he drank some more water. "Where did you learn to fly like that?"

"My father taught me."

"Well what's his name? I want to tell him he's raised a demon."

Ike laughed. "His name is David as well."

Mit paused in mopping his brow. "Is he also in the military?"

"He is."

"And he's an admiral, isn't he?" Mit asked, putting the pieces together.

Ike nodded with a chuckle.

"Well that would follow," Mit said. "Is he as crazy as you are?"

"Probably worse," Ike said. "I think he gets more reckless as he gets older. The only thing the old goat is afraid of is dying of old age."

Mit laughed and felt better for it. "What's the legend like, I mean, what is he really like? The history books paint such a dramatic picture."

"He's not really dramatic at all, more lighthearted and playful. He knows every man on his airship and beat everyone in cards at least twice. When he's not in his battleship, he enjoys causing havoc in his skiff across the quiet countryside. The old man just doesn't know when to retire, and the Armada certainly won't force him."

"Sounds like a pleasant man."

Ike nodded. "The very best of men."

Hearing Ike talk so about his father made Mit feel envious. His own father had been very different. Violent and abusive until his dying breath; may the Maker have mercy on his soul. What kind of man would Mit be if he'd had a father like Ike's? What kind of man would he be if he hadn't put a bullet in his own father's head?

The rest of their trip went by in relative boredom as the two passed through a cloudbank across the border and through the pass into Armstad. That first mission gave them both a tremendous boost in their perspective fields, given the wealth of information they carried back. It was the first of many missions, a partnership and a friendship. They flew into Viörn twice and the Outlands on multiple occasions. They were the most effective team in Alönia, that is, until something rather sensitive came between them. At the end of their last mission, Mit drew the short straw and had to present their findings to the intelligence committee. He asked Ike to deliver a letter on his way home, a letter to a beautiful young lady named Marguerite.

* * * * *

Mit took a deep breath as he shut the folder bearing all his old mission logs. They were filled with memories he had long since buried until the appearance of David Ike, similar in appearance to his father and every bit the pilot. He looked down from the balcony where he stood. Sounds of sparring echoed up from the exercise room below. There, David worked with Francisco, as he had been every night since his surgery, steadily increasing his strength. He'd spend his days spying on Blythe and his evening training with Francisco. His efforts were not wasted. Already he walked without hindrance or imbalance. He could eat soup with his new appendage and land most of the spoonfuls in his mouth. In sparring, he bested Francisco one in five times, though his inhuman arm contributed to that in a large way, and he could almost fire his father's triple-barreled revolver without injuring himself. Still, he progressed at an alarming rate fueled by sheer determination. He was a good boy, every bit the son Mit always wanted. It made Mit wonder if he should welcome David as the son of the only woman he ever loved or hate him for being the son of his greatest enemy: the man that betrayed his confidence and stole the life he might have had.

He opened the folder one last time and looked at the picture of him and Ike smiling, arm in arm, receiving the Ebony Cross for their acts of valor. How that had changed only a few short weeks later. Mit stood and walked away from the balcony toward the hospital ward section of the facility. He passed a few empty rooms until he came to one with a light on inside. He knocked gently before entering. There, he found Marguerite, the woman that had caused him so much grief all those cycles ago. The woman who chose his best friend over him in marriage. A small piece of him wanted to ridicule her in her misfortune, to ask her where she would be right now if she'd chosen differently at the altar. But that part of him was wrong. Perhaps the part that hurt the most was the fact that he knew in a dark corner of his heart that he lost her to a better man. The woman had suffered tremendously in recent cycles, but the happiness she had before then was evidenced in her extraordinary son.

"You have to understand, Marguerite," Mit began, but paused to look away. "I had no idea you and David were alive. I've spent cycles trying to forget you even existed. If I had known your situation, I would have interfered long before. By the time I found out, David was mixed up with Blythe, and I had to proceed with caution. It wasn't... vindictive. I swear it."

He looked at the limp body where it lay on the bed, a shadow of the immense beauty it once possessed. He expected no response, but that didn't prevent him from longing.

"He's a good boy, one of the best I've ever met," Mit said after a moment, forcing himself to go on. "He's like his father. I can see he's had good parenting, and regardless of how I feel towards Ike and yourself, your boy is evidence that you had a happy life together." He sniffed away a tear. "The truth is, I miss Ike. I missed our friendship the moment I started hating him. I should have let go of my anger long before now. Perhaps if I had, things would have turned out differently. I promise I will make it up to you. I'll watch after the boy in these troubled times. I spoke with Dr. Abraham, and he's going to attempt an experimental surgery on you. If it works, you might be able to speak again, but it could also kill you. Since you are already dying, I would imagine the risk to be worth the chance to talk to your boy one last time."

Mit sat for a moment longer, until he saw a tear roll down Marguerite's cheek. The sight threatened to overwhelm him with emotion. He didn't expect a reaction out of her—he didn't even know she could still cry—but those tears, the tears of a suffering mother, broke his heart. He rushed from the room with tears in his own eyes, unable to control his raging emotions, yet a feeling as though he'd let go of a great weight.

Chapter Seven

THE EVERPINE RESORT

David had visited House Thornton many cycles before, but given his age at the time, he possessed no impactful memories. He remembered trees, and that was all. Coming back as an adult gave him an entirely different perspective.

The office staff, as well as a whole host of political freeloaders, filled two airbuses and flew to the far southwest corner of Alönia. As these were the golden days, there were no clouds to obstruct their view. David watched out his window for the entirety of the 7-hour flight. He saw the swamps of House Franklyn, the grasslands of Ellery. Away in the distance he saw part of Hopkins' hills. But as the sun began to set on the far side of the Alönian Isle, he saw the looming shadows of Thornton's forests. If he hadn't known about the famed trees, he would have presumed their airship had dropped in elevation. The tops of the massive succulent everpines reached 200 fathoms into the air... on average. The tallest recorded everpine stretched 257 fathoms into the air and was known as none other than Big Stanley—the name of the forester who discovered it. In due time, investors built a resort around the mammoth tree overlooking the astounding forest that stretched across the entirety of House Thornton.

David's airbus descended into the trees as the sun sank behind the mountainous backdrop of Alönia. Glowlights illuminated the path through the forest giants as shadows deepened and darkness descended. David glued himself to the window as the airship slowed to a crawl and meandered between the forest giants. He tried to see the forest floor, but even in daylight, the tree trunks sank into darkness long before they touched the life-giving soil. That was the secret of Thornton's exuberant landscape. Springs flowed out of the surrounding mountains and filled millions of nutrient-rich bogs that pocked more than 200 square grandfathoms of land. The combination of the bogs and the trees gave way to a paradise rich in both plant and wildlife.

David peered through the growing shadows and saw more nocturnal beasts than he had ever imagined. Indeed, the forest was as vibrant during the night as it was during the day. For, as was the case in all of Alönia, the absence of sunlight promoted a vibrant bioluminescent ecology. Massive purple shelf mushrooms jutted out from several trunks with flat tops and intricate patterns woven by their flowing web of veins. Some were large enough to hold airships, which, of course, they did. Florescent salamanders three feet in length climbed to precarious heights to snag fist-sized glowbees with their sticky tongues. Gangly tree jumpers leapt 25 fathoms between branches, pouncing on unsuspecting rainbow-grubs. As one of the frogs leapt, fiery underbelly shimmering in the darkness, a shadow swept over and snatched it out of the air.

David gasped and pressed his face even harder against the window searching the bowers for another glimpse of the dark predator. He didn't get one. Despite only seeing a shadow, a creature that large and that agile in flight could only be a Leatherwing. David had read about them in school: the largest winged creature in the Fertile Plains, and they only lived in Thornton. They were a kind of amphibious bird that bred in the bogs and hunted in the treetops. David watched as luminescent wonder after luminescent wonder shimmered past his window until their airship docked alongside an extravagant landing that ringed one of the enormous trunks.

David collected his travel bag and followed the rest of the people off the airbus. He knew the faces: aides, assistants, secretaries, guards, Eric, but he'd taken to ignoring all of them in recent weeks. As they filed out onto the landing bay, the other airbus full of the people docked and unloaded. David saw Francisco walk down the ramp with Bethany lagging behind as she towed a gigantic suitcase far larger than necessary for the six-day retreat. Francisco joined David and then rolled his eyes as he turned and watched Bethany drag her bag across the floor. She sat on it once she reached them, breathing hard.

"How come yours is so much lighter?" She asked as she pointed to David's modest-sized travel bag.

David took pity on her and switching his bag to his flesh arm, he easily lifted her oversized suitcase with his ebony arm.

"But I already tried that, and it didn't work!" she said as she crossed her arms and huffed.

"No matter, Bethany," David said, failing to hide his smile. "I'll carry it."

"Okay, excellent," Bethany said without thanks as she spun around and marched off after the rest of the people.

The circular landing dock looked like a modern version of an old fashion lodge ringing the ancient tree that supported it. Polymer beams, made to look like everpine branches, stretched out from the central tree and sloped away. Glass panels covered the beams, which were in turn covered by real bogweed thatch, giving the entire roof a rustic appearance. Rough carved planks covered the floor of the ring-shaped room, while polished wooden railing surrounded the outer deck. To the perceptive eye, the only actual wooden structure in the whole room was the living, central tree. Everything else was a synthetic replica. A resort concierge met the party at one end of the landing and led them over a wide arching bridge toward a grand lobby, which was a massive circular building suspended between four everpines.

From the bridge David could see the majority of the resort buildings as their lights sparkled in the darkness. The resort stretched from tree to tree via sky-bridges or boardwalks all surrounding the famed everpine. Big

Stanley stood in the center of the resort with a lit circular walkway that wound up its trunk, along with several steam lifts that rocketed less vigorous patrons straight to the top. David looked up from the bridge as he walked, and despite Big Stanley being lit all the way to the top, he had a hard time visualizing exactly how high the tree reached above him.

As he stepped into the resorts grand lobby, his jaw dropped at the rustic wonder. Several water features burbled and churned with some of the local wildlife flitting within—young ones of course. The wooden floor planking formed a square pattern around smooth bluestone slabs, and as far as David could tell, it was actual stone. The weight of such a floor created an engineering wonder. Leather furnishings sprawled around lush shrubbery in wicker containers. The vaulted ceiling bore the same wooden beams he'd seen earlier, except instead of a thatch and glass ceiling, this one was all wood paneling, and it reached for 20 fathoms. At the room's center, a stone base held a roaring fire within a glass casing and a glass chimney that piped the smoke all the way to the apex of the domed ceiling and out the top.

David liked this place very much. It was one part natural and three parts comfort. As the party gathered in the room, he noted that there were no other vacationers other than the resort staff, those who were part of the retreat, and some guards. They flanked every hallway and major junction. While David glanced around the room puzzling at this, a man of ordinary stature in a pinstriped suit climbed to the top of the several stairs to the landing surrounding the fireplace and called them all to silence. Beside him stood Blythe and a pretty little brunette. Blythe flew to Thornton separately on his new yacht— generously paid for by the Alönian houses. David longed to see the airship, but as of yet, he had not been afforded an opportunity. He'd heard plenty of rumors, all of which spoke of incredible sophistication.

"Welcome, my friends to the Everpine Resort," the stranger said once they were all still. "My name is Raphael Hephnaire, and I am the owner of this establishment."

David gulped when he heard the name. Don Raphael Hephnaire, was one of three remaining Dons left in Alönia. David had already met Don Johnson, and now he had seen Hephnaire as well. Blythe seemed to attract the wealthiest of Alönia's populace.

"When Mr. Blythe requested a few rooms for his speaker retreat," Hephnaire said, "I was so overjoyed to have such a dignified and exceptional speaker in my resort, that I reserved the entire facility for him and his friends."

The crowd applauded with exuberance. David might have joined them if he didn't already know how much tax money Hephnaire pocketed in the exchange. After a moment or two, Hephnaire waved them to silence.

"You will have free rein of the resort and its amenities," Hephnaire said. "But first, a word of warning. The wildlife surrounding our resort is exquisite and dangerous, but only if you wander beyond the resort boundaries. Leatherwings are grand and majestic, and harmless unless you get too close to their nesting grounds. If you choose, you can take a guided skiff tour that will give you an up-close look at their ferocity, but please, stay with the tour, or you just might become Leatherwing lunch."

The people laughed at the carefree manner in which Hephnaire described the gruesome death.

"In addition, the forest floor is perhaps the most dangerous place in Alönia," Hephnaire said in a more serious tone. "The Colossus Horned Toad will swallow you whole and even snatch your skiff right out of the air. Nature's playground is not ours, which is why we have our own playground within the resort in the form of an open bar."

Oh, how they cheered for that. David groaned at the prospect of having such a beautiful environment ruined by throngs of people in a drunken stupor.

Not again, he thought.

"Now, you may collect your key from the concierge's desk, and a bellhop will take your luggage and lead you to your room." Hephnaire pointed to several counters with waiting staff. "In the morning, you can either order breakfast to your room, or be served in the dining room on the far side of Big Stanley." Hephnaire clasped his hands in front of him. "Are there any questions? No? Well, I wish you all a pleasant evening."

The crowd dispersed as the people collected their keys and, after making a stop at the open bar, they walked to their rooms and made plans to return to the open bar. David received his room key and map of the resort from the concierge, but before he could retire, he felt a grip on his arm. He turned and found Blythe smiling at him. Where before David had to look up at Blythe, now they spoke eye to eye.

"My, but it does take some getting used to the new you," Blythe said. "You're so much different."

"You should try being on the other end of it," David said, recovering from his initial surprise. "I feel like I'm walking on somebody else's legs, and everyone seems to have lost a few inches in height."

"Ha, I'll bet your right. It is the best imitation ebony iron I have ever seen," Blythe said as he tapped a finger on the black appendage. "Well, I was hoping you would sit with me at lunch tomorrow. Two of Thornton's representatives have requested an audience for what I can only presume to be a lobbying pitch."

"Yes, of course," David said. "Whatever you need."

Blythe nodded, and with one more squeeze of David's shoulder, he turned and lent an arm to the pretty brunette and walking off to his room with what was no doubt his evening entertainment.

David followed his bellhop through the grand lobby, across a sky bridge to a steam lift that rocketed him a few floors until they reached a ring of rooms in the midst of the tree's foliage. His room was nothing less than phenomenal. It smelled of pine and the outdoors, and it was much more than a standard hotel room. The washroom alone looked larger than David's entire apartment with its walk-in stone shower, sauna, carved stone bathtub, and two sinks. The bed sat in the middle of a twenty-foot high circular room with windows paneling one side and everpine the other. It had a rugged, yet expensive appearance. David thanked the bellhop, who set his bag down on a table and left with a nod. He did the first thing he always did when he vacationed with his parents: He jumped up on the bed and had a few hops. Once he'd satisfied himself, he leaped down and looked around the private room just to be sure nobody had seen, despite the locked door.

He walked out onto the balcony and admired the view of the resort, the trees, and the vibrant wildlife. Big Stanly stood tall and proud in front of him, reaching far beyond any of the other trees. David's balcony wrapped all the way around his room with a spa on one end. Tree branches grew around the alcove, with fresh foliage blowing in the breeze.

David stood there for a moment, leaning against the railing and admiring Jeshua's creation when a flicker of movement in the foliage caught his eye. He leaned out over the railing and peered into the clumps of finger-thick blue-green needles. Then, the branch moved, and green feline eyes stared back at him. Presently, it meowed and crawled down the branch a little further toward him. It was the size of a large cat, and David puzzled how the animal managed to climb so high. Then, it leapt. The blue-and-black-furred animal flew through the air, and folds of skin stretched tout between its forepaws and hind paws. The leap became a three-fathom glide, and the feline alighted on the railing next to David with superb balance. There, it sat and began preening itself. David stood stunned. He'd never heard of such an animal in all his life.

"What are you?" He asked. "Some sort of flying cat?"

Intricate swirls wove into the animal's blue and black fur, and its tail was abnormally long, at least twice as long as the animal itself. The end of the tail flattened into a tuft of fur the shape of an arrowhead.

David ignored the large sign on his balcony wall prohibiting the feeding of wildlife, as he proffered the last bits of the candy bar he had in his pocket. After all, the sign wouldn't be there if everybody didn't already do it. The animal stopped its preening and sniffed the candy bar. But it hesitated, walking down the railing and started sniffing his jacket. He reached a gentle hand out and rubbed between the animal's pointed ears, each tipped with a tuft of fur. Abruptly, it stopped sniffing him and gobbled up the candy bar David still held in his hand. David looked at the animal in confusion.

"Fickle little thing, aren't you?"

He admired the beast for a few more minutes before he went back in his room. He decided the evening air to be a pleasant temperature, so he only closed the screen portion of his balcony door. After cleaning up, he went to bed early, knowing that he would need his rest two days hence when they eavesdropped on Blythe's secret meeting.

The next morning, David awoke to an odd rumble in his bed. He roused himself and looked around the room with bleary eyes. Nobody was there, but he still felt the rumble through his bed. He looked down and jumped at what he found. In an instant he was out of the bed and standing over it in shock. There, lying sprawled out across his sheets was the same flying feline he'd seen the night previous. David looked back toward the balcony and saw that the screen door was open a foot or two. He looked back at the animal. It was awake now and stretching its limbs on his comforter.

"No, you live outside," he said as he grabbed the animal by the scrap of the neck and drug it off his blanket. He heard claws catch threads and had to jerk the overgrown feline several times before it came free. "and I live inside," he added as he tossed the animal onto the porch and closed the door, locking it this time.

No sooner had he turned around than the animal began to whine. David growled and rubbed his groggy eyes. He saw some fruit and cookies on a tray next to the refreshment station. He grabbed a handful of cookies and tossed them out the door. The black feline stopped its fussing and started eating.

At that moment, David heard a knock on his door.

He walked across his room, attempting to pat down his messy hair as he went. He opened the door and found Francisco leaning against the frame in a nonchalant manner.

"It's seven o'clock," Francisco said. "I would have thought you'd be ready by now."

"Had a little trouble with the wildlife," David said. "If you'll wait, I'll just be a moment."

After a quick wash David dressed, and He and Francisco headed down for breakfast. Not a single patron graced the dining room, at that early hour, and most would not rise for some hours more. This was good, as David and Francisco could speak with little concern at being overheard. They sat at the far end of the large dining room next to large, sun-filled windows.

"So I gather you've seen our objective?" Francisco asked before taking a drink of tea.

"The mission objective?" David said, shaking his head. "Where is it?"

Francisco pointed out the dining room window. "The meeting should take place in Blythe's private apartment."

"And where is his private apartment?" David asked, fearing the answer.

"I'll show you."

They stood and stepped out onto the small deck that surrounded the dining room.

"At the top of Big Stanley," Francisco said, and he pointed straight up.

David leaned out over his balcony railing until he saw the top of Big Stanly and the grand apartment ringing it. A shadow passed over him, and the same dumb flying cat alighted on the railing next to him and nuzzled his arm. Francisco didn't notice since he was cupping his eyes from the sun and examining the top of the tree.

David frowned at the animal, and while Francisco was preoccupied, he nudged it off the railing. It meowed in protest and glided away. David looked around in case anyone had noticed, but nobody had.

"We need to be up there at 11:00 pm tomorrow evening," Francisco said, uncupping his eyes and reclining against the railing. "And we won't have a lot of time to get there. There's a dinner seminar tomorrow that ends at 10:00. We'll have an hour to get from here," he pointed at a balcony where they stood, "to there," he pointed up, "and we have to do it without being seen. That winding walkway won't be much good as it will have guards posted all along it. Neither will the steam lifts, as they have guards at every stop and one inside each lift."

"Why don't we just airship up?" David asked.

"Even if we did it without running light, we'd be spotted by one of the lookouts," said Francisco. "Airdropping in won't work either. Too many branches to break our necks on. No, as far as I can see, we have one option. We need to climb along the trunk all the way to the top."

"In an hour?" David said with a snort.

Francisco nodded. "Unless you have another idea. Trust me, I'm all ears."

David looked over the railing again and groaned.

They decided to survey Big Stanley from other angles, so they went for a walk through the resort. The Boardwalk surrounded the entire facility and presented some of the most spectacular views David had ever seen. Unfortunately, he couldn't enjoy them as the impending doom of climbing Big Stanley weighed on his mind. After walking the boardwalk circuit twice, they concluded that climbing was their only option and that no particular path along the trunk was any easier than the next.

The only thing of real interest they saw during their exploration was the outline of a small carrier moored in the distance, something David presumed to be Blythe's new pleasure yacht, but it was too far away for him to identify anything other than the outline. With a heavy heart David joined Blythe for lunch that afternoon back in the dining room.

David sat next to Blythe, who had the pretty brunette on the other side of him. David had stopped learning the girls' names as they always disappeared within a fortnight. On the other side of the table, sat Hephnaire along with the two Thornton representatives Blythe had mentioned earlier. One of the representatives David already knew: Representative Donald Evanson of House Thornton's First District. He'd stalked the representative during his week of snooping around a few seasons earlier. The other was Representative Addison Mitchell of Thornton's Third District. Both men were known Pragmatics.

The representatives attempted some small talk as the wait staff served lunch, but as everyone finished eating, the men came to the point.

"We have a proposal for you, Speaker Blythe," Evanson said. "As you know, our districts are but sparsely populated and reliant on logging and mining for survival. We have no manufacturing to speak of. While we may disagree with you on most political questions, we do agree on one thing: our constituents are our greatest concern."

Blythe nodded with pinched eyebrows and a serious gaze.

"It is with that in mind that we want to propose some legislation," Evanson said.

"Why not propose it in the assembly?" Blythe asked as

he took a sip of his tea.

"In recent weeks you have been against any legislation proposed by Pragmatics," Evanson said and held up a hand as Blythe made to speak. "An understandable stance considering the past dozen cycles. What we want to communicate to you today is that our proposed legislation is bipartisan in its substance, and its purpose is solely to provide work for our populace. The mines on the far side of Thornton, which have fed this house for more than a century, are running low on minerals. However, during recent excavation, some miners found a new vein that runs underneath the bog fields."

"Gentleman," Blythe said with a smile. "I think I see where this is going. If you are asking me to grant you a variance to the mining ban on old forest lands, that is something I cannot do."

"The vein runs thousands of feet below the surface." Mitchell cut in with less tact than Evanson. "We could set depth parameters to be sure that there was no impact on the surface."

"I'm very sorry, gentleman," Blythe said in a placating tone. "My position is quite firm on this."

"But what harm will it cause?" Mitchell said, losing his patience. "Our district relies on mining to survive. What do you expect the people to do?"

"If there is one thing I know about Alönians," Blythe said as he raised his teacup, "it's that they are tenacious and resourceful. Never fear sirs, I'm sure your constituents will adapt and find new jobs within House Thornton."

"But…" Mitchell started to say, but another look at Blythe, and he scooted his chair back, threw down his napkin, and stomped out of the dining room.

Evanson managed more tact as he wiped his mouth, thanked Hephnaire for the lunch, and followed after Mitchell.

Not a moment after they had left the room, Blythe turned and spoke to David. "Start an advertisement campaign in Thornton marketing an abundance of jobs in the third for workers with mining experience."

His brunette companion giggled at that.

"Yes, sir," David said, glancing at Hephnaire. "But sir, we have no such jobs."

"No matter," Blythe said with no apparent care that Hephnaire was listening in. "When they arrive and find no work, they will join our social assistance programs. Once they get a taste for free money, they won't be able to leave."

Hephnaire raised his teacup in salute as Blythe chuckled. David looked from one to the other and decided he better laugh as well, even though he found the idea revolting.

"Blythe, you really have a mind for population manipulation," Hephnaire said. "However, their request has sparked my own memory. I too have a petition to make of the speaker."

"Of course you do, you old devil," Blythe said with a laugh. "Go on then, make it."

"The view out of my lower resort rooms is getting obstructed by some new growth," Hephnaire began. "If I could remove some of the younger trees, and when I say young, I mean, perhaps 50, 60 cycles--not more than 70. It would greatly improve the rooms' values."

"You know, I cannot tell you how pleased I am with this resort," Blythe said as he spun his teacup on the table and then looked at Hephnaire. "If the view remained unobstructed, I might even be tempted to return someday."

"Blythe, the penthouse is yours as often as you want it," Hephnaire said.

"Oh yes please," the brunette said with another giggle.

Blythe placed a hand on his heart. "Too kind Mr. Hephnaire, too kind. I suppose it is of Alönian interest to keep this resort in excellent condition if the speaker will be frequenting it. I see no problem with your petition. They are young trees, as you say."

"Truly, Speaker Blythe, the forest does not know they are missing, as I have actually already cut them down." Hephnaire pulled a document from under the table. "If you could sign this line, I already did the speaker the courtesy of filling in the date of the variance."

Blythe laughed. "How thoughtful for you, Hephnaire. You even knew the date I would have signed it, had I known about it last season." Blythe autographed the document, and the two men laughed about it for some time, offering additional jokes at the departed Evanson and Mitchell's expense. After a few more minutes, David stood to excuse himself.

"Leaving David?" Blythe asked.

"Unless there is something you need, sir."

"Oh, let him go, Blythe," Hephnaire said. "He probably wants to make the one 'o'clock balloon jump."

"You have a balloon jump here?" Blythe asked.

"On the far side of the resort." Hephnaire pointed across the dining room. "We strap a life balloon on your back, inflate it, and let you float through the foliage to a lower platform."

"Well you better be on your way then, David," Blythe said. "Enjoy yourself."

David almost corrected the assumption to tell them he was heading back to his room for a nap, but he stopped himself. Hephnaire's description of the balloon jump gave him an idea, one that just might save his and Francisco's necks when they climbed Big Stanley.

Chapter Eight
HAVOC

Blythe's dinner party and conference proceeded as they always did. A lavish meal of the most expensive dishes along with a continuous flow of fermented drink crowned with an absurd speech from a murderer. The only way David could bear staying to the end was by thinking of the day when The Houses of Alönia threw Blythe out of office. If tonight's venture proved fruitful, that day could be soon. All through the dinner, David tapped his foot and twirled his thumbs. Who was Blythe speaking with on his long-range communicator? David had his suspicions, Hephnaire making the top of the list. Who better to conspire with than the Don in charge of Alönia's unions? And he'd already witnessed Blythe and Hephnaire making quid-pro-quo transactions under the lunch table, a timeshare at Everpine for a land variance. Tonight's secret meeting meant something sinister on the top of Big Stanley.

David and Francisco slipped out of the seminar as

soon as they could, without arousing suspicion. They had to walk around Big Stanley, as running would attract attention. Once on the far side, they hopped over the boardwalk railing into the shadows of a low hanging bower. There they slipped off their suits and changed into the supplies Francisco had stashed earlier that day. They put on specialty gloves and shoes with intricate spikes along the palms and soles for gripping bark, but in the event they had to climb glass or metal, the pull of some velcro let the spikes hang on a flap and left the palm of the glove covered in a sticky grip. Their shoes bore a similar design.

But on their backs, they buckled the outlandish idea David conceived during the previous day's lunch. After leaving Blythe and Hephnaire in their budding friendship, David went to the balloon jump platform, and against his better judgment, made the jump. The resort staff asked him his weight, strapped him into a life balloon, and inflated it. David immediately felt the pull of the balloon against his restraints, and he floated a little with every step toward the edge of the platform. He looked down the jump zone into the distance and felt a twinge of pain in his arm, a phantom pain from the time he lost it. He buried the thought and jumped.

It was very like his training back at the academy, except the scenery on the way down was infinitely better. *Beautiful* couldn't quite capture the experience. He floated down at a lazy pace feeling a tingle in his stomach as his feet hung in empty space. But the sites around him soon overtook the anxiety. Sunlight filtered through the trees, accenting shadows and capturing flashes of wildlife. Birds called in different melodies of love. The exquisite smell of everpine and flowering epiphytes filled the air and gave him an unexplainable longing to explore the wild.

David marveled and gawked at the thousands of species that lived so many fathoms above the ground. It was an entire world that lived cycles without ever touching the dirt he found so necessary. Thornton during the day looked different than at night but no less extraordinary. While none of the bioluminescence glowed in their vibrancy, the natural colors of the animals were no less brilliant. But all of his observations were cut short as a dark shape detached itself from the shadows of a nearby everpine and swooped across the jump zone. He started kicking the air in a futile effort to get away. But the creature did not harm him; rather, it dove by and snatched a bird out of the air, the birds trilling tune cut short. He relaxed as the majestic leatherwing banked in a circle and glided down into the shadows below. Its oily skin shimmered as it passed through sunbeams, betraying the fact that it lived in water as much as air. As he watched the amphibious bird swoop away, his feet snagged in a net, and he realized he'd come to the end of the jump.

He rode the steam lift back to the main level and ran to tell Francisco about his brilliant plan. Thereupon, later that night, Francisco filched a box of life balloons despite his skepticism. But David cajoled and convinced and together they practiced far into the night, and despite nearly hanging himself on more than one occasion, David felt confident his idea would work.

So as he and Francisco strapped on their specialty climbing gear, they also strapped on life balloons and inflated them. Prior to stowing the gear in the foliage, they'd calibrated the life balloons to their exact weight. Their practice session told them that anything more and they would float away from the tree without any hope of getting back—an experience that nearly sent Francisco into the upper atmosphere. He was still a little bit leery of the idea after that.

"This better work," Francisco said.

"It will, I promise," David said. "Just remember what I told you. The higher we go the stronger the wind. Don't let it blow you off the tree. You'll float for hours until someone spots you or your balloon loses buoyancy. Nothing to worry about."

Francisco grunted. "I'd still rather free climb it."

"It's too far to climb. We only have," David checked his pocket watch. "forty-seven minutes to get to the top. That's not enough time."

Francisco tugged uncomfortably at his restraints, but before he could say anything else, David bent his knees a little and leapt. He soared twenty feet in the air and clung to the side of Big Stanley. He looked down with a smile on his lips. Francisco followed suit. David made another jump and caught hold of a mushroom another ten feet further. It felt a bit like swimming up from the bottom of a pond. The slightest kick of his feet or pull of his arm sent him up whole fathoms at a time. In no time at all, they reached the bottom of one of the many resort decks that encircled Stanley. Together they worked their way across the bottom of the deck to its outer edge. Twice David snagged his balloon in the floor joists, and they lost a few minutes while he fished it out. When they reached the outer edge of the platform, Francisco used a mirror to see how many guards were on patrol. He looked back at David and held up two fingers and then a forestalling palm. They hung there for a few minutes until Francisco nodded and pulled himself over the railing in one silent movement. David imitated him, but with far less grace. Once over the railing, they both jumped and let their balloons take them a few fathoms into the air before they clung to the tree and held their breath. They waited as the two guards completed a circuit of the deck and passed around the other side of Stanley. Then they were on the move again, leaping up the tree in great bounds. They fell into a rhythm as they passed deck after deck of the massive living tower.

David coiled his limbs and prepared to leap upward as he had for the past twenty minutes, but his foot slipped off the bark of the tree, fouling his trajectory. He floated into the expanse drifting further and further away from the tree. His eyes widened, and his heart quickened as he realized what he had done. He flailed his arms in a futile attempt to grab hold of old Stanly, but it was far outside of his reach. Just as he lost all hope, a hand grasped his ankle and jerked him back toward the tree.

David hugged the tree like a long-lost lover once it was within his grasp. He panted and wiped perspiration from his brow.

"What did I tell you before we started?" Francisco said with a growl. "You're going to be the death of me one of these days!" Then the man kicked off and continued up the trunk.

It took David several moments to calm his racing heart, moments in which he considered giving up the foolish venture and returning to his room. But Francisco paused a few fathoms above him and looked down. David could feel more than see the disdainful look through the darkness, and it reignited his determination. With a deep breath, he tried again, coiling and jumping to match elevation with Francisco.

Finally, after leaping nearly 80 fathoms of tree, they reached the highest tier of the Everpine Resort, the penthouse and Speaker Blythe's quarters. As the suite was sectioned into several spacious rooms, Francisco opted to climb to the roof and observe their quarry through the skylights. They arrived above the living room skylight at 10:52. Each cut free their life balloons and unstrapped the restraints. As Francisco melted a small hole in the corner of the skylight and fished in a small microphone on the end of a wire, David noticed that there were already people in the room. He started to lean over the skylight to get a better look when Francisco jerked him back. He bared his teeth at David, pointing first at the moon and then at the shadows along the floor beneath. David nodded and placed his ebony hand along the metal frame of the window and lay alongside the skylight to have a view without casting a shadow on the living room floor. He saw Blythe and Hephnaire sitting at a table having a drink.

David applauded himself for his foresight. Blythe and Hephnaire were plotting something sinister, and all he had to do was listen. Francisco placed a soft cup over his ear, and he heard the men's conversation as if he were in the room beside them.

"I'm willing to consider it, but what can you offer me?" Blythe asked.

"If you allow my unions into Public Pharmaceuticals," Hephnaire replied, "I'll hand you the Sixth District."

"An interesting boast." Blythe smiled and rubbed his jaw. "How do you plan on achieving such a feat?"

"If you grant this policy and require labor unions in every district of every house, specifically my labor unions, I'll finally have access to the workers of the Sixth District. I'll start small: demand better health benefits, higher pay, more leave, but as I require more and more, profits will wane. Usually, I monitor all my other unions to see to it we sap our providers and not strangle them. I'll do no such thing in the sixth. The workers won't realize what's happening. They'll consume their own jobs. The business owners won't like it from the start, but if you mandate unions through legislation, they won't have a choice. Eventually, the unions will be able to require whatever they want from the businesses, and the businesses will have to comply. The end result will be the total collapse of the sixth's business sector. How much of their population will come running to the third?"

"But you also want access to Public Pharmaceuticals," Blythe said as he took a sip of his favorite pink drink,

"The largest employer in my district."

"That is nothing more than an internal dispute among the dons for supremacy," Hephnaire said. "Don Johnson is an obese bovine. It's painful to watch him ruin his father's empire and embarrassing to know that he is the most powerful of the three remaining dons. I'll clip his wings, but I won't affect business or population in your sector."

"So, I have but to trust the word of a don," Blythe said as he held his drink up to his forehead, "and you'll cull my most threatening enemy. I do wish you were more trustworthy. It is a tempting proposition."

"When have I not been, Blythe…" Hephnaire began, before Blythe cut him off.

"Your whole life, Hephnaire, no, more than that. The Hephnaire family has been dishonest since its inception."

David thought Hephnaire would grow angry with Blythe, but the man only shrugged.

"It's the only way to make money," Hephnaire said.

"Here, here," Blythe remarked in a toast with his now empty glass. "I'll do it Hephnaire, but only with an insurance policy." Blythe put his cup down and leaned forward in his chair. "I'll rewrite the legislation as an employee improvement program. Your Unions will have free rein on all businesses, but only for a three-cycle term. After which the program will expire. If I am not still speaker, you will have no way to renew it."

Hephnaire frowned, but in the end, he nodded, and the two men shook hands. David wanted to spit out the vile taste in his mouth, but he resisted the impulse. He thought he had seen it all when a woman entered the room, and not just another one of Blythe's floozies, it was Bernice, his actual spouse. David looked up at Francisco and then back down at the trio. He'd supposed Bernice to be dead in a ditch or floating in the Capital Bay, not in the same room as Blythe.

"Your 11'o'clock is here," she said with a forced smile.

David gulped. *This is only the warmup?* He thought.

"Is he?" Blythe said as he jumped to his feet and check his watch. "Damn! Lost track of time. Good evening, Hephnaire. I'm sorry to rush you along, but I have a pressing engagement."

Hephnaire seemed to know a dismissal when he heard one, and he left the room immediately.

"Send him in," Blythe said to Bernice as he straightened, leaned against his chair, and then straightened again, apparently unsure how to present himself.

Bernice left, and David held his breath. A moment later she returned escorting a cloaked man of small stature. The man seated himself but refused to take off either his hat or his cloak.

Blythe looked uncomfortable, more uncomfortable than David had ever seen him.

"Welcome to the Everpine Resort," Blythe said to the stranger. "Is there anything I can get you?"

"No," the stranger said as he leaned back in his chair. "I came to hear a status report. I did not come for drinks."

"You're sure?" Blythe said. "I have Senchá."

"Please, I only want the report. Then I must leave."

"We are on schedule, ahead of schedule, actually," Blythe said, his voice faltering.

"The airships?" The stranger asked, lifting his head just enough so that David could see his chin, but no more. The man spoke perfect Alönian, but that was just it, perfect Alönian in a way that marked him as a foreigner.

"Deconstruction begins on the 38th day of next season." Blythe clasped his hands and smiled. "You see, ahead of schedule, well in advance of the wedding."

"What assurances can you give me to guarantee that date?" The stranger asked, not sharing Blythe's enthusiasm. "You have made promises for the past five cycles and only now show results. We cannot adjust the image once the tapestry is sown."

"The assembly has already approved the deconstruction. The airships are steaming toward the Third District as we speak. My enemies are powerless to intervene; yet I am still hacking away at their limp corpses. In another few seasons, I will be the only power in Alönia. The die is cast, and there is no changing it."

"Your confidence is commendable," the stranger said. "I wish I could share it. Too many times I've seen a total victory transform into a complete loss. I have even orchestrated it myself on several occasions. You will forgive me if I feel skeptical."

David risked a little more pressure on the window frame as he leaned out as much as he could without casting a shadow. He couldn't see the man's face, and as of now, he hadn't a clue of his identity. If only he knew the man's nationality. But then, a black shape thudded against the roof on the other side of the skylight. David jumped, and such was his position, that he clenched his fist on the frame of the skylight, his ebony fist. The frame crinkled beneath his grip, and the glass fractured into a spider web of cracks. A pause of absolute silence followed, a moment that allowed David to look up and see the cause of his fright. The flying cat lay on the other side of the skylight licking a paw, ignorant of its mischief. Then, the fractured glass crumbled into a thousand pieces that skipped across the living room floor. David saw Blythe look up in shock, but the stranger was nowhere to be seen. He'd vanished.

"Time to go!" Francisco said, and he lifted David by his shoulders. David heard guards yelling from below as he turned to run. He even saw one poking his head up to the roof of the penthouse. Several gunshots rang out just as David and Francisco leapt from the rooftop and dove into empty air. David heard the shots whiz by his head, but then gravity overtook him, and he fell face-first toward the forest floor.

He kept his body straight as the wind whistled in his ears, a sound tainted with pain and turmoil. He could almost hear his mother's screams and see his father disappear into roiling flames. David shuddered and gritted his teeth. The resort's main floor grew larger by the millisecond. At the last possible moment, he and Francisco pulled their ripcords and inflated their secondary life balloons. David felt his body jerk with the counter force and slow considerably. He landed on the boardwalk with no more impact than if he'd dropped a fathom's distance. He followed Francisco's lead and shrugged off the secondary balloon. Then, they ran.

Guards poured out of every doorway and blocked every entrance. David and Francisco's only advantage was that nobody knew what they looked like or what level of the resort they were on. All at once, Francisco leapt off the boardwalk and started climbing the everpine that held it up. David hesitated for an instant, but hearing boots thud on the boardwalk behind, he swallowed his fear and jumped. There was a moment where he hung in the air that separated the boardwalk and the tree. He saw between the gap and the darkness below, then his hands felt bark, and he gripped with all his might. The spikes on his gloves and shoes dug into the tree, and he found that climbing the knobby bark was far easier than he'd originally thought. He used his ebony arm to his advantage, and after a moment he'd caught up with Francisco. The guards ran by on the boardwalk below without ever looking up. After about 30 feet of climbing, they swung over a ledge onto some scaffolding. David ran to the door marked *Service Entrance* and tried the latch.

"It's locked," David said in a whisper.

"David, you have an ebony hand. Unlock it."

David looked down at his arm and then comprehended. He put a few fingers between the door and the frame and bent the frame just enough that the latch swung free. The two of them slipped through, and Francisco placed some foliage in the doorframe so the door would stay closed. A moment later, they ran down a hallway with suite doors along one side. Francisco grabbed David by the arm and pulled him to a stop. David looked at him with wide eyes.

"This isn't my room," he said as Francisco fumbled with a lock pick.

David saw the shadow of guards approaching from around the next corner. At the last possible moment, the door swung open, and Francisco shoved David inside before closing it as quietly as he could and locking it. David stood in the middle of the room holding his breath until the guards marched by without stopping. Then he breathed a sigh of relief.

"But this isn't my room," David said again. "Is it your room?"

Just then, Bethany stepped out of the washroom dressed in her nightgown.

"Oh, hello Bethany—" David began, mind racing to think of a cover story, but she cut him off.

"Were you seen?" She asked.

"I don't think so," Francisco said. "They'll be checking rooms any minute. Find something to do with David." Then he ran across the room and disappeared off the balcony.

"Huh?" David said. "Find something to do with me?" He looked at Bethany who stood with her hands on her hips. Then she threw back her head and groaned.

"Sometimes I really hate that outlander," she said as she grabbed David by the hand and led him over to her bed as the sound of men busting down doors echoed down the hall.

"Outlander? Where did he go?" David asked, now thoroughly confused.

"Shut up and do exactly as I say," Bethany said as she pulled back her comforter. "Get in."

David looked aghast. "What?"

But Bethany didn't wait for him to comply. She shoved him into the bed, and then crawled in beside him and pulled the covers over them. She rubbed her hair with a hand until the static left it in a mess. Then she huffed and said, "Whatever you do, only let them see your face."

David nodded, beginning to feel himself perspire in his clothes under the blanket.

Bethany waited until she heard the guards bang on her door, then she said, "Don't come in!"

That was as good as an invitation to the hunting men. They kicked the door in, and the sound of it slamming against the wall made David jump. At the same moment, Bethany squeaked and held the covers up to her neck, despite the fact that she was fully clothed. David poked his head up over the covers and looked toward the door. Just beyond the threshold stood Gerald and Hans, each with a hand cannon pointed at them. The pair of them looked back and forth between David and Bethany, until they roared with laughter.

"Didn't mean to interrupt you two," Hans said.

"My, did you ever see a pair of more guilty faces," Gerald added as he holstered his hand canon.

"Quite!" Hans said. "Never mind us, we'll leave you to

it then." And then the pair of them left and shut the ruined door behind them.

Bethany jumped out of the bed the moment they left and braced the door shut with a chair.

"Why did they leave?" David asked as Bethany walked back toward the bed.

"Really, David?" She said with folded arms. "You can't be that naive."

"And...and who are you?" David asked. "Who are you really?"

"I work for the man in the shadows, same as you," Bethany said.

"Is everyone a fraud?" David asked as he slumped back into the bed.

"The only fraud I care to deal with right now is the one where you and I pretended to be sleeping together," She said as she put her hands on her hips again.

David turned bright red as he put all the pieces together.

"Now get out of my bed," She said.

David moved to comply, but not fast enough for Bethany. She reached down and grabbed him by the ear.

"Ow, ok, ok, ok," David said as he stumbled behind her. She towed him to the balcony and pushed him out.

"But what am I going to do out here?"

"Goodnight, David," Bethany said, as she shut the door and locked it. Then she gave a little wave through the glass and shut the curtains. A moment later the light winked off.

David stood for a few seconds in the dark until his

eyes adjusted, and the moon and surrounding bioluminescence illuminated his surroundings. For a moment, he considered climbing around the structure till he found his own room, but one look over the side, and he decided he'd had enough climbing. He settled down on one of the reclining chairs in preparation for a long night, but before he had a chance to close his eyes, the dark shape of a large flying feline sored into his alcove and alighted on the railing. It jumped down and crawled into David's lap.

"I hate you. I really do. You nearly got us killed up there!" David paused and decided to stroke the feline's back. "Do you have a name? No? Good. I shall call you *Havoc* since it seems it's all you're good for."

Chapter Nine
VICE

Around 100 fathoms higher, Blythe stood in the middle of his suite's living room glaring at the mess of broken glass on the floor as a maid swept it up. Every single piece infuriated him. Of all the moments for intruders to make themselves known, tonight was the worst. He had just finished a confident speech to his benefactor, one that boasted imminent success and the impossibility of failure. Then the roof fell in and rained glass on his moment of triumph. It was indeed aggravating, infuriating . . .

"Humiliating!" Blythe screamed as he threw the glass in his hand on the floor and added its bits to the mess.

The maid uttered a little shriek and sat up on her knees. She kept her head down as she clutched the broom and dustpan, both shaking in her hands. Blythe cocked his head as he looked down at her, but then there was a knock at the door, and his wife strode in and stood beside him. She looked down at the glass and the shaking maid and evidently spotted the broken wine goblet among the rubble.

"Losing our temper, are we?" She said with a mocking smile and then turned to the maid. "Leave us."

The girl jumped up and left the room in a rush. Bernice walked around the remainder of the mess on the floor and sat in one of the plush chairs near the window. Blythe walked over to the refreshment station and poured himself another drink and one for his wife as well. He handed her the glass and then sat in a matching chair across from her. They sipped in silence for a while.

"You realize this may have been a mercy for us," Bernice said.

"How could you possibly think that?" Blythe replied as he rested his head against the chair back and groaned. "I looked like a weak fool to one of the only people in the Fertile Plains who's still a threat. This arrangement was meant to be a steppingstone, but now it's becoming more and more like a vice squeezing me out."

"Look beyond your own pride, darling," she said, and then she took a drink.

He hated it when she toyed with him like this, and she only did it when he was frustrated, so he cut to the quick of the matter.

"Why is it a mercy?" he asked.

She took another drink and furrowed her brow. "We have a spy in our office," she said after a lengthy pause that tried Blythe's patience. "If this little," she twirled her finger around as she pointed at the mess on the floor, "...incident hadn't happened, we would be ignorant of it."

Blythe wanted to chastise her stupidity if only to have a victory over her, but as he thought about her words, he knew they were true.

"This meeting was top secret," he said, and he shut his eyes and sighed. "The only way it could have been discovered is if someone listened in on our transmissions. It pains me to say it, but I doubt any slipups on their side. I certainly didn't divulge anything, and I only communicated with the utmost secrecy."

"Really?" Bernice said with a roll of her eyes. "Your sure none of you many midnight friends didn't coax it out of you?"

"I'm not a fool, Bernice," Blythe said.

"What of Samille and that foolish escapade?" She said and snorted in her triumph over him. "Do you ever get tired of your dirty little habit?"

"All the time. That's why I keep changing partners," Blythe said, jabbing back at her supplanted role as wife. "And what of you? Are you so innocent in your fidelity? I'm not ignorant of the flames you've kindled. Have you divulged information during your pillow talk?"

She scowled at him. "My antics are few and far between, and I never discuss politics or our plots. Though, during my last romance, the suitor did ask a lot of questions."

"It's a bad time to be asking questions," Blythe said. "Who is he? You don't mind if my lads pay him a visit?"

"Perhaps that might be best," Bernice said without a hint of remorse. "He's become vexing anyway. Do you remember Nathaniel?"

"The solicitor?" Blythe said with a gag. "Really, must you be so drab?"

"Let's not point fingers, darling," she said as she gritted her teeth.

After a moment's consideration, he nodded. "Well, if nobody coaxed it out of us, that only leaves a few options. Either the device was cloned, or they've been watching us the whole time."

"How could they clone the device?" Bernice said. "It was in your vault the whole time." Then she covered her mouth as Blythe nodded with meaning.

"Himpton?" she asked.

"Or David," Blythe said.

"Do you really think it could be David?" Bernice frowned and looked into her drink.

Blythe stood and walked around the room, glass crunching beneath his heals. "I don't know, Bernice. A moment ago, I believed our office impregnable."

"Perhaps, but not *impregnatable*," Bernice said with a laugh that grated Blythe's ears.

He gave her a tight smile and continued. "I said as much to our benefactor, but now I am compelled to recognize a spy. It could be either of them, or neither, I don't know." Blythe looked up at the broken skylight and puzzled at the odd bend in the frame. He sighed and sat down, holding his cold glass to his forehead to nurse his growing headache. A knock came from the door.

"Enter," he said.

Gerald and Hans walked into the room, and their

presence eased his frustration.

"Anything?" He asked.

"Nothing of interest," Gerald said. "Though, with the amount of staff that seem to be doubling up in rooms, we could have saved Alönia a good deal of tax money."

Blythe ignored the man's jest and gritted his teeth. How was he supposed to find a spy when he had nowhere to look? Then, a thought came to him.

"Get Hephnaire up here. Drag him out of bed if you have to."

Gerald and Hans left in a hurry, seemingly hearing the urgent tone in Blythe's voice.

"You've had a premonition, Husband mine. Won't you share?" Bernice said as she sat sideways in her chair and let her feet dangle off the armrest.

She always used pet names with him, even though the arrangement between them was anything but romantic. It was as though she wanted to remind him of the bargain they'd struck all those cycles ago. Their marriage was not born out of romantic inclination or sexual attraction. They'd both been born in the slums, they both craved power, and they were both willing to do anything to gain it. That was the attraction between them. They loved each other as much as they hated each other. They loved the power that came through their union, but they hated the fact that they could only have it through each other.

"Not a premonition, a gamble," Blythe said, but he would say no more until Hephnaire arrived. The Don walked in with bleary eyes that looked more for show than in earnest.

He looked at the glass in shock. "What's happened here?" he asked.

"Don't demean me with your games, Hephnaire," Blythe said. "I'm in no mood. I'm trying to catch a spy, and you have the means to help me."

"Well, my services are always available... for a price," Hephnaire said.

Blythe smiled and nodded to Gerald, who sank his oversized fist into Hephnaire's paunch.

"How's that for a down payment?" Blythe asked. "If it's not enough—"

"No, no it is more than enough," Hephnaire said with a grimace.

"Excellent. Like I said, I'm in no mood for games." Blythe crossed his legs in his seat and took a sip of his drink. "I need copies of all your recordings of my staff's rooms."

Hephnaire froze in his massaging of his stomach. "Recordings?"

Blythe nodded at Gerald again, but the movement alone this time loosened Hephnaire's tongue.

"Yes, Yes, Recordings. What about them," he said, shying away from Gerald's clenched fist.

"I know you have them because we found dozens of listening devices when we took up residence in this room," Blythe said. "A don with a resort? The infidelity that goes on here is too much a temptation to refuse the lucrative trade of blackmail. I want all the recordings of my staff, and I want my men at the listening outpost for the remainder of our time here. Do we have an understanding?"

"A perfect understanding, Speaker Blythe," Hephnaire said.

"Good. I hope this episode does not frighten you," Blythe said as he swallowed the last of this drink. "I see a very profitable relationship between us in the future."

Hephnaire smiled, but it was a tight smile.

"Gerald. Hans," Blythe said. "Go with him. And check Himpton and David's room recordings first. I want to know of anything out of the ordinary."

The men left the room, and Blythe and Bernice sat alone again.

"Your latest toy is still waiting for you in your bedroom," Bernice said.

"Send her away. She's a spoiled brat, and I'm tired of her annoying giggles."

Bernice stood and snorted.

"And bring that maid back to clean up this mess," Blythe said as she sat her goblet down on the table. "Then, have her sent to my room."

"You are disgusting," she said as she walked away.

"It's what you love about me, darling," Blythe said, a sneering smile on his lips.

He sat back in his chair and pondered in his solitude. In the last few seasons, he'd almost achieved everything he'd ever wanted. He was one of the most powerful men in the entire Fertile Plains. He'd denied himself nothing, and yet, he had an emptiness inside him. Why did he feel like he still lacked everything?

Chapter Ten
BURDEN OF PROOF

David looked down, unable to meet mother's gaze in the middle of the kitchen. She looked the way she always did right before he got punished, hands on her hips and a stern, unwavering expression. He prodded his puckered, black eye, but he knew all too well that his injuries would not soften his mother's fury.

"Don't touch it!" she said, and she pulled his hand away from his eye. Then she pressed a piece of meat against the bruised side of his face and replaced his hand.

"Hold it there," Mother said.

David did as he was told. The meat felt cold and sticky against his face, but not unpleasant to his burning skin.

"Why did you hit him?" Mother asked.

David looked at the floor and kicked at the wood paneling with his feet.

"Look at me, David!"

David looked up, tears welling up in his eight-cycle-old eyes, though the raw meat kept one from spilling over.

His lip quivered, not from pain or from fear, neither of those made him cry. He was ashamed, and the thought of disappointing his parents brought on tears more than anything else.

"He said father was the worst armada captain in Alönia," David said in the midst of a sob. "He said father told lies just so he could get famous like grandfather. He even said—"

"I didn't ask what he said," Mother interrupted. "I asked why you hit him."

David opened his mouth to reply but closed it again. Did she not understand? He hit Darius because he insulted his father. What other reason could there be. His mother must have seen the confusion in his face, for she replaced her hands on her hips and looked at the ceiling with a sigh. Then she crouched down and knelt on the floor in front of him, so their faces were at the same level.

"You struck him because you were angry," she said as she took his shoulders in her hands. "You struck him because you lost your temper."

"But he was lying about father!" David said, a tear rolling down his cheek. "I had to hit him."

"Does that make it right?" Mother asked. "Is it ever right to lose your temper?"

David looked away. He wanted to say yes, but he knew it was the wrong answer.

"David," Mother said, taking his chin and forcing him to look at her again. "You can't decide when you can and cannot obey Jeshua's commandments. Jeshua commands us not to lose our tempers, and then he gives us self-control for the times when we are tempted. You have a duty to do what's right."

"I know that's what He commands, but... I just..." David trailed off as he drew in a breath.

"You can't just know about Him, David," Mother said. "You have to know Him, know Him like you know father and me." Mother's eyes filled with her own tears. "He commands you to do justice, love kindness, and seek the humble path, but it's more than that. Do you know Him? Do you? Do you really know Him..."

* * * * *

David shook himself awake with the memory. Sunshine warmed his face, and a kink bent his neck. A few tears rolled down his cheeks leftover from his dreams. His mother's voice still echoed in his ears as though it had really been there, but he hadn't heard that voice in cycles, and he might never again. However, not hearing her in the present didn't keep the echoes of her voice from filling his memory. Her question had remained in his thoughts for more than a decade. *Did he really know Jeshua, or did he just know about him?* Then again, over the cycles, David had changed the question. *Did he want to know Him?*

Something warm and fuzzy along his side brought his mind back to the present. He looked around and realized where he was: still locked on Bethany's balcony. Havoc lay beside him, purring on his back in absolute contentment.

"Don't get used to this," David said as he scratched the animal's belly. "I'll be locking my door from now on, and you will sleep outside alone."

Havoc yawned and rolled onto his paws. David stood and rubbed his eyes. He looked off the balcony at the amazing view and noticed whole fleets of gunships patrolling through the air around the resort and across the entire forest. Evidently, he and Francisco's little stunt had shaken things up. He turned and rapped on the balcony door at a polite volume. Then he stood back and waited. Five minutes later he knocked again with a little more firmness. The same result. Havoc rubbed against his knee, and David could feel the deep rumble of his purring.

"Well at least somebody wants me," David said as he banged on the door with his metal fist, all pleasantries forgotten. It didn't help.

45 minutes later, he still stood on the balcony, leaning against the door and making a continuous thud with the back of his head. All at once, the door opened, and he fell on his back inside the room."

"Good morning!" Bethany said. "How did you sleep?"

David rubbed the back of his head. "You're fired," he said and climbed to his feet with a groan. But Bethany didn't seem to hear him.

"Ah! And who do we have here?" Bethany said as she picked up Havoc and nuzzled his head. The feline filled her arms and then some. Its long tail hung down her robe and trailed along the floor. "If I'd known such a gorgeous creature slept on my porch, I'd have let it in."

"He sort'a came with the room," David said.

He looked away with a snort as Bethany scratched Havoc under his neck. But then, the room's main door rattled and pushed up against the chair Bethany had placed there the previous night.

"One time!" She said as she stamped her foot and dropped Havoc to the floor, who ran out to the balcony with a fright. "I get seen with a man in my bed one time, and now everybody's banging down my door!" She removed the chair from the door and swung it open.

Francisco stood on the other side, and he stepped in and shut the door behind him, as best as it could be shut.

"I trust last night went well," he said after he'd secured the door.

Bethany forced a smile and a shrug. "You're so amusing, Francisco. Well, here's your man back safe and sound and well-rested."

"She locked you on the porch, didn't she?" Francisco asked.

David nodded, and Francisco laughed.

"Now you are acquainted with the real Bethany," Francisco said. "Loud, sharp-tongued, and salty as ever."

She curtsied, and then held up a rude finger.

"So you, Bethany, and Mercy were all working together?" David asked. "Was anyone in the office not a spy?"

"Surprisingly enough, Samille wasn't. She was just a little too ambitious," Francisco said, wincing at the last part. "I regret framing her now, especially after what Blythe did to her."

His words put a chill in the room.

"Well," Bethany said. "I'm going sunbathing, and none of you are invited."

It was then that David realized why the girl wore a robe and her blond hair hung in a ponytail.

"Just a minute Bethany," Francisco said. "We need to discuss what happened last night."

"I locked him on the porch!" Bethany said, legitimately offended this time.

"Not that," Francisco said. "What David and I overheard on our mission. I need you to play back the recordings we took so we can try and figure out the identity of the stranger in the meeting."

"Oh," Bethany said, relaxing some. "But I think we should do it in David's room, as his door isn't broken. We'll order breakfast."

Upon reaching David's room and ordering breakfast, the most obnoxious keening sounded from the balcony.

David groaned and walked to the balcony with the last of the room's snacks.

"Of all the rooms, how did I get stuck in the one with a pet?" David said as he opened the door, and Havoc came bounding in. David dropped some nuts and dried fruit on the floor in front of him. Havoc sniffed the snack and then looked up at David.

"What!" David said. "You already ate everything else!"

Francisco took one look at the animal and then back at David with a pinched brow. "Is that the same feline that startled you last night on the roof?"

"Unfortunately. The blasted thing won't leave me alone."

"Do you have any idea what it is?" Francisco asked.

"I know it won't leave?" David said.

Francisco started laughing, and he kept on laughing until David grew frustrated. Bethany looked back and forth between the two of them.

"Well? Do you know how to make it go away?" David asked while Francisco took a breath between chuckles.

"That's a Glide Panther," Francisco said with an obvious look. "They're very rare."

"Yes, I gathered the glide part when it flew onto my balcony," David said. "Why won't it leave, and why is it following me all over the resort?"

"You're feeding it?" Francisco said.

"Maybe. But what's that got to do with it?"

"Glide Panthers are bonders." David's confusion must have been evident because Francisco continued. "They bond for life with other creatures, usually other Glide Panthers."

Someone knocked at the door, and Bethany went to see who it was.

"Well," David said, "I don't exactly see any other Glide Panthers in here, so why does it persist in staying."

"It bonds as a cub when someone else feeds it. In the wild, they are very community-oriented animals, but they are rare in these parts. This cub may not have been bonded till you fed it," Francisco chuckled. "Just wait till it gets bigger, much bigger."

David opened his mouth to comment when the meaning of Francisco's words finally clicked.

"It bonded to me?"

"Seems like it."

"When I fed it?"

Francisco nodded.

"How do I un-bond it?"

"You can't."

"Why not? I'll just leave it out on the balcony until I leave."

"It's a Glide Panther," Francisco Repeated. "If it did bond to you, it will track you for grandfathoms if it has to. And if you sail away in an airship, it will wander until it starves."

"But... But I don't want a Glide Panther!"

Bethany giggled at David when she returned with a large tray filled with sausage, bacon, eggs, toast, and an assortment of fruit.

"You shouldn't have ignored the signs," Francisco said.

"You mean the sign that says *don't feed the animals?*" David said in frustration as the three of them sat down for breakfast. "That's the kind of sign you find next to duck ponds where they simultaneously sell duck feed. Maybe they should hang a sign that says, *If you feed the animals, you are accepting a responsibility for life.*"

"Bethany, you feed him," David added. "You like him, don't you? Maybe he'll bond to you."

"No, thank you," Bethany said. She smiled and sat primly on her chair.

"I miss the old Bethany," David said. *Stupid and docile*, though he didn't say that part out loud.

He filled his plate with some of the steaming food, and

the smell made his stomach growl, as well as Havoc's. David looked over and saw the glide panther sitting on its haunches and staring up at him with its luminescent eyes.

"You are a pathetic moocher," David said as he dropped a sausage link. Havoc snatched it from the air. "I'm only feeding you, so you'll get big enough to make a coat."

Bethany set up a phonograph and played back the recording David and Francisco had gathered the previous night. They listened several times to what the mysterious man said while they finished their breakfast. Bethany, as it turned out, served as a technician for Mit and the underground, something that completely baffled David, coming from a girl who couldn't even turn on the tea machine without assistance.

When they'd all finished eating and were no closer to discovering the strange foreigner's identity, David sighed and asked, "Would anyone like any tea?"

He looked at Francisco and then Bethany. She held up her knife and wrinkled her brow.

"Do not ask me to make tea, or I will stab you with this knife," she said and poked him several times with the point to emphasize her words.

David held up his hands. "I was going to make it."

"Oh. Okay then. I'd love a cup," she said, redirecting the knife and spearing a piece of dragon fruit.

David yawned, walked over to the refresher station, and started heating the water, but when he opened the tin of Jorgan leaves, he frowned, a section of the recording coming back to mind. Then his eyes widened.

"We have Senchá Tea!" he said with understanding.

"Ew. That brew is awful," Bethany said, and she wrinkled her nose. "Jorgan, please."

"No, I mean, that's what he said on the recording, the foreigner," David said with barely contained excitement. "Don't you see? Alönians hate Senchá as do the Bergish. The only people in the Fertile Plains who like it are the—"

"Viörn!" Francisco said, finishing David's thought.

David started pacing around the table as Bethany and Francisco considered what he said.

"Of course, it could just be someone with terrible taste in tea," he mused aloud.

Then Bethany's eyes brightened, and she shook her hands in the air. "The... the tapestry. His analogy about the image being fixed once the tapestry is sewn. Don't women in Viörn sew tapestries?"

"Their marriage tapestry," Francisco said, nodding along with Bethany.

"I didn't think of that," David said. "At a Viörn engagement, girls begin a tapestry of themselves and their husband to be. Once the tapestry is finished, the marriage commences. The tea, the tapestry, that precise way of speaking... He could be Viörn."

"Possibly," Francisco said. He leaned back in his chair and rested his chin in his hand.

"Why would Blythe be talking to a Viörn?" Bethany asked.

"...about the deconstruction of our warships," Francisco added with a shake of his head.

"Those are important questions," David said, "but I think the most important of all is why He was scared of him. You could even hear it in the recording. It was tenfold in person. Why would Blythe, the speaker of Alönia, be terrified of a little Viörn?"

"Bloody Nora!" Francisco exclaimed, causing David and Bethany to jump. "You're right. A few cycles back we had an intelligence report from Armstad on Viörn. It described the Emperor as weak in his rule and his only daughter as a simpleton. The report went on to introduce a new political figure, one on whom there was very little information. They knew him to be an admiral of small stature, and that he was the true power in Viörn. Since then, there hasn't been a single report out of Viörn as all our spies in the country have been reported missing or dead."

"Isn't that treason?" Bethany asked? "Talking with the enemy?"

"Technically the speaker can talk with any head of state," David replied, "but striking deals with a declared enemy must be approved by a majority of the assembly."

"So... yes, then?" Bethany said as she rolled her eyes. "It is treason?"

David nodded, but his thoughts were far off. Then he smiled. "All we have to do is record a complete conversation and photograph the Viörn. The assembly will have no choice but to remove Blythe as speaker." David looked at Francisco with a wide-eyed smile.

"It could work," Francisco said, nodding back at David.

"We got him," David said, his tone growing excited. "We've got him! They're bound to have another meeting soon. We only have to record it."

"Perhaps, if you refrain from breaking any more skylights..." Francisco said.

"That wouldn't have happened if Havoc hadn't pounced on me," David said as he pointed at the panther sprawled out on his bed and purring contentedly. But his heart wasn't in the accusation. As the implications of their discovery flooded his mind. They now knew exactly how to snare the slippery speaker, and they were all perfectly positioned to catch him in the act of treason. They had but to wait.

Francisco laughed, stood, and went over to the refresher station presumably to finish the tea David had begun making. But as he neared the wall, he slowed and looked at random points along its surface. Then he ran to a couch and slid it across the floor, wedging it between the suite door and the wall.

"What is it?" David asked.

But Francisco didn't answer. He sprinted to the bed, flipped the mattress, and snatched a repeater from a hidden pouch. Havoc rolled onto the floor and crawled under David's chair.

"Have I been sleeping on top of that this whole time?" David asked as he got to his feet and pointed at the repeater.

But then the room echoed as something slammed into the other side of the suite door. It might have collapsed inward, but for the couch Francisco had braced against it only seconds before. The assassin lifted the repeater and fired a single shot. Somebody yelped from the other side of the wall, and then several counter shots penetrated the door, leaving holes in it and the wall opposite. David threw Bethany to the floor and crouched down beside Francisco. Francisco pointed his repeater along the wall and fired a single shot at several points. David heard yelps after every shot and wondered how the man could be so accurate with blind shots. Then he remembered Francisco's bionic eye.

"Do you have another gun?" David asked over the racket.

"I can handle this," Francisco said as he reloaded. "Find us a way out of here. The hallway is not an option."

David looked around the room, but there were really only two ways in or out: the main door and the balcony. He ran to the balcony and saw the same gunships he'd seen that morning banking toward his room. That removed climbing as an option. They didn't have any gear, and even if they could manage it, the gunships would spot them. He stepped back into the room, conscious of their limited time, but unable to come up with a viable escape.

"David?" Francisco said. "They're bringing out their big guns. Any time now."

David looked around the room and saw a box in the corner, the same box Francisco had filched from the balloon jump excursion the day before. He ran over and tore it open. They'd already used most of the safety balloons, save two.

David adjusted the buoyancy on each, and without hesitation, he stooped and grabbed Bethany where she lay on the floor with her ears plugged. He fastened the restraints around her torso.

"Do you know how to work one of these?" He asked as Francisco let out a long burst of rounds.

She nodded. So he picked her up and tossed her petite frame off the balcony. It wasn't entirely necessary, but if he were going to die today, he'd have some comfort in the fact that he'd gotten even with her for locking him on her balcony all night. The sour look she gave him as she fell certainly warmed his heart.

David ripped down the rope that drew the curtains and tied it under his arms. He tied the other end to one of the restraints on the only remaining safety balloon. Then he slid a knife from the breakfast table into his sleeve.

"Francisco, I'm ready when you are."

By this time, so many holes riddled the wall that David could see figures moving along the outside hall. Francisco fired a few more shots, and then he turned and ran to him. But he came up short when he saw what David had planned.

"Oh, bloody hell!" He said. "I'd rather die from a gunshot then smash into the forest floor."

"It will work," David lied. "I promise."

In truth, if the balloon could not support their combined weight even on the maximum buoyancy setting, as he expected it could not, he planned on cutting himself free with the knife in his sleeve. All too well he remembered the last time he'd shared a life balloon. That time he'd lost his arm, and his mother lost her mobility. He and Francisco weighed considerably more than they had.

Another few shots blasted the last of the door to bits. Francisco groaned as he fastened the restraints around his shoulders. Together he and David walked onto the balcony, where Havoc crouched with a wild expression in his eyes. David picked the panther up and tossed him over.

"Perhaps he won't come back after that," David said with a nod.

He and Francisco straddled the railing. He heard men forcing their way into the room behind him and saw the gunships swoop in front of the balcony and swivel their chain-guns toward them.

"Lad," Francisco said as he gripped David's hand. "You've done well by me."

David smiled. "On the count of three, then. One... Two... Three!"

Together they jumped and sored far out into the expanse. Time slowed down as it always did whenever David courted death, which seemed to be becoming a habit. He saw the gunships try to follow their decent, but they couldn't maneuver in time, and as David fell, he could see the ships growing smaller in the sunlight. He heard Francisco fire off a few more shots with his repeater—good shots that brought a guard down from the railing. Francisco didn't seem to fear death as long as he met it with a gun in his hand, a cry in his throat, and enemies at his feet.

Together, he and Francisco left their pursuers behind. They fell beneath the lowest platforms of the alpine resort, and as they fell, the light of the golden days dimmed. They fell further and further until the tree foliage disappeared and only stout trunks remained. The forest floor materialized out of shadow into a variety of greens and yellows. It wasn't until David could distinguish the algae-covered bogs from the moss-covered dirt that Francisco inflated their life balloon. David felt a jerk as the rope around his torso pulled taut. Its tension drove the air from his lungs, and he found himself gasping for breath. Yet, they still fell at an alarming rate. At this speed they'd hit the ground and remain alive just long enough to experience the excruciating pain of breaking every single one of their bones. He knew what he had to do. He wouldn't be responsible for crippling another person in order to prolong his own life. If he cut himself loose, he would die, but Francisco would live. He gritted his teeth in determination and reached for the knife he'd hidden away in his sleeve.

Chapter Eleven
FEEDING THE ANIMALS

David rummaged around in his sleeve, but the knife wasn't there. The jerk of the rope had knocked it free. He pulled on the rope as they fell, and the ground grew closer. He dug his fingers into the knot, but it had tightened considerably with the tension. He could have loosened it if he had had more time. He even tried biting it, but it was no use. The ground raced toward them, and they fell precariously close beside the trunk of Big Stanley.

"David!" Francisco called. "What are you doing with that rope? Let it be."

David looked around in frustration and felt the same hopelessness he'd felt all those cycles ago. Memories flooded his mind and brought the taste of bile to his mouth. This time, it was him trying to sacrifice his life for another. He despised the injustice of the whole situation. How many people had to die while Blythe, a murdering scoundrel, sat in peace? Was there no justice in all the

Fertile Plains? Was there no Maker at all who cared?

David screamed as his anger got the better of him. He reached out with his ebony arm and dug it into the side of Big Stanley. It sank deep into the bark and jarred his shoulder. He felt the heat of the friction on his face and saw woodchips and splinters in their wake. He dug his fingers in with all his might until they were only a few short fathoms from the ground. Then his hand broke away from the tree, and the motion swung him and Francisco away from the trunk. David braced for the impact, gritting his teeth against the pain of breaking his legs. But the pain never came. Instead an entirely different sensation flooded his senses. Chilled water washed over him and rushed up his nose.

David sat up and spit some algae out of his mouth. A second later, Francisco sat up beside him and coughed. David looked around in shock. His mind reeled as he deliberated on how he still lived. They had landed in a bog. Until their disruption, its green surface was indistinguishable from the rest of the forest floor. As he looked, he saw the long gash he'd made down the side of Big Stanley. He held his Ebony hand in front of his face and wiggled its fingers. It looked as shiny as the day he'd first gotten it. Then he and Francisco looked at each other and uttered a nervous laugh, which grew to a roar bordering on manic. Together they waded to the side of the bog and pulled themselves up its slippery shoreline. David wiped some algae from his face and fiddled with the rope around his torso, but Francisco produced a knife and cut it for him.

"Hang on, that's the knife I grabbed from the breakfast table," David said. "How'd you get it?"

"Never mind that," Francisco said, and he handed the knife back to David. "You can have it back now that I know you won't do anything stupid with it."

David held the knife in his hand, and then looked back up at how far they'd dropped. Was it luck, or was it providence that he still lived?

"I'll have that knife," a girl said from a distance. "And I know exactly who I'll stick with it."

David looked over as Bethany stepped through some bushes. Her white robe was covered in green sludge to her mid-thigh, and her satin slippers were nowhere to be seen. Several twigs clung to her blond hair.

"You!" she said as soon as she saw David. "You tossed me off a balcony in naught but my sunbathing clothes. Now I'm stuck in a forest without shoes!"

David deadpanned. "Now that's a real shame. I don't know how I'll be able to live with myself."

"Give me the knife," Bethany said as she held out her hand. "Give it to me!"

But the sound of a gunship burner echoing through the tree canopy cut off the banter.

"Time to go," Francisco said as he reloaded his repeater.

"To where?" David asked.

"To our skiff, lad. Where else?" Francisco jumped up from the forest floor.

"You have a skiff down here?" David asked as he followed suit, ringing the water from his jacket.

"We had one hidden here in case of emergencies," Francisco said. "I think this qualifies as an emergency."

Francisco pulled back a branch of a succulent looking tree and jumped back as the head of a leatherwing filled the opening. It presented a double row of serrated teeth and emitted a hissing roar.

"Run!" Francisco said, and he led the way around the bog to the other side of Big Stanly.

Nobody needed to be told. David and Bethany raced after him. David heard large wings beating the air just behind them. All too well he remembered Hephnaire's warning about disturbing a leatherwing's nests. They ran through the low foliage of succulent and thorny bushes, staying just ahead of the deafening thud of the beating wings. Then Bethany screamed and stumbled on the ground. David had completely forgotten about her bare feet. He jumped back and dove over Bethany, hoping his body would weather the amphibious bird's talons better than hers. He felt the rush of wind as something glided over, but then the sound of the creatures flapping grew distant as other roars echoed far behind them. David looked up and saw the beast soring back toward Big Stanly, and after a moment of listening, he knew why. He heard the roar of chain-gun fire and the screech of leatherwings protecting their nests.

"Come on!" David said. He lifted Bethany in his arms and ran toward Francisco, who had dropped into a gun stance.

"That is a very large flying salamander," Francisco said.

"Well right now it's buying us time," David said. "Which way to the skiff?"

Francisco set out at a quick jog, and David ran alongside with Bethany in his arms. She didn't say anything as he carried her, but with this new Bethany, silence spoke volumes.

The boglands were nothing like the ethereal treetops above them. Town sized trunks sprouted out of sodden soil. There wasn't a single patch of bare dirt anywhere. If it wasn't a tree trunk, then it was a bog, a bush, or a carpet of moss. David found the moss strangest of all. Decades and perhaps centuries of growth had compounded into rolling blankets of greenery several feet thick. While ordinary moss grew only microscopic flowers, this moss displayed fist-sized buttercups that grew on thigh-high canes. They left a yellow smudge on anything that touched them. Dragonflies the size of birds darted around trees and bogs chasing disturbingly large mosquitos that David had trouble ignoring. Bethany swatted the beasts away as he followed in Francisco's wake.

It didn't take the gunships long to exterminate the nest of leatherwings. No sooner had the sound of the chainguns ceased, David heard the sound of men and hounds following their trail, and no matter how hard he ran, they continued to close the distance. He felt sweat pouring down his back from the exertion of carrying Bethany, despite her small stature. Finally, Francisco reached into the undergrowth and pulled up the corner of a moss-encrusted tarp. He jerked the tarp, and it slid off a Mark I

Night Hawk, an older military skiff with an open cockpit.

"Nice," David said as he set Bethany on her feet and checked over the skiff. "Somebody's updated it a bit; removed the torpedo bay and added a seat—"

"David," Bethany interrupted as she climbed into the middle seat. "I'm tired, and I want to go home. Could you talk about it while you fly?"

David nodded, remembering the hounds and men who were only minutes behind them.

He climbed into the front seat and started up the flight sequence.

"Fly south and east," Francisco said, but as he climbed into the last seat, he bumped a large blue mushroom the size of a bolder. The top of the mushroom split open and released thousands of glowing seedpods that floated up like bubbles high into the forest shadows eliminated their way.

"Over there," A voice said in the distance.

Without missing a beat, Bethany reached into a pouch beside her seat and pulled out a gas pistol. She fired three silent shots in quick succession. Two more explosions of glowing bubbles erupted in the distance.

"No, over here!" another voice said.

David looked at her with his mouth agape. "Nice," he said once he found his voice.

"That should buy us some time," she said. "Can we go now?"

David switched on the burner and flash heated the pontoons. As the skiff was not in standby, it took several minutes before they gained lift. Bethany's ruse gave them enough time to get airborne. Only moments before the skiff was ready, a dark shape glided over the skiff and next to Bethany. David looked back and saw Havoc curling up on Bethany's lap. Evidently Havoc didn't mind being thrown off a balcony. As soon as his meters stabilized, he slammed the accelerator down, and they rocketed forward. As much as he wanted to superheat his balloon and leave the bogs, he remembered what he had seen when he awoke that morning. A cloudless sky full of gunships was no place for one little skiff. If they remained at low altitude and snuck out of Thornton unseen, they might have a chance. But that chance shattered when a few shots followed them and reverberated through the tree trunks.

David banked around the next tree and had to swerve to miss a gunship on its opposite side. Evidently, they'd sent out patrols. He cut around another tree and checked his mirrors. Two gunships pursued them and, no doubt, signaled the others. He heard the whirr of a chain-gun and veered around a tree just as the gun started spitting bullets. They thudded into the tree behind them, and David saw chunks of wood flying through the air in his mirrors. He increased his speed and started zigzagging around the everpine trunks, always keeping a tree between his ship and the angry gunship.

As David banked around a tree, another gunship tried to cut them off. David dove under it and felt the breeze of its passing in his hair. Bethany screamed. The bottom of their skiff passed so close to the ground, and they left a yellow trail of dust where they'd brushed through the moss buttercups. Strictly speaking their skiff was faster and more agile than the gunships, but as more and more airships joined the fight, speed and agility seemed irrelevant. Chain-guns ripped through the forest and carved great swaths of destruction.

Presently, David heard Francisco firing his repeater.

"Their armor's too thick for that." David shouted over the rush of wind.

"Well I'm too far away to spit on them, so it will have to do," Francisco shouted back, and then he unloaded on the closest gunship.

Tracer rounds passed nearer and nearer, even finding purchase in their pontoons. The aerosol sealant did its work, filling the wholes and repressurizing the pontoon, but each whizzing bullet reminded David of their peril.

All at once, David cut around an everpine, and the forest opened up into a larger bog than the rest, more of a small lake. He veered back towards the shore and the cover the trees provided when Bethany screamed another cry of terror. A thick globular tongue shot over the skiff and slammed into the tree beside them. Veins and pimples the size of autumn melons speckled the slimy, skiff wide tongue. David heard tree bark crunch, and the force of the impact sent a shiver down his spine. He followed the long knobby tongue with viscous dripping saliva back to its source and looked into a gaping orifice in the middle of the bog. Milliseconds later he saw the tongue retract in his mirrors and snap back into a maw with lightning speed. As the mouth snapped shut, he watched a veritable hill roll under the algae-covered waters leaving two bulbous eyes with horned lids bobbing along the surface.

David grunted. "So that's what they look like."

But just before he swerved back into the forest, he saw more and more of the Colossus Horned Toads surface and spurt their tongues at gunships. Two found their marks and caved in the sides of the airships sending them spinning into the water. The sight gave David an idea.

As they passed over dry ground, David gritted his teeth and turned hard around an everpine along the lakeshore. The sharp turn pressed him into his seat, doubling his weight. As he looped around it, he sighted a gunship in front of him, and for the first time in the chase, he unloaded his military-grade chain-guns and cut the gunship to pieces. Then he pressed the throttle all the way down and raced across the lake at full speed. A few gunships foolishly followed.

At full speed, his small skiff was too quick for the colossus toads to catch. A few tried, but their tongues grasped empty air. The gunships were not so lucky. They were battered to bits. One of the larger beasts snagged a gunship with its tongue and then leapt its entire mass out of the water and retracted the bow of the ship back into his mouth.

David used those precious moments the toads provided to break free of his pursuers and race into the shadows of the forest on the far side of the lake. He didn't let up on the throttle, despite the danger, not when they finally had the lead they needed to make their escape. He only slowed down an hour later when his reflexes dulled, and he brushed the side of a tree with his pontoon. His hair and shirt stunk of sweat, and his seat squeaked with the slime of it. Thirty minutes later, the trees seemed smaller. Another thirty minutes and they were sparsely populated.

"Stay close to the ground," Francisco said.

"But why?" David asked. "We don't want to get caught down here."

"Trust me. Stay close to the ground for another few grandfathoms and then follow the fissure."

David nodded, understanding now. The Trans-house fissure ran from Thornton to Huntington. One narrow crack followed the base of the mountains weaving through the countryside. It was too narrow for any gunship to fly within, but a skiff ought to fit just fine. If by chance, anyone still patrolled the skies above or followed behind, they would never see them in the chasm. A moment later and they weaved through the smooth fissure at a relaxing pace.

"How far should we follow it?" David asked.

"Until we reach the Hopkins border," Francisco replied.

They traveled like that for the rest of the day, only venturing above the fissure to avoid a waterfall or narrow portion. Depression settled on David like a cloud as he realized the implications of their detection. They now had little to no chance of unseating Blythe or uncovering what the man had planned. Nobody spoke the whole way. They climbed into the twilight sky as soon as they saw the tell tail House Hopkins plains. Though, the moment

David pointed them toward the yawning stars, he spotted the glint of an airship high in the sky catching the last glimmers of daylight.

"There's an airship up there," David called back to Francisco. "A big one."

"That's where we're headed," Francisco said. "That's Mit."

David nodded and accelerated their ascent. As they neared, the airship grew larger, far larger than any ordinary airship. When the sun faded, lights illuminated along the sides of its envelope like stitches along the exterior. David tried to count the lights in order to estimate the ship's size, but he lost count every time he adjusted his skiff's course. Four bays lined its underbelly, and each looked large enough to carry 30 skiffs. David only knew of two Alönian airships this size, and one of them was still under construction. This ship could be none other than *The Valor*, built as an Alönian supercarrier, but sold off to a private citizen when Blythe cut the Armada's funding. There were only a handful of citizens who could afford such a jewel, and David knew precisely who purchased this one. He gulped and wondered if he'd made a deal with the devil... again.

Chapter Twelve
SILENCE IS BROKEN

The second bay door opened and admitted David's skiff passage into the carrier's immense belly. There was only one vacant skiff dock in the whole bay. Shiny new Mark 2 Nigh Hawks lined the bay armed with their torpedoes and looking ready to launch at a moment's notice. David waited until he felt the docking clamps fasten onto his skiff. Only then did he loosen his vice grip on the controls and let his head lean back against the seat rest. Fatigue rushed into his limbs as the adrenaline receded, but he wasn't ready to give in to his exhaustion just yet, not when he sat in the belly of the beast.

A guard escorted them down scaffolding that crisscrossed the top of the hanger, his stony expression slipping when he saw Havoc padding along after David. The docile beast looked as out of place as a businessman in the Third District. They reached the far end and walked across an observation platform to a steam lift. They rode it up several floors, and David saw the guard wrinkle his nose at their palpable stench. Sweat and swamp apparently didn't mix well. When they reached the sixth floor, they walked down hall after hall, each filled with guards and pilots of all variety, most looking like seasoned veterans.

The ship itself stood apart, an orchid among everpines. The floors looked like they'd never been walked on. The steel gray walls and ceilings cast a shimmering reflection. None of it felt like polymer, though it had to be, as any other material would weigh the ship down. They passed rooms of every purpose: barracks, medical centers, armories, rec rooms, dining commons. David lost track of how far they walked. His steps came unbidden as he plodded along after the guard.

At last, they reached a circular room with a dozen chairs around a large oblong table with a steam projector affixed to its center. David recognized the layout of the space, a war room. Mit sat in the middle of the table pouring over maps and reports. He looked up when they entered and forced a tired smile, but his eyebrows twitched in surprise when he saw Havoc.

"What's this?" Mit asked as he watched the glide panther cross the room.

"He will be a carpet, or hat," David said without preamble. "It depends on how fast he grows and how long I can tolerate him."

Mit snickered before saying, "Well, I'm glad you all made it safely back. Please, have a seat. I'd like a debriefing before you all take your rest."

Each of them slumped into a chair and breathed a sigh

of relief. A nod from Mit and the guard walked to the refreshment station and poured them each a steaming mug of tea. David looked at Mit anew, trying to work out exactly how this man had gotten his hands on a warship as prized as *The Valor*. There really was only one logical conclusion, but he didn't like that answer, and it tasted sour in his mouth. Yet, as Mit met his eyes, David knew it to be true.

"Can we clear up a little matter before our debriefing?" David asked.

Mit gave him a nod.

"Mr. ... Johnson?" David said, and then he looked around at everybody's reaction. It was subtle but present, nonetheless. Everybody in the room paused in what they were doing and slowly looked up. Bethany actually held her breath, but they weren't looking at Mit, they were looking at David.

Mit took a careful sip of his tea and leaned back in his chair appraising David with his piercing brown eyes.

"The airship gave it away," David said. "That and the underground's facility at the Third District. It was far too large to be a recent construction, and the third only very recently became significant real estate. What I don't understand is why you would fight against the man who has the ability to make your business empire larger than it's ever been."

Mit smiled and nodded. "That's not usually the first question people ask me. They usually want to know how I'm able to appear as a fat slob whenever I resume my role as a Don. It's fat pads and a lot of makeup, in case you were wondering. I knew it wouldn't take you long to put it all together, but I wanted you to discover it on your own. If I'd told you this at the beginning, I don't think you ever would have agreed to work with us. You have a distaste for the Dons, and rightly so."

David nodded.

"My father," Johnson continued, leaning back in his chair as he launched into his story, "was as typical a Don as ever there was one: ruthless. He took our family beyond anything my ancestors ever imagined. Our pharmaceutical empire has overshadowed every other Don. During his rise to power, an intelligent and foolish Armstadi father decided to marry his beautiful daughter off to the wealthiest man in Alönia. His greed led to his suicide and the most horrific life for a pure, young woman, my mother. My birth was the only thing that kept her from following in her father's footsteps and ending her own wretched life. I grew up watching my father abuse my mother in every way imaginable. He justified his ruthlessness by his success. But, as is often the case, his violent and wild lifestyle ended in an early death. As you can imagine, I wanted nothing to do with him or his industry empire. I very nearly changed my name and would have if not for my mother's interference. Make the name good and change centuries of history."

Johnson nodded. "That's what she told me. But I needed some time before I assumed my role as Don. My mother looked after the company for me. The only thing that outmatched my father's ruthlessness was my mother's intelligence, and our company prospered even more under her leadership. I, meanwhile, joined the Alönia's Secret Service and became a sneak. You see, as a young child my mother instilled in me a love for Armstad, as I am half Armstadi. I had my own private mission as a sneak to gather intelligence on Armstad's enemies. I had some success, and it was on those missions where I first met your father." Johnson gestured towards David. "He was... a very exceptional pilot and a good friend.

"During our exploits we learned of an imminent war on the horizon. Time had not tempered Berg and Viörn's battle lust, only modified it. They remember well their catastrophic defeats at the hand of your grandfather. So they've spent decades rebuilding and diversifying their armadas. Both your father and I screamed this message at our superiors, and on one occasion, we presented our case to an assembly subcommittee. They ignored us. Every mission they'd applaud, pin a medal on our chests and throw our report in the wastebasket. Your grandfather tried his hand at getting them to listen, but they weren't interested. That's when I decided to return to my old life. If I couldn't prevent a war as a sneak, perhaps I could prepare for it as a Don. I aligned my family's company with the Houselands and created Alönia Public Pharmaceuticals. It might have been one last jab at my long-dead father, but it also allowed me a certain amount of anonymity. I play a pompous fool in their presence, and the man in the shadows when they're not looking. The Houselands was all too happy to sink their fingers into the largest company in the Fertile Plains, and now have a vested interest in keeping the company alive.

In return, I have a certain amount of influence in the assembly, and nobody looks twice at my books. I made some allies there, a few even know my alternate identity."

"Representative Walker?" David asked, and Johnson smiled back.

"Walker and I have a secret friendship." Johnson said. "I knew that as long as he controlled the assembly, nobody would be able to use Public Pharmaceuticals for anything I disagreed with, despite multiple motions from Equalist to mandate and administer antipsychotics. But then Blythe took power, and I was faced with ruin on two fronts. My ancestral company would start operating against my will, and the war for which I was preparing would begin long before I was ready."

"Blythe told me about a new wonder drug he's administering," David said with new understanding. "He seemed hesitant to admit it worked, but eager to distribute it."

"Yes, methylphenidate 151," Johnson said with a scowl. "Blythe ordered us to mass produce and dispense on the streets earlier this season. It's advertised as a mental stimulant to expel anxiety and promote focus. In reality, it's nothing more than dope to sedate the masses, for what reason I do not know. Perhaps to make Alönians easier for him to control. Regardless, there was one unforeseen benefit from Blythe's order. He cut armada funding and redirected it to us. I, of course, am not interested in being the assembly's drug dispenser, so I'm mixing a placebo into the aerosols and slowly decreasing their potency. This leaves me with an enormous amount of surplus funds, and I have put them to good use building my own armada. So, in the end, armada funding was not really cut at all. Ironic, isn't it?"

David smiled, too tired to laugh. "I'm assuming that's what you used to purchase this vessel."

"Quite right," Johnson said as he rapped a knuckle on the table. "Blythe gave it to me for a steal. I think he might have pocketed some of the cash and cost the Houselands a fortune in one fell swoop. The Valor is the first of its kind, a new generation of warship. Designed in Armstad, assembled in Alönia. The balloon envelope has a paper-thin ebony iron over-layer adding considerable strength without any additional weight. The reinforced polymer interior gives additional strength and sheds an unbelievable amount of weight. Less weight meaning more skiffs and more armaments."

"Odd," David said, "I must have missed the gun emplacements when I flew in."

"No, we had to remove the larger ones," Johnson said with a frown. "Can't exactly have a private citizen flying around in the most heavily armed ship in the Houselands. All the small arms are still in place, and I can refit the long guns at a moment's notice. But until such need should arise, we cloak ourselves as a simple skiff carrier."

"You were probably right not to tell me who you were from the start," David said. "I've always had a prejudice against Don's."

Johnson smiled. "So have I. We both have our reason."

"Perhaps, but events in Thornton have made the

situation a little more bleak than you understand," David said. "We have no time for my prejudices. I'm not sure how, but Blythe discovered our treachery and tried to capture us."

"Yes," Johnson said with a grimace. "We guessed as much when a whole squad of gunships descended on the resort like a flock of vultures."

"It was my fault," David said, and he hung his head. "If I hadn't interrupted ruined at the mission, we wouldn't be in this predicament. Now you've lost all your plants in the speakers office, and we have nothing to show for it."

"This is true," Francisco said, and David winced. "But... we learned much before we were discovered. For one, Blythe is plotting with Hephnaire to dismantle Public Pharmaceuticals and the sixth with Hephnaire's unions. We overheard them plotting, just before the 11:00 meeting."

"So Hephnaire wasn't the one in the meeting," Johnson said as he rubbed his jaw.

"Yes, but did you hear me?" David said with a little more urgency. "We've lost every edge we had, and Blythe's going to dismantle your company and the Sixth District." David looked around the room, almost wishing they would reprimand him.

"That was bound to happen sooner or later." Johnson said in a soothing tone. "It was only a matter of time, just as it's only a matter of time before they discover I'm diluting the drugs and embezzling from the assembly. I have faith in the citizens of the sixth and my own employees to see through this plot. And if they don't, then there is hardly an Alönia left worth saving." Johnson leaned forward. "Put it out of your mind, David, we need you focused on the future and not griping about the past. Now tell me, if Hephnaire wasn't the mystery man of the secret meeting, who was?

David looked at Francisco and Bethany, but they both yielded to him to give the report. Some of his confidence returned. "We don't know the man's identity. We only know that he's small, prefers Senchá tea, and uses analogies about sewing permanent tapestries."

"Viörn!" Johnson said slapping his hand on the table as he stood. "Short you say? It couldn't be..." He looked at Francisco with a question in his eyes.

"That was our conclusion as well," Francisco said. "Especially after David noted Blythe's fear of the man."

"What did they talk about?" Johnson asked, looking between David and Francisco.

"The planned destruction of our airships," Francisco said.

Johnson froze before falling back in his chair. He rested his head in his hands. "And we have such a speaker."

"It may be time to put politics aside," Francisco said. "If he's undermining Alönia for the Viörn..."

"No," Johnson said from his hands. "We can't just assassinate him. For one, we don't have any more people in his office. And two, we know the harm he's doing because we know how sinister Blythe is, but to everyone else..." Johnson dropped his hands into his lap. "They'll laud him as the instrument that brought peace to the Fertile Plains right up until the Viörn and Berg blow Capital Orbital out of the sky. No, the people must cast Blythe out, or not at all."

"But we don't have time to wait till the next census." Francisco said. "We have half a season before Blythe destroys the armada. We don't have enough proof to convince the assembly to remove him and no way to acquire more. And even if we did, do you think they'd remove a man that 75% of them believe a god. Your band of mercenaries isn't enough to fight a war with two countries."

Johnson nodded. "Thank you, Francisco. I will take that into consideration. Was there anything else they discussed?"

"No," David said with a wince. "I sort of cut the meeting short."

"Ah, I see," Johnson said. "Well, regardless, you all did a fine job. That's more intelligence gathered in three days than we've had in three seasons. You all should get a good night's sleep."

"Good!" Bethany said. "I want a bath and something other than sunbathing clothes."

The meeting disbanded with little ceremony. Despite the dire situation, each longed for a few hours of sleep.

"Except you, David," Johnson said, and everyone looked at him. "We have had word from your mother—"

"Is she ok?" David asked as his heart started racing. When last he'd left her, Dr. Abraham was preparing for a surgery, a surgery, he'd informed David on many occasions, that might kill her.

"I think you misunderstand. We've had word..." Johnson paused, "from your mother. She sent the word. She woke up sooner than expected."

David shook his head. "She did..." Then it hit him. "She's talking! When? For how long? What... What did she say?"

"She asks that you come and visit her," Johnson said with a smile. "I told her you might be too tired, but that I'd ask anyway."

David was flabbergasted. "You... you what?"

Then Johnson tossed him something that jingled. David caught it and held up a pair of keys.

"That's my skiff," Johnson said. "This airship is heading back to the underground as we speak, but that skiff will make it in half the time."

"Thank you, sir," David said as he stumbled around his chair. "I don't know what to say."

"Well if you don't know what to say then get going and say it to your mother. Rudolph, kindly show him to my skiff," Johnson said to the guard waiting at the door.

David trod on the guards heals three times on the walk back to the carrier's bays. He wanted to run, but the guard insisted on walking. When they reached the hanger, a different one than David had landed in, David abandoned the guard and made for the only modified Mark II Night Hawk in the entire bay of stock skiffs. Johnson wasn't the type to fly an ordinary skiff. He knew he'd guess correctly as the keys unlocked the canopy, and he climbed inside. The guard opened the bay doors while

David flash heated his pontoons. The moment they reached minimum lift, he detached from the docking clamps and dropped through the partly opened bay doors. The skiff slipped through with barely a foot on either side. As soon as he was airborne, David wasted no time in maxing out the skiff's capabilities. He rocketed forward and enjoyed the exhilaration provided by the duel thrusters and the modified burner. In no time at all he'd left the carrier behind, but he didn't slow down for anything. His mother was talking, and he had so much he wanted to ask her.

* * * * *

Mercy ran across the Valor, or at least she ran as fast as was proper for a young lady. She'd just seen Bethany enter a cabin, and that could only mean one thing: David was onboard.

Surely Johnson meant to tell David she was still alive. He couldn't exactly keep the two of them on an airship together and expect her to hide away in her room the entire time. Actually, that was probably exactly what he intended, but he couldn't help it if she walked into the war room and stumbled right into David. After all, he hadn't warned her David would be onboard, and he hadn't told her to avoid him. If he didn't want them to see each other, he should have planned accordingly. Mercy looked down every hall as she passed them, just in case David had already left the war room. She almost shouted at the back of a complete stranger with a black mechanical arm and brown hair, but after another look at him and the guard who escorted him down the hall, she realized he was too tall for David, and his even gate never broke stride. She looked at every young man she passed, causing a few of them to smile and some to blush, but she didn't see David in the halls. She walked up to the war room door but paused before opening it. She looked around for a mirror but settled for the polished door latch. She brushed her hair out of her face and straightened up her gown after her rush across the ship. She couldn't help her flushed face or her wild heartbeat, so she took a deep breath and fixed her posture. She entered.

Inside the war room she found Johnson and Francisco leaning against the side of the table and chatting over cups of tea, but no David. She looked around the room once more upon entering just to be sure.

"Where is he?" She asked.

"I'm afraid you've just missed him," Johnson said.

"Where has he gone? What room?" Mercy asked, already turning back to the door.

"No, he's not onboard anymore," Johnson said. "He took my skiff and flew on ahead of us."

Mercy looked at the floor and sank into one of the chairs around the table.

"When, Mr. Johnson?" She asked, all of her excitement giving way to tears, which she did her best to hold back. "When will you tell him I'm still alive? When will I get to see him?"

"Mercy—" Johnson started, but she cut him off.

"No please, let me finish," she said as she wiped her nose. "I know it's silly, and I know this is not the time, and I don't even know why, but I want him to know that I'm alive, and I care for him. I want him to know before he forgets about me. I..."

"Mercy, before you go on—"

"He's such a good man, and it pains me to see him suffering," Mercy said. "If knowing I'm alive stops his hurt, even if he hates me afterward, I'm willing to do it. He's a good man, Mr. Johnson. I know you can trust him. He will not betray us, not now. Not now that he knows who Blythe is, and what the Equalists actually stand for."

"I know Mercy, that's—"

"Then why won't you let me go to him?" Mercy asked, as her hands clenched the folds in her skirts.

"Mercy, when we arrive back at Braxton, I want you to go to David," Johnson said.

"This simply can't continue any..." Mercy paused as she realized what Johnson had said. "You want me to what?"

"I think you should go to him while he is with his mother," Johnson said. "David is going to need you these next few days."

"Oh," she said, wiping her eyes and flushing with embarrassment. "Why the sudden change?"

"Francisco has just finished his report." Johnson nodded to Francisco. "It seems that, while David may be a long way from becoming a successful sneak, Francisco owes him his life. They had some trouble getting out of Thornton, and in the process, David proved his mettle and his resolve, and even his willingness to sacrifice his life for others. He's ready to know the truth, all of it."

"I told you he wouldn't let you down," Mercy said. She smiled and wiped another tear.

Johnson nodded. "I considered letting you see him tonight, but we had a note from his mother, and he was eager to be off."

"The surgery, it was successful?" Mercy asked.

"In a way. She has regained some limited mobility, but her body is in the final stages of organ failure. If David hadn't returned when he did, I would have sent for him. He will need you Mercy. When his mother dies, he will lose the last thread he has tying him to the Fertile Plains. You must bring him back from despair."

Mercy nodded. Slowly her excitement at the prospect of seeing David transformed to pain for his impending loss. She knew how much he cared about his mother; she'd witnessed it. Johnson had assigned her no small task.

The walk back to her cabin was much different from the walk she'd just taken to the war room. Shutting her door, she walked to her vanity and looked in the mirror. Her blond curls hung down one shoulder, and her blue eyes winced when she thought of David struggling to recognize her. She grabbed a bottle from the counter and shook it. If she had to bring him back from the brink of hopelessness, she wasn't going to do it as a stranger. She'd do it as the woman he knew, the woman he used to love, and she hoped, still did.

Chapter Thirteen
A LOVE AFFAIR

Typically Captain Ike would have felt affronted at a task as mundane as delivering a letter, but since it got him out of a debriefing with the top brass in the armada, it felt joyous. He'd never been to Livingston's Second District before, but as a favor to Agent Johnson, he'd agreed to deliver a letter to #3 Whitechurch Lane in the market sector of Livingston's Second District to one Marguerite. He had asked why Johnson was so particular that Ike hand deliver the letter, rather than just using the public system. To which Johnson said that he wanted this to be something *special.* No doubt a small portion of it was having an armada captain be his delivery boy.

Ike snickered as he walked down the cobbled street between elegant townhomes. He and Johnson disagreed when it came to women. Johnson always had a special lady in the wings, but none of them ever were special enough to make it past special gifts. Ike had never courted a lady. Whenever he met one, he always knew within a few minutes that he could not love her, and to string her along would be cruel. So he'd distanced himself from many of the opposite sex. His father had all but bribed him to marry, but he wanted to be excited at the prospect, not compelled.

A warm breeze ruffled his hair, and he followed the scent of something sweet baking over coals. Ike smiled to himself as he rounded a corner and saw what he'd been smelling. In front of him an arch rose high into the air and granted passage into crowded streets of an old fashion market. Row upon row of vendors sold fruits, grains, meats, baked goods, and trinkets of all varieties. It bustled with activity as people called out prices, and customers balked and dickered.

The market sector sat alongside the fork in Franklyn River. After Ike had docked his skiff at a public landing, he walked through the residential portion of the city and stumbled into the famed Livingston market. The smell he'd been following was that of a bakery, situated on the front edge of the market. As Ike watched, a man in a checked apron removed some rolls from a brick oven under an awning. The smell made Ike hungry. He bought one of the rolls and meandered up and down the market streets, smiling at the shop owners that hailed him, but he politely declined their merchandise. As he neared the river, the scent of fish added to the many other smells. When he saw his first fishery, he had to stop and stare at the dozens of intricate creatures chilling on ice, some with claws, some with whiskers, some with brilliant stripes and some with multiple rows of sharp teeth. He heard the owner arguing with a shopper about the oysters he'd sold him a day earlier. Evidently, the purchaser was convinced they were mountain sheep gonads. After hearing that, Ike continued down the street with a broad smile on his face. He loved Alönians.

He stopped at another shop with an excellent selection of jackets hanging at the entrance. He perused the rack, but when he looked over the top of the jackets, his mouth fell open. On the other side of the rack, a young lady with chocolate hair stood in front of a mirror, turning and appraising herself as she held a burgundy scarf around her shoulders. She wore a white blouse with brass buttons tucked into a long, navy skirt. Presently, she stopped turning, and Ike saw her face turn very sour in the mirror as she saw his reflection staring at her back. She whirled around and scowled at him with her hands on her hips.

"Do you make a habit of spying on women while they try on clothes." She asked with a huff.

Ike worked his mouth and fumbled with a few words. "Um... please, I'm dreadfully sorry. You must forgive me. I did not know you were changing, and surely I am not the first man to forget himself and stare at such a lovely young lady."

The woman flushed, somewhat taken aback. "Well, I suppose I wasn't really changing, but as long as you're gawking there, you might as well tell me what you think."

She spun in a slow circle with a very dignified face until she stood facing him again. "Well?" she asked.

Ike crossed his arms over the rack and rested his head

on his hands. "Truly, I don't think I have ever seen a woman so beautiful." Then he winked.

She blushed an even deeper shade of red, and her serious composure slipped. "No, not me! The shawl." She lifted the burgundy cloth from her shoulders and swapped it for another. "You're supposed to tell me which is better."

"Are they not the same?" Ike asked.

She snorted. "You are the most worthless gawker I've ever had to deal with."

"Terribly sorry, I don't have very much experience in the area," Ike said, and the woman laughed.

"Well, if you haven't the ability to help me, then I don't know why I'm even talking to you." She turned back around and started hanging up her shawls. It was a dismissal that was very obviously not a dismissal, for as he watched she glanced in the mirror very quickly to see what he was doing.

Ike stood up straight and sighed. "Yes, I guess I'm not an expert on shawls," he said as he rifled through the rack he'd been leaning against. "But I've been told I have very good taste in trousers." He walked around the rack to where she stood and held up a pair of pants. "... and these seem just about your size."

She turned around with an indifferent look that spoke of boredom, but when she saw the trousers, she squeaked and clapped a hand to her mouth. They could probably have wrapped around her slender waist three full times. She pulled her hand away and struggled to resume an indifferent composure.

"Not my color," she said and then turned to hang up her other scarf.

"Really? Oh bother," Ike said as he threw the trousers over a rack. "And I really thought I had it right that time."

She laughed and turned back toward him. "You're in the armada?"

Ike looked down at his uniform and nodded.

"And a captain," she said as she crossed her arms and frowned at his rank insignia. "I don't like armada captains. They're a bit like a knife dipped in sweet cream. They seem so wonderful until you look beneath the surface and discover they have a girl in every port."

She still smiled, but there was some fire in her eyes. Part of her seemed resigned to leave and go about her day, but the other part wanted to know what he would say.

Ike pondered the veiled question. "If I were to tell you that I didn't have any girls in any ports, would you believe me?" Ike asked.

"Do you?" She asked.

"No," he said without hesitating. "I'm always hesitant to pursue beautiful women, such as yourself, for fear that they would only soak up my attentions until a more exciting man presented a better opportunity."

"I see," she said through still smiling lips.

"That, and no one seems to appreciate my most excellent wit," he added, and she laughed again as she exited the shop.

"Well it was very nice to meet you, Mr. Armada

Captain."

"That's it then? You're sure you won't be needing any more assistance from me in picking out trousers?"

"I'm actually quite sure on that matter, but..." She paused and bit her lip. "If you wanted to escort me and help me with my groceries, I wouldn't be opposed to the idea."

Ike smiled and offered her his arm. "Madam, there is nothing I'd rather be doing."

She took it with a toss of her hair, and they walked together to the grocer at the end of the lane. By this time, Ike could see the river where it forked and house Braxton on its opposite shore. He escorted the young lady through the grocery market and held her basket as she filled it with a wide assortment of fruits and vegetables. Everyone that passed smiled at her and stared at him, something that made Ike wonder who the girl was, as everyone seemed to know her.

"You haven't told me your name yet," Ike prompted.

"No, I haven't," she said. "You will have to earn that."

"I'm carrying your groceries. What else am I supposed to do to earn it?"

"You're going to have to win my heart before I'll tell you my name," she said as she added some tubers to the basket. "Too many young men have learned my name and dogged my heals because of it."

"Doesn't your father own a gun?" Ike asked.

"He does," The girl said in a conspiratorial manner, "and he's even used it on occasion."

"Hmm," Ike mused. "Well, some lovesick men need

to be shot twice before they'll learn their lesson, lest they think the first time was an accident."

She laughed. "That is a very astute observation. I'll have to tell my father."

"Yes, but do wait until after I've left," Ike added. "You know, if you buy much more, I think we will be needing another basket."

"I think your right," she said and picked up another basket and handed it to him. "I have a long way to go before I'll fit those trousers you picked out for me."

Ike smiled while she filled the other basket as well. He didn't know why she required so many groceries, but he played along. They paid for the groceries and then walked across the street and delivered them to a restaurant that sprawled out along the water called *The Yachtsman*. The beautiful woman directed Ike to hand the baskets to a kitchen girl who blushed whenever she looked at him. Then after depositing the groceries and receiving no compensation, Ike and the woman walked back down the lane.

"You must know the owner of *The Yachtsman*," Ike said. "Is that where you work?"

"Are you still fishing for a name," the girl asked as she twisted the ends of her brown hair around her fingers.

"Well, I'd like to know something about you. Isn't there anything you can tell me before I win your heart?"

She smiled. "So certain, are we? Perhaps I'm not so easy a target. I warn you, many have tried and failed."

"A girl as beautiful as you, who is still unwed, cannot possibly be an easy target," Ike said. "But, perhaps no one has ever tried as hard before me."

"You are more persistent than most, and definitely more bold," she admitted. "But, alas, this is where I must leave you," she said as she stopped in the middle of a lane. "I have other errands to attend to, for which I need no assistance."

"Then perhaps we should have dinner tonight after you've completed them."

She laughed and looked away. Then she looked at him again and pursed her lips.

"Come on," he said as she considered his offer. "Think of it this way, either you will meet a new friend and enjoy a lovely dinner, or you'll meet a megalomaniac that you will have the pleasure of watching your father shoot, or—if we are both very lucky," He paused until she smiled, "We'll each find something a little deeper than friendship."

She bit her lip and took a breath.

"Oh, get on already!" A girl said from a grain vendor across the street. "Just have dinner with the man."

"Shh, Sarah, you stay out of this!" She said, and then turned back to Ike with a calm composure, but the flushed cheeks were unmistakable. "Fine. I'll meet you at sunset at the restaurant we delivered the groceries too. We can both eat dinner, and then I'll have dessert while my father shoots you."

Ike made a show of thinking about it for a moment, before he offered an extravagant bowed. "Madam, you have yourself a deal."

She laughed. "Until then, Mr. Armada Captain," she

said as she gave him her hand and he kissed it. Then she turned and walked away down the alley.

Ike watched her leave, then he turned and stepped up to the grain vendor and found a very red-faced Sarah.

"I won't be telling any secrets, so you might as well not ask," she said, unable to keep the smile from her round face.

"Will you tell me her favorite flower?" Ike asked.

"Oh." Sarah squealed before fanning herself. "Well, of all the suitors who've pursued her, you might actually win her heart. Alright, I'll tell ya. White buttercups, that's what she likes. You'll find them down the lane there at the flower vendors. Now don't let her scare you off. That girl needs a good man in her life."

Ike thanked her and continued down the street. He checked the sun. There were about two hours before sunset, and he needed to make the most of them. He set out along the street at a quick march. In his excitement, he completely forgot about the letter he was supposed to deliver.

He visited the candle vendor, the fabric vendor, and finally, the flower vendor. By that time, the sun hung low in the clouds. He hurried down the street and back toward *The Yachtsman*.

Once he'd reached the restaurant, Ike spoke to a dignified gentleman about his father's age. "A table for two, please. And could I request waterfront seating."

"But of course," the man said as he looked at the items Ike had brought along with him. "You're here to woo a young lady, and there is no place better for wooing than a riverside table at *The Yachtsman."* The gentleman led Ike through the restaurant, shaking the hands of patrons as he passed. He took Ike out the back of the restaurant onto a balcony that overlooked the water. Ike wasted no time in placing the candles in the middle of the table and laying a large bouquet of white buttercups tied up in a gold ribbon across the chair opposite his. The gentleman obliged him by lighting the candle.

Ike took his seat once he was convinced everything was perfect.

"Shall I bring you some drinks?" The gentlemen asked. "Water, or perhaps something a little stronger?"

"Water for me," Ike said. "And some tea for the lady."

The man nodded and walked off. Ike checked everything on the table twice more. In moments the sun would set, and he started to wonder if the young lady had abandoned him. But then, he saw her.

She stepped out of the restaurant onto the balcony. She too had been busy during the last few hours. She wore an elegant floral gown that wrapped around her shoulders leaving the tops bare. Her flowing brown hair wove down her back and over one shoulder. Her gown was beautiful yet tasteful. At her neck lay an ebony iron locket in the symbol of Jeshua. Ike and several others stared at her as she walked across the balcony.

She smiled when she saw him gaping, and her blush reached her neck. Then she saw the bouquet and the candles, and she covered her mouth with a hand.

"Aw, they're beautiful," she said as she scooped up the buttercups and smelled them. She sat in the chair, and the light of the candles played off her face as the sun faded in the distance.

Ike smiled at her. She truly was beautiful. Then the man returned with their drinks and set them down on the table.

"Thank you, sir," Ike said, and he looked up and nodded at the man, but the gentleman seemed somewhat changed from before. He returned a tight smile to David.

"What can I get you this evening?" The man asked.

"Oh," the girl said before Ike had a chance to answer. "Shall I order for us? I'll have the rainbow snapper with shallots, and the gentleman will have the special."

The man nodded and turned to walk away.

"Thank you, papa."

"You're welcome, dear."

Whatever question Ike had on the tip of his tongue slipped away with that one tidbit of information. "Papa?" He asked.

"Mhm." The girl nodded and took a sip of her tea. Her eyes sparkled with mischief. "Didn't you know? He owns the restaurant."

"No, I didn't know," Ike said as he nodded. "But that would explain why we bought all those groceries and handed them over."

She laughed. "You'll be eating those soon."

"Does this mean you're going to tell me your name?" Ike asked.

"Not until you win my heart," she said. "But it might be a start if you tell me yours."

Ike smiled. "David."

"And... your surname?" She asked as she looked down her nose at him.

"Ike, David Ike," he said and then looked down.

"Oh? No doubt the son of the famed Admiral," she said with a laugh. "You probably get asked that a lot."

"More than you can imagine," Ike said.

They talked on until their dinner arrived, the sound of the river laughing and churning alongside the restaurant. They learned that he was eight cycles her senior, both of them were born in their parent's later cycles, and both of their mothers had passed on just a few cycles earlier. When at last the girl's father delivered their meals, Ike stood and proffered his hand.

"Forgive me, sir," Ike said. "I did not know you were her father. My name is—"

"I know who you are," the man interrupted, and then he shook Ike's hand. "I fought as a gunner in the Protectorate War. You're the spitting image of your father. It's a pleasure to meet you, Captain Ike. I'm Alistair." He looked up and down Ike's uniform. "You're a very young captain," he said when he spotted Ike's rank insignia. "Your father must be proud."

"He is, sir," Ike said, "and it's a pleasure to meet you too."

The girl looked back and forth between Ike and Alistair. "You served with his father?" She asked her papa.

"For once, my dear, I think the joke is on you," Alistair said. "This is the son of the legend. Careful of that dish, lad," Alistair said, glancing back at Ike before he walked off chuckling. "It's damned spicy."

Ike looked at his plate, and then at the girl who looked at him with a shocked expression. "I'm not sure if your papa is talking about my meal or you?"

She blushed and looked down, and for the first time that day, Ike felt as though he'd gained the upper hand in the strange game the girl played with rules that appeared and disappeared at her whim. That is, until he took a large bite of the red fish on his plate and felt it's spices sizzle up his sinuses.

She laughed uncontrollably as tears rolled down Ike's cheeks, and he gulped down his water. They talked on as he struggled through his meal and drank whole tankards of water. The conversation ranged from their interests to their future plans. When at last they'd finished their meal and dessert and tea, and it had been some hours since the sun disappeared, Ike stood and helped the young lady out of her chair. She had not put her bouquet down since arriving, something Ike perceived as a good sign. He led her through *The Yachtsman*, and after saying goodbye to her father, he offered his arm to escort her home as every gentleman should. They walked back up the market alley, where she waved at people she knew. It was just as alive in the night as it was in the day, people thronged about in boisterous conversations. Boys played street games, and men played chance games. Though Ike and the intriguing woman walked through the market life, they purchased nothing, and neither one seemed interested in the prospect. He escorted her past the market, and she directed them down one of the residential lanes. Finally, they stopped, and she turned to him.

"I must thank you for the evening. I had a lovely time," she said. "I think, seeing as my father didn't shoot you, I may have found something a little more than friendship in you this evening."

She slipped her arm out of Ike's and climbed a few of the townhome steps, smelling her buttercups as she did. She turned on the third step and hid her smile behind her flowers. "If you should want to call on me again, you can find me here at #3 Whitechurch Lane." Then, after a small pause and a giggle she continued. "Ask for Marguerite." With that she turned, glided up the last few stairs, and disappeared inside the home.

Ike felt a brief feeling of triumph that was almost immediately swallowed by a feeling of dread. He rifled through his pockets until he'd found the letter and its address on the back. He thought for sure he'd heard that name before, and after reading the back of the letter, he realized he had.

Miss Marguerite #3 Whitechurch Lane,

Livingston's Market Sector

It only took Ike a moment of contemplation before he popped the seal on the letter and read the contents beneath a streetlight.

Marguerite,

I know that I did not win your heart, but you certainly captured mine. You left me with enough information that I was able to find you. I would beg that you allow me another chance to show you that I am the man you want to spend the rest of your life with. If you should not desire my affections, I will abandon the quest with but a word. I beg you to grant me an afternoon. I am confident that such time will be all you need to see me for who I am: A man desperately in love.

    With all my heart,

    Don Hezekiah Johnson

Ike groaned. Fate had dealt him a cruel blow. A choice was never so hard: his greatest friend or a wondrously beautiful woman. However, the more he thought about it, the more he realized that it really wasn't his choice at all. It was Marguerite's. And, if he truly did capture her heart, she would not entertain pursuits from other suitors. He refolded the letter and did his best to reseal it.

Stepping up to the letter slot on #3 Whitechurch Lane, he reached to insert the square of paper, but hesitated at the last second. He felt his fingers pinching the parchment, refusing to let go. If she had already given him her heart, there was no reason to bother her with this trivial matter. She might even thank him for shielding her from a determined stalker, and at the same time he would save Johnson from a stinging rejection. Ike withdrew the letter and tapped it against his pursed lips. He sighed and made up his mind.

Chapter Fourteen
RISE

It took David 4 hours in the modified skiff to fly back to the underground's facility in Braxton's third. He tapped his foot through every minute of the trip and checked to make sure that he was flying at full throttle twice an hour. All of his previous weariness washed away the moment he heard his mother was speaking. After so many cycles of silence, he could talk to her, and she'd actually answer him!

When he finally touched down at the old warehouse where the underground made their base, he leapt from the cockpit before the docking clamps had fully attached. He ran down the halls and startled more than a few guards in his haste, arriving at the hospital wing in a rush and nearly knocking Dr. Abraham to the floor. However, the doctor caught hold of David's shoulder before he could enter his mother's room. David looked back at Dr. Abraham with a wild expression, part excitement and part annoyance at the holdup.

"She's asleep, lad," Abraham said. "And the good maker knows she needs it."

David looked at Abraham for a moment before the words penetrated his excited mind. "But, why?"

"It's the middle of the night, David," Abraham replied. "Most people sleep at this time. Considering your mother's condition, I would expect it and even induce it if she were awake."

David sighed and rubbed his eyes, but something in the doctor's tone caught his attention. "Wait, what is her condition? They told me she was talking. Has there been any improvement?"

Abraham put a hand on David's shoulder and looked him in the eye. "She is talking. I was able to restore that much, but I couldn't repair what cycles of paralysis has wrought. She's in her last days, David. Tomorrow, the next day, I don't know when, but soon, very soon. We've kept her alive as long as we could and restored her speech so she could talk with you, but when you do finally speak with her, she won't be entirely herself. Her condition lends to delirium. When she wakes up, make the most of the opportunity. It may be your only chance to speak with her while she's lucid."

David swallowed hard and nodded at the bittersweet realization. He thanked the doctor and stepped into Mother's room as softly as he could. In the dim light he saw her degraded state. A dozen tubes ran under her blanket, and multiple machines hissed and warbled. The fact that anyone could sleep at all in that din leant to how tired Mother must have been. She lay in an elevated position with a device attached to the back of her neck and a thick cord running to one of the nearby machines. Someone had shaved most of her hair off, hair that had once been her glory.

The sight of Mother brought him to tears. He'd come all this way just to watch her die. He walked as quietly as he knew how and sat in a chair beside her bed. He saw her pale, thin face, and he wondered if Abraham had really told him the truth. Could she actually speak?

He dozed through the rest of the night, rousing himself each time his head bobbed, forcing himself to stay awake for the moment when she woke and called his name. At dawn, he saw the sun peek through the buildings on the last golden day. Clear blue sky shown above, and its contrasting appearance made the city look more rank than it did in constant rain. Mother's room lay three stories up in the old warehouse, and the one-way windows allowed him to see out of the sophisticated surgical center, while anyone looking in would only see a dirty, old building. Mother still slept, her chest rising in falling in time with her breathing. A nurse walked in with a tray of breakfast for David, and she laid it down on a small table beside him before stepping up to some of the machines and reading their displays. David looked at his breakfast without much interest after the nurse left the room, but beside his plate of fried tuber and eggs lay a newspaper. He would have had no interest in the news in that moment, except for the fact that he saw his name on the front page. He scooped up the paper and smoothed out the main article. After reading it once through, he wished he hadn't.

MAN HUNT

The late aide to Speaker Blythe, one David Ike, is wanted for the murder of three women. Speaker Blythe discovered the truth during the Speaker's retreat at the Everpine Resort. However, despite authorities' best efforts, David Ike escaped and is on the run. "No one is as disappointed in David as myself. I loved David as a son, and this betrayal cuts to my heart." Blythe said.
...

David gaped at the paper. Ghostly white faces flashed through his mind. The thought of him committing the heinous murders made him sick. Torturing women to death? Torturing Mercy to death! It was unthinkable. He remembered her awful stab wound. He was so engrossed in the article that he almost missed the small voice that called his name.

"David?"

He looked up and glanced around the room before he realized the voice came from his mother. He looked at her and saw her looking back, tears running down her cheeks and a smile that only curved half of her mouth. David dropped the paper.

"Mother!" He said. In an instant he was at her side clutching her hand. "Mother, it's been so long!"

"I love you, David," mother said. It came out slurred, but they were the words he'd dreamt of for cycles. "I've wanted to tell you for so long," she said between sobs. "I wanted you to know."

"I do know, Mother," David said as he wiped his face and tried to clear his bleary vision. "I could never forget that, not even if you were silent for a lifetime."

She sobbed, and he leaned in so she could kiss his forehead. "I've been praying for you, David. I've been praying for you for five cycles. I never stopped."

David felt a pang of guilt wash over him. In Mother's turmoil, she had apparently turned to Jeshua for strength. In his turmoil, he'd turned to himself and his own strength, and his strength was failing while hers remained strong.

"I don't know if he's listening anymore, Mother," David said between sobs. "Everything is crashing down around me, and I don't have the strength to try and hold it up."

"David," Mother said as she looked in his eyes, a look he used to loathe, but now desired with all his heart. "He's always listening. Maybe he's just trying to get your attention."

"He had my attention when father died, and when Grandfather died, when you were paralyzed, and when I was crippled. Then he took my only friend, and the doctor says he's going to take you too, soon." David fell against Mother's chest and shook with sobs.

"I know, David," she said as she kissed the top of his head. "I watched the whole time, and there wasn't a thing I could do to help, except pray."

"The authorities want me for murder, Mother," David continued with another sniff. "Murder! I'm trying to do what's right, but every step of the way, it only gets worse. Why mother? Why is he doing this to us!"

Mother rested her chin on his head attempted to rock him as she had done so many cycles earlier, but her body was still partially paralyzed, and only her head could move.

"You can't blame Jeshua for a Fertile Plains racked with turmoil. We did that on our own." Mother rested her head back against her pillow and sighed. "We ruined his perfect creation with our pride and lust. It's not the way he intended it to be. You can see it every once in a while, when the sun rises and shifts over the mountains and all of the intricate creations, you see a glimpse of a time long past. The time before the plains felt the weight of our evils. But when the sun sets and the light fades away, for the briefest moment you can see... a hope for the future. A memory of the past and a hope for the future."

Mother's eyes glazed over as she lost herself to memory. "It's interesting because one can hardly tell the difference between a sunrise and a sunset, when they're captured in a photograph, but when you're there, watching it in person, they leave you with completely different feelings. The Fertile Plains may be wracked with pain and suffering, but everyone knows that it wasn't always like this, nor will it always be like this. There is hope in the life to come. I don't fear death, David. I know it's just a new beginning, one where I'll see my husband again, and my father and mother, an eternity without the pains of this life. That's why you keep going when everything seems hopeless. Even if everything collapses in this life, follow the path Jeshua has laid out for you, and you'll find yourself at peace with him in the end."

"But I'm so tired," David said. "I'm so tired, and I don't know where my path is anymore. What will I do once you're gone? What will I have left?"

"You will have your duty," Mother said looking at him with kind yet concerned eyes. "Same as always."

"But Alönia is ruined," David said. "What duty is left?"

"Not that Duty," Mother looked taken aback. "Every person in the Fertile Plains has the same duty regardless of where they live, the duty to do what is good."

David looked away sniffing back tears. "I'm not sure I know what good is anymore," he said. "This past cycle has been so confusing. The people I thought were good have turned out to be false."

"David, oh my sweet David," Mother said as she looked at him with a longing in her eyes. "After all these cycles, do you not know Jeshua?"

David tried to meet her eyes, but he couldn't. "I thought I did, but..."

"Knowing him gives you purpose," Mother said. "Not knowing him means hopelessness as all the things you cling to in this realm pass away. Knowing him means knowing good."

"What good is left for me to do?" David said. "Everything is clouded. I see things that need to be done, but I can't help but ask why. What good will it do?"

"I know David. I've been watching, remember?" She

said as she leaned her head back against her pillow, and he looked in her eyes. "But good never changes, no matter what. No matter how bad it gets, you have but to do justice, love kindness, and pursue the humble path. It will not fail you. You just have to know Jeshua and trust him."

David nodded, remembering the words even before she said them from his earliest childhood lessons. The memory of those simple charges brought warmth, a thought that if all else failed, he could fall back on the three tasks. But even still, he wondered what the point of going on was when there wasn't the slightest chance of happiness as long as he remained in the physical realm. Justice, kindness, and humility seemed so trite when he was watching his friends die. Or when he was being accused of murdering them. If the only hope he had lay in the afterlife, perhaps he should ask Johnson for the next suicide mission. But he could not say these things to his mother in her weakened state. Despite the fact that he had longed for the chance to share his troubles with her, now that the chance had finally come, he found himself holding back to save her from further pain.

"Did you know the whole time that Blythe was false?" he asked after a moment, and then he told her all he had discovered up until that point.

"Not to the extent you say," Mother said after David finished. "We tried to keep politics out of the family, as you know. But towards the end of your father's career in the armada, we started to wonder if we might be of more use in politics than in the armada. Not many people knew it, but your father had intended to take his PLAEE and run for office as a representative."

David nodded. He'd guessed as much after he found the PLAEE book in his father's satchel. "Why did he leave the armada? What was it that drove him to politics? He told me his superiors were angry with him, but he never told me why."

"It was many things, really," Mother said. "The armada wouldn't believe that the Berg and Viörn were plotting against us. The last straw came when he returned from the Outlands after defeating their overlord. They just couldn't understand his plans, and they threw them in his face."

"Did Father really know Don Hezekiah Johnson?" David asked. "Did he really go on missions with him."

Mother nodded. "They were very close friends... until something came between them."

"What came between them?" David asked.

Mother pursed her lips. "I think Mr. Johnson should probably tell you that. But you can trust him. He's a good man."

"He's not the man I expected to be trusting," David said with a sigh.

"What about that dishy redhead?" Mother asked with the same slanted smile. "Mercy... wasn't that her name? She came to see me a little while ago."

David looked away. The doctor had warned him of her delirium. She apparently didn't know that it had been four seasons since He'd brought Mercy to visit her. He didn't have the heart to say she was dead, either for mother's sake or for his.

"She was pretty, wasn't she?" David said with a nod.

"Pretty? She was gorgeous!" Mother said. "And don't you go losing her! A girl like that has to be chased. Your father had to chase me, you know."

"Yes, but he still won your heart in a day," David smiled at mother.

"True, but it was a very long day of chasing," she said with a smile of her own. "If you want her, you're going to have to get off your duff and chase her down."

"Get off my what?" David asked with a laugh.

"You know very well what I mean," she said as a blush touched her pale cheeks. Then she looked at him very seriously. "It makes it easier if you have someone to share life's burdens with. Don't wander alone, if you don't have to."

If only she knew how much her words made his soul ache, but he swallowed his discomfort and nodded. "I'll do my best," he said.

"You better!"

David smiled, but turned to wipe away secret tears. They continued to talk until lunch, conversations David had desired for whole cycles, questions he'd wanted answered for far too long, but as he talked, he watched his mother's strength ebb away until she spoke from hooded eyes. Over and over she told him how proud she was of him, how he was every bit the son she'd prayed for, and how his father would say the same if he were there. It pained him to let her sleep, knowing that every word she spoke could be her last, but in the end, he pulled her blanket up to her neck and kissed her on the forehead. She didn't need much prompting. As soon as he stopped speaking, her eyes shut, and she slept.

David ate a few bites of what the nurse had brought, but for the most part he sat beside mother and waited for her to rouse and speak with him again. She slept through the afternoon, and he paced her room while she did. Dr. Abraham entered a few times, but only for a cursory check, and then he left them. At five minutes to five 'o'clock, David stood at the window watching the passersby and the Úoi Season clouds blow in from the West.

"Darling, is it really you?" Mother asked. "It's been so long!"

David turned and looked at her. She favored him with the same lopsided smile he'd seen that morning. He smiled at her even as his heart broke. She had already forgotten their earlier conversation.

"I'm here," David said, and he walked to her bedside and grasped her hand.

"Oh, my dear husband, I've missed you so much," she said in the midst of sobs. "I know it hasn't been long, but it seems like an eternity since we were together. How I've missed holding hands on our walks. I've needed you these past few cycles."

David felt a lump form in the back of his throat. She thought he was his father. Did he really look so much like him? He'd spent cycles as half the man, but now his own mother confused them in her delusions. It hurt him to see her so confused, a woman famed for her wit. He felt pride at knowing he'd finally measured up to his father's stature, but pain that his father couldn't see it himself.

"I know," David said, becoming the mirage mother had manifested. "But I'm here now, and I'm never going to leave."

"David needs our prayers," mother said. "He's struggling to find his way, and he's giving into despair. You need to talk with him!"

"I will," David said, struggling to hold back his raging emotions as he spoke. "I'm sure he'll be fine."

"He's hurting so much," Mother said. "So many things have happened to him in the past few cycles, and I haven't been able to help him. The beasts want him for murder now, our David. It's even worse now than it was before, like you predicted. David needs hope again."

"He'll be fine now, I promise. I'm here, and I'm not leaving." David's body shook as he spoke. He didn't know how much longer he could maintain the charade in his present state.

"Now that your back, you can finish what you started," Mother said. "Run as a representative and start rebuilding the assembly. David has been having so much trouble with them. They... They..." She paused and shook her head with a confused look. "They've accused him of murder."

"Everything will be fine," David repeated, but most of it was lost in a sob. He leaned in and held his mother. "Everything will be fine."

"I'm so glad your back," mother said, smiling her crippled smile. "I'm so happy." She rested her head against his chest and sighed.

David continued to hold her for a few minutes while her mumbling grew more and more incoherent. Eventually, she stopped speaking at all. He felt her chest rise and fall with feeble breaths, each one fainter than the last.

All at once, she turned and looked at him with her deep chocolate eyes. "Walk in the truth, my son. Don't forget the truth!" Her voice sounded far away, but her eyes looked clear and coherent. "I see you... I see you standing victorious, rising above your enemies, soaring in an airship black as night. You're going to save them, all of them." Then she smiled and grew still.

David's looked on in shock. He shook her body, but there was no response. After five long cycles, the constant rhythm of her breathing had stopped, the one outward sign indicating the life within. Now, it lay still. He heard an alarm ring on one of the machines, but he knew what it signified even before it rang. He'd didn't let mother go. He held her long after doctors and nurses rushed into the room. None of them disturbed him. His mother was gone, and there was nothing to be done. Someone turned off the alarm and the racket of the other machines, and then they left him in peace and quiet.

It came suddenly, the feelings of emptiness and loneliness. He'd had a purpose for so long, the purpose to keep mother alive, and now she was gone. Even when she couldn't speak, she could still listen. Now she was nothing, just an empty shell. He had held her when she passed, but his holding did nothing to stop her passing.

She had slipped through his fingers and into eternity. Death had snatched her from his grasp, but she was still in his arms. His throat felt raw, and his eyes clouded with the tears he'd been holding back for so long. The sobs came a moment later, and his body shook violently with the emotion. He looked up in the midst of his lament.

"I want to hate you," he said to the empty room, but he knew that someone was listening. "I want to hate you so much! Doesn't that bother you? Do you want me to hate you? Why?" David fell forward and sobbed into Mother's blanket again. "Why did you do this to me? You took everything. My friends, my family, my job, my home; I have nothing left." He tore at the blanket with his hands. "I don't have any strength left to go on. I've run out of people to love." Hopelessness closed in around him, and he choked on its noxious fumes with gags and tears. "I need a reason to keep going. Right now, I don't have one. Please! Please speak to me! Answer me!"

As he sobbed over his mother's body, he heard the sound of bells in the distance. He realized what they were: the call to the evening sanctuary. At first the sound infuriated him, but the longer they tolled, the more his mother's words rang in his own head, and the words drove and compelled him. He had to see it for himself, the hope mother had described, the flicker of hope in the sunset. He needed a hope for the future, and even if he couldn't admit it, he knew he needed Jeshua to give it to him. Without wanting to, he found himself walking through the facility. He took the stairs to the top floor and stepped out onto the roof.

Clouds had congregated above in recent hours, driving the last light of the golden days to the far western side of Alönia. Only a few small patches of blue sky remained, but the areas around them were brilliant hues of pink, indigo and ruby red. The green hillsides beyond the city with their fresh foliage and thousands of different colors of wildflowers faded into navy blue the further out he looked, as the distance blotted away the green. David wasn't sure why, but he looked back to the east and saw the dark rainclouds of the new season approaching, filled with the black of night and devoid of hope. As they crept overhead, he heard the first drops of rain tap the roof and felt its coolness on his head. It chilled him, and he turned forward again. The golden light of the sun glistened off the droplets and formed a brilliant rainbow circling the sky, one with more hues than David had ever seen before. The sunlight banished his chills and caused him to gasp. He stumbled to the edge of the parapet and sank to his knees. He reached a hand toward the distant light, grasping at something that seemed just out of reach. His eyes overflowed with tears, and he fell against the parapet.

"I want to know you," he said between sobs. "Forgive my stubbornness. Please don't leave me here alone. Help me. I can't go on without you."

No sooner had he said the words he felt a surge of peace wash over him, as though he had been holding his breath beneath the water and had just broken through to cool fresh air. David closed his eyes, and warmth flooded his body as though someone was wrapping him in an embrace. He felt more than understood that he had just met someone. Someone who cared more for him than anyone he had ever known. He opened his eyes and watched the brilliance of the sunset anew.

He could see it. He could see what mother spoke of. As the sun ebbed lower and lower behind the Alönian mountains, he felt no loss in its passing, only hope. The feeling was different than the sunrise he watched seasons earlier after Mercy died, just as his mother said. Then, he saw purpose, an understanding that Jeshua had a path for him and would direct his steps, but he had only seen it in part. Now, he saw Jeshua's eternity in all of its splendor. The sun would rise again, not only on the morrow but also in the glory of the afterlife. Life in the Fertile Plains was only a moment compared with that eternity, Jeshua's eternity. As the last light of the golden days played across his face, he knew Jeshua, more than ever before. He knew him as he knew a close friend. He knew he wasn't alone, and he knew a new sense of peace and purpose. He'd do his duty. He'd do justice, love kindness, and seek the humble path. He'd make his parents proud, Jeshua rest their souls, and someday, he'd join them in eternity.

Chapter Fifteen
A NEW HOPE

Mercy walked through the underground's facility toward the surgical center. She'd been there several times before, once during its construction when she'd reported to Johnson her findings on David, once when the underground decided to bring David in for questioning, and once just a few weeks ago when she'd visited David's mother. This time, she needed to convince David she'd never died, and console him at the eve of his mother's death. She shook her head as she walked, a mixture of excitement and terror amidst questions and confusion. She really didn't know what emotion to feel, only that she needed David to forgive her for hurting him. But on the other hand, how could she justifiably ask him for anything. She'd abandoned him by faking her death after he'd expressed feelings for her, and now she'd come back at the time of his mother's death, and she wanted to ask him for forgiveness? Her mind was flooding with doubts. What if he threw her out the minute he saw her? What if he told her he didn't care she was alive? What if he never wanted to see her again?

Mercy paused as she walked up to Marguerite Ike's surgical room and looked at the shut door. Perhaps his mother had told David she was alive. Mercy wondered if she'd also told him to be wary of her.

She closed her eyes and went over the speech she'd rehearsed a thousand times in preparation for this moment. But the words seemed so trite in comparison to the emotions raging inside her. She struggled to master her emotions before knocking three times. Nobody answered. She knocked again with still no reply. Finally, Mercy cracked the door open and looked inside. The room lay empty, the bed stripped and the multiple machines she'd seen earlier wheeled off into the corner. Mercy turned back to the hallway and caught a nurse by the arm.

"There was a patient in this room," Mercy said. "Has she been moved?"

"Not moved, no," the nurse said. "She passed on less than an hour ago."

"Was there a young man with her when she passed?"

"Aye, he'd been with her all day," the nurse said. "Poor dear sobbed for quite some time."

"But where did he go?"

"I'm not sure, miss. He walked out in a daze after the woman's passing and took the stairs."

Mercy forgot to thank the woman as she turned and rushed toward the stairway. She stepped into the stairwell and looked up and down its center. Nobody was there, and she couldn't decide which way she should go. She looked up and decided she'd check there first. There was only one story above her and several below. She stopped off at the top floor of the facility and asked a guard if he'd seen someone with David's description. The brawny man shook his head, so she raced back into the stairway and climbed the last flight to the rooftop. She opened the door and stepped out onto the expanse, turning as she went. There was only one other person there, standing on the far western side, leaning against the parapet. The sun's last rays were twinkling across the sky as she looked at the man's back. Light rain pattered on the roof around her, soaking her auburn tresses and red dress. The man she saw had David's hair but not his body. This man's square shoulders and muscular physique stood in stark contrast to David's crippled form. But who else would stand on a rooftop in the rain except a man who'd just watched his mother die?

"David?" She called, unsure of what she was seeing.

The man's head twitched to the side. Then he turned and faced her. Everything Mercy planned on saying stuck in her throat. She opened her mouth to speak, but all she did was gasp, as she saw a man with David's face on someone else's body. He stood several inches taller than her, and his shoulders were broad and square. His mechanical arm no longer hung lower than his natural arm, and it drew the surrounding light into its black gilded depths. But his face remained, as it always was, strong and bold featured. He looked at her as though she did not even exist, smiling at a memory. A tear rolled down his cheek, and he began to turn back toward the sunset. If he had ever loved her, he certainly did not anymore. Mercy put a hand out and took a step forward. David jumped as he saw the movement, falling back against the parapet wall.

"You! You're dead!" he said, and he clung to the wall behind him as though it were an anchor.

"No, I'm not," Mercy said. That was it. Whole seasons of rehearsing and planning precise words, and they washed away the moment she saw his face. She took another step.

"You're not real!" He said. "You're a fake, a mirage of someone I used to love."

Mercy's step faltered when she heard his denunciation. A sob contorted her body, and she covered her mouth to choke off the sound. Tears mixed with the raindrops that ran down her face. She felt water soaking through her red dress, the very same dress she'd worn when she interviewed with Blythe and David. He hadn't even noticed.

A fake, that's what he'd called her, and that's exactly what she'd been. Had anything about the Mercy he knew been the truth? He was right. He'd fallen in love with a mirage, an image he'd cast with the lies she told. Lies, so many lies, and now she hung in the web of her own making. She started shivering as the rain and the cold of her own dread seeped into her bones.

He shut his eyes and shook his head. "I can't believe I'm even talking to you," he said as he slid down the parapet wall to a seated position, seemingly uncaring of the rain that fell around him.

Mercy's tears flowed freely now as she watched him. He rested his head against the wall and shut his eyes. It was clear he wanted nothing more to do with her. Mercy hung her head, all her fears realized in one fell swoop. He hated her for what she'd done. She'd exploited a good man to do her duty, and now she was paying the price. She wanted to turn and run back down the stairs. She wanted to hide; she wanted to be anywhere else but on that roof with David. Before she would have given anything to see him, but now that she knew he couldn't stand the sight of her, she longed to be away so she wouldn't have to feel his disdain. But she'd come on a mission other than the one to make her own heart whole. His mother had passed on, and she had to bring David back from the brink.

"I'm sorry," she said. "I'm sorry about your mother."

He wiped his face of tears and rainwater and nodded. "It's better this way. She had suffered for so long, only staying alive so she could deliver me one last message. As soon as she told it to me, it was like her life concluded, and she fulfilled her final desire. She's with my father now."

"What was her final message?" Mercy asked, and she risked another step toward him. They were only a few strides apart now.

"Purpose," David said. "She gave me purpose again, or at least, she pointed me back to the purpose I should have been pursuing the whole time. It's interesting, in her final moments, she hallucinated my father, the thing she loved the most in all the Fertile Plains. Now I'm hallucinating you scarcely thirty minutes later." He started to laugh. "It's not enough for you to haunt my dreams. Now you're in my waking thoughts as well."

Mercy's mouth fell open. "Hallucinating?" She said, and her tears ceased to flow. In three long strides she reached David's side and slapped him, hard.

His eyes popped open with the impact, and he looked up at her with an expression like a hurt puppy.

"Has a hallucination ever done that?" Mercy asked.

David rubbed his cheek in confusion. "But... but I held your limp body! Your bloodstained my clothes!"

"It wasn't my body," Mercy said as she crossed her arms and shut her eyes. "I had a plaster cast made a few weeks prior, and my brother rigged up a dummy corpse. That was sheep's blood."

David stared at her and rubbed his cheek as she looked down on him. Very slowly, he rose to his feet and stepped close, looking full into her green eyes. Mercy's seasons' long agony melted away as he looked at her. He touched her cheek, and she smiled.

"It really is you?" he asked with faltering words.

She nodded and tried to smile, but fresh tears spoiled her attempt. He shut his eyes and shook his head. But when he opened them again, he smiled and drew her into an embrace. His warmth brought immediate comfort and security.

"How?" He asked as he buried his face in her now limp hair. "... and why did you wait so long to tell me?"

Mercy took a deep breath. She made to pull away so

she could speak to him face to face, but he didn't let her.

"I'll tell you everything, but can we first get out of the rain?" she asked. The sun had set, and cool evening air blew across her wet dress. She shivered.

"Yes, of course," David said. "I'm sorry."

He took her arm and led her back into the old warehouse. After he found her a blanket and brewed some tea, she started her story, her real story.

"I was born in Armstad, and my first name really is Mercy, and a few other things you know are true, but most of what I said was a lie." Mercy waited for David to show some form of disapproval or anger, but he only looked curious.

"I'm not estranged from my parents," Mercy said. "Every single member of my family is involved in the effort to keep Armstad safe. My oldest brother, Corvin, is a sneak, and one of the best ones Armstad has ever had."

"Corvin?" David asked. "I know that name." He looked at the ceiling and then snapped his fingers. "But of course," David said with a snap of his fingers. "A few weeks before you *died*," He drew quotation marks in the air as he spoke, "I did a little snooping on Representative Walker. A man named Corvin landed an airship at Walker's mansion and gave a report."

"Yes, that was my brother!" Mercy said. "He made regular reports to Walker back when he was speaker."

David chuckled as he looked into his mug of tea. "Sometimes the Fertile Plains seem very small."

"Well, he's the oldest. Bibi is next oldest," Mercy continued. "He's a part of the Armstad assault force.

Most people in our army consider him the deadliest man in the Fertile Plains. Then there's Yoni. He made the plaster cast dummy that... well, anyway... He's an inventor of sorts. He's built all kinds of weapons and airships and expanded our knowledge in multiple sciences." Mercy chuckled as she thought of him. "He's been blowing things up since he learned to walk. I'm the youngest. I trained as a sneak, but since I was not able to serve in the same capacity as my older brothers, my father sent me to Alönia. He'd long feared that Alönia's Equalist party would take power and leave Armstad to face their enemies alone, just as Blythe has done. So he hatched a plan with Don Johnson and implanted me into the office of the leading Equalist threat."

"How did he know Johnson?" David asked.

"Johnson's mother was Armstadi, and Johnson did some sneak work himself and made several presentations to Armstad," Mercy said after a sip of tea as David gave a knowing nod. "He and my father formed a friendship and an alliance around the time of my birth," Mercy continued, "though I never met Johnson until my aideship with Representative Herald, and even then, our meetings were few and far between. He's a very stern man, and sometimes he even scares me, but he's always good, and he always makes the right choice."

"That's how my mother described him," David said

"Well," Mercy continued, "I worked for Herald for two cycles, and though he boasted his ability to unseat Speaker Walker, he lacked the inspiration to actually follow through. None of us expected Blythe, or should I say, you."

David looked away from her, and she could tell he was ashamed of his accomplishment.

"Whether you revere the achievement or not, it was a remarkable feat," Mercy said. "Besides, if you hadn't elevated Blythe, we never would have gotten acquainted with each other."

He perked up at that.

"The moment after Blythe's grand speech, Johnson moved me to the Blythe campaign," she explained. "I assumed it would be a simple matter to dismantle the office from the inside out. We all underestimated you, and after you evaded every trap we set, and navigated Blythe though a dozen pitfalls, I realized that the only person who could remove Blythe from power, was the man who put him in it: you."

David choked on his tea, but as she looked in his eyes, his gaze faltered, and he looked away and nodded.

"The trouble was that you wholeheartedly believed in Blythe and his ideals, but I could tell that Blythe's character was not congruent with your own. I knew that if you saw the true Blythe and what the Equalists truly stood for, you'd turn on them. I was right, but I acted too late. Killing myself seemed the only way to get your attention and get you to start asking the right questions."

"Oh, it definitely did that," David said with a sigh.

"I confess I grossly underestimated how deeply it impacted you, and the ten days I'd hoped you would use to dismantle Blythe, you spent in mourning. I'm truly sorry for what I put you through. Had I known... how you felt, I would have tried something different." She looked away, unable to meet his gaze as she wiped a tear.

He reached across the table and gave her hand a squeeze. "I'm just happy you're alive, and that it was all a farce."

Mercy nodded with a sigh and continued. "We planned my death, and the census fraud money trail. It was a two-pronged attack. If you didn't realize the truth during the campaign finance investigation, I knew you find it out after I died. We had Speaker Walker put together the census oversight committee and hand pick an inspection team. The night I left you at the office, the last time we saw each other, I met up with the team, and we prepared my apartment, placed the corpse and such. I knew it would only be a matter of hours before you came looking for me. I was across the way at an adjacent apartment congratulating myself on so apt a prediction, when I saw your face as you entered. I knew then that I had struck you far deeper than I could have imagined, but once you entered, we were bound to that course of action. The census oversight committee arrived after you'd had time to confirm my death. They bagged the dummy and erased any evidence to prove I still lived. That's why neither you nor Winston ever found a body."

David nodded. "It's all so simple, looking back. In my grief, I never thought to examine the body beyond a pulse. I'm sorry it took me so long to realize who Blythe really was. I didn't find out his true character until moments before his oath of office, by then it was too late."

"Don't blame yourself. We all botched the job where Blythe is concerned. It's just that nobody saw him coming."

"Someday I might finally learn to look where no one else is," David muttered, more to himself than her. "Regardless, Blythe never would have got as far as he did if he hadn't received foreign aid."

Mercy nodded. "Francisco told me what you discovered in Thornton. It's disgusting. I was in the gallery when you took your seat at the assembly for Blythe's acceptance speech," she said. "I could tell the moment I saw you that you'd discovered the truth. That's why I saw you when you wrote that note and slipped it into the House Law book. After the census, I sneaked down and got it. I wanted to see you the moment I knew you'd changed your mind about Blythe, but Johnson told me to wait. He said my death was the only reason you changed your position, and that if I miraculously reappeared, you would question your decision."

David sighed and nodded back and forth, apparently considering the statement. "He's not wrong," he said at last. "I held to Equalist ideals until a few days ago. I suppose I began to doubt them when I got an up-close look at the people who championed them, but it wasn't until Thornton that I truly rejected them in favor of a Pragmatic perspective."

"Well," Mercy said, "because of that, my existence was concealed from you. I saw you on several occasions, and I had to bite my tongue to keep from calling out. I was at your interrogation only a few floors down from here."

David froze in the middle of drinking his tea. "You were?" He asked as he looked at her. "What did I say?"

"Only some very sweet things about me," Mercy said as she looked in her cup. "You even cried over me." She looked at him as she blew on her steaming tea, doing her best not to smile.

David blushed vibrantly, which made her start giggling.

"What made Johnson change his mind and let you come today?" he asked once she'd had her laugh.

"He knew your mother was at death's door," she said, in a more solemn tone. "He thought I might be able to bring you back from the brink of despair. But, when I found you, when you thought I was a hallucination, you didn't seem to be in despair. You spoke of a purpose."

David nodded. "I'm sad she's gone, but I'm happy as well. It was no life to live, being trapped inside her body and such. I'm not sure what pains me more, seeing her suffering or knowing she's gone. I... I got to say goodbye." He sniffed and nodded. "It's bittersweet. She reminded me of my duty to seek good, and that part of that good is to do justice. Blythe's justice is long overdue, and a war that could kill thousands is right around the corner. I don't know how yet, but I'm going to remove him from office and lock him away in a prison where he can rot for a lifetime."

"Oh?" Mercy said, and she saw David's eyes glinting with determination. "I see. Do you have a plan yet?"

"No," David said as he rested his head in his hands. "I feel like Blythe is carving Alönia to pieces, and I'm trying to catch the fragments before they dash to oblivion on the ground. One thing is for sure, I know we need to save the forward fleet before he has it decommissioned and dismantled. The Viörn admiral, if that was indeed who he was, seemed very keen about the airships' deconstruction. I can only imagine a terrible fate if Viörn invades a defenseless Alönia."

"Jeshua works in mysterious ways," Mercy said.

"I know." David nodded his head. "I know he's got a plan, but I just can't tell what it is yet. I suppose he will reveal it in good time."

Mercy noted the difference in the tone David spoke of Jeshua as compared to the last time they had a conversation about him. The last time, when they'd sat on the sunbeam after the prowler attack, David had avoided the subject, looking away whenever Mercy mentioned Jeshua's name. Now, he spoke of the name reverently, as though it had a special place in his heart.

David used his hand to massage his temple again and continued. "There's more. Blythe has undercut a lot of my influence and my ability to work." He stood and walked over to a trash receptacle. He rifled through it until he drew out a newspaper with some tea stains marring its corners. Her turned it to the front page and dropped it on the table in front of Mercy. As she read it, her hand slipped up to cover her mouth.

"Murder?" She said when she'd finished the page. "He's accused you of the crimes he committed!"

David snorted as he resumed his seat. "Probably the smartest thing he's done since I've met him. It prevents me from speaking out without risking my capture, and it also discredits anything I might say. I can't show myself in public without risk of arrest, or worse."

"Well, part of it is easy to disprove," Mercy said after a moment's thought. "I'm still alive, so you obviously didn't murder me."

David smiled. "It also proves that Blythe has no idea about your ruse or your involvement with the underground. We might be able to use that to our advantage in the future. Still, the situation is bleak."

"They'll have to get past Armstad first, you know," Mercy said, searching for something happier to discuss, "Viörn and Berg, that is. We are not as defenseless as many would believe, despite our size."

"True," David said with a smile. "But If Berg and Viörn attack..." He shrugged. "We are at a tipping point, and we must act fast. Did Johnson tell you when he'd be joining us?"

"He dropped me off and continued on to the Sixth District for a meeting with Walker," Mercy said. "He wanted us to come along if and when you were ready. Are you sure you are?"

David nodded. "I'd like something to do. A task would be beneficial."

"You're... different," Mercy said, cocking her head and wrinkling her brow. "Much different than I expected you to be. Given everything that's happened, especially today, I expected you to be more... in despair."

David gave a tight smile and brushed away a tear. Mercy wondered if she had said too much.

"I am sad, but despite everything that's happened, I found hope today. More than I've ever had."

Mercy smiled, but as she looked at him, she realized he was not referring to her. "What hope?" she asked.

"The hope of eternity," David said. "The hope that one day Jeshua will reunite me with my mother and father. I've been running from him for a long time, knowing about him but not really knowing him. My mother said some things to me before she died, things she'd told me a long time ago, but her death drove them into my heart." David sighed. "I came to the end of my strength, and I realized how tired I was of running, tired of the weight of my shortcomings, and tired of my hopelessness. I realized my need for something more than this physical realm to fill me with purpose. So I called out to him, on the rooftop, and he... he..." David looked around, apparently struggling for the right words. "...came to me. I don't know how else to explain it. I felt warmth and love and joy filling my being. The same feeling I got when my mother embraced me or when my father squeezed my shoulder and told me I did a good job, but more, a thousand times more. And now I feel hope, real hope."

Mercy felt her smile grow and tears roll down her face as David spoke. Once he'd finished, she leaned over and gave him a hug. "Oh, David! There's no better hope."

"So you know what I'm talking about?"

She nodded. "I know exactly what you're talking about. My mother and father told me about Jeshua when I was young. Growing up in Armstad with the ever-present threat of invasions... well, even as a little girl I'd hide in my closet and speak with him, asking for strength and peace and safety for my family."

"I'm glad," David said. "It makes life so much easier knowing death is just a new beginning, and... I'm glad you feel the same way I do."

She nodded and felt her cheeks color. "Well, at least now you'll have me to help you with your efforts in life instead of working against you."

He smiled. "Just don't die, again. Once was enough."

"I'll do my best," she said as he helped her to her feet. Together they left the facility and climbed into Johnson's skiff. It was a tight squeeze, but Mercy didn't mind, and David looked as though he thoroughly enjoyed the proximity. He powered up the skiff, and they soared through the light rain into the clouds. They made a quick stop at a floating refueling station, and Mercy had a moment to admire the stars and the brilliant glow of the moon. She watched David as he paid the attendant, and felt a strange feeling, one she had never felt before. She knew that ahead lay a monumental task, as well as war, death, and destruction, but during this evening, as she sat so close to David and rested her head on his shoulder, everything seemed right in the Fertile Plains. She felt entirely happy, and she wasn't even quite sure why.

Chapter Sixteen
THE SIXTH DISTRICT

Economy thrived in the Sixth District. In fact, before public pharmaceuticals established its headquarters in the third, more business operated in the Sixth District of House Braxton than in Braxton, Livingston, Hopkins combined, despite being one of Alönia's smaller districts in square fathoms. Such was the prosperity and growth of the city that it sprawled across the entire landscape of the district, one continuous municipality. When the city first reached capacity, rather than capping expansion, the city planners simply added another layer of factory orbitals above the industrial sector, creating the first multi-level metropolis.

David had flown over the sixth on many occasions from an airship at two grandfathoms in elevation. Even from that distance the sixth looked impressive, but as David and Mercy dropped through the early morning clouds and merged into bustling air traffic, David gaped in utter shock. It was unlike any city he had ever seen, as modern as Capital City, as crowded as the third, yet cleaner than both, despite the many factories. Thriving industrious people hurried through the streets and along the orbital walkways. Air traffic teamed in expressways at four different elevations, each of which traveled at different set speeds. Enormous turbofans pulled air from above the highest orbitals and continuously ventilated the lower levels.

David understood now why people described it as the *city that lived*. He glided beneath the city's orbital level and watched everything churn with activity, and not only the rail lines and airships. Buildings moved with rotating turbines, cogs and gears, pumping pistons and compressing hydraulics. Complex cranes ferried shipping containers along overhead steel lines. Trains traveled on top of elevated tracks or hung on rails that ran beneath the orbitals. Yet, the thing that David found strangest of all was the fact that the light shone as bright beneath the orbitals as it did above, and it didn't take him long to figure out why. The city planners evidently foresaw the orbiting level's shadows and implanted a system of mirrors at crucial points to reflect light on the lower portions.

David flew through the well-organized traffic according to Mercy's direction, until they approached a towering pillar reaching from the ground level all the way to the upper orbitals, but the closer they flew the more David recognized the pillar for what it really was. There were twelve in total, and each provided a crucial service. Not only did they ground the orbital layer of the city, they also powered the entire district. All of the rainwater that fell on the orbital flowed through a system of gutters in such an efficient manner that engineers claimed the ground never felt a drop. This water flowed down the center of the twelve towers through hydroelectric generators. No columns of steam vented from cooling towers and, by the look of it, no rank air from an overpopulated industrious society. The local populous called them the twelve pillars of Alönian industry. The pillars also supported a few floors of offices around their middles. These offices were the headquarters of 11 different industries, most of which constructed different components of airships; 11 industries for 11 pillars, and one, as far as David knew, lay vacant.

He docked the skiff at a landing below the pillar's offices, and together he and Mercy ascended in a nearby steam lift. David asked where they were going, but Mercy only told him to wait and see. The view from the glass wall of the steam lift created a perfect observatory of the multi-leveled city's innerworkings. David had never dreamed this much industry existed in Alönia. The sight made him doubt the third's greater population, and the cleanliness baffled him. The air tasted fresh when he'd stepped out of the skiff, as fresh as the air on the Capital City orbital. He was a long way up from Alönian soil, but as far as he could tell, the clean streets and shining windows continued far past the mid-levels all the way to the original ground level.

He turned as the steam lift door opened behind him, and he stepped into a hallway that looked to wrap around the square pillar. He and Mercy walked a little way down its length and then turned and passed through a wide arch that opened into a grand observatory. There were several people in the room, Johnson, Francisco, and Bethany, but the face that drew David's attention was the solemn countenance of Representative Walker, former speaker of the Houses of Alönia. Everyone turned and looked at David and Mercy when they entered the room. Johnson stood and clasped David's hand.

"I was very sorry to hear about your mother, David," he said. "You have my condolences."

"Thank you, sir," David replied with a tight smile.

"I do believe you know representative Walker," Johnson added after he'd released David's hand, "even if you've never met him."

Representative Walker approached David from the window where he'd been spectating and smiled at him.

"So this is David Ike," Walker said as he appraised David. "The most famous aide in Alönian history. I must say, you look very different from the first time I saw you sitting in the Third District booth after Blythe's grand speech. Now, you look as regal as your father and grandfather." He too took David's hand and shook it.

David did his best to smile but found the exchange awkward. It was unsettling to shake hands with the man he'd once called enemy, and it was odder still that Walker would receive that hand in friendship after David destroyed his career.

"We didn't expect you so soon," Johnson said after the exchange. "I had thought it would be at least a week before Mercy revived you from your loss. Are you sure you're ready to return so soon?"

David nodded, doing his best not to think about his mother as they all alluded to her. "I left the Third District with more hope than I've had in a long time," David said. "I'm ready to do my duty and right a lot of wrongs." He nodded toward Representative Walker.

"You found hope at a time like this?" Francisco asked after everyone had found a seat around the room.

"What Francisco means to say," Walker said as he rested his index fingers against his chin, "is that we have been in conference for some time and our situation is dire. We cannot conceive of any reasonable means to unseat Speaker Blythe before he slashes the armada and prostrates Alönia before her enemies."

The former speaker frowned. "As you know, in weeks Blythe intends to put the squeeze on both public pharmaceuticals and the Sixth District, both from legislation and corporate espionage. This district is the Pragmatic's stronghold, and its passing would doom our party and Alönia. Whatever Blythe's intentions, he's leading Alönia into the mouth of the beast." Walker ended with a great sigh and looked out over his magnificent city.

David fought against feelings of pain, guilt, and regret and prepared his mind for thought. "I think our greatest hope is still inspector Winston," he said after some consideration. "If we can pin Blythe with multiple murder, there is a decent chance we could have him removed from office."

"Have you seen the papers from the past few days?" Francisco asked.

David nodded. "I know. He's blamed me with the murders, but pinning them on me won't counter all of the evidence Inspector Winston has on him."

"But we've looked for him non-stop ever since you gave us his name," Johnson said. "The man's a ghost. More than likely, Blythe had him disposed of weeks ago in light of what he knew."

"That may not matter," David said. "You can't really erase evidence, just like you can't erase history. You can try and cover it up, but in the process, you just create more evidence of its existence. Maybe we're looking for Winston in the wrong place. What we should really be doing is backtracking Blythe's interaction with the Orbital Police and see when it was that Blythe inquired after Winston."

Johnson and Walker looked at each other and then at Francisco.

"Seems like a fair idea," Francisco said. "So far we've got nothing from watching Winston's house except we spotted a few other people watching his house as well. That and we also discovered that it's not just inspector Winston that went missing."

"What do you mean?" David asked.

"There's about a dozen inspectors missing," Francisco said. "All of them disappeared around the same time. We posted a watch at a few of their houses, but there's no sign of them either."

"Somebody cleaned house," Johnson said.

"That's the going theory," Francisco said. "There doesn't seem to be any connection between the inspectors. They come from a range of departments within the Capital City police; white-collar crimes, security, orbital traffic, and none were of particular importance."

"I'm assuming your men already looked for connections with Blythe?" David asked, and Francisco nodded. David rested his head in his hands. He needed to broaden his scope of inquiry. Perhaps the focus wasn't on Blythe's criminal history, perhaps there was some other connection."

"No connection in academy class or training groups?" David asked.

"None of note," said Francisco. "Most of the orbital guard were born and raised on the island and trained at the Capital City Academy. But this lot comes from all different cycles."

Bethany slapped a hand against her forehead. "Oh, but of course!" she said, and everyone looked at her. "It's not like the information is public, but I'll bet if you asked around their friends and colleagues, you'd find a common political affiliation."

"That would solve it," Francisco said with a nod to Bethany. "It would be difficult to prove, but it fits. Blythe would want a capital guard loyal to him."

"True," David said. "But if we'd have a hard time finding out, how would Blythe know? You said all the men disappeared at the same time?"

Francisco nodded.

"If one or two disappeared each week as their leanings became public knowledge, I'd agree with Bethany," David said. "But to have them all disappear at once... It's almost like they upped and left."

"Francisco," Johnson said. "Let's try altering our search and look into if and when Blythe inquired after Winston. At the moment, I think that's all to be done with our missing inspector. What about Blythe and his slippery little Viörn friend? Any more communications between the two?"

"Not through our cloned device," Bethany said. "It's been silent since the Thornton meeting. They probably guessed we'd been eavesdropping and switched devices."

"So proving Blythe's involved in treason is off the table for now," Johnson said and massaged his brow. "Too bad. That would have been easy. Any other ideas?"

Nobody said anything. David looked around at the downcast faces. All of them seemed hopeless, all except Mercy's. She looked at him with an encouraging smile, a look that gave him confidence.

"Why don't we wait on Blythe and his removal until we have more answers," he said. "We should face the problem we have answers too."

"Which is?" Johnson asked.

"The airships," David said. "We need to rescue the airships from their deconstruction. Without them, it won't matter if we retake the speakership. Viörn and Berg will crush us in one fell swoop."

"We don't have the personnel to succeed in such a heist," Francisco said.

"We don't need to rescue all the airships," David said. "We can leave all the support craft and focus on the larger vessels. Skiff Carriers are the major players these days anyway. And, I'll bet with a little bit of recruiting, we could find a few hundred Armada vets willing to help us smuggle them away."

"But away to where?" Francisco said. "Where will we hide a few hundred thunder class carriers, not to mention, when we fly them away, what will keep the orbital guard from chasing us down? It's like robbing a vault and trying to escape on the back of a bovine. I don't know about you, but shooting down our own guard won't create sympathy for our cause."

"We cannot possibly hope to survive without those ships," David said, letting his hands fall to his lap. "That is an absolute in this situation. How we snatch them, and where we take them only requires better planning, but not having them means complete disaster."

"Why not take them to Armstad?" Mercy asked. "The capital guard can't pass into our airspace without permission."

"Where are the ships now?" Johnson asked.

"At Veteran Shipyards on the north side of Capital Island," Walker said. "To be deconstructed on the 39th day of Úoi Season."

"That's only an hour from Armstad airspace at a carrier's pace," David said hopefully. "We could make that." He turned to Francisco.

"Perhaps," Francisco said. "An hour is a long time in a chase." He lifted his arm and pulled up the sleeve, revealing the pulse emitter strapped to his arm.

"39th day of Úoi Season?" Mercy said as she leaned close to David's ear. "Isn't that the same day as the third's election?"

David looked away from Francisco's fidgeting to nod at Mercy. "I know what you're thinking, but he's got 80% of the popular vote behind him, and he's running unopposed."

"So no campaigning against him then," Mercy said and frowned.

David shook his head. "Francisco?" he said at length when the man had his entire sleeve unrolled and his emitter partially disassembled. "Are you going to tell us why you're disrobing in front of us?"

Francisco opened his mouth to speak, but then cocked his head and continued to fiddle with the wires strapped to his arm. At length he said, "Bethany, what would happen to a gunship if we shot it with a pulse emitter."

"Nothing," Bethany said, nodding to the little emitter on his wrist.

"No, not like this one, one of a much larger scale," Francisco said.

"Oh," Bethany said with a roll of her eyes. "No lasting damage to the gunship. It would take the crew a few minutes to rouse themselves and a few more minutes to restart the burner. It's not a new concept, just not effective in battle because it won't kill the enemy, and the range is very limited."

"But we don't want to kill the enemy," David said, nodding along with Francisco as he saw where the idea was heading. "We could mount them on the carriers and disable any gunships that got to close."

"But... I thought we didn't have enough men to man the airships," Johnson said. "If we have to man their guns as well, we won't have nearly enough."

"We don't need to fully man all the airships," David said, "only the ones at the rear."

"Yes," Walker said, with a flourish of his hand. "But when you start shooting at the gunships, they will undoubtedly shoot back."

"Orbital gunships aren't armed with torpedoes," David said. "They really won't be able to do anything but scratch the paint with their chain-guns. Their greatest threat is boarding, but if we stun them when they get close..."

"They won't be able to," Francisco said, finishing David's thought.

"Hmm," Johnson said as he leaned forward in his chair. "The Armstadi would be more than grateful to have the forward fleet back as most of them came from the Armstad border anyway. But what will Blythe do?"

"He won't declare war," Mercy said with a snort. "Even he would hesitate to do something like that. He's marketing himself as a peacekeeper. Declaring war isn't his style."

"Even so, Armstad can't abscond with several hundred airships and expect the assembly to do nothing," Walker said.

Mercy looked up for a moment, apparently deep in thought. "When warships enter Armstadi airspace without authorizations, there is an automatic quarantine by our border control. After all, Armstad would have no idea the airships were stolen. It could be an invading armada. And, given the number of airships *invading*, as it were, it may be some time before Armstad could return Alönia its airships. The paperwork alone would be a nightmare."

Mercy gave an exasperated expression, and David smiled at her.

"Could you contact Armstad and inform them of our plan?" Johnson asked.

"Of course," Mercy said. "I don't foresee any objection from them."

"So what we're proposing is," Johnson said, and he squeezed his eyes tight in apparent concentration, "recruit old armada veterans, sneak into the Veteran shipyards, disperse a skeleton crew to all but the rear vessels, which we will arm with large pulse emitters and a full gun crew, charge out of the docks and race across the channel into Armstad airspace pulsing any gunship that ventures too close. Once in Armstad their border control will confiscate the ships and hold them until the paperwork can be finalized, which might take upwards of..."

"I should say three seasons," Mercy said, filling in when Johnson paused. "Maybe even a cycle."

Johnson turned to Walker with a questioning look.

Walker huffed. "I think you might need to start distributing your antipsychotics to the underground," he said. "You've all gone insane. That's the riskiest plan I've ever heard."

"Desperate times, representative," Johnson said as he nodded. "Desperate times."

Everyone looked around at everybody else, but no one had anything further to add.

"Start preparing for the operation," Johnson said to Francisco. "We have some time to reconsider, but if we're going to pull this off, we'll need to start mobilizing immediately."

Francisco nodded.

"As for Blythe," Johnson continued, "We will need to wait until he makes his next mistake. Keep an eye on him, David and Mercy. If he slips up, it will be you two who'll catch him in the act."

David felt the weight of those words, and as everyone stood to go their separate ways and see to their duties, he lingered. Mercy turned at the arch, apparently noticing that he hadn't come with her, but David waved her on and smiled in a reassuring manner. Johnson and Walker had stayed as well, both looking out the large glass windows at the expanse of the Sixth District as the thrum of its air traffic buzzed around the pillar.

"Sir," David said, "Might I have a word?"

The two men turned around, and David gave a tight smile to Mr. Johnson. Walker, seemingly recognizing the need for privacy, excused himself. Once he had gone, Johnson looked at David in an encouraging manner.

"I was wondering," said David, but then he paused, unsure how to ask what he wanted. "I was wondering what it was that estranged you and my father. I asked my mother, but she told me that it would be better if you explained it."

Johnson bit his lip and looked at the floor with a nod.

"I suppose I knew this question was coming eventually," he said. "Your father and I were very close during our earlier cycles, very, very close, the best of friends, really."

"But he never mentioned you," David said, "Neither did my mother."

"Yes, that would follow," Johnson said. He took a deep breath before turning back toward the window and looking out at the busy city. "I met your mother before your father did. I met her, and I fell very much in love. She did not feel the same, and after some time of fruitless pursuing, she dismissed my affections without even giving me her name. I am a don and not accustomed to people telling me I can't have something. I redoubled my efforts, and after some digging discovered her name and address. However, as fate would have it, I asked your father to deliver the letter. I'm not sure what my reasons were. Perhaps I thought she would be impressed that an armada captain was transporting my love messages. In any case, he agreed to deliver my note, but that same day he and your mother fell in love. I think you know that story better than I. Your father stumbled upon your mother without knowing who she was or that she was the same woman I had affections for. It really isn't surprising, when you think of it. Your mother was incomparable in beauty and charm."

David nodded. "She wouldn't tell my father her name until he won her heart."

"Yes," Johnson said, "She told me the same when she met me, but I never won her heart. I accused your father of betrayal, and as your parent's relationship progressed, your father's and my relationship deteriorated."

"Did he ever deliver your letter?" David asked.

Johnson nodded. "Yes. By his own admission, he struggled with the undertaking once he knew your mother was the same woman for which I had affections. But in the end, he delivered my letter, and your mother chose him over me. I was hopelessly envious of his victory, and I blamed his interference for my shortcomings. Your father was a better man than I, plain and simple. It's taken me cycles to figure that out, but your mother knew it the minute she met him."

"I see," David said, finally understanding the mystery surrounding Don Johnson.

"The ill will I bore toward your father and Mother all these cycles was jealously placed on two very good and very kind people. I intend to make it up to them by assisting you in their absence. If there is anything you should need, anything at all, you have but to ask."

David looked away to wipe an unbidden tear. "Thank you, sir," David said. "You have already done so much for me. You really have no cause to do any more. I'm sure all is forgiven."

Johnson laid an arm across David's shoulders and sighed as the two of them looked out across the expanse in front of them.

"It really is an amazing city," Johnson said after a moment.

David looked out the window and nodded, thankful for the subject change. "It's not anything near what I expected," he said. "I expected vast slums separated from pockets of ostentatious wealth."

"There are slums here," Johnson pointed to the far-right corner of the cityscape. "They're just in smaller proportions here than anywhere else in Alönia. There is no such thing as utopia, not in this life anyway. There will always be rich, and there will always be poor. The only thing that will change is the proportions. The Sixth District recognizes that and makes a grand effort to incentivize and reward anyone striving to better themselves. Walker has a saying. *Everyone who wants to be rich in the sixth, is. The only people who are poor are those who want to be.*"

"But, wouldn't everyone want to be rich?" David asked.

Johnson laughed. "Laziness isn't a disease, it's a mindset," he said. "You choose when to sleep and when to strive. You choose when to sacrifice and when to indulge. Look at your own situation. In the end, who was it that helped you more than anyone else?"

"You did," David said.

"Wrong," Johnson said with a grin. "You helped yourself more than anyone else did. Was I there when you decided to spend every waking minute studying for your PLAEE? Was I there when you worked yourself to the bone to provide for your mother? If you hadn't put forth that effort, would either of you have survived for five cycles? Tell me, you lived in the district with more social assistance programs than any two other districts. Did they assist you?"

"No, they never had enough funds," David said.

"And why is that?" Johnson asked, but David only shook his head.

"Because," Johnson continued, "by the time the tax money reaches the hands of the needy, it's reduced by 85%. They have to pay to have the taxes collected, pay to have them accounted, pay to have them divided, pay to have everybody's needs assessed and categorized, pay to decide who should receive assistance and who is well off, and finally, pay to distribute. By the time everyone has withdrawn their hand from the pot, and I think you know firsthand how many withdraw more than they should, there's hardly 15% left for those for whom the funds were intended. You could rely on 15% of the population's generosity with better results if you just left the money in the hands of those who actually worked for it. Had you applied your same work ethic in the Sixth District, instead of the third, you would have had a much easier life. There are no social assistance programs here at the sixth, and yet, there are fewer poor than anywhere else. There are jobs in abundance, and many companies have employee assistance programs you might have used to help your mother. Do you see what I'm saying?" Johnson asked.

David nodded. "People here are free to live how they like, and the result is a happy, prosperous community. But how is it so clean?" he asked. "I don't think I've ever seen a cleaner city."

"The citizens of the sixth are proud of their city,"

Johnson said. "Each citizen had a hand in building it. That means they have a vested interest in keeping it valuable."

"And Blythe wants to destroy it," David said. "He doesn't care about the prosperity or the people who live here, he just wants the power. He is happy to feed his constituents a failed system as long as it keeps them dependent on him and tied to his district."

"Yes, though, not all Equalists are like him," Johnson said. "There are some who are as you were, sincere in their beliefs and honestly seeking to help people. Some of them spend their whole lives striving to help Alönia's poor with a flawed system." He sighed and leaned against the window.

"We are at the close of a very dangerous game, you and I," Johnson said after a moment. "The Fertile Plains are collapsing around us, yet we are still betting against the odds."

"I'll do, I'll unseat him," David said after a moment. Then he looked at Johnson. "I will unset Blythe."

Johnson looked at him with his stern, unwavering gaze. "I have no doubts you will. You're an Ike, and if there is one thing at which Ikes excel, it's achieving their goals even when the odds are stacked against them."

David smiled and looked over the city, thriving and blissfully ignorant of the impending siege from its neighbors. After a long moment, the two of them departed, not speaking as they left, but nodding in the fashion that men often do, a nod of respect and admiration. Seeing the sixth gave David even deeper conviction than he had before. It gave him a people to fight for, and a people who would appreciate his fighting.

Chapter Seventeen
THE OLD CITY

"If you don't learn to move your feet, you're going to wind up on your ass every time!" Francisco said as David looked up from the ground.

David groaned and rolled to his feet. His sneak training had intensified on every level. If he was going to participate in an airship heist, he needed to be capable, and Francisco had raised the "capable" bar significantly since the last mission in Thornton. They went running every morning, and not just ordinary running; they ran along rain gutters of the Sixth District's highest orbital level. The Úoi Season rain made the gutter's slick and left a good three inches of water in the bottom of the gutter. Every time David fell, he enjoyed a wet landing before he slid a few fathoms. It didn't take him long to step lightly and run with a bend to his knees. Francisco called it balance training, but it felt more like drowning.

This morning's drench was only the beginning of Francisco's hellish training. Next they spent an hour with weights where David wasn't allowed to use his mechanical arm. Francisco seemed determined that the right side of his body be as strong as his ebony left, something everybody else knew to be impossible. Then he spent some time in the range, balancing on a bar and firing his father's revolver at a moving target. Francisco had suggested he start with a smaller caliber weapon, but David wouldn't dream of using any other weapon. After the range, when he felt exhausted enough to climb back into bed and call it a day, they stepped out onto a sparring mat so Francisco could knock him down and practice a few vulgar insults.

"It's not that I don't want to move my feet," David said once he'd found his footing, "It's that they won't move." He leaned over to rest his hands on his knees and pant. Then he felt a foot kick his shoulder, and the world spun as he landed on his back, again.

He looked up and saw Havoc lounging on top of a mat beside the sparring ring, his tail flicking in wide arcs. He cocked his head and gave David a curious look.

"I can see why nobody's ever bothered domesticating glide panthers," David said as he lay on the ground. "I could be in dire need, and you'd just sit there licking your paws." As if on command, Havoc raised one of his growing paws and rubbed it against the side of his head. True to Francisco's claim, the animal had hardly left his side since he'd returned from the Third District, following him around the facility, even braving the rain to track him as he ran the gutter circuit, and, in just a few short weeks, it had grown considerably. However, Havoc never seemed to care when Francisco beat the stuffing out of David on their sparring sessions. Bonding evidently did not encompass guarding.

David looked up at Francisco with an annoyed look.

Francisco didn't say anything, as was his style, but his expression spoke volumes. *Get up, you lazy cur; the enemy will be twice as tough on you.*

David climbed to his feet again, this time fixing his eyes on Francisco the entire time. He took up a stable stance and lifted his hands in front of his face. Letting out a slow breath, he focused on Francisco's movements. He'd learned much since they'd started their training. He now knew what the Sneak was going to do before he did it; he just wasn't able to stop it from happening. Francisco's movements were quick and flawless. He always played to David's weak side and avoided his ebony arm like a red-hot poker.

David knew how dangerous his arm was even in practice. He'd crushed several pistol grips at the shooting range and several more skiff controls. Every time he saw the arm's strength, he wondered if someday it might hurt someone he loved. He'd had nightmares about it. He was holding hands with Mercy when something startled him, and he broke her dainty fingers. After that, he'd refused to touch her with anything other than his actual fingers.

David turned as Francisco stepped toward his right side, forcing the man to confront his mechanical arm. Francisco jabbed twice at David's face, forcing David to block, and while his own hands momentarily obstructed his vision, Francisco dropped to a crouch and kicked at

David's legs. David knew the move was coming, as he always did. This time, he decided that if he had to fall, he was going to fall forward on top of Francisco rather than on his back. He lunged forward as Francisco's kick swept his feet out from under him. Surprisingly, his gambit worked. As he fell on top of Francisco, he grabbed the man's shirt with his right hand and shoved him on his back. At the same time, David closed his ebony fist and slammed it into the mat an inch away from Francisco's head. The impact punctured the leather and squished out stuffing. Everyone else in the gymnasium stopped and turned when they heard the thud. Francisco's breath hissed out as the full weight of David's body pressed against him. His bionic eye swiveled to the side and observed David's ebony hand where it was buried in stuffing, and then he smiled.

He spoke to David in a very low voice. "When you're fighting a real enemy, don't hesitate to crush skulls and spill blood. Don't hold back your fury, only your temper. Throw yourself into the fight with equal parts thinking and feeling, anticipating your enemies' actions and reacting with natural, fluid movements."

David nodded, then he heard a giggle and saw Mercy standing at the edge of the mat with a newspaper in one hand and the other over her mouth.

"Well, this is awkward," she said.

David threw himself off of Francisco, the sweetness of his victory soured by the realization of their proximity and Mercy's presence.

"And all this time I thought you were sparring in

here," Mercy said.

David grinned and blushed. He stood to his feet and wiped the sweat from his brow. He became acutely aware that he'd left his shirt at the side of the mat, but Mercy only smiled at his blushing.

"Don't suppose you'd like to have a go at sparring?" David asked and gave her a half smile.

"Oh?" Mercy said. Then to David's shock she dropped the newspaper beside the mat and slipped off her heals. She lifted her white skirts with red trimming and stepped onto the mat with her small bare feet. She walked toward David with slow steps, never taking her eyes off him. She didn't stop until she was only a few inches from his face, a nearness that quickened his heart and shortened his breathing. He could smell the floral scent of her perfume and feel the warmth of her breath on his skin. He could see the depth of her sparkling green eyes and the wave of her red hair as it flowed over one shoulder. She clasped her hands behind her back and rose up on her tiptoes so that her eyes met his.

"I don't need to use my muscles to subdue and overpower my opponents," she said in a whisper, a whisper that made the meaning of the words all the truer.

David knew he'd already lost, and he knew Mercy understood the same, but he maintained some semblance of control and said, "Prove it, pretty girl."

Mercy smiled one of her dazzling smiles, and David felt his knees wobble.

"Maybe next time," she said. Then she turned and sashayed off the mat employing just a little more feminine movement than was entirely necessary. There was no doubt about it, David found her to be the most attractive woman in all the Fertile Plains.

"I think I like sparring with her better than you," David said to Francisco, as he watched Mercy retreat.

Francisco grunted.

"When you're done playing," she said as she bent to retrieve her newspaper and slip on her heels, "come have tea with me in the dining room, and I'll show you what I discovered. Oh, and do take a bath. You smell of sweat."

"What did you discover?" David asked before she walked out of the gymnasium.

She turned and smiled at him. "Didn't I say? I found Inspector Winston."

David had never washed and changed so quickly in all his life. He'd chased after Mercy with a torrent of questions after she'd exited the gymnasium, but in the end, she'd only grinned and waved as the steam lift doors closed between them, and she rocketed away. He dressed in a fresh set of clothes and ran all the way on to the dining room on tired limbs. He found her on the far side of the comfortable café-looking establishment at a romantic table for two with an excellent view of the city. She waited there in her white dress trimmed in red, sipping tea and reading the newspaper. David hurried across the room, Havoc at his heals, and sat opposite her with an anxious expression on his face.

She looked up at him and smiled. "How did the rest of the sparring go?"

"Huh?" David asked, somewhat taken aback. "Oh, we

didn't spar anymore after you left. My final match with you left me weak at the knees."

She laughed and patted Havoc's head.

"Come on now, don't keep me in suspense," David said. "What did you discover about Winston?"

Mercy held up the newspaper. "Haven't you learned to read the morning newspaper yet?" She asked with a disappointed look. "Until you do you will be the last to discover anything at all."

"Oh," David said. "Well, I've been somewhat busy as of late. Training with Francisco, hiding as a fugitive, planning an airship heist." He counted off on his fingers as he spoke. "Did I mention training with Francisco?"

Mercy rolled her eyes, unfolded her newspaper and plopped it down in front of David. He perused it and saw an article Mercy had circled in the job opening's section.

Help wanted from former legendary aide in restoring IKW from the old city tubes. Sanctuary faith required. Working hours: 7:00-8:00 daily. See site for details.

David read through the peculiar solicitation several times before looking up at Mercy.

"Don't you see?" She said. "The *former legendary aide* is you, and IKW could only be Inspector Kenneth Winston."

"Yes, I gathered that, mostly, but what the devil are the old city tubes? And what site am I to see? It's all so cryptic. We could research for cycles and never find the meaning in the message. And, how do we even know IKW is referring to Inspector Winston?"

Mercy rolled her eyes. "Because it's in the same line as

you. Former Legendary Aide? Honestly David, the chances that this message refers to anyone other than you and Inspector Winston are very remote. As for the *see site for details* part, well that must be talking about the job location."

David opened his mouth to inform her that the solicitation did not give the job location when he put it together. "Oh! If the job solicitation is *restoring IKW from the old city tubes*, then the site location must be the old city tubes."

Mercy nodded.

"But," David said as he scratched his head. "I have no idea what the *old city tubes* are."

"It must allude to something he said to you," Mercy said. She took another drink of her tea. "Some sort of conversation in passing."

"We never talked about old city tubes," David said. "...but we did talk about some of the older buildings in Capital City. Did you know that the police station is one of the oldest—" David gasped and raised his hands up to his head. The motion sent the newspaper flopping onto the floor. Havoc jumped from where he lay and tried to crawl under Mercy's chair, a spot in which he no longer fit.

"The lava tubes!" David said. "When we were walking through the lower levels of the police station, he told me about how Capital Island was once a volcano and that, supposedly, lava tubes connected all the old structures." Then David checked his enthusiasm when he remembered what else Winston had said. "But he also told me no one had ever found them."

"Well, obviously somebody did," Mercy said, and she grabbed the newspaper from the floor and replaced it on the table. "How else could Inspector Winston be alive down there?"

"You think he's down there right now?" David asked.

"Well, how many people were a party to your conversation about the lava tubes?"

"Just the two of us," David said with a nod.

Mercy shrugged. "That probably means it's him. He must have gone into hiding when Blythe took the speakership."

"Even if somebody found the lava tubes," David said, "I still don't know where they are. How am I supposed to find them?"

"That could be more difficult," Mercy said, "but he did give us a lead."

"A lead?" David asked.

"The old city?" Mercy gave him a weren't-you-listening look. "I don't think that's just referring to the older city buildings. The old city is a particular sector of Capital Island. Some of it is newer, but most is original construction from back when the Houselands were still separate houses, and Capital Island was a kingdom of its own."

"You know," David said with a grin, "sometimes I forget how much of a genius you are."

"Oh stop," Mercy said. "I already did my fair share of blushing at this morning's sparring match. We need to stay on topic. Where is the secret entrance to the ancient lava tubes? I would assume it would need to be at a very old part of the city."

"I'll bet there is more than one," David said. "Inspector Winston told me that the tubes used to connect all the old buildings in the city. Wouldn't that mean there was more than one entrance?"

"Yes," Mercy said with an impressed look. "That will certainly make things much easier."

"How big is the old city?" David asked as he leaned back and interlaced his fingers behind his head.

"A little over two square grandfathoms."

"What!" He exclaimed slack-jawed. "We'll need some help then."

Mercy nodded. "Even then, it would still take weeks."

"We don't have weeks." David sighed. He leaned against the table, then, unable to help himself, he stood and started pacing back and forth. Mercy crossed her legs and sipped her tea, she and Havoc following him with their gaze.

"We could always search the city permits?" David said after a few minutes, and then he stopped and shrugged. "The entrances have to be in ancient basements or down original drainage pipes through old foundations. If we checked the city records, we could make a map of which of the standing buildings are the oldest and search them in chronological order."

Mercy smiled behind her teacup. "It would only take a few days to search the oldest buildings, and most of them are vacant."

"*Working hours from 7:00-8:00, daily.*" David quoted as

he resumed his pacing. "What do you suppose that means?"

"Could mean that Inspector Winston will be waiting for us from seven to eight daily."

"True," David said. "Or it could mean that that the entrance is only open from seven to eight daily."

"AM or PM?"

David frowned and hunched over the newspaper solicitation. "You know, it wouldn't have killed him to be a bit more specific. We'll have to search at both times."

It took David and Mercy five minutes to convince Johnson to give them a team to search the old city. They sent a group of sneaks to collect building permits from the city records so as to prevent any suspicion from one single person collecting all the records. David took a map of the old city and started marking the oldest buildings. It was lucky that Alönia, even before the formation of the Houselands, kept very detailed property records, and the city chose to organize them by date. About two dozen buildings fit David's portfolio: pre house unification, original foundation, and located in the old city. Two days later, David, Francisco, Mercy, and Bethany sored through the air in a skiff as the sun rose in front of them on their way to Capital City.

There were six teams, each to search 4 buildings from the hours of 7:00 to 8:00 in the morning, and then again during the same hours in the evening. Hopefully, one of them could find an entrance to the old lava tubes. For the obvious reasons, David and the rest of his team each wore disguises. He and Francisco wore outlander sand masks, while Mercy and Bethany colored their hair and concealed their features with makeup and contact lenses. Both selected black hair and brown eyes for this excursion. David wondered if there was any hair color that Mercy did not look good in, because thus far, she had dazzled him in three.

He landed their skiff at an old abandoned dock nearest their team's grouping of buildings. As with many places on Capital Island, he had never been to the old city before, other than the police station. Most of it appeared dingy and broken down, especially the buildings primarily constructed of wood and plaster. The stone structures still stood, their solid surfaces untouched by time like the old Capital City police fortress. None of the old towers stood more than twenty stories tall, though most connected by grand arching walkways high enough for air traffic to fly beneath. All of the roofs were tiled with slate or clay or paneled in copper or lead. It felt romantic in a way, like the setting to an old love tale, and without even knowing it, David grasped Mercy's hand as their party of four walked the ancient cobbled streets.

"Are we really going to have to watch you two ogle each other all day?" Bethany asked. She made a gagging face and covered her mouth. "You should tell Mercy about that time you and I hid in my bed together."

David flushed and looked at Mercy with an expression of panic. Mercy's eyes widened, but the corners of her mouth twitched, and then she burst out laughing.

"Mercy!" Bethany said before she groaned. "You've ruined it. We could have played that up all day if you'd kept it together."

"I'm sorry," Mercy said. "Here, let me try again." Mercy looked away and then turned back to David with an expression of disgust. "David! How could you?" She gave him a noncommittal slap, before placing her hands on her hips with a huffed.

"No," Bethany said. "It's no good anymore. He knows you're joking."

David looked back and forth between the women unsure what to say.

"I couldn't bear to see him so upset," Mercy said with a shy smile at David. "I know he's too innocent to ever do anything naughty."

"You are both equally no fun at all," Bethany said as she looked away.

Mercy grabbed David's arm and leaned her head against his shoulder as she giggled.

"I... I slept on her balcony." David stammered awkwardly, half smiling and half serious as he spoke.

"I know David," Mercy said. "I heard about the whole thing. Bethany told me the story after you left to see your mother. She had everyone in the dining common rolling on the floor with laughter."

"Oh," David said, feeling relieved and embarrassed at the same time. "Did she tell you I threw her off my balcony in naught but a robe and her sunbathing clothes?" David spoke loud enough for Bethany to hear.

"No," Mercy said. "She must have forgot about that part."

"Ha! I wish I could!" Bethany said with a snort. "I still

have stickers in my feet from that maker forsaken swamp." She wriggled as she walked, apparently shuddering with the memory.

But before she could complain any further, Francisco spoke up. "Here we are."

All four of them stopped in front of a simple stone building with tall arched windows and a high-pitched lead roof with intricate metal spikes along the peaks. The inscription above the door read *Public Library*. The four of them made a quick circuit around the outside to see if there was any drainage pipes or exterior cellars, but in five minutes, they were back where they started at the main entrance to the library.

"This building is still in use," Francisco said, "And its operating hours are not until nine."

David checked his pocket watch and saw that it was a few minutes before seven. The light from the sun that penetrated the haze was just high enough to reach over the rooftops.

"Luckily," Francisco continued as he pulled a pick out of his pocket. "Someone lent me the key." He stepped up to the front door and unlocked it with a pick as easily as if he had used the actual key. All four of them slipped inside, and Francisco locked the door after them.

The only light on the inside shown through the widows along the outside of the building. The light stabbed across the central expanse of the library in great shafts that sparked with dust particulates. David looked through an arch and saw a great domed central room with row upon row of bookshelves. It smelled like foul breath and moldy parchment. As the four of them moved through the foyer, the floor squeaked with their passing.

"We'll take the left side," David said. "You and Bethany take the right."

Francisco grunted, and the party split apart. David and Mercy started by walking the exterior of the room, and then moving inward to the center. David felt a little disappointed at finding nothing, but the chances of finding a forgotten entrance to ancient lava tubes in the first building he searched were extremely remote.

A moment after he and Mercy returned to the foyer, Francisco and Bethany joined them.

Francisco shook his head at David's questioning look. "We found a basement, but nothing inside," he said.

The next building they searched was an old abandoned residence, and David found himself missing the scent of foul breath and moldy parchment in comparison to pigeon poop and human urine. Users had evidently frequented the old residence in their desperate states of addiction. Again, other than one sleeping homeless man, they found nothing of interest. It was the same result for the remaining two buildings. By nine 'o'clock, and after meeting with the other team leaders, they learned their morning's work was a complete bust. Nobody found so much as a sewage drain larger than 4 inches across.

"Perhaps you're right, and the entrance will only open at 7:00 to 8:00 PM," Mercy said with a hopeful tone.

David smiled, but as he sat in the old café poring over their map as he had been all afternoon, he knew that was incorrect.

"Even if that were true," He said, "They would have at least found some sort of evidence of an entrance." He ran his fingers through his hair and sighed. He'd removed his mask sometime earlier, choosing instead to conceal himself in the corner. "No, I'm becoming increasingly concerned that we are either looking in the wrong place or chasing after ghost stories."

"Perhaps there is something we are missing in the message," Mercy said. "Help wanted from former legendary aide in restoring IKW from the old city tubes. Sanctuary faith required. Working hours: 7:00 to 8:00 daily. See site for details," she recited.

"It's that part at the end that bothers me," David said. "7:00 to 8:00 daily. It means something more than just a time, but what?"

Mercy shook her head.

As the 7:00 pm approached and the clouds above faded with the setting sun, David and Mercy met up with Francisco and Bethany to search the buildings again for good measure, despite none of them even hoping to find something. As they approached their first building, the one they'd searched last in the morning shift, David heard the toll of bells from a nearby sanctuary. He never used to notice them before he'd spoken with his mother. Now, they were an ever-constant reminder of his duty and the hope that awaited him.

This time, the sound gave him another thought. He paused as his party walked up the stairs, cocking his head to listen to the bells. Then he pulled out his map of the old city and looked searched its contents.

"What is it, David?" Mercy asked.

"Um, a thought. Could be nothing, but still." He ran a finger down the map, and Bethany and Francisco paused at the door.

"We need to hurry," Francisco said with an anxious look. "We'll need the full hour if we are to search all the buildings."

"You go ahead," David replied. "I want to check something else."

Bethany and Francisco disappeared through the door, and Mercy stepped up to David's side.

"The sanctuary," He said. "The old city sanctuary is really old." He tapped a finger on the map where it sat.

"Yes, but it's not on our map of oldest buildings," Mercy said.

"I know," David replied. "That's because it's *too* old. It predates building permits. And," he said with some excitement, "I've been thinking of the end of the message, the part about sanctuary faith is required. I thought before that Winston was trying to tell us to trust him, but now, I think he means the actual sanctuary."

"The sanctuary is on the other side of the sector," Mercy said, and the bells stopped tolling as she did. "Do you think we could make it in an hour?"

"We can try," David said as he took her hand and led her down the street at a brisk trot.

They reached the other end of the city in forty-five minutes, brows slick with sweat. It was indeed a very old sanctuary. High stone walls stood with the aid of great aching buttresses blossoming from their sides. Spires and columns reached higher than most of the surrounding buildings, and a great copper dome covered the center of the great basilica. David slipped inside and was relieved to find it empty. The old city was sparsely populated, and very few of those living there attended sanctuary. They walked through the candle-lit rooms surrounding the great circular sanctuary in the middle. The marble floor felt smooth as polished glass to David's shod feet, most likely due to the millions of people who had walked it smooth over hundreds of cycles. As they finished their search of the outer rooms on one side, they entered the central sanctuary to pass to the other side of the building. It glowed with the light candles. They passed through the middle of the room, and David looked up at the dome and gasped.

He pulled Mercy's arm and pointed up. "Look at that!" he said.

Above them was a spectacular mosaic on the walls that trimmed the base of the dome. It depicted a map of the old city and the original buildings within the ancient walls. At one end sat the Capital City police station, though, at the time the mosaic was made, it was the main fortress of the old city. There were half a dozen other buildings that must have been destroyed because he didn't recognize them, all except for the sanctuary on the opposite end of the map.

"So the sanctuary has been here since the beginning of the city," Mercy said.

"Exactly!" David felt giddy with the realization. "And, those other buildings must have been the other entrances to the ancient lava tubes. Probably a secret method of travel in the event the city was taken. Look there." he pointed to the old fortress. "That's the Capital City police station. That must be how Inspector Winston knew about the tubes. Somehow he found the entrance and fled into the tubes when Blythe took office."

Mercy nodded, but then they heard a door shut, and both of them dropped to their hands and knees and crouched behind some long benches. David peered over the bench and saw a round little man clad in the traditional garb of the priests of the maker, walk all the way down the sanctuary and out a door in the back of the immense, domed room. A moment later, the sanctuary bells started ringing.

David had never been so close to the bells before, and the sound reverberated around the domed room and buzzed in his ears. That's when he had another thought.

"Mercy!" he said over the top of the buzz. "The evening and morning sanctuary is from 7:00 to 8:00 AM and PM. The bells sound it off." He grabbed her hand as her eyes lit up with comprehension. Together they raced across the sanctuary toward the door that the man had disappeared through. They stepped inside a dimly lit room echoing with the sound of the bells. A circular stairway wound up and down. David stepped to the edge and leaned out over the railing. He saw the same priest operating a system of levers on a platform above him. Above the priest shown the last light of the day through the windows of the bell tower. Chains extended all the way down the tower past where David stood and down into a circular cellar where they attached to massive square stones that rose and fell with the chime of the bells.

David led Mercy down the spiral staircase to the base of the bell tower. Darkness cast so much shadow that he could barely make out Mercy's face, but he could still feel more than see the movement of the great stone counterweights around him. He reached into his coat and pulled out his electric torch. Switching it on he scanned the bell tower's inner workings. He let go of Mercy's hand and walked out into the center of the circular tower.

"David, be careful!" Mercy said over the sound of the bells. She didn't have to warn him why.

The stones rose and fell in a circle around him, and each one was large enough to squish him flat without even slowing down. There was barely enough space for his square shoulders. He turned in a circle and shone his light at each of the stones and the space behind them. All were the same, save one. He paused at that one and held his light at an angle. As the stone raised the height of five feet, it paused for the space of a second before sliding back down into its trough. In that second of time, David's light illuminated a cave with steps leading down into darkness. He turned to Mercy and smiled.

Chapter Eighteen
THE FORGOTTEN

David waved his arm at Mercy and called out, "Come on! Before the bells stop ringing!" He could just make out Mercy's troubled face in the dim light. He shined his torch at the narrow path leading to the center of the massive counterweights, where they stood, so she could step with assurance. Mercy reached down and grabbed her skirts. She bundled them around her knees and shuffled down the narrow passage with hindered steps. David knew her concern. If her billowing skirts got caught under one of the counterweights, it would probably pull her dress and the girl within into the heaving stones. David felt his heart pumping with anxiety, knowing that any second the bells would stop ringing, and their entrance would be sealed shut behind several feet of solid stone. As soon as Mercy reached the center space directly behind him, David turned and shone the torch at the stone with an entrance behind it. He heard Mercy gasp.

David listened to the stone rise and fall in time with the bells. He watched the tunnel behind flash in an out of view. He handed his torch to Mercy, then he bent his knees, took a couple quick gulps of air, and dove under the stone as it rose to its zenith.

He flew through the air for a split second of misery before his feet stumbled and tripped down a few of the stone steps on the other side of the counterweight. He had barely found his footing when everything went black. He put his hands against the cave walls and held his breath. Then, light flooded the tunnel again as the huge counterweight drew back up. David turned and saw Mercy on the other side, shining the torch through the opening before the stone dropped again.

When it rose again, he put out his arms in a gesture he hoped communicated his readiness to catch her. It was well he did, for as soon as the stone reached its zenith, the light from the torch shook, and a bundle of fabric flew through the space. David felt the weight of Mercy's body thump into his chest and her arms wrap around his neck. He cradled her in his arms and found the burden scarcely twenty pounds more than Bethany, despite Mercy's taller stature. Three clangs of the bells later, the stones stopped moving, and the passage sealed shut.

"David, you can put me down now," Mercy said in a whisper from beside his ear.

"Do I have to?"

"Yes."

David sighed dramatically as he lowered Mercy to the ground.

"Probably for the best," He said once her feet rested on solid stone. "My back was about to give out."

Mercy gasped. "Rude!" She said and slapped his arm. David chuckled as he took the torch from her and pointed it down the stairway, which wound around in a circular descent.

He started down the stairway and heard Mercy following close behind. He did his best to split the light of the torch between the two of them so that both could see where they trod. After about twenty to thirty steps, the stairs came to an end beside a long narrow tunnel about ten feet high. Its sides glimmered in odd ways as they caught the light from the torch and threw it back. David illuminated one wall with his torch. It looked gilded as though someone had plated it with polished silver, though it shown in different colors along different levels of the wall. He lengthened the light down the side of the passage and saw that the metallic surface continued as far as he could see. He ran his hand along the wall. But for a few bubbles here and there that pocked its surface, the wall felt smooth as glass. He took a step and almost tripped on the uneven floor. Shining his light down, he saw why. The floor rippled, though, not in a jagged way. It looked like the surface of a pond frozen in time after someone tossed a rock into its center. He tapped a foot down and felt solid rock, his leg jarring with every impact. He looked up at Mercy with a puzzled face. She stood a few feet away, her outline clear in the darkness.

"Welcome to the lava tubes, David," she said.

He looked back at the floor, and realized he stood on

molten lava froze solid with the passage of time and the cooling of temperatures. He looked back at the wall.

"Did lava do all of this?" He asked.

"It's really not my area," Mercy said, "But I imagine that if molten lava formed this tube when it was forced between the rock strata by the eruption of the volcano, it had enough heat to melt the metal ore right out of the rock."

"Gilding the surface," David said with a nod. "It's beautiful in a... terrifying sort of way."

"Which way do we go?" Mercy asked, looking up and down the tunnel. "We can't get out the way we came, at least not until the morning sanctuary meeting."

"Bethany and Francisco will be wondering where we are right about now," David said. "What direction would you reckon that is?" He pointed his torch down the tube to the right of the stairway they'd descended.

Mercy looked up. "Um," She put her hands out and turned several times, apparently working her way backward till the last time she'd seen the sun. "I can't be sure, but either west or south.

David nodded. "That's what I thought as well," he said. "Toward the police station. I say we go that way. If Inspector Winston is down here, we might find him that way. In any event, we can always come back here in a few hours and wait for the entrance to open again."

Mercy agreed, and they struck out along the tube in the direction they guessed led toward the police station, though after the tunnel curved and turned, and after so long in the darkness, they couldn't be sure which way they traveled. Mercy clung to David's arm with a vise-like grip. Several times her heals caught along the uneven floor, and she used his support to keep from falling. Twice David bumped his head on the tunnel ceiling when he failed to notice the height of the tunnel drop away. He found it difficult to look both up and down at the same time when there was only light enough to illuminate the ground. After thirty minutes of careful walking, they heard the trickle of water from up ahead. A few minutes later, they came upon a stream flowing down one wall and burbling across their path before disappearing beneath a crack in the rippling basalt floor. The flowing water drew wildlife. Fat mole crickets with oversized eyes and clear carapace bodies that revealed internal organs hopped along the narrow stream and nibbled on mold, moss, and lichen.

Mercy stepped around the crickets, apparently trying not to squish them. David looked up as he stepped over the stream—something he learned to do after the second time he bumped his head—and saw grass blowing in the breeze along the roof of the tunnel. It struck David as strange to see grass growing on the ceiling and swaying in a breeze he couldn't feel. He pointed the torch up and realized he was mistaken. It was not grass.

Hundreds—perhaps thousands—of harvestmen clung to the ceiling like a thick carpet, their long spindly legs looking like shoots of grass.

"Oh," He said. "That's why it was moving."

Mercy looked up and squeaked. She dug her fingernails into his arm. The harvestmen and mole crickets disappeared as they walked further and further away from the stream, though that did not stop Mercy from looking up every few seconds. After another fifty strides or so, the tunnel forked. David pointed his torch down each fork, but both extended further than the light illuminated. After some little consideration, David chose the left tunnel, as the right had a fine layer of mold along the path that appeared untouched by footprints. If anyone had been down that tunnel within the past few weeks, there would have been evidence. David's confidence grew as they continued down the left path when he saw a clear footpath along the center of basalt. Fallen rocks lay to one side or the other, and David even found the butt of a cigar. At one point Mercy thought she might have heard something, but after a few minutes of listening and hearing nothing, they continued. Ten strides later, a blinding light flooded the tunnel. David shielded his eyes from the display. He heard boots scuffing rock in front and behind him.

"Who are you?" a voice called from the direction of the blinding light. It sounded calm and collected.

"At the moment," David said, "We're lost. Who are you?"

The voice chuckled. "You're here because you're lost. We're here because we don't want to be found. What an interesting paradox."

"What're your names?" another voice said, this one rough and suspicious.

"David Ike, at your service," David said. He wanted to reach into his coat to unholster the gas pistol Francisco taught him to conceal, but as one hand shielded the light from his eyes and the other held a flashlight, he doubted he could retrieve his revolver without arousing suspicion. In any event, he knew he couldn't aim with the light in his eyes.

"Of course you are," the suspicious man said. "And who's she supposed to be, the Mrs.?"

"Take them," the calm voice said.

David felt rough hands grab his shoulders and tie his arms behind his back. They took his father's pistol, but not without a few remarks about its quality. The man that searched Mercy for weapons visibly blushed as he rifled through the folds of her skirt. Then, their capturers guided them down the tunnel, past a row of lights that had previously blinded David and Mercy. Once past, David perceived about a dozen men, all of them armed. The group huddled around him and escorted him and Mercy a few hundred strides further along the tunnel. As they walked, David watched a faint light grow from a dull glow to as bright as day. The men shoved him through a crevice in the rock into a massive cave a dozen fathoms across and as many high. At least a hundred men filled the cave floor, and a hundred more peered down from chambers and overhangs along the cave walls. Their captors frog-marched them to the middle of the cave where three men stood around a flat stone that acted as a table, clearly the leaders. The three men turned and faced David. All three appeared somewhere in their forties, and each bore the bearing of an armada man.

"What's this about then, Charlie?" the leader in the

middle asked. "Find this couple making love in the caves?"

The men laughed.

"Not exactly," Charlie said.

His voice matched the confident man who'd first called out to them in the tunnel. In the light, David saw the fellow for what he really was: a dirty man of 25 with several weeks of unshaved face and a crop of greasy brown hair. Every man in the room looked the same, though each of different ages and bearings. Only the three leaders bore trim faces and combed hair.

"We caught them exploring the sanctuary passage," Charlie said. "The lad says his name is David Ike."

The leader on the right laughed. "Don't they all?" He said as he stepped closer to David and examined his face.

"And how about the lady?" The center leader said. "What's she got to say for herself?"

"I'm called Mercy," she said.

"A pretty name for a pretty girl," the center man said. "We've never had a pretty girl in the caves before. Should we invite her to stay lads?" He asked with his hands outstretched.

The men roared with a mixture of whistles and jeers.

"She can room with me," a man called from above. "I don't mind."

Mercy stood tall under the barrage of catcalls and hazing, but David had seen enough. He twisted his ebony wrist and snapped his bindings like a piece of straw. In the next moment, he reached out and grabbed the closest leader by the throat and lifted him several inches off the ground. The man grabbed David's wrist and gasped for air, but David maintained his grip. All the men around him drew weapons and lunged for him.

"Move and he dies!" He said. Then he pulled down his sleeve and revealed his mechanical arm. Several of the closer men gasped as they threw up signals for the crowd to halt.

"That's an ebony arm," the leader in the center said.

"It is," David said.

One of the men nearest him shuffled back a few steps.

"Now, let the girl go," David said in a slow firm voice, "and I'll let your leader live."

"David! Stop!" A man said from the outskirts of the cave. He had just entered through another passage with a score of men. The sound of his voice gave David pause.

"David, put the man down. He's not your enemy!" The man said again, as he fought through the crowd. He pushed to the front, and David gasped.

"Inspector Winston?!" David asked. The man looked haggard, but his face and eyes were still the same.

"Yes, David," Winston said. "Now trust me. Put that captain down. He's not your enemy."

David hesitated a moment, but then set the leader's feet on the ground and released his throat. The leader shuffled back a few steps, choking and rubbing his sore skin. Some of the men surrounding David drew weapons again and moved to take him, but the center leader held up a hand.

"Wait," he said, holding up his hand. "Winston, you know this man?"

"He's the one I told you about," Winston said. "He's the one who can take down Blythe."

The room echoed with murmurs as the men talked amongst themselves.

"You got my message then?" Winston said. "The one in the paper?"

"Yes, well, Mercy found it, actually," David said. "You remember Mercy, Don't you?"

"Mercy? Aren't you dead?" Inspector Winston asked.

"I faked my death to escape Blythe," Mercy said.

"Wish I'd thought of that," a man said from the crowd around them.

"That will do lads," the leader in the center said. "Go about your business while we talk with Mr. Ike and Ms. Mercy."

The men dispersed into packs of ten or twenty around the cave's circumference, but anyone that watched could tell they were still listening.

"Charlie," The leader David had held hostage said as he continued to massage his throat. "Go back to your post, and later on you and I are going to have a chat about properly securing prisoners, one you're not going to enjoy."

Charlie nodded and took his men back out of the cave.

"I put that note in the newspaper through one of my contacts with the Voxel," Winston said. "I thought you might find it because I remembered how you found Ms. Samille's death notice."

David nodded. "We found it, but we had a hard time parsing it out," He said. "Most of our team is still up searching the old city, and by now they've probably noticed our absence."

"Sorry for the puzzle pieces," Winston said. "Most of us down here are wanted men. We can't afford to advertise in an obvious way."

"I suspected there might be a dozen or so of you down here," David said, "but who are all these people"

Winston pointed to the three leaders around the table. "These are the ring leaders of our merry band. This is Admiral York." The man in the middle nodded in acknowledgement. "This is Captain Pellión." Winston pointed to the man on the left who thus far had said nothing. "And the man you tried to strangle, that's Captain Hobs."

Hobs gave David a tight smile.

"I know your names," David said. "Each of you. You're all well known for your strategic brilliance and military prowess."

The men looked away with bitter expressions.

"Quite," Winston said. "That's what they used to be," Winston continued, "but when Blythe took power, he cooked up false charges of sedition, murder, or embezzlement to send them to prison."

"Why?" David asked.

"To shut us up," York said. "We were the last of the armada officers warning of an impending attack from Berg and Viörn. Our superiors wouldn't listen to us, and when Blythe replaced Walker, we lost our last ally."

"And you came here?" David asked. "Why?"

"It was the inspectors who came here," York said.

"We didn't know about this place till we each received secret messages or visits from one of the inspectors."

David turned to Winston. "So you knew about the lava tubes all along, even back when you led me through the police station?"

Winston nodded. "A few of us did," he said. "All of us close friends of similar mindsets."

"But what drove you down here?" David asked.

"The purge," Winston said. "After I heard Blythe took power, and after you discovered it was he who committed all the murders, I knew my days at the station were numbered. That night, the night after the census, I collected some supplies and disappeared into the tubes. It was well I did, for less than a week later, some guardsman came to the station and started asking around for me. I even spotted some spying on my flat. I knew I made the right choice when Blythe removed the Capital City police commissioner based on the most ridiculous accusation. There're a dozen inspectors here who fled into the tubes not long after receiving threats or refusing bribes, or perhaps they had the simple misfortune of knowing me." Winston shook his head. "You see, I knew Blythe's dirty secrets because I worked his case. He's gone to great lengths to bury me, and anyone I might have talked too. Some of my friends are dead," Winston said as he bared his teeth. "Money is passing under police station tables like you would not believe. Blythe's already replaced a good portion of the officers and chiefs, the rest he's bought outright through his new commissioner. So we hid. I'm not proud of it, but we had little choice. We invited others to join us who we knew were under similar persecution." Winston gestured to the armada men.

"What about everybody else?" David asked. "There must be several hundred men in here."

"Just over a thousand, actually," York said. "They are all sorts. Many of them are men who served under us in the armada. Many are veteran soldiers cast aside for serving disgraced commanders imprisoned on false charges. A few are doctors and pharmacists who spoke out against Blythe's miracle drugs. All have the same enemy and the same oppressor. We call ourselves *The Forgotten*. We were Alönia's finest, yet we were cast aside. Each of us was top of our respective professions, but all our hard work and profits were assigned to others when we dared to contradict the speaker. We built Alönia, but Alönia forgot our labors."

A murmur rose throughout the cave as men agreed with York.

"I wondered what had happened to you that night, the night of census when you ran out of the station to try and stop it. For seasons I presumed you were dead too, but then I saw your name in the paper," Winston said. "I saw that Blythe accused you of the murders he committed, but I had no way of finding you after you left Thornton. That's why I placed the advertisement in the paper."

David nodded as everything fell into place, and he understood the situation. "We were discovered during Thornton retreat," he said. "We barely escaped with our lives."

"I gathered as much, but I knew that you were the

only one who could remove Blythe from office," Winston said. "That's why I risked the advertisement to find you."

"Me?" David said. "But that's why I was trying to find you! I've had the entire Underground looking for you for whole seasons."

"Who's the Underground?" York asked.

"Well, we're rather like yourselves," Mercy said. "Except better funded and with infinitely better living conditions." She glanced around the cave and wrinkled her nose.

"More than a decade ago, the founder of the underground foresaw the approaching storm and the failure of Alönian politics," David said. "He started a secret organization to counteract the inevitable." David proceeded to sum up the basics of the underground without betraying any sensitive information. "I told them you were the linchpin to accusing Blythe." He added to Winston once he'd finished explaining.

Winston laughed. "And how would I do that? I can't even show my face above ground without somebody trying to shoot it off. You're the genius."

David massaged his temples. All the day's excitement and success leached away with the inspector's words.

"Well, I had a plan," David said. "But it dried up in Thornton when they discovered me."

He sighed. He didn't know exactly what he expected Inspector Winston to do once they found him; He just thought a Capital City inspector would know how to charge a man with murder. At the very least he hoped Winston would share with him the burden of unseating

Blythe, but it seemed that the inspector, like everyone else, hailed him as a miracle worker. He felt like a magician pulling rabbits out of a hat.

It made David wonder if this was what his grandfather felt like the day of the Protectorate War? Was this the burden of command everyone spoke of? Why did it keep falling to him? Blythe had played his hand well. The only people who knew of his villainy and cared to do anything about it were either powerless or pushing up daisies, and everyone had turned to a lad barely 20 cycles old simply because he shared blood with the houselands greatest hero. But, after all, he was an Ike, and he had one idea left, one rabbit still in his hat.

"We do have one other option, a long shot. Could you get us into the Police station?" He asked Inspector Winston.

Inspector Winston paused to consider it. "I could get a few in. They patrol during the night and day now, but it's possible. Why do you ask?"

"If we could get into the station," David said in a contemplative tone, "we might be able to find Ms. Paula's evidence. That is... if Blythe hasn't already destroyed it all."

"Evidence?" Winston said.

"Yes, our last hope is to make a formal charge through the assembly," David said. "They're the only ones who have the power to convict Blythe, though, it would take some cajoling to turn the Equalist assembly against their savior, especially with such an outrageous assertion. And, in the event that Blythe is removed, the speakership would fall to his first aid until his district's next election. That means time is short."

"Who's Blythe's first aide?" York asked.

"Eric Himpton," Mercy said with a note of disgust.

"He's just as bad as Blythe except stupider," David said. "The Third District's vote is on the 39th day of this season. If we could oust Blythe before then, we would have a chance to put our own man in the speakership, especially if Eric and the Equalists didn't have time to mount a full-scale campaign."

"But that's..." Winston looked up as he seemingly did some mental math, "That's only 23 days away! Not nearly enough time to plan an accusation and convince an assembly to act on it."

"And that's only half the battle," David added.

"Half?" Winston said as some men around them started muttering.

David looked at the armada men and said, "I'm sure you heard about the airship deconstruction plan."

"Yes," York said with a snort. "It's a damn good way to enslave all of Alönia to its enemies."

"Well, the deconstruction will also commence on the 39th day of Úoi Season," said David.

York nodded. "Our ship is among them. The lads and I have been considering a way to sneak her out before they rip her apart."

"One ship isn't enough to fight a war," David said. "If Viörn and Berg attack, we would need all of them."

"Fat chance of that," Pellión said in a sad voice.

"Perhaps," David admitted, "But it must happen.

While at Thornton, the last thing we discovered before escaping into the everpines was that Blythe had a master, a Viörn Admiral. We spied on one of their meetings."

"A Viörn admiral?" York said. "You're not referring to *the* Viörn admiral, are you? The one from the Armstad intelligence reports who's supposedly running the People's Republic beneath the old emperor's nose."

"That is our presumption," David said.

York leaned against the stone table as though overcome with fatigue. "So," he said. "Blythe is not only a murderer, he's a traitor."

"Now you see why he's planning to destroy the airships?" David said. "The Viörn general is hoping to defang us before his attack, and all under the guise of peaceful unification. We must rescue all the airships else we face a war without our weapons."

Admiral York nodded.

"What would you do if you had the evidence?" Winston asked, and he nodded to several men who disappeared through a corridor.

"Well, granted it would take some doing," David said, "but if we had the evidence, we might be able to convince the assembly to vote on an inquiry and then hear our charges, and…"

The men returned and worked their way through the crowd. David trailed off as he saw them. They looked to be carrying something. As they reached the stone table, they slid several boxes across its surface. David walked slowly toward the table, not believing what he saw. He turned one of the boxes around and read the inscription.

"This is Paula's evidence!" David said with a gasped. "All of it!"

Winston smiled. "Nearly all of it," he said. "I nicked it when I went into hiding. It was my insurance policy if they ever found me. The problem is, I'm missing the most important piece. I looked everywhere, but I can't find the locket, and that's the only bit we had that tied Blythe to the case."

David looked at Winston, and a smile crept across his face. He loosened his collar and grabbed hold of a silver chain from where it hung around his neck. He pulled it free and dangled a circular broach in front of his face.

"I think I can help you with that."

Chapter Nineteen
ANOTHER KIND OF LEVERAGE

It took some doing, a lot more than David expected. After everything the individual members of both organizations had experienced, both *The Forgotten* and *The Underground* harbored a healthy distrust of strangers. But in time, and after several meetings between Johnson and Admiral York, the two groups merged, and their collective resistance was of considerable strength.

The Underground wasted no time creating a staging ground for the airship heist out of the Forgotten's cavernous bases. The old lava tubes provided an excellent means of sneaking men across Capital City to the Veteran Shipyards without detection. The Underground transported food and supplies to the Forgotten refugees. This helped the groups meld together without difficulty, and it was well they did. Time was short.

Winston revealed a latch to raise the counterweight without having to wait until prayer time as well as a concealed bay door built into a city drainage pipe. This allowed people to pass in and out of the tubes at will. As it turned out, Bethany and Francisco, along with the other teams, spent the better part of the night searching for David and Mercy after they disappeared beneath the ground. Francisco used every curse in the book when the two of them reemerged from the sanctuary and called in.

Twenty-Four hours later, David stood in the conference room back at the Sixth District pillar facing men who had more experience, knowledge, and wisdom than he. Yet, there he was preparing to present his brilliant plan, the plan to save Alönia and the Fertile Plains. He felt ridiculous. But when he looked at Mercy where she sat with perfect posture to the side of the conference room, he gained confidence, not in his abilities, rather, confidence in his resolve. He would fight with all his might in the pursuit of his duty, because it was right, and because it meant a Fertile Plains where she would be safe.

"Ladies and gentlemen," He began, "most of you know the gist of the plan I am about to lay out, as many of you had a hand in its conception. However, it was not until recent events we had the resources and personnel to implement it. That is why we are fleshing the plan out in full detail today as a real-world scenario." David paused and looked around the room, then continued.

"The time to act is upon us. We dare not wait any longer, or else we may lose the little freedom we have left. This, the Sixth District, the pillars of Alönian manufacturing, and our refuge, will crumble within the cycle by Equalist legislation and financial ruin. Our financier, Public Pharmaceuticals, will dry up at the same time when Hephnaire's unions invade, and the placebo is discovered. And most importantly, war is upon us, and we are not prepared. For these reasons, we are accelerating our strategies for an all-out assault against Blythe and his administration." As David spoke, he saw resolve in the eyes of his audience as well as unity.

"Our plan has two objectives, each of equal importance. First, we will rescue the Alönian Airships from decommission and deconstruction. No heist of this magnitude has ever been attempted. There are more than 1000 airships in Veteran Shipyards. We intend to steal the most valuable of the lot, or 572 skiff Carriers to be precise. Even with the combined forces of our new allies," David nodded to York and his captains, "we don't have enough men to man all the carriers. As it is, we will only be able to fully arm ten of the carriers and fill the rest with skeleton crews." David pressed a key on the steam projector in front of him and waited till a map portraying Capital Island, the Alönian Channel, and the Armstad Bay in the top corner appeared.

"We will begin the heist by sending in a team of sneaks and commandos led by Francisco to infiltrate the shipyards and neutralize the guards." David saw Francisco offer one of his dangerous half-smirks. "Once the coast is clear, Admiral York will take command of the airships and cover the retreat of the skeleton crews as they cruise away at full burn toward Armstad airspace. Admiral York will direct the rearguard of ten ships armed with non-lethal pulse emitters to forestall any pursuit by capital guard gunships. The rearguard will take the brunt of it in this mission as you won't be allowed deadly force but will most certainly receive it."

"We'll do our part," York said. "Besides, they're only guardsmen. How hard could it be?"

The audience of commanders chuckled. Everyone knew about the rivalry between the armada and the capital guard.

"Best we can tell," David continued, "it will take an hour to reach Armstad airspace. So that means an hour of toying with the guard before relief. Are there any questions before I continue onto the second objective of our plan?"

When nobody said anything, David cleared his throat. "Now the hard part." Everyone chuckled again. "The second objective has two prongs: we must both remove Blythe and replace him with our own man. First, we are working with all our remaining contacts in the assembly to try and force an inquiry on Blythe. In addition, we found several points of leverage against popular Equalists leaders, which should grant us the votes we need. At the risk of repeating what you already know, I would remind you that an inquiry does not prove anything against Blythe, it simply allows us to present our case before the assembly in a formal hearing.

"During the hearing, Representative Walker will present a case against Blythe using the evidence and testimony provided by Inspector Winston, Don Johnson, Mercedes Lorraine, and a few others. After our testimony and the evidence we provide, the assembly will have no choice but to remove Blythe from power. Our hope is that they will not see this as an attack against Equalists, but rather an opportunity to fill the speakership with a puppet called Eric Himpton."

"Who's that?" York asked.

"Blythe's first aide," David replied. "You see, if Blythe is removed, his position will fall to his first aide, in this case, Eric. The first aide will hold that position until the next district election. The speakership does not belong to Blythe, it belongs to the most populous district, the Third District." Does that answer your question, Admiral?"

York nodded.

"That brings us to the second prong of our second objective. The Third District election is on the 39th day of Úoi season. Therefore, if we can remove Blythe from office at the eve of his district election, we stand a good chance of filling the seat with our own man, and in turn, filling the speakership with a Pragmatic." David paused again and looked around the room.

"Who?" Walker asked, and everyone in the room nodded along with the question.

"Don Johnson," David said.

Johnson gagged on his tea, sputtered and coughed. When he finally regained control of his faculties, he looked up at David in shock. "I am not a politician," he said. "I'm a sneak and a don. I'm the furthest thing from a politician."

David frowned and said, "Name one politician who's not wealthy and sneaky, and I'll concede the point." With the exception of Johnson, everyone laughed, Walker hardest of all. "More to the point," David said, "You're also the only popular and credible name we have to work within the Third District. No one else commands even a smidgen of respect in that depressed district. And, you have a perfect cover to throw your name into the race prior to the election without arousing any suspicion or concern."

"Humor me?" Johnson said as he crossed his arms, though he did not sound in the least bit humor-able.

"Tomorrow, you need to meet with Speaker Blythe," David said. "Inform him that you are aware of his plot with Don Hephnaire and tell him from now on he can count you as his enemy. Then announce your candidacy in the Third District race. He'll think you a buffoon."

"And he'll be right," Johnson interrupted.

"You'll be a laughingstock for three weeks," David continued. "Until Blythe is removed from power on the eve of his own race. His campaign will be thrown into disarray, and his aide won't be able to pull things together in time to counteract your popularity, small as it may be."

"What popularity?" Johnson asked. "I'm a fop to all the Fertile Plains."

"What is the general opinion of your employees toward you?" David asked.

"Excellent," Johnson said. "Excellent pay creates excellent opinions."

"You are the largest employer in the third," David said, "more than that, you're the largest employer in Alönia, and all of your workers love you, despite your personified eccentricities. Your popularity might even rival Blythe himself. Just by announcing your candidacy in the race, you could easily have the support of all your employees. That is probably enough in and of itself to beat Eric."

Johnson scowled at David, apparently fully aware that David had purposefully concealed this part of the plan until the presentation. "What else did you have in mind?" Johnson asked.

"That's it," David said with a shrug. "After the assembly removes Blythe from power, you will already be a part of the election and perfectly set up to win."

"I have reservations about our second objective," Walker said from the back of the room.

"You see!" Johnson said, pointing a finger at David. "I'm not the only one."

"No," Walker said. "Not that part of the objective. I actually agree that you should run for the vacated seat." Johnson let his hand drop to the table with a look of betrayal, but Walker didn't seem to notice. "No, my reservations are about me presenting the case before the assembly. I don't think I'll carry much force anymore."

"You're the former speaker of the assembly," David said. "Surely that in itself carries force."

"Respect is no longer valued in politics," Walker said. "I don't think it ever was. Old faces and old voices disappear into the background, and mine is as old and worn out as any of them. I wouldn't be surprised if they accepted my motion just to have the pleasure of denying it at the end of the presentation. They'll hardly even hear the evidence, despite its potency. If we want to capture the assembly's attention, we need to make a splash, something new and different."

"Yes... I think I see your point, Representative Walker," Johnson said with a smile that gave David the impression he was not going to like what the don said next. "If it's a splash we want, why not use a name that's both new and respected, one that will capture interest and hold it till the end of the motion. I think Representative Walker can make the motion, but David should present the case before the assembly."

"I'm wanted for murder for the exact same cases," David said. "That's a huge conflict of interest. They will never believe me."

"How is his name both new and respected?" York asked, eyes suspicious.

"My dear Admiral York," Johnson said dramatically, "May I have the pleasure of introducing you to David Ike III, the son of David Ike II, the son of Admiral David Ike, hero and legend of Alönia."

York's mouth fell open, and he peered at David with new interest. "I saw the legend once, at a distance." He said slowly. You have his bearing. Every person in Alönia, whether Equalist or Pragmatic, would stop and listen to anyone claiming your lineage."

Walker tossed his head back and forth, apparently weighing the idea in his mind. "That would certainly steal the wind out of Blythe's sails. And, you enjoy an ironic advantage over Blythe in that he once called you his greatest supporter and the hero of the Equalist party."

"Don't remind me," David said with disgust. Then he

looked around the room at all the intent faces. "Are we honestly considering this? Do you want me to present the case?"

"I can't see a downside," Walker said. "Your presence will spark instant interest in the situation. I warrant every Alönian with a phonograph will tune in to the broadcast, and every pub will have the frequency on their loudspeaker."

"That is until Blythe cuts the feed," Johnson said. "He always does when someone starts talking sense in the assembly."

"We're in agreement then?" Walker asked with a look at Johnson and York.

Johnson nodded and gave David a smile that seemed somewhat vengeful. David felt a lump form in his throat. He looked at Mercy, but her dazzling smile only made it worse. He swallowed hard.

"All right then," he said. "Representative Walker will make the motion for an inquiry, and I'll present the case to the assembly, granted, only if I can make it past both checkpoints."

"I think we can manage that," Johnson said. "You won't get out of it that easy."

"I have a question," Captain Hobs said, speaking for the first time. "If we can assume the speakership, what need have we for the heist?"

"Blythe is intent on destroying the airships," Johnson said. "not only for himself, but also for the Viörn Admiral. If he were removed from power before that could happen, we fear he might sabotage them in his last moments of office. And, like David alluded to—surprising as it may be—the heist is the easier of the two objectives. If we fail in removing Speaker Blythe, at least we have preserved the Alönian Armada, though the Maker only knows what we'll do with it."

They fielded several more questions, simple details that needed discussing, and then they dismissed, each heading to prepare for their respective part in the grand plan.

David collected his notes and maps as the room emptied. He felt like a vast weight had been placed on his back, though he concealed it as he busied himself. A small hand rested on his shoulder, and he knew whose it was without looking.

"That didn't go as expected," he said, and she giggled. He turned and looked into her beautiful face. It made him smile.

"Well," Mercy said, rolling her eyes. "If you don't want to play a part, you have to stop doing such a fine job."

David smiled, but then he looked at her seriously. "I don't have a clue how to convince a whole assembly of representatives that their hero is a fraud and a murderer. I've never even addressed the assembly before. I don't know what I'm doing."

"Who's the most successful politician you know right now?" Mercy asked.

David thought about it for a moment. "Blythe," he said in a bitter tone.

"Exactly!" she said, "and yet, He's nothing more than a swamp monkey in a suit. Was there any formality in his grand speeches that won him his speakership?"

"I suppose not," David said.

"The only intelligence in all of Blythe's accomplishments came from an overworked, underpaid aide." Mercy poked his chest with her finger. "I've said it from the beginning, you are the only one capable of unseating Blythe."

David nodded. "Will you help me write my speech?" he asked.

"Of course," Mercy said with a smile.

"Good," David said, "because, for the life of me, I can't decide how I'm going to convince people to believe something they don't even want to hear."

"That's a lot easier than you might think," Mercy said. "You stroke their pride by flattering their intelligence, fueling their emotions, and tickling their humor. Then, you convince them that there is something better, a hope they've never seen before.

"But the assembly doesn't want hope," David said. "What they want is exactly what I want to take away. What if they reject my hope?"

"That's really not up to you," Mercy said. "If Alönia doesn't want to be saved..." She gave him a knowing look.

"Then Alönia doesn't deserve to be saved," David finished. "In my heart I know that, but it seems as though the people of Alönia would want to be saved if they knew everything that was going on. The representatives have lost touch with their constituents. They conceal as much as they represent. They don't think as I do. I've always operated under a conviction of what is right and what is wrong. They operate on greed and self-preservation."

"Well, perhaps you should present your case in a manner that forces their hand." Mercy sat on a nearby chair and bit her lip. "The thing they fear the most is losing their seat on the assembly," she said. "If you put them into a position where that is at stake, they might put aside their prejudice and see reason."

"Might..." David said with a sigh. "That's exactly what concerns me. Everything hinges on their conviction of Blythe, and I have to ask myself, what if they don't? What if they are so drunk with their lust for power that they're willing to do business with the devil? What then? We have no contingency."

The issue bothered David for three straight weeks. He and Mercy wrote and rewrote dozens of speeches. They rehearsed until David's tongue felt as though it were made of lead. On several occasions, David gathered Walker, Johnson, York, and a few others to play the assembly as he made his case before them. They commented and critiqued, though the general impression was complimentary. But something bothered David about it, an itch in the back of his mind.

He was not the only one who slaved away in the Sixth District pillar. The facility was never quiet. As engineers worked on experimental emitters, Admiral York ran simulations on steam projectors, and Francisco commenced relentless drills and conditioning, though the bionic man was not without his games.

Each night, he selected a team of sneaks and

commandos and sent them on a raid into 20 private rooms to filch a pair of underpants without awakening any of their victims or being seen by the double watch. The next morning, they hung them in the dining common. If any of the guards or sleepers caught them, the team wore the underwear on their heads the next day as they ran a double circuit along the gutters.

And, as if the intensity of David's inquiry preparation wasn't enough, the teams bore a special dislike for him, or rather his glide panther. While David's tireless efforts left him in a deep sleep every night, Havoc and his feline senses caught the thieves in the act every time and sent them running with deep panther roars. Havoc grew larger every day, and he was now nearly the size of a hound. His dark swirling fir drank up the darkness and eluded all in the night, save Francisco himself. Nothing is more disconcerting than the sound of a deep, guttural growl and not knowing from whence it comes. David wished Francisco would assign the teams to another room as he was running out of underpants, but Francisco saw Havoc as excellent training.

Even Mercy's room became an accidental target of a special training mission when one of the commandoes took a wrong turn in the darkness. The next morning David watched the red-haired beauty with a matching red face of fury march into the dining room, point her gas pistol at a commando's head, and inform him that if he did not take her garments off his head and give them back that very moment, she'd shoot him between the eyes. David couldn't help but laugh as she snatched the rosy red garments from the smiling commando and stomp from the room, pointedly looking away from David. It was one of the rare instances when she lost her proper composure. From then on, she assumed Bethany's harsh method of using a pulse emitter on any man foolish enough to set foot in her quarters.

Mercy, sweet, proper Mercy, became David's taskmaster during his diligent efforts in writing his speech. Encouraging when needed and driving him during all other moments. Her work ethic rivaled his own, and her knowledge and intuition helped him craft a grand speech. Though neither would speak it aloud, both felt that no matter how strong the evidence, and no matter how convincing and convicting the case, whether it possessed all the arts of oration or not, the assembly would never remove Blythe. He was the source of new wealth and comfort, and the provider for their lusts, whether physical or otherwise. He'd created more than a need for himself amongst them; he'd created a social addiction. David needed something more. He needed a stronger form of leverage.

Chapter Twenty
THE INQUIRY

David felt a trickle of cold sweat run down his back as he sat in Representative Walker's Windward VX2. Though he'd never been in a plusher skiff, he later recalled none of its splendor, as he had also never experienced greater apprehension. He tapped his foot on the thick white carpet and drummed his ebony fingers on the matching white leather armrest. Mercy sat beside him, her fingers interlaced with his and her head resting on his shoulder. Every few minutes he heaved a great sigh, letting his breath out slowly in hopes it would calm his raging nerves. It didn't.

The sun shone through the windows as it slid past its zenith in its prolonged dive behind the Alönian mountains. Clouds drifted by, their white fluff tinged with golden rays. But no matter how much beauty passed by the window, David's mind fixated on the same agonizing thought.

Would his speech be enough? Would it be enough to convince a fickle people?

As the sun inched lower and lower, marking the approach of their arrival and the afternoon assembly, David reminded himself over and over again that if Alönia did not want to be rescued from Blythe, then Alönia did not deserve to be rescued. He would inform them of the truth and pray they believed it, and pray he did. He pleaded with Jeshua the entire trip, not rousing until he felt the familiar bump of the skiff sliding against docking clamps.

"Ready?" Walker asked. Everyone nodded.

The skiff hatch opened, and Walker and Johnson stepped into Walker's private assembly office. Johnson wore his customary fop garb and false girth. Winston walked off next, with a box of evidence under each arm, followed by Bethany carrying a curious purse full of electronics. Lastly, David and Mercy emerged, both wearing disguises, and David carrying two additional boxes of evidence. He posed as Walker's new assistant, though anyone who knew him would see through his disguise in an instant. After considerable thought back at the sixth, David opted for a simple disguise knowing that he would have to discard it once he began the inquiry. Mercy did the same, wearing tinted contact lenses, an overcoat, and an extravagant hat to hide her distinctive hair. They gathered in the midlevel office with twenty minutes to spare before the assembly.

As it was a midlevel office, there was no window floor, something David greatly appreciated. It reminded him of

Blythe's old Third District office, except there were several round windows along the walls and no scandalous women. His secretary was an older woman, and she smiled at them as they entered. His aide, Benjamin Wilks, looked a quiet, intelligent man, though not handsome by any account. He walked with spindly legs and had an odd way of coming up on his toes with every step. He also eyed David with a sour expression.

"Welcome back, Representative," he said. "Is there anything I can get you?"

"Ha, a sedative would be nice," Walker said, "but, no. Thank you, Mr. Wilks. We need to leave for the assembly as soon as possible, as we'll be taking the back way. David, there, can't be seen."

"Yes, representative," Wilks said. "I'm sure that would be a terrible tragedy."

David thought he sounded insincere. And, Wilks did have cause to be. David stripped his mentor of power and reduced both of them to an assembly laughingstock. It never ceased to amaze David that Walker bore him no ill will, despite all the trouble David had caused.

Wilks opened the office door and looked down the outside corridor. He nodded to Walker, and the party exited. David kept his head down as they walked through the halls, the first of which was empty, as was the second, but as they neared the center of the assembly, the passages filled up, and passersby eyed him, growing numerous enough to bump shoulders. Bethany left them there, and with a nod she disappeared into the crowd to fulfill her part. For a second, it made David feel guilty sending such a dainty little thing on a mission all alone, but then he thought better of it. Bethany was not the helpless little girl she appeared. If anything went wrong, she could always harangue them with her salty personality and send them away with red faces of shame.

Walker's office was as far away from the assembly room as an office could be, another slight from Blythe after he assumed the speakership. David realized it would have been faster to take the public entrance and wait through the security line, but he didn't have a prayer of making it through the checkpoint without being discovered and escorted straight to the Capital City police station never to be seen again. The thought reminded him that if he didn't succeed in his mission, he might spend the rest of a very short life in prison.

Wilks put a hand behind his back and motioned them to stop as they approached the main foyer. David faced the wall and stacked his evidence boxes on top of each other, pretending to look through folders inside the top one. Walker stepped up to Wilks and leaned forward in a mock-serious conversation. David overheard Walker whisper to Wilks, "If Blythe approaches us, start apologizing."

A moment later, Wilks said, "I'm very sorry, Representative, it's completely my fault."

"Wilks," Walker said, putting his head in his hand. "Of all the days to forget, it had to be today. What am I going to do with you?"

"Representative," Blythe said, placing unusual emphasis on the title. "You shouldn't berate your aide.

He might be your last friend in the assembly."

"Not now, Speaker Blythe," Walker said. "I haven't the time."

Blythe smiled in his handsome way. "Temper, temper. This wouldn't be something regarding the motion you intend to make today. I saw a notice on the docket. Are you sure you don't need any help? Me and the lad could search that box much faster together."

"I'm upset for my own reasons," Walker said between gritted teeth. "It's none of your business."

Blythe laughed. "But it will be my business in a very short while," he said as he stepped closer, "When I veto it. Though I might not even have a chance to do so if nobody seconds your motion."

Blythe put his hands in his pockets and walked away with a smile on his face. David realized while he'd been listening, he squeezed the box lid so hard his fingers punched holes in the top. He replaced the lid and leaned against the box with a sigh. He looked around Wilks and Walker and saw the crowded foyer. Any one of those people might recognize him. Bending, he lifted the boxes in front of him, and the stacked boxes completely covered his face. However, the stacked boxes also prevented him from seeing where he walked. The party started out across the foyer toward the entrance to the Assembly. David tried his best to follow in the footsteps of the others, but an enthusiastic assistant cut in front of him, and he knocked her to the ground.

"How rude!" she said, and David shifted the boxes to see what had happened. The girl climbed to her feet and straightened her dress.

"Terribly sorry," David said. "I can't see very well."

"Clearly!" The girl said before she turned and marched off with a huff.

David felt slender fingers wrap around his arm and pull him forward. Mercy leaned her head against his shoulder as she guided him through the rest of the Foyer.

"What is it with you?" She asked. "You're always knocking little girls down in this Foyer."

David smiled as the memory of how he and Mercy first met warmed his nervous bones.

Finally, they entered the assembly and worked their way up the stairs along the side of the egg-shaped room to the Sixth District booth, where the other witnesses had already gathered. Only after finding a secluded bench in the back where a shadow would conceal his face did David finally put his boxes down. Mercy joined him there and gave a nervous shrug. The crowd of representatives and aids slowly meandered around the auditorium until everyone had found a seat. Blythe took his place at the central dais with Eric Himpton sitting behind him. Blythe waited till the steam projector puffed out his commanding form, then he spoke.

"Welcome, representatives, to the 8th assembly of the 3242nd cycle," Blythe said. "I see on the docket that we might be entertained by a motion from Representative Walker." The room echoed with laughter. "It's probably best to save that motion for last," Blythe said as he scratched his jaw, followed by more chuckles from the audience. "Let's start with Representative Arnold."

David sat through six agonizing motions from six Equalist representatives, all of them requesting financial assistance for various social programs. All passed. It looked dark by the time the Equalists had finished their motions, endless black filling the glass top and bottom of the assembly. However, before Walker had a chance to make his motion, Blythe looked as though he were going to end the assembly without letting him.

Walker rolled his eyes, stood, and keyed his motion.

"Oh, yes!" Blythe said. "I almost forgot. George Walker wishes to speak with us."

Walker nodded and shouldered the humiliation with good-humored dignity. He leaned forward and spoke into his microphone.

"Honored Representatives—"

"Denied," Blythe said, interrupting him.

The rest of the auditorium laughed louder than David had ever heard. The laugh broke into applause as they ratified Blythe's decision. It was some time before the people calmed down enough for Walker to begin again."

"Honored Representatives—"

"I'm joking with you, Walker," Blythe said, interrupting him again. "Go ahead, you can make your motion. I promise I will listen to the whole thing before denying it."

A few snorts this time, but Walker only smiled.

"Thank you, Mr. Speaker," Walker said. "My motion is simple. I wish to ask this assembly to launch an inquiry into Speaker Blythe."

The sound that followed was as though all the air had

been sucked out of the room. Mouths fell open followed by a few gasps, a couple of snickers, and then the general din of conversation. Blythe looked mildly amused.

"Alright, Walker," Blythe said. "Rather than listening to some drawn out and well-rehearsed accusation, let me first ask if there is anyone else willing to place their political career on the line to second this motion. If not, we might all be able to go to dinner early."

A significant pause hung in the air, one Blythe seemed more than willing to let draw out. David watched several of the few remaining pragmatics turn their heads away, unwilling to risk their careers for such a serious and probably fruitless motion. Then, someone stood, and everyone in the room gasped. Even Blythe looked taken aback.

Representative Harold, the same representative Mercy used to work for, raised his hand and said, "I second."

What followed was an interesting spectacle, a confrontation between new and old Equalists. Herald was the more senior and for many cycles, the leader of the Equalist party. Blythe was the charismatic savior, the rising star, and the face of the new Equalist party. Both had power, and the members of the assembly were hard pressed which side to choose.

David smiled as he saw events unfold as a result of careful planning. Earlier that week, Mercy paid a visit to her old boss. He had always liked her, never actually realizing that she was a spy, and seeing her alive and well brought joy to his heart. Mercy explained that she faked her death in order to avoid being Blythe's next victim. At first he disbelieved her, but the longer she explained the more he questioned Blythe's character. With her prodding, she orchestrated a meeting between Herald and the parents of Samantha Samille, which included her powerful admiral father, a constituent and contributor of Herald's campaign. Herald had no choice but to accept the meeting, not knowing that earlier that week, Johnson had also met with Samille's parents, having met her father during several political events.

Ms. Samille's parents were not difficult to convince of Blythe's villainy, as they already hated him for making their daughter into something worse than a courtesan. Believing him to be her murderer was a small step. Johnson had but to make the accusation, and they believed it wholeheartedly. With their prompting and Mercy's coaxing, Herald agreed to second the motion and hear the evidence before a formal inquiry. In truth, David wondered if a large part of Harold's acquiescence rested in the fact that he still harbored resentment that Blythe stole his speakership. That same suspicion had once prompted David to spy on Herald, and seeing Herald turn on Blythe only reinforced the thought.

"I have a constituent involved in this inquiry," Herald said almost apologetically. "And I see no harm in hearing the evidence. If it is fruitless, my constituents can at least have closure."

Blythe didn't look happy, but he nodded, none the less, to his fellow Equalist. "Let us put it to a vote then," He said. "Assembly rules require a sixty-percent majority to go forward with an inquiry."

The steam projector formed into the number 2, then clouded as more votes registered. David found himself praying again, hoping they would reach the 46-vote threshold. The number thirty-eight materialized, and his heart sank, but then the projection clouded again. Apparently, interest had gripped a few more representatives, and they decided to cast their vote out of pure curiosity. The number forty-four formed, and David held his breath. The moment stretched out, and his face turned red from oxygen debt. Blythe opened his mouth to speak, but the projection clouded one last time and resolved into the number forty-seven. Blythe rolled his eyes, and David resisted the urge to jump into the air and whoop as he did so many seasons earlier. The auditorium buzzed with excitement, both for and against the inquiry.

"All right, Walker," Blythe said. "You have your inquiry. Let's try and make it quick. I have a date waiting for me. What is this inquiry about?"

"I am merely making the motion, Mr. Speaker," Walker said. "My colleague will present the case before the assembly."

Mercy squeezed David's arm and gave him a tight smile. He stood, castoff his disguise, and walked out of the booth and down the stairs toward the central dais with a box of evidence in his arms. Gasps and whispers followed him as he descended and passed different district booths.

"Is that Blythe's old aide?" someone asked.

"What was his name?" another said, and the man beside him replied. "Same as everyone else's." A few snickered at that.

Blythe's head followed David as he walked nearer the central dais but seemed not to recognize him until he reached the glass floor at the bottom of the stairs.

"You!" Blythe said with a snarled before looking up at Walker. "You expect me to allow an inquiry by a criminal? This man is a murderer!"

"I beg to differ, Mr. Speaker," David said, and he set his evidence down beside him. "I am merely a man accused of murder by a man who committed the very murders of which I am accused."

"That is absurd!" Blythe said. "I won't stand for this—"

"Then maybe you should sit?" David said. "After all, I am the one doing the inquiring, not you."

Blythe looked at David, his red face burning with fury as a couple of people snorted. Blythe knew the assembly rules, of that much David was sure. Which meant, he knew he had no power during the inquiry and had to answer every question posed him from the inquirer. Rather than embarrass himself further, Blythe sat and collected his composure.

A wise choice, David thought.

"I wish to begin this inquiry by asking you what evidence you discovered, which compelled you to accuse me of murder in every single tabloid in Alönia?"

"I am an eyewitness," Blythe said confidently.

"So, you were there then... when I committed the murders?" David asked.

"No, I witnessed you admit to all three torturous

murders of all three innocent women," Blythe replied. A murmur of disgust rippled through the assembly, but David cut it off with another question.

"So what you're saying is that the strongest evidence you possess is your word against mine?" He asked. "You have accused me of murdering women in a torturous manner, and I am accusing you of murdering women in a torturous manner. We seem to be at an impasse. Have you any other evidence?"

"I would think the word of the Speaker would be considered stronger than the word of an outcast aide?" Blythe said, regaining his casual manner.

"I have been shot at by the capital guard and others. My face is on a security watch list with a shoot-on-sight designation. According to what you just said, you are claiming that with naught but the word of the Speaker, anyone can be accused, convicted, sentenced, and shot. If I recall my house law correctly, you need a magistrate to sentence and a trial to convict? Am I not correct?"

"You are correct," Blythe said coolly. "in most cases. However, in situations of treason and Houseland security, the speaker may issue a shoot-on-sight order."

"So I'm accused of treason now?" David said, widening his eyes. "Treason and murder, my but I have been a bad boy." That got a few chuckles and a dangerous smile from Blythe. David knew how much Blythe hated it when somebody made sport of him, and he hoped Blythe's fury would cloud his judgment.

"In any case," David said, "You're incorrect in your assumptions. Even in the event of treason, Houseland citizens are still entitled to a trial. You have grossly abused your power. As speaker you are not a monarch or a tyrant. You are the voice of your district, and you serve the people."

"Please," Blythe said. "Spare me your boring speeches and move on with it."

"I wish I was given boring speeches and a proceeding when I was accused of murder," David said. "The first thing I knew of it was chain-gun bullets hissing over my head."

Blythe's face twitched.

"But I digress," David said. "We begin this inquiry with the simple established fact that I am no more a murderer than any other man. Accusations are but words. Evidence and procedure convicts."

"Would that the three women you slaughtered could accuse you today!" Blythe spat, leaning over the dais. "I've seen your work. Beaten to death, that's what your victims endured. Beaten and beaten until their breath grew smaller and smaller and finally, mercifully stopped. That's my evidence."

Again, the assembly groaned with disgust.

"Poor dears," somebody said.

"Dirty bastard," another said.

David knew what Blythe was doing. Every time David gained the upper hand, Blythe would again remind the assembly of the horrid crime and call for justice for the atrocity. His passionate finger pointing at David and the vulgarity of which he spoke drowned out David's logical display of evidence. It was as though Blythe dazzled the assembly with a bright light, so bright they couldn't see the monster directly in front of them. David and the speaker were playing a very dangerous game of tug-of-war, and Blythe had the upper hand. However, David knew a thing or two about tug of war. If his opponent pulled too hard without proper footing, he'd end up on his backside.

"It just so happens that one of the three women is here today, and she does have a voice and an accusation," David said, reading the situation and deciding to play a bit of his hand early. "I call my first witness. I had hoped to proceed in a different order, but Speaker Blythe seems intent to remind this assembly that I committed three brutal murders, Ms. Paula Carbone, Ms. Samantha Samille, and Ms. Mercedes Eleanor Alexandra Lorraine. I submit to this assembly that this assertion is not only absurd but also impossible. I call Mercedes Eleanor Alexandra Lorraine to testify as my first witness."

The assembly gasped as Mercy stood and began walking down the stairs. She too had shed her disguise, and she descended with her auburn hair up in a bun, but for one flowing lock that curled around her shoulder. She wore a red and white gown, the color she was most known for, and it reached all the way to the floor in folds of fabric that cascaded like melting ice. The contrast accented her tall, comely form as the white and red shifted back and forth with every step. She held the hem of her skirts up with a dainty hand, her other sliding down the rail with elegant grace. Each footfall enveloped the next stair beneath her bell-shaped dress. When she reached the bottom and stepped out onto the glass floor, she released her skirts, and they swirled around her like a swath of cloud.

Blythe looked utterly dumbfounded. He gawked at her with open-mouthed astonishment.

"Ms. Lorraine, would you state your name for the assembly's records?" David asked.

"Mercedes Eleanor Alexandra Lorraine," Mercy said.

"What is your occupation, Ms. Lorraine?" David asked.

"Political aide and spy," she said.

Several in the assembly gasped.

David smiled. Mercy always had a dramatic effect on people, especially men. "Ms. Lorraine," He asked, "would you be so kind as to describe the events that led up to your supposed death."

Mercy nodded. "I was assigned to the Blythe office specifically to investigate his financial records. While in his employment, I uncovered vast amounts of financial fraud, though what I discovered that concerned me most was evidence that he had murdered two of his staff when he suspected them of political espionage. One such employee was murdered after her dismissal from the office. The situation scared me, as I knew that leaving the office would not grant me safety if my actions were ever discovered. So I faked my death."

Blythe swallowed and sealed off the expressions leaking onto his face. "Is this assembly honestly going to consider the stories of a murderer and a political spy? This is absurd!"

"I think every member of this assembly understands the value of political espionage," David said. "They just prefer not to have them in their own offices. In the past, political spies have uncovered several sinister plots within this room." David turned as he spoke, observing the many representatives. "Fraud, embezzlement, treason... Murder." He looked back at Blythe as he said murder, and his subtlety was not unnoticed.

Blythe frowned at him, and David could just see the muscles in his jaw bulging as he clenched his teeth. Then, he leaned back and said something to Eric while making a chopping motion with his hand across his throat. David pretended not to notice as he turned a page of the folder he'd pulled from the evidence box. Out of the corner of his eyes, he saw Eric stand and slink off of the dais and down the dark corridor behind it.

"Ms. Lorraine, could you describe the events that led you to believe the speaker murdered two of his employees." David walked around the dais as he spoke, and while Mercy answered, he saw Eric in the shadows of the corridor speaking with one of the guards. If the breadth of the guard's frame was any indication, David would guess it to be either Hans or Gerald. Not a moment later, David saw the doors surrounding the auditorium close and mysterious, broad-shouldered shadows lurking in front of them. At the same time, a few guards cleared the handful of observers in the gallery.

David swallowed. Blythe had set the course and jammed the rudder in place. There was no going back or deviating now; David had but to surge forward to victory or failure.

Chapter Twenty One
VETERAN SHIPYARDS

On the far side of Capital Island, a few dozen grandfathoms away, a group of six men meandered down a dingy, poorly lit sidewalk beside a massive compound. Twenty-fathom-high cement walls topped with any number of ship-killing armaments surrounded the installation, as this particular facility usually housed a significant number of military craft. It was called the Veteran Shipyards.

While on most occasions Veteran Shipyards refitted, restocked, and repaired all the military ships that entered its walls, tonight its many berths lay full to capacity with ships condemned to deconstruction. It almost seemed a betrayal, like coming home and discovering you are no longer welcome.

But the group of six men paid no mind to the high walls or the threatening armaments along its top, nor did they seem to mind the three statue-like guards they approached. They stumbled onward appearing drunk as they moved through the light rain and sloshed in the puddles. One of them possessed a very peculiar bionic eye. As they got nearer the guards, one of the men whispered something to his companion, and the man barked out a rasping laugh.

"Your right!" he said. "They do look a bit stiff. Oi, you!" he called to the guard nearest in a provocative manner. "Did someone put a stick up your bum so you wouldn't slouch."

All six of the men laughed now, far too hard for something that wasn't actually funny. The guard didn't move, apparently uncaring of their banter. Though, if they'd been close enough or sober enough to notice, they might have seen his frown.

"Yeah, I think they did," the man continued. "They tell you to stand real straight so you can pretend you're tough in your fancy, pompous outfit." The man flitted around in front of the guard mocking him and nearly tripped several times. "I'll bet they issued it to you with ladies undergarments."

His fellow drunks laughed harder at that, one of them falling over face first in a puddle, which caused even more laughter.

"Guardsies in lady's undies," one of the other drunks said as he slapped his knee. "Go on, Karl. Say it again. See if the lad blushes."

"I don't even think that gun works," The man called Karl said as he stepped up to the guard and leaned in close. "and if it does, you wouldn't know because you've never even fired it." He smiled as the guard winced, though if he had known any better, he would have realized it wasn't his words but rather his foul breath that affected the guard so. He looked back at his mates and said, "Poor lad's flinching." He leaned forward again, and, seemingly in a surge of over-confidence, he reached out and pushed the guard's shoulder.

The guard reached the end of his limited patience and lashed out at the drunk. He swung the butt if his repeater up and buried it in the drunk's paunch. The drunk doubled over and fell into the guard, knocking them both down. It was difficult to follow what happened next as all three guards began brawling the six drunken men. The guards' original confidence in besting six intoxicated men proved unfounded as all the men floundered about on the street rolling in an out of puddles. Karl even managed to steal his assailant's repeater and fire it above his head as he danced a jig along the sidewalk and hummed a merry tune. Bullets impacted off the compound walls and hissed overhead.

"Help!" One of the guards said as he staggered back toward the gate, apparently realizing that he and his fellows were in over their heads. "You, gatesmen, help!"

He needn't have called out, for as he spoke the gate was already rattling open. Evidently the commotion and the sound of the repeater had drawn some attention. The gate swung open, and five more guards stepped out and joined the fray. Somebody grabbed Karl and wrenched the repeater from his hands.

"Hey, that's mine," Karl said as he reached for the repeater, but the guard who took it responded by swinging it at Karl's head.

A whirl of coats and hats and fists followed, but the result was inevitable. In the end, six drunks in tattered old jackets lay sprawled and drooling on the cobbles; although, they must have been a bit more than they seemed as two guards lay drooling with them.

"You two, secure this gate," one of the guardsmen said. He had his hat slanted to the side, where a curious-looking bionic eye swiveled about. "The rest of you, take these wretches to the guard room. I want them tied and gagged. We'll let the Capital City police deal with them in the morning."

The six remaining guards complied with military precision. All six drunks and the two guards were drug through the gate and into the guardroom on the other side, which was built into the twenty-five-foot thick wall, where they bound and gagged all eight guards and drunks alike. As they worked, a phonograph buzzed on the far end of the guardroom. The guard with the bionic eye motioned to one of the other guards who stepped up to the phonograph and flipped a switch.

"Main gate, this is Commander Lewis. What in the fertile was that gunfire I heard?"

"A couple of drunks got into a brawl with our guards. They have the look of former aeronauts. We subdued them and tied them up, though one of them got ahold of a repeater and fired it into the sky."

"Aeronauts," Commander Lewis said in an annoyed manner. "Probably some of the rabble that used to fly the worthless tubs we've got inside our docks. Carry on then, and make sure they feel welcome," Lewis said the last part with a sarcastic tone.

The line switched off, and the guard looked up at the man with the bionic eye, who nodded. Francisco adjusted the ill-fitting jacket and pulled his capital guard hat down as low as it would slide without falling off. He stepped from the guardroom and looked into Veteran Shipyards. Over a thousand ships moored there divided along twenty-three rows of docks and stacked two or even three ships high. It was a significant force to be reckoned with by any apposing armada.

"The forward fleet," Francisco muttered to himself. "We'll see you fly again."

He turned and opened the gate. Without a signal, sixty men ran from the opposite side of the street and rushed through the gate, each wearing a guardsman hat and coat. The group split into ten teams and ran toward different sections of the facility. One ran to an adjoining guardroom, and Francisco heard some dull thuds and saw the flash of a pulse emitter. The sight made him smile. He turned to the three guards behind him and said,

"We're moving."

To anyone watching, everything at Veteran Shipyards looked perfectly normal, other than the fact that there were about twice as many guards on patrol as usual. Francisco led his team of sneaks across the facility beneath a few of the massive airships and toward a fortress looking communications tower on an adjacent wall. Francisco chanced a glance at the top of the walls and saw the flash of a pulse emitter. He smiled at his men's efficiency.

They passed a guard standing at his post beside a steam lift, and Francisco and the three lads behind him saluted as they marched past, though as soon as they'd passed him, the rear man in the troop turned and tazed the guard with his pulse emitter. The guard crumpled to the ground with a thump. They reached the steam lift where another guardsman stood, this one slouching at his post.

The sneaks lined up in front of the steam lift, and Francisco cleared his throat. The guard straightened up and saluted. The steam lift door opened, and the troop of sneaks marched inside. However, before the final man in the line entered, he raised his arm, tazed the guard, and pulled the limp body inside the steam lift. With a hiss, the doors slid shut and rocketed the sneaks and the unconscious guardsman to the top of the communications tower. They hid the guardsman's body on the side of the lift so it wouldn't be seen when the doors opened. A moment later, the four of them stepped out of the shaft into a square room surrounded by windows and filled with phonographs, steam projectors, and maps. During the ordinary operations, 20 guardsmen would occupy the room, directing air traffic in and out of the landing. However, given the docks were filled to capacity and the evening hour, only four men remained on duty, two of which were sleeping. Francisco raised his hand at one of the guards in a salute. His men did the same. Then, as one, they pointed their pulse emitters at the four guards and tazed them.

Francisco checked his watch before saying, "Shultz, two minutes."

The sneak didn't need telling. Shultz had already stepped up to one of the phonographs and tampered with its settings. He removed a curious looking device from his coat pocket with several wires dangling from one side. After splicing a few wires on the phonograph, he twisted them together with the wires on the device and then switched it on. A few of its lights blinked, and then Shultz looked at Francisco and nodded. The thought of all incoming and outgoing transmissions being redirected to an underground switchboard a few grandfathoms away filled with colorful personalities made him smile.

Francisco then walked to the far side of the tower and pulled a torch from his pocket as his men bound and gagged the unconscious guards. He pointed it out the window toward the far end of the facility and switched it on and off three times. He waited for three agonizing minutes before a torch flashed back three times. Francisco breathed a sigh of relief and walked to the other end of the tower and flashed his torch down at the main gate they had entered. A light flashed back, and within moments, men started pouring in through the gate, hundreds at a time. Several pulled canvas-covered pallets suspended beneath balloons. Francisco watched for a moment as the men continued to flood the facility, then he turned back to his men and the four bound guards.

With a nod, he turned and entered the steam lift once again, but this time keying the lowest floor. The shaft dropped, and he felt a tickle in his stomach as they dropped lower and lower below the ground level. As they rode along Francisco ran through the list of responsibilities on the mission. The hard part was over. Now they had but to deal with two nightshift engineers, shut off the facility's power, and spirit away to safety while Admiral York did the hard part. The doors opened, and the four sneaks stepped out into a very different environment.

A dull glow illuminated a narrow hall that led a few strides in one direction toward a brighter lit room. Several dozen thick conduits ran along the hallway, and the sound of rhythmic hissing and pumping echoed. Francisco and his men ran along the hall until they reached the room at the end. The sound of machinery increased in volume as they entered; however, there Francisco and his men froze in place. Three guards and twice as many engineers turned and looked at them in unison. They sat around a pile of game pieces on top of a makeshift table. The room thrummed for a few seconds as two groups of men looked at each other, and the Veteran Shipyard's generator carried on its endless work. Francisco thought fast.

"What is going on here!" he barked in his best sergeant's voice.

The guardsmen stood at attention, but the engineers folded their arms and scowled, all except one who took advantage of the situation and peeked under the guard's cards while they were faced away.

"I asked, what is going on here," Francisco said again. He positioned himself beside his sneaks so as not to get caught in the crossfire when the shooting started.

"Just a bit of gaming, sergeant," the shortest guardsman said.

Francisco nodded and noticed the guards' repeaters resting to one side of the table within reach of the engineers and that the guards still had their pistols holstered at their sides. There was no way they could taze all nine men before they started shooting back. Unless…

"Whose idea was this?" Francisco asked. "One of you greasy faced engineers?"

The engineers' frowns deepened.

"Answer me!" Francisco said.

One of the engineers rose to his feet with confident defiance before saying, "That's chief engineer to you, sergeant. I don't have to take any of your cheek."

Francisco smiled, and then he looked at the three guardsmen and pointed to one side of the room. "Line up," he said.

The guards hopped to and lined up exactly on the spot he pointed. Francisco stepped up to the gaming table and kicked it as hard as he could, sending its crate top flipping end over end on top of the repeaters. In the same instant he raised his hand and tazed the nearest engineer. The chief had already raised his fists for a fight when Francisco heard the other sneaks' pulse emitters buzzing away. One of the engineers dove at Francisco, but he easily sidestepped the man and tazed him, sending him to the cement floor with a thud. Just at that moment, when Francisco's focus was otherwise engaged, the chief engineer reached under the broken table at his feet and pulled out a repeater. Francisco whirled to face him at the clinking sound of a round sliding into the chamber, and for a brief moment stared into the triumphant eyes of the chief engineer who held the repeater pointed at Francisco's head. But before the man could fire, a glowing blue pulse struck his chest, and he crumpled to the floor with a blank, drooling expression. Francisco turned around and saw Shultz with his pulse emitter still extended.

"Much obliged, Shultz," Francisco said, and then pointed to the other two sneaks. "Tie up these clowns. Shultz, shut down the power to the armaments. We're behind schedule now, so double time."

In five minutes' time, the guards and engineers were tied and gagged, but Shultz still busied himself in a mess of wires at one side of a power grid.

"Shultz?" Francisco said as he checked his watch. "We're out of time."

"I just need a couple more minutes, sir," Shultz said as he held a screwdriver in his mouth. He clipped some wires with his pliers and twisted two, exposed copper ends together. "If I turn all the power off, we won't be able to use the steam lift to get out."

"You have one minute, then we'll take our chances," Francisco said. He replaced his pocket watch and checked the charge on his pulse emitter. Two minutes later, the group of them piled into the steam lift and rose back to the ground level. When the doors opened, they reemerged into the light rain, and the cool air was a pleasant change from a stuffy engineering room. During their time below ground, Admiral York had been busy. Already, the running lights of 500 odd airships glowed as they awoke from their sleepy berths. Men scurried around below the stacks of ships loading munitions and armaments. In the dim light of the facility, Francisco could see aeronauts scurrying around on carrier decks as they bolted down gunship-grade pulse emitters.

"Sir," a man said as he ran up to Francisco. He was one of the other team leaders responsible for clearing the walls of guards.

"Ah, Eric," Francisco said. "Nice work on clearing the far wall. That was a whole minute faster than we expected. Where do we stand now?"

Eric smiled before replying with a voice that did not match his small stature. "We had one incident where a guard drew his gas pistol and got off a few shots. Most of them missed, but two of our men have minor injuries. The carriers are all powered up and should have minimum lift in another few minutes. Admiral York is just finishing his rearguard's refit. Barring any unforeseen events, we should be ready for extraction within the hour."

Francisco checked his watch again. "Excellent. It looks like everyone is ahead of schedule except us. Perhaps I'll make the run tomorrow with my underpants on my head."

Eric smiled at that.

"Have the men ready for the extraction but maintain guard over the perimeter. I want the team leaders ready to check in with their torches once we lift off. We're not leaving a man behind."

"Aye, sir," Eric said. He saluted and marched off.

Francisco led his team across the compound at a quick march, and they splashed along the puddles until they passed beneath a massive carrier. He could just see the seams to the large bay doors that concealed the seventy skiffs inside. They joined some other engineers and aeronauts in a steam lift and rose up to the carrier's main level where gold letters marked the airship as *The Barlet*. It was a second-generation thunder class carrier named after house Barlet, the house in which Admiral York was born. Francisco crossed some scaffolding and boarded. The ship had a slightly beveled top deck that concealed the large cylindrical internal balloon. Francisco crossed to the front of the ship and stepped inside the armored bridge.

"Admiral, our sneak teams have completed their portion of the mission," Francisco said. "We await your orders."

Admiral York looked up from a map and nodded. "Fine work, Francisco. Our crews are nearly complete with the refit. The pulse emitters draw more power than our usual explosive armaments, so we had to run several tests. It would be a shame to launch ourselves into the sky only to burn out and drift uselessly across Alönia." York smiled as he rubbed his hand along the ship's wheel with obvious admiration.

"Yes, that would be anticlimactic," Francisco said dryly. "I have ordered my teams to divide up between the ships of the rearguard when the time comes. If any gunships manage to drop borders unto their decks, my men will do their best to repel them."

Admiral York nodded his approval, and Francisco exited the bridge to wait with the rest of his men on the top deck.

Within the hour, York sounded the all-clear, the rest of the sneak teams boarded, and the thunder class carriers began to rise above their berths one hundred at a time and soar out of the shipyard. Francisco tapped his fingers against the railing in frustration. The process of mobilizing five hundred ships took far longer than he preferred. The carriers with skeleton crews departed first, most of which had never before flown a carrier, or even an airship. The underground had scoured the houselands looking for Armada Vets and former crewmen from the doomed carriers, but in the end there hadn't been enough time, and they'd settled for cooks, cleaners, physicians, and pharmacists. York had issued crash courses in airmanship using make-belief controls and photographs. The hope was that when the capital guard realized what was happening, the crews would have a head start, and the rearguard would cover their retreat.

The communication's relay they'd installed at the tower had been a last-minute idea from Bethany, and just might give them the extra time they needed. If guardsmen saw the carriers departing Veteran Shipyards, and they contacted the tower to see what the issue was, the relay referred them to the underground's switchboard, and the underground would allay suspicion... in theory. They'd distributed scripted answers, like: *we're reorganizing the airships to make more room* or *we received an anonymous tip that airmen were going to storm the shipyards, so Blythe has ordered the airships moved?* But it was only going to be a matter of time before some blockhead went off script and said something like: *you're seeing things, mate* or *it's none of your bloody business.*

Francisco blanched as he considered the possibility. But at the very least, the relay would give them another few precious minutes to make good their escape. If all went according to plan, and they were very, very lucky, they might even reach Armstad airspace before the guard could mobilize.

At long last, Francisco felt a jolt as *The Barlet* began to rise. The skeleton crews were on their way, and now it was the rearguard's turn. He watched the top of the shipyard walls come into view and something else that made the grizzled sneak laugh. A flagpole stood on the top of the wall flying several pairs of underpants in place of a flag. Francisco turned to the rest of his team.

"We had to leave our mark, sir," Shultz said.

Francisco shook his head. "I don't think they'll forget us."

The Barlet rose above the shipyards with its nine other sister ships. The rearguard maneuvered with expert precision and departed in half the time it took any other ten carriers. As soon as they were clear, they switched off their running lights and disappeared into the blanket of cloud. In minutes, they were two grandfathoms out into the channel and a grandfathom in elevation escaping into the night sky.

The men snickered and joked quietly as they went

about their business checking and rechecking munitions. There were a dozen watchmen scanning the black expanse with specialized telescopes. Francisco stood at the rear of the ship, examining the clouds below and counting off the minutes. Cool high-elevation air blew around him and filled his lungs. It felt good after the exertion of their mission, cooling his sweaty back and soothing his tired limbs. But he did not allow his senses to dull. His bionic eye swiveled as he scanned the clouds, which is why he saw it first. It started as a glow beneath the cloudbank.

"Ship," Francisco said, with a sigh. "Ship!" He said again, louder this time. "Below us and to the southwest!"

All conversation ceased as every man looked off the side of the carrier and waited for the lookout to announce the ship type. Francisco didn't wait, he already knew. He manned a pulse emitter and swiveled it towards the approaching ship. The enlarged version of his wrist emitter had a chair and firing controls mounted beside a row of several flat disks skewered by a central shaft. The hastily built contraption contained parts from obscure places: a dining room chair, hydraulics from a lift, controls from an old skiff, and electronics from a generator. Wires protruded at multiple points in a haphazard fashion along with several notes that read, "Touch and die" or "press for immediate sterilization." Static filled Francisco's hair, and he wondered if, perhaps, they should have used more than a piece of wood to separate the gunners from quite a lot of electricity. He ignored his misgivings and lined the prongs of a fork mounted on the end of a metal skewer with the nearest clump of gunships. The chances were slim that any ship other than a capital guard gunship would be crossing the channel at this late hour and at this elevation. On the other hand, it was also far too soon for any pursuit, and this fact troubled Francisco.

"Osprey class gunship," one of the lookouts called, and the other crewmen groaned. Only the guard used the Osprey class gunship.

Then another lookout called out. "Ship, three ships, five, at least a squad."

Francisco saw it too. Dozens of gunships rose out of the cloudbank, and in moments the dozens turned into hundreds. The lookouts stopped calling out the ships as they stared through their telescopes with open-mouthed astonishment.

"How did they mobilize so fast?" One of the crewmen asked in a mainland accent. "This was supposed to take them half an hour. Even then, I never expected them to gather that many ships."

"They expected a rescue attempt," Francisco said as he closed his natural eye and stared between the fork prongs with his bionic eye, waiting for the gunships to fly into range. Francisco thought Blythe foolish, but he never presumed him an idiot. He'd obviously anticipated and prepared for just such a heist.

In the light of the partial moon, Francisco could see each of the approaching gunships silhouetted against the clouds. On the other hand, the moon also gave the gunships a partial view of the carriers as they cut across the sky. Within moments, the entire mass of gunships veered upward in pursuit of the carriers coming ever nearer. He rested his finger on the trigger as he gaged the distance. He noticed that all the other armaments were also swiveling into position preparing to ward off a massive boarding action from hundreds of angry gunships. However, he and the crews waited, each knowing their orders to fire only at point-blank range.

Ten seconds. Francisco thought, and he began a mental countdown. But, before he'd reached five, he saw something impossible, something none of them had accounted for. The gunships nearest, the one he had his emitter trained on, flashed for a split second and something small and oblong rocketed away, racing toward the Barlet with impossible speed.

Then a lookout bellowed at the top of his lungs, "Torpedoes!"

Chapter Twenty Two
THE VOICE OF THE PEOPLE

David watched Mercy leave the glass platform and ascend the stairs in all her grace and beauty after she'd finished her testimony. He wished he could stay near her the entire time she walked the orbital to keep her safe. Now that Blythe knew she was alive and that she was the true spy who'd infiltrated his ranks, he would stop at nothing to kill her. But Mercy had her part to play, just as David did.

David looked back at the assembly and smiled. "I know I am not as pretty as Ms. Lorraine, but I would ask that this assembly hear me out." Some of the men in the audience nodded their heads. "But I am getting ahead of myself and have skipped my introduction. You know me as David Ike."

Many of the representatives and aides smiled at that. There were probably a dozen David Ikes in the room that very moment.

"However, my full name is David Ike III." He saw

some of the mocking smiles falter. "My father was Captain David Ike II, a highly decorated officer in the Houseland Armada. But, it is my grandfather with whom this assembly is most familiar, as he was Admiral David Ike, legend in the armada and Hero of the Protectorate War." David turned and faced Blythe as he finished.

To the casual observer, Blythe's face looked impassive, but David knew the man well, and he knew the look of veiled shock when he saw it. The rest of the assembly was not so restrained. Women gasped, and men snorted.

"He's got to be joking," one man said, and a general murmur followed.

"You're lying," Blythe said. "You're as much a part of the Ike legend as the other Ikes in this room."

David stepped up to the steam projector and keyed in a code. In a moment, the projector flashed an image of himself, his father and grandfather all smiling after David's first academy skiff race. While the people gawked with open-mouthed astonishment, David smiled with fond memory at the image. A tear rolled down his cheek.

"Regrettably, my family members are all dead," David said, "and I am the last surviving member of the Ike legend. A terrible airship accident maimed me, killed my father, and eventually my grandfather and mother as well. I tell you this because I wish you to know whom it is that Speaker Blythe accuses of horrible atrocities, and who it is that accuses Speaker Blythe of the same horrible atrocities. I am not some run-about from the streets. My parents raised me under the principles of our family. They raised me to pursue my duty through kindness, justice, and humility. That is the duty of all men, and it is that duty that drives me to make these accusations at great personal risk."

Blythe, for once, sat speechless, gazing at the image of David and his family projected on the steam cloud above his head. David pressed a few keys, and the image vanished. Blythe returned his gaze to David with a mixed expression of anger, fear, and a hint of curiosity.

"Speaker Blythe," David asked as he began the inquiry in earnest, sensing that he had grasped everyone's attention. "How did you know Ms. Paula?"

"She was my secretary," Blythe said in a flat tone.

"And what was your relationship with your secretary?" David asked.

"Strictly business," Blythe said without hesitation.

"You never had any romantic... entanglement with Ms. Paula?" David asked.

"None," said Blythe.

"I would remind you that the speaker's dais binds all who sit upon it in an oath of honesty," David said, laying the final snares of his trap.

Blythe nodded coolly.

David felt giddy inside. "I will call my second witness, Mr. Mallory Shackleford."

Mallory stood and descended the stairs from Walker's box with his hat in his hands. His nervous manner was not nearly as refined as Mercy's elegance, nor was it as polished as the time David had first met him nearly a cycle earlier when Blythe and himself first dined at The Dancing Skyfish, when Mallory led them to their table. It struck David as strange, all those seasons ago, that Mallory knew Blythe by name and had a particular table permanently reserved. And David didn't believe for one moment that it was only because Blythe was a representative. He had a hunch that Blythe frequented the establishment, and his hunch had been correct.

David rushed through the introductory procedures, so he could ask Mallory a question while Blythe's business relationship was still firmly in the assembly's minds.

"Mr. Mallory, how often did you see Mr. Blythe at The Dancing Skyfish?" David asked.

"Oh, perhaps once or twice a week," Mallory replied.

"And did he visit alone or with company."

"Always with company," Mallory said, and nervousness tingeing his voice as he twisted his hat in his hands.

"Do you recognize this woman?" David pressed some keys on the steam projector again and a picture of Ms. Paula in her teardrop hat and light pink fingernails resolved out of the steam.

"I do, she came with him to dinner on many occasions," Mallory said. "but I haven't seen her there for about a cycle."

"I don't see where you're going with this," Blythe said, cutting into the questioning. "I also took you to dinner at the Dancing Skyfish. Did we also have a romantic relationship?"

The assembly laughed, and Mallory looked at his hat, but in a small voice, he said something that only David could hear, and what he heard made him smile.

"I'm sorry," David said when the assembly had quieted. "I didn't hear the last thing you said, Mr. Mallory. Could you repeat it?"

"I… I did see them kiss once," Mallory said.

"A kiss?" David said as he faced Blythe. "Is a kiss also part of the business relationship?"

Blythe frowned at Mallory. "Evidently I didn't tip enough." The assembly laughed again and continued to do so as Blythe went on. "On the other hand, it seems to me that you're feeling a bit jealous, David."

"Not at all sir," David said as the assembly again laughed. "But I do wonder if you were telling the truth when you said there was no romantic entanglement between you and Ms. Paula."

"Let me clear this up," Blythe said. "She kissed me not I her. I had no romantic entanglement with Ms. Paula, though she may have had one with me."

"I see," said David. "and did your interactions with Ms. Paula ever advance beyond *her* kissing you?"

"Never," Blythe said.

"That's all Mr. Mallory. You may go," David said.

Mallory ascended the stairs as quick as a man could without running.

"Next I would like to bring up the doorman from Ms. Paula's apartment," David said. "One Mr. Wade Bristol."

A very round man with a stern manner and a halo of hair waddled down the stairs and took up a stance beside David, his wide girth separating his small feet from his narrow shoulders.

Again, David rushed through the introductions and

pressed Bristol for any knowledge he had about Blythe, particularly knowledge of Blythe at Paula's apartment. Blythe frowned when he saw Bristol, but he offered no comment, not even when Bristol described Blythe walking through the complex at 8:00 in the morning in naught but a Bathrobe, and that on several occasions, he paid for Ms. Paula's rent.

David thanked Ms. Bristol and returned his attention to Blythe.

"Am I to understand," David said, "that you still maintain that you never had any romantic interaction with Ms. Paula beyond a kiss?"

"That is correct," Blythe said. "None whatsoever."

"So we're to believe that you paid for Ms. Paula's rent in naught but a bathrobe in the early morning because..."

"I couldn't find my trousers that morning," Blythe said, filling in David's sentence.

The assembly laughed once again.

"Did you try looking under Ms. Paula's bed?" David asked, snagging Blythe's momentum as the audience continued to laugh. "Really, Mr. Speaker, your story is an obvious fiction. Do you really expect us to believe such a ludicrous tale?"

"I'm not responsible for what anyone believes," Blythe said. "I'm responsible for telling the truth."

"He's got you there, lad," a representative called from the audience to more snickers.

David did his best to smile, but more and more he wondered if this was one giant, elaborate show, and everyone was an actor save him.

"Really, David," Blythe said. "Even if I did enjoy a romantic flair with Ms. Paula, such antics are not unknown by this assembly, and they are hardly a crime. You began this inquiry with an accusation of murder, yet all I've heard are headlines from the juicy section of a tribunal."

"You're quite right, Mr. Speaker," David said. "Let me continue to this second box of evidence. I wish to call Inspector Kenneth Winston to assist me in establishing the evidence."

Blythe flinched a little when David mentioned Winston's name.

"Inspector Winston," David asked when the inspector reached the floor in front of the dais. "How are you connected to this case?"

"I was the inspector assigned to investigate the case," Winston said. "This is the evidence I collected during my investigations." Winston gestured to the boxes on the glass floor.

"And what of Ms. Samantha Samille?" David asked.

"Since the cases had a strong connection," Winston said, "I was also assigned that case."

"Could you explain what you mean by *strong connection*?" David asked.

"Both victims were killed in the exact same way," Winston said. "Blunt force trauma all across the body. In short, they were beaten to death. And, since they both worked in the same office, sat at the same desk and worked the same position, we can presume with nearly one hundred percent certainty that they were killed by the same person."

"I don't think I need to ask Speaker Blythe if he had any romantic interaction with Ms. Samille," David said.

"I'll admit to that one," Blythe said with a smile. "I enjoyed every minute of it."

David walked to one of the evidence boxes and drew out a small note.

"Inspector Winston," David asked, "could you explain what this is?"

"This is a love note from Ms. Paula. She was having an affair with a married man and wished to end it with marriage."

"Could you read the letter in its entirety?" David asked.

"*A divorce would ruin me, and you cannot offer me enough to justify the loss. Are you not happy with what we have?*" Winston read from the note.

"What does that tell you, Inspector Winston?" David asked.

"That Ms. Paula had a lover, a married lover."

David took back the letter and flipped over to another bit of evidence. The onlookers made no sound, but he saw curiosity in their eyes. Perhaps their curiosity would grant him the upper hand.

"What is this Inspector?" David asked.

"That is Ms. Paula's personal notebook."

"Is there anything of interest in that notebook?" David asked.

"Yes, there is a very interesting page in the back. It contains a list of addresses in the Third District and their general increased value."

"When was the note written?" David asked.

"After the announcement that Public pharmaceuticals' would move to the Third District," Winston said. "We know this because their values remained the same for ten cycles, and because the increased values in that notebook are representative of their values after the announcement."

"And who owns those properties?" David asked.

"According to the district property records, all of them are owned by Speaker Blythe," Winston said.

Blythe looked in shock as David put an image of the page in question on the steam projector.

"What does this tell you, Inspector?" David asked.

"It tells me that," Winston said, pausing to collect his thoughts, "Ms. Paula was keeping a personal record of Speaker Blythe's net worth and financial dealings. And, it was one of the last things she did before she died."

The assembly murmured when they heard that.

"How do you figure that, Inspector Winston," David asked.

"Our original autopsy report established Ms. Paula's time of death between 24 and 48 hours after Mr. Blythe's grand speech. Therefore, she wrote that note after Speaker Blythe's grand speech but no more than 48 hours after the grand speech."

"Very good, inspector," David said. "On another note, in your investigation of the speaker, did you ever calculate his total net worth?"

"I did. As of a season ago, I calculated it to be in

excess of 20 million sterling."

"20 Million?" David asked as he looked at Blythe.

But Blythe only shrugged and said, "Business has been good."

David reached into the evidence box and pulled out one last item, his crowning jewel.

"Could you tell me what this is, inspector?" he asked.

"That is Ms. Paula's locket," Winston said.

David held it up for all to see and enjoyed Blythe redden when he saw it.

"Ms. Paula always wore this locket," David said. "In fact, I never saw her without it, despite the fact that she had a fine collection of jewelry."

David let that sink in for a moment, gnawing at the minds of the representatives. Then he turned the metal locket, and the two halves came apart revealing the writing within.

"Ms. Winston, could you tell me what it says on the inside of the locket?" David asked and handed the locket to Winston.

"On the one side there are the letters, *WJB*," Winston said, "and on the other side *IV*."

For once, the assembly remained absolutely silent, every one of them staring at the tiny locket Winston held in his club-like hands. None of them dared to make a sound.

"So, sum up what we have established, if you would, inspector," David said. "Tell me your professional opinion of the evidence and the conclusions we can draw from it."

Winston bit his lip before he began. "Speaker Blythe and Ms. Paula were having a love affair. Ms. Paula wanted marriage, but Speaker Blythe refused, not wanting to jeopardize his political standing. So, Ms. Paula threatened him with blackmail, then she was tortured to death—

"This is slander," Blythe said. He jumped up from his seat, interrupting Winston.

"Is it?" David said, fury tainting his voice. "You did not feel so when you accused me of the same crime."

Blythe fumed. His face reddened and mouth opened and closed with unspoken words.

"As it is," David said, "My inquiry has come to an end. I would now ask the assembly to vote on this matter. A three-quarter vote of no confidence will strip the speaker of his power until a magistrate trial either convicts or acquits him. His first aide would fill in his speaker duties during the interim, or until his district's next election."

"Thank you, David," Blythe said. "We are all aware of the assembly rules. Before this assembly votes I would remind them all of the prosperity we have all enjoyed these past few seasons and the continued peace and prosperity we will feel for many more to come... while I am speaker." He said the last part with particular emphasis, almost as though he was warning them that if he went down, he would take them with him.

The steam projector showed two tallies, one for yeas and one for nays. A murmur began and rose to a rabble as representatives talked amongst themselves. But the discussion ended as soon as it began. David felt his blood chill and his heart pound as he paced on the glass floor in front of the dais.

He wondered. *Had they already come to a decision? That was too quick.*

He looked up at the tally and saw fifteen yeas for Blythe's removal, but he needed fifty-seven votes to remove Blythe, and the nays' tally had not resolved from the mist yet. Thirteen nays appeared, and David bit his lip, then the number thirty, and David gawked. Just like that, it was over. He'd failed to convince the assembly. It didn't matter that there were still votes outstanding, there weren't enough votes left to reach fifty-seven yeas.

David felt himself screaming inside his own head. *How could they? How could they ignore such overwhelming evidence? They hadn't even considered it. It was as if they always intended to vote as they did.*

But the number of nays continued to grow, while the yeas remained at fifteen. Forty-nine nays, then fifty-two, and at last, sixty-one. The nays had the vote by an overwhelming margin. Very few, if any, Equalist voted against Blythe. Evidently, they didn't mind having a torturous murderer as their speaker, as long as he let them prosper off the sweat of the taxpayers. David looked at Blythe and saw a cold smile, a smile of triumph.

"Well, David," Blythe said. "I'm sorry you had to go through all that trouble. I could have told you that would be the result even before you started. What did you think you would accomplish through all of that, hmm?"

David maintained his gaze at Blythe, but he said nothing.

"It's hard for me to believe I once called you brilliant,"

Blythe continued, "because, that was a very foolish thing to do. You've given yourself to me and accomplished nothing in your sacrifice."

"It wasn't in vain," David said. "The people heard the truth. They'll rise up against you."

"The people!" Blythe said, barking out a laugh. "What people? I switched off all broadcasts of this assembly the moment you called your first witness. You think I would allow them to hear all of that? And even if they had heard, they wouldn't care. Why would the ignorant, doped up masses care what kind of man is sending them their social assistance checks? The money, the drugs, and the ease are all they care about."

"You mean your pacifying wonder drugs? The drugs you're using to control the populous?" David said. He turned and looked at the representatives around him. "Don't you care what he's doing to Alönia? He's forcing Don Johnson to issue pacifying drugs, so the people will accept whatever he says. He's destroying our democracy from the inside out while you sit by and do nothing!"

Nobody spoke, nor did they meet his eye. The only sound in the room was that of Blythe's chuckling. David turned and faced Blythe, disbelieving what he saw.

"They know, David," Blythe said. "They all know. That fact is: they don't care. They get to live very comfortable lives because of my legislation."

"By comfortable lives," David said, feeling himself sweat as Blythe looked at him with his sickly condescending smile, "are you referring to the fact that your administration has spent more sterling in its first few seasons than Walker spent in his entire tenure as speaker? You're enjoying and wasting our peoples' hard-earned money."

Blythe shrugged. "A small price for a unified party."

"But what of our democracy?" David asked. "What of our Houseland government?"

Blythe sighed. "What is democracy but two Voxils and a mountain lamb deciding what's for supper. The people still vote, they just don't realize that I've dissolved their will to work and survive without my assistance. They're dependent on me, no... they're addicted to me."

"But that's wrong!" David said. "It will destroy the houselands, and you know it."

"You know what the problem is with Pragmatics ideology?" Blythe asked. "You're always bogged down disputing between yourselves what's right and wrong. We Equalists don't bother; we simply unify behind what's easiest, profitable, and popular. The houselands died some time ago, David. Sure, Walker got a few last kicks out of the old girl, but the era of Alönia is over, and the era of a unified Fertile Plains has begun, and I will lead it."

"The people of Alönia did not elect and pay for your extravagant lifestyle so you could sacrifice them in favor of other realms," David said while looking at the representatives. "You represent Alönians, not Bergs or Viörns, or even the Armstadies. Do you even know about the speaker's Viörn friend," David asked and enjoyed seeing Blythe's face twitch out of the corner of his eye, "the one giving him orders?"

"They are fully aware of my peace talks with Viörn and Berg," Blythe said, interjecting.

"Alönia will not be so easily thwarted," David said, turning back to Blythe. "You can say whatever you want about us, but we are a proud, strong people. We will not fall so easily to a dictator eager to prostrate us to our enemies. The Viörn and Berg are coming—"

"That's enough out of you," Blythe said. "Guards, take him away so we can hang him."

"They are mass-producing their airships and positioning them along the border." David continued as five guards walked across glass floor and toward him. They surrounded him and closed in like a noose around his neck.

David pointed a finger at Blythe. "Justice will find you one day. It will knock on your door and demand recompense for the crimes you've committed, the innocent lives you have wasted."

"I said that's enough!" Blythe shouted, standing to his feet. "Shut him up."

A guard lunged at David, but David was not the simple aid he had once been. He easily dodged and elbowed the guard in the face. He felt a crack through his sleeve and saw blood seep from the man's nose.

"And not just you," David said after he punched another guard and sent him sprawling. "All of you will meet justice," David said, projecting his voice so that it echoed across the assembly. "I presented the crime at your feet, and you chose to ignore it and condemn innocent blood."

David faced the last three guards, but he positioned himself in such a way that only one of the guards could attack him at a time. The closest guard swung at him, but David caught the man's forearm in his ebony hand. The guard screamed as David constricted his fingers and snapped the man's wrist. He kicked the man and sent him sprawling into his fellows. But a strong hand grabbed David from behind, and a thick muscular arm snaked around his neck. David wriggled as Hans and Gerald each grabbed one of his arms, and Hans constricted David's neck in a chokehold. David felt his vision blur in matter of seconds. He writhed and kicked Gerald's leg. The huge man grunted with pain but maintained his grip. The three of them fell to their knees, and David could see Blythe leaning over the dais through his watery eyes.

The sight of that smirking face sickened him. David clenched his ebony iron fist and started bending it at the elbow. Gerald, big as he was, could not match the incredible strength of his mechanical arm, but time was short. Already David felt himself passing out. He could hardly hear the yells of the assembly. But he had enough wits about him to close his mechanical fingers around Gerald's thick hand and squeeze. Several pops sounded in David's ear followed by a wail. Gerald kicked himself free and cowered away from the inhuman appendage. Hans slacked his grip on David's neck when he saw his partner's fear. David used the opportunity to lean over and slam his ebony fist into Hans' gut.

Han's eyes widened, and he slumped to one side. David stood from the floor and rubbed his neck as he gasped for air. More guards had arrived and crowded around him, but none seemed interested in stepping within range of his unique arm. They didn't need too. One of them pulled a pulse emitter from a holster.

David, sensing that his time grew short, pressed a button on the side of his mechanical arm, and a curious device rose from a compartment. It looked like a tiny ray-gun. He pointed it at the glass floor.

"You wouldn't!" Hans said from where he sat massaging his stomach, and every other guard froze when they saw the ray gun attached to the side of his arm.

"I believe in the people of Alönia," David said with a look at Blythe. Then he squeezed his fist, and the curious device on his wrist buzzed and emitted a high-pitched sound.

Everything slowed down in David's head. The glass flour below them dissolved into sand, and a breeze from the air below carried it away in an enormous cloud. Guards yelled and reached for the steel girders. Blythe screamed in fury.

But David, for his part, felt weightless, so weightless he thought he might be nauseous. He slipped through the floor as though it were made of water. He fell out the bottom of the assembly and saw the light of the room rising above him as he did so. His worst fears were realized. Panic took him as he flailed, gasped, and coughed on the cold, sandy air. He looked around and saw an endless expanse of night and cloud.

Chapter Twenty Three
SACRIFICES

Francisco watched the torpedo as it streaked through the air directly toward the Barlet. Nobody had expected torpedoes, so no one had bothered to man the flack cannons or any of the other countermeasures. Crewmen stared dumbfounded as the deathly cylinder ate away the distance with a ravenous appetite, counting down the fathoms till it sank its teeth into airship hull. Every muscle in Francisco's body braced for the impact, and he felt the back of his gunning chair press into his spine. But he was a warrior, and he'd seen and expected death for many cycles. One thing he knew for certain, he'd meet it in a fight. In one final act of defiance, he squeezed his emitter's trigger and felt his entire body tingle with static. Then, he gritted his teeth and waited for the inevitable.

His aim was true, but the substanceless glowing wave of electricity passed through the torpedo like a wisp of cloud. The burner behind the torpedo shut off, but its momentum drove it on until it slammed into the side of the carriers' hull with a solid thrum like a hammer on the side of a metal drum.

Francisco looked over the side of the ship and saw several torpedo pieces falling from the sky until they disappeared into the cloudbank. It took him a second to realize what had happened. His pulse emitter had shorted out the torpedo's ignition sequence, and it struck the carrier's thick armor with no more force than a cannonball. But circumstances did not permit him to ponder further as dozens more torpedoes launched at the ship.

"Shoot them!" Francisco yelled. "Short them out with your pulse emitters!"

The order sent the well-trained crew into action. They knew the danger of torpedoes well, and every available aeronaut manned flack cannons and chain-guns and emitters alike. The other ships observed the effect of the emitter on the torpedo and followed suit. Within moments, the air roiled with exploding bursting flack canisters, golden tracer rounds, blue-tinged electricity, and exploding torpedoes. Several more thrums of echoed through the ship as shorted torpedoes glanced harmlessly off their armor.

In addition, as the gunships released their torpedoes, they flew in range of the powerful emitters. Dozens of pulses crippled gunships and left them gliding on their last known trajectory until the crew awoke from their stupor and restarted the burner, something Bethany insisted would take at least ten minutes. That was all fine and good when they expected to face less than half as many gunships firing nothing larger than chain-guns for a maximum of 30 minutes.

"Expect the unexpected!" Francisco said as his pulse emitter thrummed and sent another gunship gliding away for ten minutes of bliss.

That was the last thing David had told him before they each left for their separate missions. If he ever saw David again, he planned on punching him in the face. This was his crazy plan, and while he sat in a plush chair at the assembly, Francesco sat in an electric chair, hair full of static, and staring between the prongs of a fork at pursuing torpedoes. Yes, he and David would most certainly have words.

"I'm aiming with a bloody fork! Does that qualify as unexpected?"

Then, the inevitable happened. One of the many torpedoes slipped past the rearguard's countermeasures and exploded into the side of a carrier's hull. Francisco watched as an entire bay door blown free by the explosion tumbled through the sky in a cloud of smoke and burning debris. The carrier listed for a moment before resuming its course. The armor had absorbed most of the explosion, but another hit like that, and the carrier would come apart at the seams. The other carriers repositioned their formation placing their injured sister in the center, but the hit proved the inevitability of the battle.

Francisco checked his watch in between shots and winced when he realized it had only been twenty minutes. They had another forty minutes of flight time before they reached Armstad airspace. They weren't going to make it, and if they didn't last for another twenty minutes, neither were the other 500 carriers. If the rearguard fell, the gunships would catch and destroy the rest of the carriers in five minutes' time. They needed a new plan.

"Airman!" Francisco called to one of the lookouts. "Take my position."

Francisco jumped from his gun and did not turn to see if the airman had followed his order. He ran to the ship's bridge as fast as he could. He burst through the door just in time to hear York speaking into his radio.

"Capital guard! This is Admiral York. You are using deadly force against my ships. If you do not cease immediately, I will be forced to do the same."

A wash of static sounded in the speaker.

"Capital guard, do you read me?" York said. "We are carriers, and we will loose our skiffs on you if you force our hand."

Francisco knew the last part was a bluff. They didn't have enough men to man their 60 skiffs. Apparently, the guard knew that as well as static continued to rasp from the speaker. York replaced the microphone on the side of the radio and leaned over the map table with a sigh.

"I'm all ears, Francisco," York said. "I've used my last bluff. We've just been caught with our trousers down."

"I have one idea," Francisco said. "But you're not going to like it." Francisco relayed his plan to York and watched the admiral's face fall into a deep frown. He looked around at his ship with pursed lips, and then at its men. Then he nodded.

"Do it," he said. "I'll notify the other carriers."

Francisco nodded and ran from the bridge, but he did not return to the top deck. He ran down a narrow corridor that led through the bowel of the airship. He found a very round chief engineer and several engineering assistants, and together they made their way to the ship's generator. Francisco explained his plan to the chief as they ran.

"No!" the chief said once they'd reached the generator. "I can't do that!"

As he spoke, Francisco heard the explosion of another torpedo impacting against a sister carrier. Time was running out. He drew his gas pistol and held it underneath the chief's nose.

"I want you to listen very carefully," Francisco said in a dangerous voice. "There are men dying out there, your friends and mine. I've got the ability to stop it from happening, but there's a fat, idiot, engineer in my way. You can either help me, or I'll see to it that your assistant gets a battlefield promotion." The watching assistants gazed with expressions of shock.

The chief's eyes crossed as he looked down the barrel of the pistol. He nodded vigorously.

"A wise choice," Francisco said as he put his pistol away. "Now work quickly. In five minutes we will be nothing but ash and ember."

The engineer ordered his two assistance to gather some supplies, and then he began welding sheets of metal to a space beside the generator and laying some power lines. Another explosion made Francisco shiver with fury.

Had that one downed a carrier, or just injured her? Within a few minutes the chief stood up and nodded to Francisco.

"Will it work?" Francisco asked.

"How should I know?" The chief said. "I didn't come up with the bird-brained idea, and I put it together under gunpoint. It might just short out all the conductors and send us drifting across the night sky."

"How do I start it?" Francisco asked.

The chief held up a small box that looked like a light switch with several cabled snaking out of its bottom. "Just flip this switch."

Francisco took the box in his hands and raised it up until the fathom long wires pulled taught. "You couldn't have made it any longer?" he asked and then frowned.

The engineer scratched his head. "In hindsight, I suppose that might have been—"

"It will do," Francisco said. "You." He pointed a finger at one of the assistants who jumped with the motion. "Inform the Admiral that we are ready. And you two," he pointed to the chief and the other assistant, "collect everyone else below deck and get to the hanger bay."

After they'd left, Francisco picked up the switch and waited for the signal, but just then, a deafening explosion rocked the ship and sent him hurtling into the wall of the cramped engine room. It took him a moment to shake the stars from his vision and climb to his feet. Then he realized he no longer held the switch. He looked around the dimly lit space for a pair of heartbeats. In that time he heard the carriers bay doors opening. Spotting the switch on the opposite end of the room, he stooped and picked it up, only then realizing the wires were no longer attached.

"Typical!" Francisco said as he grabbed the wires from the floor and threaded them into the two holes on the back of the switch box where they'd once been. He had neither the tools nor the expertise to do any better than that. He bit off a curse when one of the wires fell out, and he stuffed it back into place. Then, the engines shut off, which was the admiral's signal for the all-clear. Francisco gritted his teeth and flipped the switch.

Nothing happened. He flipped it off and on a few times, but the box refused to work. He yelled into the silence and banged the box with a frustrated fist and used every curse he knew. Then the small space illuminated with the bright light of electricity, and he felt static course through the air. Bolts of energy arced around him and left black smudges on the walls.

Francisco dropped the box and ran down the hall as fast as he could. He didn't slow as he bounded down the narrow corridor and careened around the tight turns. The whole ship began to buzz, and the air smelled of crisp ozone. When he reached the bay doors, he didn't stop to look for a skiff. He grabbed a life balloon off the wall and jumped out the open bay doors without even fastening it around his shoulders.

Francisco tumbled through the air, one hand clutching his life balloon while the other tried to find the shoulder restraints. All the while wind tugged at the life balloon and threatened to rip it from his grasp. He struggled with the straps, knowing he only had moments before he'd lose consciousness. Finally, his arm found the restraints, and he shouldered them on and snapped the clasp. He reached up and pulled the tabs of the balloon and felt the comforting tug against his restraints.

At the same moment, *The Barlet*, or what was left after it suffered two torpedoes, pulsed with a growing electrical surge that filled the night sky with a bright blue light. The surge arced out from the broken pieces of the Barlet and engulfed a majority of the gunships that were at that very moment swirling around the wounded carrier. Francisco smiled his warrior's smirk as several more electrical surges exploded in the distance when several other rearguard carriers followed suit. Then the pulsing energy reached him, and he screamed as it surged through his body and arced off his mechanical eye. The surge dissipated, and he hung as limp as a man at the gallows, dangling from his bobbing life balloon in the midst of falling wreckage and several hundred drifting gunships. His sacrifice had not been in vain. Away in the distance six battered carriers and a little less than 200 skiffs, the remnants of the rearguard, soared through the night sky and passed into the free Armstadi airspace. The mission was a complete success, but for the brave few who made the ultimate sacrifice to save their fellows.

Chapter Twenty Four
A WOMAN'S TOUCH

As David's group headed toward the assembly room to make the inquiry, Bethany separated from them and continued down another hallway. Nobody usually ventured down this hall, and the only sound she heard was the echo of her own heels clicking on the ground. She had been rather peeved when David transferred her out of the switchboard team to come to the assembly with him and Mercy. She'd spent hours fiddling with her relay device so that even a blockheaded sneak couldn't possibly mess up the connection with the Veteran Shipyard tower. Then she wrote several pages of possible responses she might use when guardsmen called in to the switchboard.

Her current favorite was, *Thank you for calling the manslaughter direct phonograph. If you are currently being slaughtered, press 1. To hear in Bergish, press 2. If you are being slaughtered, but are not a man, this line is not for you.*

Bethany giggled to herself as she thought of all the fun

she might have had at the switchboard. Yes, she had been very peeved at David until he explained exactly what it was he wanted her to do. Then, she'd decided that this would be twice as fun. Reaching a T at the end of the hallway, she checked a small napkin sized map David had drawn her the day before. This had been a last-minute addition to the plan, and there hadn't been time to acquire anything other than a hodgepodge of materials. She frowned at the hand-drawn map and rotated it several times. She knew she was getting closer when she heard the rhythmic sound of machinery, but the map confused her. She chose right at the T, but after three steps, she turned the map around again and decided to go the left.

The longer she walked, the louder machines whirled and hissed in the distance, but she wasn't looking for those particular machines, rather, some close by. Such machines were not her specialty. She had a pact with the underground: she would not touch anything that used grease or oil. She worked with electronics, and she knew them well.

She arrived at another turn and spied around the corner. A guard stood rigid beside a door to one side of the hall. Unlike the rest of the Capital Guard, this hulking man looked as though he knew which was the dangerous end of a repeater. Bethany crossed her arms and huffed.

David, you mentioned one capital guard, she thought to herself, *not a tall, muscular*—she spied around the corner again—*ruggedly good looking brute.*

A smirk replaced her frown as Bethany removed her hat and touched up her hair. Looking in a pocket mirror, she doublechecked her makeup and general appearance. Though she had never said it to anyone, she had been very disappointed in herself and the slightest bit jealous that Blythe had completely overlooked her in favor of Samille back in the Third District office. To the Third District she had only ever been a doe-eyed idiot. That had been a miscalculation on her part. She'd completely misjudged Blythe's attractions and the extent of his depravity. Of course, Samille was an escort and also dead. It might have been the miscalculation that saved Bethany's life.

But even David ignored her in favor of Mercy. She hadn't actually wanted either David or Blythe's affections. David talked too much, and Blythe was old, promiscuous, and perverted. But a girl does tend to wonder if any of the boys are noticing her. When she finally found a man who could make her heart throb, would she make his heart throb as well?

Bethany looked down at her white satin dress, tight through the bodice and loose through the skirts, a large bow over one shoulder. She snapped her mirror shut and replaced it in her purse along with her hat. *Of course I will,* Bethany said to herself. *Sweetheart, you're gorgeous!*

She took a few steps down the hall from whence she'd come, breathed a couple of deep breaths, and charged forward as fast as her heeled feet would allow. She skittered around the corner and collapsed against the wall with a gasp. She turned around, peeked down the hall, and breathed a sigh. She turned, yelped, and put a hand over her mouth when she faced the guard, acting as though it were the first time she'd noticed him. He still stood at his post, but he eyed her with stern curiosity.

Bethany looked at the guard with her large blue eyes. Then she removed her hand from her mouth and whispered anxiously.

"Can you hide me?" she said.

"This area is off limits," the guard said, sounding bored.

"Well so am I, but that doesn't seem to slow Blythe down," she said as she lifted her skirt and walked toward the guard as fast as ladies were allowed. "What's down that there? Does he ever go down there?"

The guard smirked. "I don't think I've ever seen the speaker in these halls."

"Well he's coming now," Bethany said. She was only a few feet from the guard now. He towered over her petite form despite the heels she wore. Unfortunately, his knuckles turned white as his hands tightened on the repeater in his arms. He suspected her. Bethany redoubled her efforts.

"Please," Bethany pleaded. "I just need a small cupboard where I can stay out of his hands and in my dress. I've slapped him twice, and he won't leave me alone!" She put her hands on her hips and pouted.

It was working. The guard's eyes flicked away for an instant, eying her pretty dress. His hands loosened on the repeater, and he sighed.

He pointed down the hall with one hand and said, "There's a broom closet down that corridor and around—"

He never finished his sentence, for as soon as he looked in the direction he was pointing, Bethany took a handheld pulse emitter from her purse and tazed the man on the side of his neck. He crumpled to the floor with such a loud clatter it made her jump.

"Shhh!" She said to his limp form. She turned her head and read the man's name tag. "Someone will hear us, Tristan."

Bethany checked both ways down the hall before she stepped up to the door behind the guard. Pulling a lock pic from her hair, Bethany fiddled with the lock. It wouldn't budge. She bit her lip and tried again. She was no sneak when it came to locked doors but on occasion..."

"Ah-ha!" Bethany said as the door swung open. She bent down, grabbed Tristan by his shoulders, and attempted to drag him into the room. He didn't budge. She pulled harder, but she only managed to slip and fall on her backside. She got up and kicked the guard in annoyance.

"That's no way to treat a lady!" She said.

She grabbed his arm this time and braced herself against the doorframe. He moved at a painfully slow rate, and his face squeaked as it slid across the polished floor.

"Why did you have to be so big?" She said, huffing and puffing as she pulled him into the room. "Tristan seems like a little man's name." Finally, she shut the door behind them and breathed a sigh of relief.

She bent and retrieved the guard's repeater. She emptied the magazine and then fiddled with the trigger.

When she'd finished, she dropped the repeater on the guard's chest. It would be hours before he awoke, and she would be long gone, but she still enjoyed her little games.

The room looked like the inside of a power plant. Wires ran this way and that. Pipes and conduits crisscrossed along the walls and ceiling. In the middle, a long antenna as wide as Tristan's waist reached through the glass ceiling and continued on for several fathoms above the top of the orbital. A wide dish crowned the apparatus. Bethany smiled. Someone had collected all of her favorite toys into one single room.

She set to work, first at the phonograph on the left side of the room. In moments she heard the general din of the assembly room and watched representatives find their seats in the light of a small steam projection. Next, she took her little purse and stepped up to the control terminal on the side of the enormous antenna. She ran some wires from the terminal to the phonograph, but for the moment, she left the terminal's power switched off. She had to wait until the appropriate time, something David reiterated over and over again until she'd groaned in frustration.

She heard the call to assembly, and several representatives give their motions over the hum of the phonograph, but she still waited, not touching the power switch on the terminal. Rather, she used the time to check and recheck her work. She even found a roll of tape to secure all the loose wires on the floor so nobody would trip. As she sat in a makeshift chair and prepared herself to watch the dullest assembly ever, waiting for a precise moment that seemed hours away, she heard a groan from behind her.

She spun around and saw Tristan standing to his feet and shaking his head. He looked toward Bethany and wrinkled his forehead. Then a grimace soured his features.

"You!" he said with venom in his voice. "You tazed me!" He raised his repeater to his shoulder and pointed it at Bethany.

Bethany looked at him with wide eyes. "You weren't supposed to be awake so soon," she said. "Everyone else takes longer."

Tristan grunted. "I hope I'm on guard duty where they lock you up. I'll taze you and watch a few programs while you're drooling on the floor."

Bethany slipped her hand inside her purse.

"Aw!" Tristan said as his fingers tightened on his repeater. "Not so fast, little missy. You move that hand again, and I'll squeeze this trigger. I got no problems shooting a woman, even one as pretty as you."

Bethany whimpered.

"That's right, now you hold real still," Tristan said.

"Don't you want to turn the safety off?" Bethany said as tears rolled down her face.

"Huh?" Tristan said with a scowl. He looked at his repeater and then flicked the safety off. In that same instant his body stiffened, and a buzz issued from his repeater. He dropped the weapon and crumpled to the floor. Bethany withdrew her hand from her purse and pulled the cap off some lipstick. She freshened up and popped her lips a few times.

"Oh, Tristan," Bethany said as she stood and walked over to his prone form. "If you keep electrocuting yourself like that, you're bound to get brain damage."

She used her lipstick to draw several hearts on his cheeks. Then she jumped up as Walker started making his motion for the inquiry. She stepped over to the steam projector and watched the scene unfold. She saw Blythe mock Walker and the vote for the inquiry. She watched David's triumphant return followed by Mercy's miraculous appearance. Then she saw it; it was he cue. Blythe leaned over and whispered something to Eric, who immediately left the dais.

A moment later, Bethany saw a few doors close from the limited perspective her projector presented, but Eric did not return. Bethany raced across the cramped room, stepping on Tristan to do so. She turned off the light and put her back against the wall behind the door. There she waited.

Within a few moments, she heard footsteps approaching. They neared and paused at the door.

"Tristan?" a voice called.

But after a moment, there was the sound of keys unlocking the door. Then it opened with a creak, and a heavily tanned man entered the room. He reached behind the door to turn on the light, and a flickering blue light filled the dark room as Bethany tazed him. He crumpled to the ground. Bethany closed the door and turned on the light. In front of her lay Eric Himpton sprawled out on top of Tristan. She stepped over them and walked up to the antenna terminal. She rubbed her hands together, savoring the moment. She flicked the power switch and heard several generators groan to life. Lights eliminated up the side of the antenna and around the dish at the top.

Bethany smiled. David had been concerned from the start that Blythe would shut off the assembly broadcast, and the Houselands would never know what happened during the inquiry. He had agonized over this fact for weeks on end, and finally dreamed up one of his typical, crazy-brilliant plans.

When Blythe sent Eric to shut down the broadcast, Bethany intercepted him and ensured that the broadcast stayed active. In addition to that, she'd projected it on the orbital emergency frequency, a system the orbital used whenever all of Alönia needed to hear something in a hurry, like an invasion or a cyclone warning. The enormous antenna sent out a signal to several other relay stations, and collectively they broadcasted across all Alönian frequencies, with the exception of military channels. This meant that every single Alönian radio and phonograph now projected the inquiry.

The plan was ingenious. Blythe wanted and believed nobody could hear him, but instead, everyone could. Every single Alönian currently using a phonograph or listening to the radio was now listening to the juicy inquiry of William Jefferson Blythe IV. If Bethany had to guess, the news would spread like wildfire, and the whole Houselands would tune in. But that wasn't even the best part! The reason David had been so adamant on the timing was to ensure that Blythe wouldn't discover that all of Alönia was listening to the inquiry. He'd sent Eric out to terminate the broadcast, and then cleared the gallery and locked down the assembly so nobody could report on the event, but in this case, it just meant that nobody could tell him he was national news.

Bethany watched the assembly for a few more minutes while David pressed his case, then she headed for the door. There, she paused and looked back at Eric. She pulled her lipstick from her purse and bent down over his face to draw some hearts. She could spare a few more minutes.

Chapter Twnty Five
A NIGHT IN THE CLOUDS

David fell for a few moments of terror before landing with a thud on something white and padded. He'd fallen perhaps ten feet through the sky onto a skiff hovering below the assembly's glass floor, and the impact of his landing bruised his tailbone. Considering how far he could have fallen, though, he decided he didn't mind so much. He grunted and rubbed his backside.

"I worked for three hours dressing up and making myself beautiful," a voice said from beside him, and he turned to see a rather distraught looking Mercy.

He opened his mouth to speak, but his stomach had yet to decide what was up and what was down.

"At your request!" She said as she pointed a finger at him. "And now you've completely filled my gown with sand!" She shook out her bodice.

David looked around and saw the fine layer of particulates covering the entire 71 two-seater cockpit and grimaced. However, when he looked back at Mercy, there was no trace of annoyance. She smiled at him.

"I think it worked," she said with a hopeful smile.

David remembered himself and scooted across the white leather bench seat to the controls. Guardsmen dangled from steel girders only ten feet above them, and it wouldn't be long before one of them spotted the skiff in the darkness. With expert hands he adjusted the throttle, and the skiff shot forward leaving behind a cloud of sand filtering down to Capital City. As soon as he had a chance, he leaned forward and switched on the skiffs onboard phonograph. Though the wind whistled around him, the speaker projected unmistakable sounds of panic and yelling. Over the top of all the chaos he could hear Blythe's screams of rage. David smiled.

"He doesn't sound very happy," Mercy said.

"Just wait till he discovers we've stolen all his airships," David said and Mercy laughed, a sweet sound that carried across the night sky. The open top allowed chilly, high-elevation air to flow around them, and the current made Mercy shiver. David reached an arm around her, and she snuggled close. She'd released her hair from the bun, and it flowed behind her like a flaming torch in the wind.

David had wanted this for a long time: a flight in an amazing skiff through the starlit evening with Mercy clinging to his arm. He wanted to say something nice.

"I'm sorry about your gown," he said. "I can help you get the sand out later."

"Thanks, but it's not in places you're allowed to go."

David gulped. "Oh… um… right." He tried to think

of something *else* to say.

"Are you blushing?" Mercy asked.

"Probably not as much as you are," David said.

She laughed and slapped his chest.

"So where are we going?" she asked as David banked the skiff through a cloud.

"You know where we're going," he said with a sideways glance.

"Can't we at least pretend we're doing something romantic?" she asked.

"What? Stealing airships isn't romantic?" David asked.

"Men!" Mercy groaned and shook her head.

"All right, we're flying to the Seventh District resorts on our way to a romantic dinner."

Mercy sighed and rested her head against his shoulder again. "That's a happy thought."

David weaved between clouds for a few extra moments, purposefully taking the long way and enjoying his close proximity to Mercy, but eventually he slowed the ship and raised the cloth top.

Mercy sighed and drew a compact gas pistol out of her skirts. "So much for my imaginary romantic evening."

David smiled and dropped the skiff through the cloud cover and heard the familiar pitter-patter of raindrops splashing on the windscreen.

"Trust me, this is going to be a lot more fun," he said.

Mercy gave him a doubtful expression.

Below the clouds, light pollution from Capital City lit up the sky. David turned the skiff toward the Victorian sector, and there, moored alongside several other yachts, sat Blythe's newest pleasure cruiser, designed in Armstad, crafted in the Third District, and paid for by the general taxpayers of Alönia. It was the flagship of the armada. He'd only seen it once before in House Thornton and, even then, only at a distance, but he knew an advanced airship when he saw one.

David glided his skiff closer. The yacht looked about the size of a small to medium carrier. The bay doors along the underside looked large enough to hold between thirty and forty skiffs. While the other yachts all enjoyed extravagant paint jobs that were visible even in the darkness, Blythe's yacht looked black as pitch in comparison. Wherever the light touched, it seemed to slip around its oily surface without any reflection at all. The surface reminded David of his own arm.

As he drew alongside, something else caught his attention. There was no top deck. The ship's envelope sloped around in one continuous curve, interrupted only by a tower protruding from the middle and several spherical armaments looking like bubbles. David guided his skiff toward the rear of the yacht and notice one central turbine coring the entire hull with duel rudders forming a cross over the thrust nozzle. The Cloud Cutter 71 had a similar design though on a much smaller scale. The closer David got, the more details became visible. On either side of the stern, he saw gyroscopic turbines folded alongside the envelope; though, these folded so tight they didn't interrupt the envelope's smooth curves.

David looked at Mercy with a dangerous smile.

"Sometimes I wonder what your devious mind is

thinking?" Mercy asked with narrowed eyes.

"I'll bet that's the most sophisticated airship in the sky," David said. "And that's precisely why I'm stealing it."

"It's not enough for you to take away his speakership," Mercy said, "you wanted to take his toys as well."

"Well I'm not going to let Viörn take them. When war finally comes, we can't risk technology like that in enemy hands."

"Well then," Mercy asked as she checked her pistol's magazine, "Let's get this over with."

She handed David a cloth bundle, and he unwrapped his father's old revolver. He attached the holster to his belt. Its weight against his hip gave him comfort.

"Right, well there should be a..." David said as he rummaged around in the skiff's storage compartment. "Ah-ha!" He said and produced a small square device with several buttons on one side and a long antenna protruding from the front. "A bay-door-opener."

David veered the skiff below the yacht and pressed one of the buttons on the device in his hand. Nothing happened. He checked the device to make sure he was pressing the right button and frowned when he saw that he was.

"Perhaps he doesn't have a personal opener yet," Mercy said, but David couldn't believe that Blythe would not afford himself such a luxury at the earliest possible moment, especially considering his nocturnal lifestyle.

"Oh!" David said, and he tapped the control against his forehead.

"What?" Mercy asked.

"I'm an idiot. It's a private garage."

David maneuvered the skiff up around to the top of the yacht. Sure enough, a skiff sized hatch with blinking lights along its side lay open beside the control tower.

"This is going to be easier than I thought," David said, and he guided his skiff through the opening and landed in a small, single-skiff garage. He closed the private hatch and opened their skiff's cloth top.

"Smells like new airship mixed with Úoi season rain," David said in a whisper.

They listened for a moment, as Francisco had taught them to do before entering an unknown situation. Once satisfied they were alone, David climbed from the skiff and alighted on the ground, before helping Mercy do the same. Her billowing skirt made it difficult.

"Not the best heist attire," She said in a whisper as she lifted her skirt and slipped off her heals so their clicking wouldn't give them away.

David crept to the far end of the skiff compartment and opened the door. Dim light and the sound of sweet music drifted through the open door. David crouched down and slipped inside the room, followed by Mercy. While she held her gas pistol, he slunk through the room with his father's revolver at the ready. However, the compartment adjoining the skiff garage looked to be empty.

David rose to his feet very slowly and looked around the opulent three-room suit. Plush couches and thick carpets graced the floor, while an impressive refreshment station covered one entire wall. David tried to check the adjoining room as quietly as he could, but his wet shoes squeaked against a section of uncarpeted floor.

"Dearest, is that you?" a woman called from the next room over, a bedroom by the look of it. She emerged a moment later holding a glass of wine and dressed in the most peculiar aeronautical uniform that was at least three or four sizes too large. Sleek black hair flowed over one shoulder.

"Who the devil are you?" The woman asked as she placed a hand on her hip and huffed.

"What are you wearing?" David asked with a squint at the uniform, and then David put it together. Blythe said he had a date this evening, and this black-haired beauty must have been the one he was referring too.

"Speaker Blythe asked me to wear it and—" She said, but David put his hands up and interrupted her.

"Ok, ok, ok," he said, "I don't want to hear anymore."

"But you didn't answer my question," she said and spilled some wine on the white couch as she spoke. "Who the devil are you? Why is she here?" the girl asked with obvious jealousy as Mercy stepped into view in her flowing red. "Blythie said we'd be alone tonight," she added with a humph.

"If there's one thing I know," Mercy said, "it is that you are never the only girl in the life of William Jefferson Blythe. Tell me, dearie, do you know airship regulations require passengers to wear life balloons at all times."

"No," the girl said, her eyes narrow. "I've never had to wear one before."

"Oh, but they do," Mercy said, and she grabbed one of the vests of the wall and started helping the girl into it.

"But we're docked right now," the girl said as she reluctantly let Mercy fasten the restraints around her arms. "And you're not wearing any life balloons."

"We've only just arrived," Mercy said. "And let me show you something about docked airships," Mercy said as she half guided, half pushed the frustrated, and slightly intoxicated girl in front of her. "While we might be docked, we're still dozens of fathoms in the air. You see?" Mercy opened an emergency hatch along the airships exterior and pointed down."

Although the girl was frowning, she leaned out the opening a little so she could look down. In that moment, Mercy pushed the girl out the opening and pulled the ripcord of her life balloon. David heard a distant scream as she fell and then a grunt as her life balloon inflated and pulled against her restraints. Mercy shut the emergency hatch and dusted off her hands.

She couldn't stop giggling the entire way down the corridor leading away from the private cabin. David tried to orient the ship in his mind, but its halls did not match any other airship of which he knew. Several times he and Mercy had to backtrack to find a different passage. Eventually, they found a hallway that led to the airship bridge. Although they heard a voice or two echoing down the halls, they never saw a single soul.

"I think the crew is as undisciplined as the speaker," Mercy said. "No doubt they are enjoying their own revelries in the cargo hold."

They climbed a circular stairway that led beyond the airship envelope and into the control tower, or *the bridge*, as aeronauts preferred to call it. David looked around the oblong room. A row of square windows surrounded the entire space granting a panoramic view of the carrier's smooth envelope and the landscape beyond. There were ten control consuls around the room's edges, and in the center of the open space sat a white leather chair on a swivel, the captain's chair. David had been in many control towers in his life, several of which were warship towers, but oddly he felt more at home in this one.

He closed a circular hatch that sealed the tower off from the rest of the airship. Then he walked along the consuls until he found what he was looking for, the communications consul. David pressed a large red button on the side of the consul titled in large white letters, *emergency alarm*. A bell rang below deck, and at the same time David leaned over and spoke into the ship's intercom.

"This is the bridge. We have an unknown emergency warning light flashing. Ship's manual recommends immediate evacuation. Please depart through the closest hatch and await emergency personnel." David closed the line and looked out the window. In the dim light, he saw dozens of shadows leaping off the side of the ship and bobbing along below emergency life balloons. He smiled and stepped up to the pilot's station. Pulling a lever, he unhooked the docking clamps and watched the landscape around shift ever so slightly.

"So far, so good," David said.

Mercy groaned and strapped herself in the captain's chair. "Why is it that every time I fly with you, it's your first time piloting the airship?"

But David didn't respond as he eyed the many switches beside the ship's wheel. He flicked the top one and felt the ship begin to drop.

"No! Definitely not that one," he said as he switched it off. The ship bumped the moorings, and he winced. He flicked the next switch and felt them rise. "That's better." He turned and smiled at Mercy. She didn't smile back.

The airship rose in elevation, but a lot slower than David liked, so he turned a nob beside the switches and was rewarded with a more rapid ascent, much more rapid than any normal carrier. Once he reached a minimum safe elevation, he placed a hand on the throttle control.

"Let's see what she can do," David said, and he pressed the throttle all the way down. The ship lurched forward with the acceleration of a skiff. David gripped the steering wheel to keep from being thrown to the floor. They rocketed over the Victorian sector with their central turbine emitting a terrible scream. No doubt the sound awoke every resident on Capital Island. In no time at all, David saw the dark waves of the channel below them. He turned and looked at Mercy with a half excited, half panicked look.

"This shouldn't be possible!" he said over the whine of the engines. And then he laughed at Mercy as she clung to her chair's armrests with a white-knuckled grip.

David was so lost in the thrill that he almost missed the warning alarm buzzing on a control terminal two stations down from the wheel.

"What is it?" He asked as Mercy leaned over from her chair and looked at the station.

"A proximity alarm. There are some ships ahead," she said after squinting at the consul.

"How many?" David asked.

"I'm not sure." She replied. "They seem to be above us, but the sensor is having a hard time breaking through some sort of static interference."

David angled the carrier up through the clouds. The vapor flowed around the bridge like a stream around a rock. Then the control tower broke through the surface, and he got a good view of the expanse by the light of the moon. Hundreds of gunships littered the sky. He gripped the wheel in surprise and prepared to angle back into the clouds. Perhaps it would conceal them long enough to reach Armstadi airspace. But before he did, he noticed that the ships were not flying any particular course, in fact, he wasn't sure if they were flying at all. They seemed to be running dark and drifting with the wind. David expected York and Francisco would see some resistance during their crossing, but this was ten times what he expected.

"Evidently the Capital Guard mobilized faster than we thought," Mercy said.

"Or they expected the rescue attempt all along," David added, and the words sent a cold chill down his spine. Their men were not prepared for such an attack. Most of the ships were not even armed. Did any survive? He couldn't see any carrier wreckage, but in order to immobilize a ship that size, there usually wasn't much left in the air. His eyes drifted to the clouds and the sea below. He almost dropped down to see if there were any survivors, but the futile gesture wasn't worth risking Blythe's flagship.

"How did they immobilize this many ships?" Mercy asked. "Their pulse emitters weren't nearly this effective."

"I'm not sure," David said, returning his gaze to the drifting gunships. "Evidently Admiral York had a trick up his sleeve. Let's hope it didn't cost him his life. Either way, I don't want to stick around long enough to find out."

"It might be too late for that. Look!" Mercy pointed across the sky toward a few gunships.

As David looked, their running lights flickered to life, and their random drift corrected into a controlled glide. More and more joined those few, and the night sky sparkled to life with a hundred airships.

"They're everywhere!" Mercy said. "There is no way we can avoid them all, and we have no armaments."

David watched as the ships rolled and angled their flight toward him. It was too late to hide in the clouds. His curiosity had caused him to delay a moment too long. He looked around the bridge for something he might use to defend the ship when his eyes landed on the communication station.

"Not exactly," David said. He locked the wheel, stepped over to the consul, and switched it on. "Let's hope they discovered Bethany's little prank by now. Otherwise this message will never be heard." He toggled through a few channels, but they didn't hear a chaotic assembly room anymore, only static. He raised an eyebrow at Mercy, and then switched to an emergency channel.

Leaning over the microphone, he spoke. "Capital guard, Capital guard, this is the speaker's flagship in pursuit of captured vessels. Why are you not in pursuit as ordered?"

David waited for a few moments, each one tempting him to veer away from the gunships and make a run for it. If he super-heated the balloon, he might be able to rise above them before they could fire. He almost gave in, but then a voice sounded from the phonograph.

"Flagship, this is commander Lewis. We were in pursuit of the stolen airships when a few of the ships exploded in an electrical pulse and crippled the majority of my force."

"Which way did they go, commander. Those ships cannot be allowed to reach Armstad. If they do, we will never get them back."

"That was their heading last we saw. They are most likely already beyond our reach."

David hissed. "I refuse to believe that, Commander. We will pursue as far as the border and see if we can't intercept at least one of the ship thieves."

David's reached to switch off the channel when the commander spoke again.

"I'm afraid I cannot allow you to leave, flagship. We are under order to allow no airships to leave Alönia."

David's blood froze, and he felt icicles creeping up his

arms. He grasped for words, but they seemed just out of reach for his weary mind. He opted for a bold approach, rather than witty.

"Commander Lewis, we were dispatched by the speaker himself to report on a mission you have already failed to accomplish. You were out of radio contact, and new orders were issued. If you don't have the stomach to probe the border, fine, but don't get in the way of those who do. You will either let us pass or suffer the consequences."

Another long pause tested David's patience. He was now too far along this course of action to abort. A few gunships were close enough to make out their many armaments. There could be no escape, only deceit.

"Flagship, proceed as ordered. We will regroup and fly in your wake."

David didn't bother answering. He accelerated to full speed, leaving the gunships behind. As he suspected, they did not follow. They'd had enough for one night and would only carry out the bare minimum of their orders.

He didn't slow the ship until they reached Armstad airspace, by which time his ears rang with the sound of the central turbine. Finally, he throttled down and sored toward the famed city at a much more controlled velocity.

"Bloody brilliant ship!" David said, and he worked his finger around the inside of his ear to try and stop the ringing.

Mercy removed her hands from her ears and nodded. "Though, if we ever have another romantic evening, let's take the Cloud Cutter."

But just then, the communications station crackled to life with an incoming transmission.

Mercy unbuckled and rose from the captain's chair. She pressed a key on the console and played the transmission over the phonograph.

The voice spoke in Armstadi. David knew a little of the language, but the only words he picked up were "airship" and "destroyed." Mercy leaned over the speaking piece and responded to the message in Armstadi. When she finished, David looked at her with questioning eyes.

"Well, what did he say?" he asked.

"He said if he has to stay up any later to intercept one more wayward airship, he'll destroy it on sight," Mercy said, and then laughed. "Also, we are to proceed to the other side of Mt. Eluh where the rest of our airships await."

"Did he say how many," David asked, "...how many airships made it across?"

"He didn't say how many. He just said *fleet*."

Twenty minutes later, their sleek black airship coasted into a docking berth, and David saw what the Armstadi official meant by "fleet." It was difficult to see everything in the darkness, but it looked like hundreds of carriers, each twice the size of his, crowded around a landing bored into the side of Mt. Eluh.

"They did it, Mercy," he said. "I think they did it. They got them all."

They opened the control-tower hatch and climbed down the stairs, before rushing through the halls to the ship's main docking-bay door. A few Armstadi officials met them on the dock and directed them to where the rest of the wayward Alönians waited.

They ran through the rain into a large bay carved into the side of the mountain. The men cheered as they entered, all of them apparently hearing part of the inquiry on a phonograph. David shook hands with the team leaders and was overjoyed to learn that they'd escaped with all but four carriers. Hot drinks were passed around.

However, the cheering stopped, and the smiles vanished when David said, "So, Where's Francisco?"

Chapter Twenty Six
SPEAKER OF THE HOUSELANDS

Things seemed unusual in Capital City on the afternoon of the 41st day of Úoi Season, especially the weather. Light rain still pattered atop the cityscape as it always did, but in the distance whole patches of cloud cover had melted away during the night, and shafts of rare sunlight pierced at an eastern angle and bathed the luckier portions of the city with their warm rays. One such lucky portion lay in the very middle of Capital City at the juncture of the commerce sector and the old city where the mossy stone walls of the Capital City police station stood.

A man walked along the street wearing a smart blue and black suit with his hands folded behind his back. He stood above average height with broad shoulders and a strong-featured face. As he plodded along the cobbled streets, people did the most peculiar things. They smiled at him, one stranger to another, something that hadn't been seen for a long time on the Capital's streets. Men tipped their hats to him, and a few saluted. Young women curtsied with wide eyes and giggled when he smiled and greeted them back. Mothers pointed him out to their children, if their children had not already pointed him out to their mothers. Boys stopped their street games and looked at him as he passed, a few were brave enough to wave in front of their fellows.

He stopped along his way at a street vendor and ordered some tea and a sweet bun. The young girl managing the cart reddened when he spoke to her, and such was her state of excitement that she failed to add cream and sugar to his steaming tea. He paid her a full sterling, much more than the asking price, and she clutched the coin in a white-knuckled grip and gazed at him long after he'd left her cart. He passed a boy selling that morning's Voxil Tribunal. The boy greeted him in a pleasant manner and even called him "sir." The man nodded and passed by, but after a few paces, stopped and turned back. He purchased a copy of the paper. The boy spoke in excited tones and asked if he could shake the man's ebony hand.

He continued down the street, sipping his unsweetened tea and glancing at the front-page news articles. After finishing his sweet bun, he walked about a block before entering a large, old building with a large, grumpy secretary. The man produced a piece of paper, and the secretary grudgingly granted him entrance through a sturdy door into a dimly lit stone foyer. He walked down one of the four circular staircases and continued until the air felt cold and moist. The stairway deposited him at another Foyer with many adjoining halls. He spoke to a guard and produced the same piece of paper he'd shown the secretary. The guard handed him a key and directed him toward one of the hallways.

Iron bars lined either side of the dark passage, and the further the man walked along the stone floor, the worse it smelled. Every few paces, a door interrupted the iron bars granting entrance to small, identical prison cells. He stopped at the fifth door on his right and looked into the cell at a medium-sized, disheveled man lying on a cot. A few days' worth of scruff clung to his face like a fine layer of dirt.

"Francisco?" David said, leaning close to the iron bars and smiling. "You look awful."

Francisco rolled his head and looked up at David with a single good eye. His ruined mechanical eye swiveled in whatever direction gravity pulled. As soon as his eye rested on David, he jumped up and grabbed the bars.

"You!" he said in an angry tone. "I have a score to settle with you! You said no torpedoes!"

"I know, I know," David said, his smiled fading. "They weren't supposed to. We lost a few from that. I'm sorry, but other than that, the men describe the mission as a rousing success."

"They should have been on the ships that blew up." Francisco said. "I don't think I'll ever have children after having that much electricity flow through my nethers. What does it matter anyway how successful our mission was?" Francisco rested his head against the bars. "The assembly denied your motion. I heard the capital guards laughing about it."

"I think your nethers are the least of your concerns," David said. "You'll have to find a girl willing to make children with you first. Honestly, I've seen things come out the back end of a bovine that look better than you do right now."

"Go away," Francisco said as he returned to his cot. "I'm in no mood for talking, and if they're putting you in a cell, make sure it's not anywhere close to mine."

David frowned, but Francisco only lay back down on his cot and rolled to face the wall.

"Well, that's a waste then," David said. He turned and walked away. "I've worked for two straight days negotiating your release, but if you'd rather stay here, I guess I'll be going." David smiled and made a silent count. He only got to the count of three before he heard Francisco scrambling out of his bed.

"What!" Francisco said.

David heard the bars rattle with an impact. He continued walking.

"David! You get your ass back here right now!"

David turned and strolled back to the cell with an ear-to-ear grin.

"What do you mean by *negotiated my release*? And why aren't you locked up yourself? Instead, you stand there grinning, smelling like a recent bath, and wearing your nicest suit. Why?"

"Because I'm on my way to the orbital." David continued to grin to Francisco's obvious frustration. "And, you're being released by special request of the speaker, so you can come with me."

"Why?" Francisco asked. "I don't want anything to do with that desert turd. I won't go to an assembly full of monkeys so they can mock me. If he lets me out of here, I'll shoot him where he stands like I should have done seasons ago."

"That's not very kind of you, repaying a good deed with a bullet. And the speaker was so very keen that you were there to hear him swear in."

"What do you mean? Swear in for what? Wipe that grin off your face, man!"

David laughed and tossed Francisco the copy of the Voxil he had folded under his arm. Francisco caught it and held the front page up to the dim light. His voice mumbled within the stone cell as he read aloud. His voice started out drab but quickly turned to curious and then excited.

"A star falls. Four days ago, in a strange and stunning turn of events, Speaker Blythe was broadcasted on Alönia's emergency frequency during his inquiry. The inquirer, the long-lost heir of the Ike legend, produced convincing evidence and testimony against Blythe regarding two murders. The assembly ignored the inquiry and acquitted Blythe with an overwhelming majority. However, the citizens of the Third District voiced their disapproval of Blythe after he called them ignorant, drug-abusing dependents by voting him out of office the morning after the inquiry. With only two seasons as speaker, Blythe is replaced by his one-time friend Don Hezekiah Johnson!"

Francisco looked up in shock. David produced a key from his pocket.

"So, uh... do you want to leave now?" David asked.

"You are a dirty, no good, pile of Voxil..."

Francisco continued to call David every foul thing he could think of as David unlocked the cell door with his wide grin. Once the door swung open, the two looked at each other through the space. Francisco lunged forward and punched David in the gut. David doubled over with a half-moan, half-laugh.

"Get me out of here, you bastard," Francisco said, "before I kill you on principle!"

They walked out of the police station and toward the commerce sector, each explaining their recent exploits to the other. David led Francisco to a clothing vendor where they purchased a new suit. They didn't have time for a shave and a wash, but they did find a black velvet patch to cover up Francisco's ruined mechanical eye. In an hour's time they sat in an air-taxi, rising above Capital City and soaring toward the orbital.

After a ten-minute flight, they strode through the security checkpoint and down the gold and blue halls. It felt like a ghost town. Very few people walked the corridors, and the people they did see spoke in hushed tones in groups of two or three. Some glared at David as he passed, but he only smiled back. When they reached the assembly room, only a handful of people sat in its many chairs. David smiled when his eyes met Mercy's. She blushed and looked down as she stood at the base of the auditorium speaking with Bethany. Bethany rolled her eyes when she looked back and saw who Mercy was blushing at, but she smiled in the end. Walker, York, Pellión, and Hobs spoke and laughed in a group by themselves, While Johnson and Winston shook hands with the assembly's few remaining Pragmatic representatives. For the obvious reasons, Blythe was nowhere to be seen. David and Francisco descended the few steps from the hall toward the assembly dais where large pieces of wood covered the once glass floor. A splotch of blood smeared the side of the dais, and there was a dent in one of the lower booths.

"It looks like a bar fight broke out in here," Francisco said.

David mulled over the statement. Then he nodded. "More or less."

He stepped onto the wood floor and felt it creak beneath his weight. A breeze whistled between two of the boards and gave him a chill. He walked with light steps and a frown, but when he looked up, he saw someone he did not expect. Representative Herald sat a few rows up in his usual place, his hands resting on a cane. David smiled as the man seemed to be looking directly at him. After a moment's hesitation he decided to approach Herald.

"Representative Herald," David said and put out his hand. "I don't believe we've met."

Herald didn't shake the hand, but rather, he looked at David's face for a long moment, a moment that felt awkward as the silence drew out.

"I never met your father," Herald said. "But I did

know your grandfather a bit." He looked down and twisted his cane. "I was a new representative back then, about a decade after the Protectorate War. Your grandfather came before the assembly urging us not to cut the Armada's funding. You have his bearing. When I saw you there four days ago, I swear I thought I was watching your grandfather."

David smiled and looked down.

"I didn't agree with your grandfather then," the older man said, "and I'm not sure how much I agree with you now, but I can't deny that my party has progressed beyond propriety. We've forgotten our principles."

"I don't think there are two Alönians in all the Houselands that agree completely on everything," David said. "But there is always common ground with footing for both if they look hard enough. War is coming. My grandfather foresaw it, as did my father. I didn't want to believe it, but the evidence is undeniable. I think that is common ground enough for a Pragmatic and an Equalist to share." David put his hand out again, and Herald took it and nodded. "We are going to need Pragmatics and Equalists when the war finally comes," David said after they'd shaken hands.

"Aye, lad, that we will," Herald said.

"David," Johnson called from the dais, "get down here and swear me in. You got me into this political debacle, time to pull your weight."

With one last nod at Herald, David turned and descended the stairs. He joined Johnson on the dais and looked around at the empty room. It was so much different than the last time he'd observed the speaker's oath. It wasn't the same momentous event demanding front-page space in all the tabloids, but for some reason that made it feel more real. When Johnson raised his hand for the oath, surrounded by his friends and colleagues, David knew he meant it.

"Repeat after me," David said. "I, Don Hezekiah Johnson,"

"I, Don Hezekiah Johnson," Johnson repeated.

"...do so swear to faithfully fulfill the role of house speaker."

"...do so swear to faithfully fulfill the role of house speaker."

"I pledge to guard the sanctity of the Houselands from acts both foreign and domestic,"

"I pledge to guard the sanctity of the Houselands from acts both foreign and domestic,"

"...and to provide for the needs of the people by moderating the will of the Assembly."

"...and to provide for the needs of the people by moderating the will of the Assembly."

"I swear to uphold the House Rules in accordance with magistrate opinion,"

"I swear to uphold the House Rules in accordance with magistrate opinion,"

"I do so swear."

"I do so swear."

The applause that followed seemed trite in comparison to the roar that cheered Blythe, but everyone who congratulated Johnson did so with heart-felt joy, every one of them having had a hand in the achievement. Johnson was not a man who sought the position; rather, he accepted it when it was thrust upon him. He had everything most men would want in life—money, power, comfort—but he now pledged all of that to protect the Houselands from certain doom.

Johnson's acceptance speech was short and unemotional. He thanked each person by name and praised their remarkable achievements over the past few weeks. He appointed David as his first aide and Mercy as his second. He placed Francisco in charge of intelligence and all sneak operations, and Bethany over the department of communications. He assigned York *The Valor* and promoted him to Chief Admiral of the Alönian Armada. In a much more solemn tone, he ordered York to prepare the armada for war. It wasn't a flowery speech—David doubted he'd even prepared it ahead of time. It told of the long road ahead, and the storm they had yet to weather.

After a round of handshakes, most of the few attendees left, and David led Johnson, Walker, Francisco, Mercy, Bethany, and York out of the auditorium and toward the speaker's private office. The closer they got to the entrance, the more they saw litter strewn along the halls. No guards stood at the entrance, and when David tried opening the door, it wouldn't budge.

"It's locked," David said after he'd lifted the latch several times without success.

"You just don't have the right key," Francisco said as he produced his lock pick. Ten seconds later the door swung open, and everyone gaped at what they saw. The entire office looked trashed. The halls they'd just passed through seemed clean in comparison. They moved through the entrance and into the donut-shaped second floor. David could hear a few panicked voices and the sound of ripping paper from where he stood beside the balcony railing.

"No, all of them!" A woman said. "He wants them all destroyed."

"But," a second girl said, "I can't tell the difference between financial records and—"

The first girl interrupted her. "It doesn't matter, just get rid of them."

David saw a girl in her late teens run across the bottom floor with an armload of papers.

"You there," Francisco called. "What's going on?"

The girl squeaked and dropped her armload of papers.

"They're here!" she called, and then she ran back across the bottom floor toward the exit. Several other people ran from different portions of the office, all of them young and impressionable. They glanced around with concerned expressions. A young lad emerged from the office next to David and gulped. He looked at them with wide eyes and scooted by with his back to the wall edging toward the exit.

David looked at Francisco with a puzzled expression. Then his eyes widened, and he charged up the main stairway toward the speaker's office on the third floor.

"David, wait!" Francisco said, and David heard the sound of someone running after him.

David didn't stop. If Blythe had ordered the office to shred documents, his minions could do unspeakable damage if their path of destruction included Alönia's Documents Vault. He reached the office door in a few seconds and burst through without pausing. The first thing he saw were documents scattered across the entire office, whole reams of paper, though nothing looked damaged, yet. The sound of ruffling paper echoed across the room, and David looked up and saw shadows dancing within the light cast through the vaults open door. Someone was inside. Francisco joined him at the door, and together they ran across the office to the vault.

David looked inside at a man with wild graying hair and a disorderly blue suit. As David watched, the man overturned whole boxes of documents and spread the contents across the floor so he could see it. His face had a scraggly scruff of facial hair marring its features, and he trod upon several inches of documents crinkling their edges and mumbling to himself as he read their titles.

"What should we do with him?" David asked as he stood with Francisco next to the vault entrance.

Blythe looked up with a start and dropped an armload of documents. He stared at them with bloodshot eyes, and his untied cravat hung limp about his neck.

"Kill him," Francisco said. "Less paperwork to deal with."

"You!" Blythe said, pointing at David with his index finger. His other hand clutched a roll of papers. "You ruined everything!" Blythe took a few steps toward David but stopped when David drew his triple-barreled revolver.

"Whatever ruin you feel, you brought upon yourself," David said. "I only shined a light on your vile ways. Now drop those documents and come on out. There's no need for things to get any worse than they already are. For you anyway."

"Worse?" Blythe said with a chuckle. "You have no idea what's coming. None of you can even comprehend the forces at work here! Go ahead; shoot me! I'm a dead man already."

"Sounds reasonable enough to me," Francisco said. "If the capital guard hadn't taken my gun when they arrested me, you'd already be dead."

"We need him alive," David said. "He knows things in detail that we can only guess at."

The office door rattled, and the rest of their party entered.

"Aw, I see my replacement is here," Blythe said, smiling. "You look like you've lost some weight in recent days, Johnson."

"Good clean living," Johnson said, and he looked around the ransacked office with a frown. "I think I'll have a conversation with your housekeeper, though. This place is all a clutter."

"She quit when I refused to marry her," Blythe said with a smile. "She's dead now. They killed her to make sure there weren't any loose ends."

"Just shoot him, David," Francisco said. "It's best for everyone."

"Now, now, Francisco," Johnson said as everyone

crossed the office and stood beside David and Francisco. "We have a nice cell waiting for Mr. Blythe. You warmed it up for him the past few nights. Once he's there, I'll let you interrogate him for information. He might even have some tips for you on how to beat it out of him. Then he'll hang."

"I didn't do any of those things," Blythe said with gritted teeth. "It was all the Viörn."

"But you allowed them to be done!" David said. "I'll bet you even watched it. Every time you needed something dirty done, you called up your butchers, and the next day we picked up the mangled bodies in a Capital City alley. There's no difference between you and them."

"You have no idea what they're like," Blythe said, his eyes wild with fear.

"Who," David said. "Who were you working for? I want a name!"

But before Blythe could say anything, David saw the office door open again from the corner of his eye and Hans and Gerald entering. They immediately drew their weapons when they saw the scene inside the office.

"Sorry, David," Blythe said. "I'd love to chat, but it looks like my ride is here. Somebody stole all my airships, so Hans and Gerald had to acquire another."

"You're not going anywhere," David said, pointing his pistol at Blythe's forehead. "You move, and I'll put one between your eyes."

"Do that and Han's and Gerald will shoot your friends," Blythe said. "Starting with the ladies."

David gritted his teeth, but there really wasn't anything

he could do. Blythe shouldered his way past, his one hand still clutching some documents. David kept his pistol trained on the traitor's head, but he had no choice but to let him pass. Hans and Gerald waited until Blythe was outside the office, and then they backed through themselves. As soon as they were out of sight, David and Francisco sprang forward and scrambled for the door. Papers rustled with their passing. Mercy tossed Francisco her compact gas pistol. They reached the door and threw it open, but several gunshots sent them diving for cover. The glass on the door shattered and crumbled to the floor. More shots rang out and echoed through the hall, punching holes in the wall directly above where David and Francisco crouched. Francisco leaned forward and picked up a piece of glass from the floor. He used it as a mirror and spied out the door and around the corner.

"They're heading up to the roof," he said, but more shots rang out and shattered the glass in his hand. He pulled his hand back and picked up another piece.

"Tell me when we're clear," David said.

Francisco watched the reflection in the glass for a few more moments. Then he nodded.

"Go!"

David and Francisco sprang through the door and rushed around the third-floor balcony toward the roof. David opened the door leading to the promenade deck, and Francisco looked up the stairway in a quick motion before he charged up the stairs and threw open the exterior door. Cold air chilled David as he and Francisco exited and took up positions behind a planter box. David saw Blythe, Hans, and Gerald climbing into a waiting skiff, which started rising from the deck the moment they were seated. David and Francisco both fired at the skiff, but the craft shot away before they could cause any serious damage. Francisco swore and continued to empty his magazine long after the skiff disappeared into the clouds.

"It's fine," David said. "That airship is too small to make it any great distance. Besides, he doesn't have any power anymore. He can't do any harm."

"Men like that always cause harm. You should have let me shoot him in the office," Francisco said with a sign. "What do you suppose those documents were that he had?"

David shook his head. "I don't know. Maybe incriminating evidence tying him to the Viörn. I don't think we'll ever be able to find out. There were thousands of documents in that vault, and not all of them were recorded."

Francisco sighed. "Best go down and start cleaning the place up," he said. But as he turned, David didn't follow.

"You go ahead," David said as he holstered his revolver. "I'll be right down." He'd forgotten just how beautiful the view from the Promenade Deck was, and the sun looked minutes away from setting.

"Suit yourself," Francisco said.

David walked around the planter boxes and leaned against the railing. He realized with some humor that he was standing in the same spot he'd stood when he and Blythe smoked cigars. That seemed cycles ago, but it was, in fact, only a season and a half earlier.

He looked out over the railing and watched the sun as it sank behind the Alönian Mountains. Ever since his mother had died, the sunsets meant so much more to him, and he watched as many as he could. Each one gave him new hope, new purpose, and a new reminder that Jeshua was alive and working, and someday in the future David would join Him and his mother and father forever.

"I did it, Mother," David said. "I did it!" A tear rolled down his cheek, glistening in the sunlight.

He heard the sound of the door closing and turned as Mercy walked around one of the planter boxes. The wind blew her auburn hair like tongues of flame, and her face shined with the last light of the sun. They smiled at each other, but neither said anything as she walked up and joined him on the rail.

"Remember the last time you found me watching the sunset," David asked after a few moments.

Mercy nodded. "You thought I was a hallucination," she said and then laughed.

David smiled and nodded. "You're the girl of my dreams... a hallucination is not that far removed."

Mercy blushed so deeply her cheeks blended with her hair. She looked down and smiled, but David lifted her chin. He brushed her hair out of her face and looked into her eyes. This time, he was really going to do it. He would say something nice, and he wouldn't mess it up.

"You're the most beautiful girl in all the Fertile Plains, did you know? And... and I love you... very much?"

She stopped breathing for a pair of heartbeats. "Oh,

I... I didn't," she said. She obviously did know, but she seemed shocked to hear him say it.

David nodded. "It's true." Then he did something he'd never done before, but something he'd always wanted to try. He leaned forward and kissed her. She stiffened, apparently surprised, but she didn't pull away, and after a moment, she wrapped her arms around his waist in an embrace. The sun glinted off the orbital and bathed the couple and the clouds around in brilliant hues of red and orange, reflecting off the brass railing and every single one of the Alönian star's thirteen points. A terrible war approached, a war to overshadow all other wars. But in that moment, as the sun set, the only thing David cared about was the woman in his arms.

EPILOGUE

David knocked on a large metal door with pieces of wood covering up broken out panels of glass.

"Enter," a voice said.

He pushed open the door and walked into Speaker Johnson's orbital office. He saw the man on the far end of the office tapping a pen against his head with his eyes pinched shut.

"Ah, David," Johnson said once he'd opened his eyes. "Thank you for coming." He made a mark on the piece of paper and placed the pen on the desk.

"Of course, sir," David said and crossed the office to sit in the large leather chair opposite Johnson.

"I wanted to meet with you to ask you a favor." Johnson leaned forward.

"Ever since Blythe took the speakership, we lost contact with our outlander friends in the north. We can only assume that Blythe discovered our secret relationship with them and cut it off. Either that or the outlanders were only interested in working with the head of the

Houselands."

David nodded.

"Well, now that we are back in possession of the speakership, we'd like to re-establish communications. You see, they are working on a very important operation."

"What operation, sir?" David asked.

"Something that might even the odds when the war finally comes," Johnson said. "Something that has never before been attempted in the Fertile Plains: a tunnel beneath the Rorand Mountains."

David blanched. "A tunnel? Beneath the mountains?" But Johnson's expression never wavered.

"Rather ingenious, isn't it?" Johnson said. "An old idea of your grandfather's, actually."

"But... but that would take cycles," David said, trying to conceal his disbelief. Johnson had to be joking.

"Ten cycles, to be precise," Johnson said. "At least, according to the original project plan."

"You're serious? How long has this been going on?"

"Ever since we made peace with the outlanders, say about six and a half cycles ago. The fact is: we need that tunnel more than anything now. It would allow us to sneak behind Berg and cripple them from the inside out. Unfortunately, we haven't heard from our project manager in the outlands for a few seasons now. If progress has stopped, it could mean the loss of vital time."

David nodded, but couldn't help his frown. "Yes, but what do the outlanders have to do with the tunnel?"

"They're the best miners in the Fertile Plains. Who better to punch a hole through more than a hundred grandfathoms of solid rock?"

"But they're outlanders," David said, "wild and uncivilized. I can't imagine them accomplishing anything so monstrous."

"I'll admit they are a bit wild, habitual brawlers with non-existent table manners, but we managed to pacify them, a little. After that they were more than willing to do some work for us at only slightly above a standard cost. It all has to do with their political structure, which is why I think you would be a perfect envoy to check up on them and see how things are going."

"But I know nothing of outlanders," David said. "or their political structure. I didn't even know we'd made peace with them until a few seasons ago. Why not send someone more informed of the situation."

Johnson paused. "There is another reason I want you to go." He pursed his lips and chose his next words carefully. "What do you know of your father's work in the outlands?"

"I know he served two seasons there as a hunter. He destroyed so many prowlers that the outlanders lost interest in Alönian raids."

"Not exactly," Johnson said. "Not even the armada knew the extent of his work there, and it has been a closely guarded secret ever since. There are some things you need to know about your father and his last seasons as an Alönian captain."

* * * * *

Distance made the journey wearisome, distance and the sweltering heat of the barren valleys. It might not have been so bad, if a majority of the journey had not progressed on foot—grandfathoms and grandfathoms and grandfathoms of endless walking. Within no time at all, clothes disintegrated, and shoes dissolved beneath the stress of the march. How could a country survive when everything was trying to eat you? Millions of biting or stinging insects filled the air. Nothing but snakes, thorns, and carnivorous plants inhabited the jungles. They had thought the cool streams refreshing until they discovered the leeches.

They smelled the city long before they saw it. The thick air carried the heavy sent of refuse with it. Then they saw the famed junk piles of Viörn spanning as far as they could see. After a few conflicts with territorial Junkers, they decided to travel at night using the light of glowing mushrooms as a dense smog concealed any star.

But, at long last they'd arrived at their destination, Xiang city. Blythe climbed the wooden steps inside the intricate building, leaving Hans and Gerald at the entrance. Each step felt like a mountain. He reached the top and stumbled toward a door between two guards, half the size of his own but no less deadly. They looked at him, but not in concern. He looked too haggard for that. He lifted his fist and knocked twice on the door.

A man said something from within, and Blythe presumed it was permission. Mustering his remaining strength and pride, he pushed the door open and stumbled inside. A man stood on the opposite end of the octagonal office looking through an octagonal window behind an octagonal table atop an octagonal rug adorned with octagonal patterns. Octagonal paintings hung on the walls displaying eight airships flying in a formation. Blythe walked across the room, but the man did not turn to look. Blythe moistened his dry mouth to speak, but the man cut him off.

"William, you are an imbecilic fool," he said. "You had every advantage, every support, and still you managed to fail by tripping on the finish line."

The man turned and glared at Blythe with his peoples' naturally narrowed eyes. His tanned skin contrasted with his red uniform. He stepped away from the window and looked up at Blythe from behind his desk, a full foot separating their difference in height.

"As a result," The man continued, "I've had to move my entire timetable backward after we had already begun to mobilize. Do you know how much money that cost us? Not to mention how close we were to forfeiting the entire operation. You failed on every count. What use are you to us now, especially now that I know you are incapable of achieving the smallest challenge."

He never shouted; in fact, he appeared as calm as a man reprimanding a wayward child. Blythe hated it. He hated the humiliation of a sniveling man, half his size, treating him like a fool. It reminded him of his first days as an aide, penniless and pitiful, surviving on the goodwill and good fortune of his superiors. He would never return to that state, not after how far he had risen. But, for the moment, he bit his tongue and endured. He had but one card to play, and he had to play it well.

"Why should I shelter you?" the man asked. "Answer me that? Why shouldn't I behead you and write you off as a failed investment."

Blythe swallowed hard. He knew that, despite the man's tone, beheading was a very real possibility in this culture.

"Did you think I would come to you empty handed?" Blythe asked. "If I truly was as much of a failure as you've described, I would have thrown myself from the orbital and saved you the trouble of a beheading, but I didn't. I knew I had a bargaining chip, something valuable enough to balance the loss of your investments." Blythe paused, choosing his words carefully. If he played his card to quickly, the man would simply take it and order his death. Blythe had to convince him of his future value.

"I know the costs of a future war with Alönia and Armstad," Blythe said. "I know their strengths and weaknesses. I've seen their armadas and fortifications, and I can exploit their weaknesses."

The man snickered. "Prove it. Tell me something I don't already know, and I'll let you live."

Blythe smiled with dry lips. Then he reached inside his coat and pulled out a tight roll of documents. Unlike the rest of him, the documents looked clean. He'd handled them with extreme care the entire journey across the channel and across Armstad, while patrols chased them across the countryside. He'd kept them out of the dust and wind after their airship ran out of fuel, and the three of them were forced to walk across the Viörn wastes until they reached the city of Xiang.

He handed the documents across the desk, and the Viörn unrolled and examined them. He glanced briefly and turned the page to the next document and looked at it, and the next few after that.

He looked up at Blythe. "This is all of them?" he asked.

Blythe nodded. The Viörn sat and began looking through the papers again, slower this time. "You've regained my favor." He said at last. "These documents are worth cycles of planning. You have purchased a life in Viörn, and if you ensure our operation is successful, a place in my new government. Fail me again, and we will torture every last bit of information out of your brain until you die a miserable failure."

Only then did Blythe relax enough to sit on the chair opposite the Viörn. "I won't fail you again. There won't be any Ike's around to foil me this time."

The Viörn laughed. "A poorly planned life has many surprises. You had the last living member of the Ike legend in your office, and you didn't even know it."

"It had nothing to do with poor planning. I presumed the family dead," Blythe said with a meaningful look at the Viörn.

"Never presume anything about your enemies," the Viörn said. "It is ironic, though. The Ikes threatened our operations, so we snuffed them out like a spark before it became a blaze. But we missed one, and he rose from the ashes a stronger man. The irony is that we gave him the very position, which led to our undoing. Fate can be fickle."

Blythe frowned. "If your men had done a better job of destroying that airship, he would have died with his father."

The Viörn's eyes flicked up in a look of condescension. "If you would have killed all your staff like I suggested when you suspected a traitor, we would not be in this position. But you were too busy in your bedroom to bother yourself."

Blythe smiled and conceded the point, but he balled his fists behind the desk. The truth was, he hadn't the stomach for blood, but his lust for power allowed him to appreciate its results. So he used others to do the job for him while he could pursue other ventures with clean hands. He'd let the staff live for personal reasons. David and Francisco ran his campaign. Bethany would have, at some point, filled an interim between mistresses, and Mercy would have been one of those mistresses, willingly or not.

"It is of no matter anymore," the Viörn said. "Though the next time we have dealings with David Ike, we will not leave him alive. Come, we must call a meeting with our allies," the Viörn said as he stood and walked around his desk. "Our Bergish friends will be very interested in the new advantage you've given us."

The two of them left the office, neither fully trusting the other. They left the documents on the table, documents of invaluable worth to both Armstad and

Alönia. Sunlight poured through an open window and illuminated the pilfered goods revealing a crisscross of lines. The papers formed a precise blueprint of the, as of yet, impregnable Armstad mountain fortifications. They displayed gun emplacements, lines of fire, secret tunnels, communication towers, supply lines, all of the fortification's strengths... and weaknesses. The blueprints ruffled gently and lifted with the breeze.

THE END

FROM THE AUTHOR

I love writing fiction, but more than that, I want you to love my fiction. Write a review on amazon and help me improve my craft. If you are looking for updates on future books or just want to chat, contact me through my website at sashaffer.com

S.A. Shaffer

Made in the USA
Coppell, TX
05 July 2021

58572216R10246